KY

IN THE COMPANY OF SNIPERS
Book 13

IRISH WINTERS

COPYRIGHT

Ky; In the Company of Snipers, 13

Cover design and author photo by Kelli Ann Morgan,
http://www.inspirecreativeservices.com

Interior book design by Bob Houston eBook Formatting

Editor: Lauren McKellar, McStellar editing,
http://mcstellarediting.blogspot.com

Editor: Rocky Palmer, RVP the Man Editing,
mailto:rvptheman@gmail.com

ISBN Paperback: 978-942895-36-7
ISBN eBook: 978-1-942895-35-0
Library of Congress Control Number: 2016950172

Irish Winter's websites: http://www.irishwinters.com
 and irishwinters.blogspot.com

In the Company of Snipers

You can find Irish Winters on Facebook:
https://www.facebook.com/author.irishwinters

On Twitter: https://twitter.com/irishwinters1

For news on upcoming releases, sign up for Irish Winters' Newsletter at IrishWinters.com.

For more information about all my books, visit IrishWinters.com.

IN THE COMPANY OF SNIPERS

This series revolves around ex-Marine scout sniper, Alex Stewart, and his covert surveillance company, The TEAM, home-based out of Alexandria, Virginia. An obsessive patriot and workaholic, he created the company to give ex-military snipers like him a chance at returning to civilian life with a decent job.

This is not a serial with each book ending at a cliffhanger. I wouldn't do that to you. *In the Company of Snipers* is a collection of passionate love stories involving women and men who are tough enough to take on the world alone. Each is a stand-alone read, where in the course of an active TEAM operation, one agent comes face to face with his or her demons. The men and women I write about are all patriots and warriors, dealing with what they've lived through or the mistakes they've made

Spoiler alert: Every novel contains adult scenes including sexual situations (some explicit), language, and violence. I don't write sweet romance, so be forewarned.

At the end of each story, it's my hope that you, along with my heroes, will come to realize...

Love changes everything.

Prologue

A man without hope will pray to die.

USMC Lance Corporal Ky Winchester had.

It was five days since Coalition Forces had sent him and his squad to track down Hasim Nizari, to bring him to justice. The United States Army wanted the monster dead or alive for his crimes against Afghan women and military prisoners. The ANA, the Afghan National Army, wanted him, too. They'd hunted him for months, but the Teflon-coated degenerate had managed to stay one step ahead of the game. Until a couple of ANA soldiers had betrayed Ky and his men, leading him and his RTO, his radio tech officer, down a dead end and straight into hell.

Ky had taken one round to his body armor, just enough to knock him down. Not kill him, damn it. He didn't recall how he'd gotten from that stinking alley to this modern day pit of despair. He only knew that since he'd come to, torment visited him daily in the ways of cruel men. Fists. Leather belts with sharp buckles. Metal rods. Knives for sport. And worse.

Now Ky knew exactly where the bastard was. Nizari. The treacherous, cold-blooded banker to the Taliban commandeered his own torture chamber. Always dressed in a business suit, a linen shirt, and a clean silk tie when he soiled his victims, he retained cool, aloof control while he worked his dark designs on human flesh. He never lost his composure that Ky could recall. Not once.

What Ky didn't know was how many men were in this place with him. He'd heard screaming. He could only imagine. *God, the depravity of man.*

Nizari had yet to make his appearance for the day, but that didn't mean Ky hadn't been sorely tried. Hell, no. Nizari had plenty of soldiers in his band of merry men. They'd left Ky hanging so long he'd lost all feeling in his arms. He hadn't eaten in days—was made to endure at the edge of death until he broke.

"Ky." The single word came to him softly, too quiet to be real, but too loud to be imaginary. He strained to hear it one more time. Dared to believe it was real. His broken nose twitched, and despite the dried clots stuffing it closed, the poor thing still detected a cooling hint of menthol. His nostrils flared, drawing the scent in along with another that was— good. Distinctly female. No man in this hellhole smelled like that.

"Ky." His name again. He had heard it. He had! The shiver of hope raced up his spine and over his sweaty scalp. Was this his descent into delirium or the onset of death?

A vision materialized that would've made his eyes water if he could've opened them. An imaginary angel he guessed, more blur than shadow, more light than darkness. A hazy halo of gold. Cool, green eyes. Not Kelly green. Not emerald. But a clear, mint green that refreshed like the brisk bite of wintergreen in cold December. He *did* see her. He did. Maybe...

She drifted toward him, those green eyes too big for her face, and that was the cruelest nightmare of all, because he could—not—see. His heart thumped at the awful paradox he was caught in. His eyes were too swollen and bruised to work. If seeing was believing, what was she? Another nightmare? Torture could certainly drive a man crazy. But then...

That same drift of menthol and camphor filtered up through his tender nostrils and into his throbbing sinus cavities. He sniffed it in, as painful as the effort was, relishing the calming scent of eucalyptus as it soothed the damaged membranes in his skull. That he knew the distinctive fragrance only proved how close he was to losing his mind. But then...

She. Touched. Him.

Silky, soft fingertips traced his broken orbital bone. Warm palms cupped his bloody chin. *Impossible.* He swallowed hard, not ready to believe the end had come, that his brain was shutting down, offering hallucinations during his transition from life to death. *Just wait. There'll be a tunnel of light. The pain will cease. My time will end, and I'll be free, and...*

The light-as-breath brush of delicate arms encompassed his ragged, sweaty body. Another heartbeat echoed against his ears as if this gentle apparition cradled his head to her breasts, his ear to her heart, and God! This hallucination felt so good. He would've cried if he could have.

Perhaps it was merely the onset of his dying heart begging to be set free from torment, but it seemed so real. Greedily, he turned his face into the softness and warmth of that imaginary female body, seeking the comfort she offered. Wanting so much to believe. Needing her to—please, God! Be more than a wish and a prayer, more than his slippery descent into insanity.

Her warm breath caressed the curl of his ear. He didn't understand how it worked; he only knew that his dream whispered loud enough he could no longer doubt her. *"I'm here, Ky. I'm not leaving you."*

She'd no more than stopped speaking when the wooden door to his sweatbox banged open. The sharp metallic tang of a lighted propane torch struck his nostrils. Oh, God. Another twist to the torture.

"Hold onto me," she commanded, her grip tighter.

God, he wanted to, but frantic panic crawled up his spine like a living thing, a sinister ice-cold dragon with serrated talons, an icicle tail that wrapped around his neck. It came with the despair of reality, the shuddering fear of the living damned. He clenched the chain instead of his imaginary angel and prepared to meet his maker.

"You talk now?" Nizari's brutal lackey asked, smacking something against his open palm with an intimidating *thwack, thwack, thwack.*

That was why his angel had asked Ky to hold on. Somehow she'd known. This was it. His last moment on earth.

His soon-to-be murderer landed a sharp fist to his gut. The unexpected impact sent Ky spinning into the wall. He wouldn't cry out, not to this bastard, but he did want to tell that patient angel, who lingered at the edge of his mind, *"Thanks for trying. Leave now. Never look back. Save yourself."*

Instead, the menthol scent grew stronger. Her hands grew tighter. *"I won't let you go."*

Yes. You will.

His captor muttered a bizarre gurgling curse. It sounded as if someone had joined the guy with the torch, no doubt both licking their chops for the despicable pleasure they derived from torturing Americans. *Bastards. Every last one of them.*

Ky bowed his chin to his chest and prepared to die. He didn't dare guess which appendage this bastard would burn first. Toes. Hair. His face. It didn't friggin' matter. He could take no more. *Just get it the fuck over with! Kill me!*

But then a hand steadied Ky's trembling body. A big hand. A kind hand. "You gonna make it?" a gentler voice asked. Strong and clear. An American.

The chain lowered Ky to the floor, but his feet couldn't support his own weight. He collapsed, even as his ears strained for another word, needing to know for certain this was no trick or dream, that this person was not Afghan. Not Mideastern. Not even from this part of the goddamned world.

"You okay?" The man spoke again, softer this time. Tenderly. Definite West Coast accent.

Thank God. Ky groaned a raspy, "Hell, yeah."

Careful fingers travelled over his neck and shoulders, down his arms and across his ribs, physically checking without leaving pain in their wake. How odd that he flinched anyway. That it took the last of his willpower *not* to scream after all—that.

Freedom hurt so damned good.

He gave West Coast the best answer a jarhead knew. "Ooh-rah," he choked, his tongue parched, his lips swollen and ragged. "God bless... America."

"Whatever," the guy muttered. "Can you walk?"

"Yes," Ky ground out through clenched teeth. *I can run, just get me the hell out of here!*

But rolling to his side took his breath. His mouth filled with blood. Drawing his arms down to his sides hurt like a mother. He wasn't going anywhere.

"What's your name, Marine?"

Ky faced his rescuer like a man. "USMC Lance Corporal Ky Winchester, sir." Damn, he'd mumbled like he had a mouth full of marbles.

West Coast didn't seem to notice. "Damned good to meet you, Ky. I'm USMC Corporal Lee Hart, buddy." Lee pushed a knife handle into Ky's bloody fingers. "You kill the first bastard that lays a hand on you, understand? Gut him like a fish. Make him pay for everything he did to you."

"Yes, sir." Ky clutched the knife, but he shook so hard. Every bone and muscle screamed as he was no longer forced to stand on his toes. No longer stretched to the point of breaking.

"I've got another person to rescue. I'm coming back for you. You hear me?"

The knife slipped to the floor. His heart spoke before his brain could rein it in. "Sir." Shit, he was bawling like a baby. "Please don't... don't leave me here."

And there in the dark, USMC Corporal Lee Hart did what any brother would do for another brother. He lifted Ky off the filth of rot-gut Afghanistan and gathered him into his strong arms like a damned kid. Lee's fingers spread wide. He cupped the back of Ky's bobbing head to hold him still, as if Ky was the weaker baby brother. As if Lee wasn't going to leave.

Ky fought for restraint and lost it. He pressed his forehead to Lee's collarbone, shaking and breathing hard. Nothing felt as good as this American-born shoulder. *Don't go!*

He dug his shredded fingernails into this brother's bare arms and struggled to hang onto what little dignity he had left. Not much. A guy who'd been made to dance on the short end of a rusted, iron chain was a damned humble man. *Please don't leave me!*

"How long you been in here, son?" Lee Hart, God bless him, had the rumbling voice of an older, wiser angel. Brought tears to a guy's eyes, not that Ky knew what dripped down his cheeks. Could've been blood.

"F-five days, I think. Maybe more." *Seems like forever.*

A growl rumbled deep in Lee's chest. "Marines never lie, do we?"

Damned sneaky question. *Get me to feel valiant and brave when I'm—not.* "N-no, sir. W-we never lie. We never quit. We never f-f-fucking forget, either."

"Good answer. I'm not lying to you now, Ky. I will be back, but you gotta let me go. I've got more folks to save than just you." He pressed the knife handle back into Ky's palm and made sure his worthless fingers wrapped around it. "Hang onto this. There's others in this shithole who need my help. I can't leave them here any more than I'm gonna leave you. You understand?"

"Y-y-yes, sir," he replied, an obedient jarhead to the bitter end. Hell, he wanted to bawl like a baby. Instead, he sucked up a deep breath of freedom and remembered who he really was. What he stood for. Nizari couldn't take that.

"Ooh-rah," he declared from the depths of his American-born soul. He willed his fingernails to release his rescuer. He clasped the knife handle to his chest, his bloody little finger snug against the finger guard, his crushed thumb stroking the butt-end like it was a long-lost friend. The next murderer through that door would die, and Ky meant to die with him rather than endure another round of fun and games.

Lee Hart got him situated upright with his back to the wall beside the door.

"Sir?" Ky asked, not sure he whether wanted to know or not. "Was I... was I... alone?"

Lee grunted. "Except for that dead guy with the torch over there, yeah. Why?"

Ky shook his head, working his throat muscles to drum up enough saliva to swallow. "No lady with green eyes?" He hated the hopeful quaver in his voice.

Lee's solid hand gripped Ky's shoulder. "I sure as hell hope not. Stop dreaming. You've already got it made. Ladies like guys with scars. Now shut up and sit tight. I'll be right back."

Something lethal in his tone brooked no further discussion. Ky reached for him, but he was gone, and Ky was alone again.

Marines didn't lie and that was the gospel truth. But sometimes, they cried. Sometimes, the darkness got the best of them. Ky shook when his savior left. Tears oozed like molten lead between his mashed eyelids. They ran down his face, and he let them. There was no woman. No angel. None of this was real. He was all by himself. Blind. Scared. And losing his friggin' mind.

But just when the night seemed blackest...

Just when Nizari's evil spirit whispered that Lee wouldn't return...

That all was lost...

"No!" Ky spat his contempt at the darkness. "No! No! No!"

He sucked up the last of his courage, and he chose to believe, Goddamnit. He *had* seen a green-eyed woman. Okay, so he was blind, but she *was* there. It didn't make sense and it didn't have to. He knew it, damn it. He *had* seen her. She *was* real, and Lee *would* return. He would!

The cooling breath of menthol wafted into Ky's poor wrecked nose. Another miracle that made no sense. *"Ky,"* she breathed his name into his soul. He could've cried. She hadn't left him. He wasn't crazy.

"I... I tried to hold onto you," he choked out unashamedly.

The peace that surpassed all understanding invaded his wrecked soul. He couldn't explain how it worked. Didn't even try. Just leaned into the warmth of her heart and thanked God for miracles and angels.

And hope.

Chapter One

Two and a half years later

Junior Agent Ky Winchester spun a circle in the air with his index finger, signaling the Royal Canadian Mounted Police chopper pilot. Adjusting his tinted goggles, he activated TEAMshield, the built-in display that linked him with his partner, Junior Agent Tate Higgins, while it provided a wealth of intel. Temperature. Altitude. Latitude. Longitude. Compass. Wind speed and direction. Distance. In other words, just about everything.

Current position: longitude: fifty-one degrees, forty-five minutes, thirty-nine seconds; latitude: eighty-nine degrees, three minutes, nineteen seconds. Temperature? Damned cold. Frozen Hudson Bay lay a couple of hundred miles to the northeast, the Wabakimi Provincial Park to the south, and a whole lot of frozen lakes, rivers, and evergreens between. The five-miles-per-hour wind from the northwest barely buffeted his descent, but it also pushed wind chill down to three below zero. Yeah. Damned cold.

TEAMshield was the brainchild of Ky's boss, ex-Marine and current CEO, Alex Stewart. The flick of an inset button on the right temple of his goggles could convert Ky's view to night-vision. Another button controlled thermal imaging. Complete with Wi-Fi, crisp digital graphics, and a heavy-duty solar battery, about the only thing the goggles didn't do was pop corn.

He stepped to the edge of the open helicopter door, secured the thick, plaited drop-line in his gloved grasp, and ducked out of the chopper. Standing at the edge of the hatch, he clenched the rope between his knees and sturdy Caribou boots, and down he went. Fast-roping dropped a man quicker than rappelling, but Ky gripped the line tighter to slow his descent, dodging branches while he scanned the LZ, his landing zone, making sure all was as it appeared.

He didn't need to hurry like he had in the past. No terrorists waited below to murder him the second he touched down. No enemy snipers or improvised explosives were hidden from view—not there in Canada. Nothing moved. He took it slow and easy, enjoying the view. Only the crystal snowflakes dislodged by the whirring blades above showered down around him as he dropped. Just evergreen trees and winter white as far as the eye could see.

The rope spun him in a lazy circle. He landed inside the column of misty white, flexing his knees to absorb the shock of irregular terrain. Ky took no chances, not on a remote op. The all-white landscape made depth perception difficult. A hidden rock or branch could spell doom. The frigid north would end a guy with a broken leg and do it fast.

"Touchdown," he alerted his partner as he surveyed point zero. The trees were thick, but the ground beneath his feet was flat. Good enough.

Ky peeled the heavier, heat-resistant gloves off. Fast roping created friction, and friction caused blisters, something else he didn't need. He stowed the gloves in one of his many thigh pockets, but left his tactical gloves in place for warmth, and because—well, he liked gloves. They provided separation, a protective barrier between him and the rest of the human race.

Crazy? Yes, but he no longer cared what others thought about his quirk. He'd come home from Kabul with a creepy little thing called haphephobia, the aversion to human contact. His psych doctor said it stemmed from what he'd endured overseas. Said it was a common reaction in victims of traumatic physical abuse, like torture. Said it derived from the brain's natural instinct to defend its personal space and ultimately his life. Whatever. It seemed more like his brain meant to kill him sometimes. To never let him forget or heal.

All it took was the slightest accidental brush of skin on skin, and claustrophobia would rocket through him. He'd hyperventilate, sweat bullets, and basically turn to crap. He hadn't actually whimpered at the office yet, mostly because those folks understood guys like him. They'd closed ranks around him the first day he'd joined The TEAM, but they'd been smart about it. They only came close enough to make sure he knew they had his six.

The oddest thing was he could touch them, but they couldn't touch him. Couldn't even shake his hand without a panic attack sneaking up on him. Ky hated that Hasim Nizari still controlled him. Could still hurt him. The bastard's last little keepsake ruled his friggin' life. He needed it gone.

He patted his pocket to make sure his heavy-duty gloves were secure. TEAMwear, a line of rugged, lightweight tactical clothing for men and women, was another Alex Stewart concept. It basically converted an agent into walking storage as well as kept him or her warm, comfy, and dry. Pockets. Zippered pockets. Hidden pockets. You name it, if you needed anything small but handy on an op, this getup had a place to store it.

Ky wore the cold-climate version. Designed to keep a guy warm and waterproof, it came with a thick fabric liner that whisked excess body heat and sweat away from his skin. Embedded with sensors, TEAMwear also linked to his TEAMshield goggles. No matter where Ky went, his online babysitter adeptly provided intelligent feedback like: *Warning. Your left pant leg is on fire, dumbass.*

He chuckled quietly, a semi-pleasant sound in the silent world. He had yet to live down the pants-on-fire episode—not that Alex brought it up or that TEAMshield had actually called him dumbass. Mother, the know-it-all office administrator, had most likely leaked that snafu. She was like that, smart as a whip but nosey as hell and willing to share personal details. She never crossed the line too far, just enjoyed passing along the human-interest side of covert ops.

The constant feed from his goggles-on-steroids to The TEAM office in Alexandria, Virginia, was the downside of all that over-the-top technology. Above all, it ensured Alex knew pretty much everything, as in *every—damned—thing,* that went down on a team op. Not that Ky minded. He didn't mind having a rabid-dog type of guardian archangel sitting on his shoulder, either. Overseeing. Overactive. Over-nasty when the op warranted. It went with the job.

Ky looked east, toward the direction of that far-off nightmare called Afghanistan. He'd had another angel on his shoulder back then. One he'd never forgotten. Never intended to. At quiet moments like this, the grateful part of his heart lifted up to remind him he still owed every breath of this pure, frosty air to his unknown heroine. That he wouldn't be alive if she hadn't come to him and told him to hold on. That not once had he thought to ask her name.

Dumb jock move. One-night stand kind of move. One he didn't want to live down, because he still hoped that apparition was real and not invented by his tortured soul. He'd really like to meet her, to see if she was as beautiful in person as she was in his dreams.

Ky sucked in a breath of icy cold and let the mystery go. Back to business. If his intel was correct, the crash site lay five clicks east of the LZ, an easy walk, even in snow. He checked his heads-up-display for the time. Oh-sixteen-hundred hours, straight up. Four P.M. by civilian standards. If the weather held, he and Tate would soon be back aboard that chopper and on their way home with America's supposed finest black operator, FBI Agent Eden Stark, and her pilot, Charles Sweets.

Cold and snow had come early to Canada, an ungodly *gift* from the Arctic. While the sun still blessed his home in Virginia with a gentler transition from summer to autumn, winter had already blasted Kenora, Ontario Province. Not the most favorable conditions when a man had been sent to rescue what he hoped would be two survivors.

Ky knew without a doubt that he and Tate couldn't get to Stark and Sweets before dark, but that they could get close. They'd planned to hump all night. Had snowshoes in case they ran into powder. The sooner they started the better.

Tate landed on both feet with a muffled thump to Ky's left. For his size, he made a sound so soft it could've passed for a snowball dropping off a tree. Half Inuk of the indigenous Inuit tribe of Alaska, the other half Army Ranger and fiercely proud of it, Tate hailed from a little hamlet south of Anchorage on the Kenai Peninsula. Bronzed-skinned and dark-haired, he spoke little and always gave a hundred and ten percent, traits Ky respected in a partner.

Both loners, they'd worked together often. Neither needed conversation when silence served the world better. Talking was an over-rated commodity. It bred misinformation and reckless opinions, like the story circulating The TEAM office that Tate's mother had abandoned him as a baby, that he'd been raised by a white man, a fur trapper. That he'd lived on raw meat until he was old enough to fish. That kind of bullshit.

Tate might fit all of those characteristics, but it was his story to tell, and folks needed to mind their business. Hell, the whole world ought to join the M.Y.O.B. social network. Maybe then there'd be peace on earth.

"RCMP Silver Wolf to Team Arctic Fox, will stand by in Thunder Bay. Don't take too long. Over," the chopper pilot radioed from above. In other words, the Royal Canadian Mounted Police chopper pilot, a. k. a. Silver Wolf, would spend the night in a nice, warm hotel room and would only return when he had to.

"Copy that." Ky looked up and waved, but doubted the pilot could see his hand signal through the dense branches. In too few seconds, the rotor slap from the Chinook helicopter faded, telling Ky just how remote this op could be. Total silence filled the frigid void.

Team Arctic Fox had a very cold night ahead of them, not something Ky looked forward to. Two hot-as-hell deployments to Mideastern deserts had changed his internal thermostat. Humid summers in Virginia still left him chilled. He wore a jacket most days. Couldn't get warm enough.

Tate crouched to one knee and nodded to the west, his gloved index finger to his lips.

Ky glanced over his right shoulder. There in the shadows stood a black wolf, as in pitch black, its long legs and big feet a definite giveaway of its wild lineage. The animal moved forward through the filtered light of the pines, its steps as fluid and smooth as the lengthening shadows. Dark amber eyes scanned the two-legged aliens suddenly dropped into its domain. Its nostrils twitched. Ears tilted forward. But worse, a ruffled ridge of warning lifted up its back. The wolf bared his fangs.

"Shit, we don't have time for this," Ky muttered, mostly to himself. This canine thought he was top predator? Not even close. He waved the wolf off. "Go on. Beat it."

The animal didn't even flinch at the dismissal, just kept those steady gold eyes on Ky. The wolf took another step forward, his head down and his snout lowered to the snow, doing what he did best. Scenting his prey. Testing for illness or weakness. Closing in for the kill.

"You wanna play? I'll show you play." Ky took one step, too, then another straight toward the wolf, his arms spread wide to intimidate this cocky creature.

Damned if the long-legged creature didn't meet the challenge with two more very definite steps closer. Man, this big, bad wolf had some balls. Either that or he understood the concept of poker. Ky held his position, curious as to which of them was the real alpha. He'd never considered himself as such. Never wanted the title of lead dog. Just hadn't learned how to back down to a bully.

Dropping to one knee, he thumped both hands to his chest. *Come on, boy, because I'm here to tell you. I've been scared by worse. You don't even come close.*

The wolf blinked. He looked away, but gradually, those amber eyes scrolled back on target to Ky. His nostrils flared. Some might have taken it as a sign of submission, but Ky read it differently. He pushed off the ground, no longer worried. The wolf was curious, more wild brother than adversary. If he'd brought his pack with him, that'd be different, but all alone like he was, the wolf was no threat.

Ky did the unexpected. He patted his palms to his knees, encouraging the wolf to come get some. Damned if the big guy didn't slap both front paws to the snowy ground in play. "Did you see that?" Ky asked his partner. This bad boy acted more like a dog than a predator.

Tate grunted, a can of bear spray in his hand, his eyes on the wolf. "You got a death wish?"

"Put that stuff away. He's not hurting anything."

"It won't kill him, just scare him off."

"Not necessary." Ky grinned at the unlikely buddy he'd just made. "Go on, fella. Take off. Wyatt Earp here might shoot you next."

The wolf disappeared the way he came. Silently. One minute there, the next gone.

Tate stuffed the bear spray back in his pocket. Ky didn't have time to wonder why this predator had shown up—didn't want to think of it. Wolves scavenged more than just caribou carcasses. They culled more than the elk and deer herds, and if she was injured, Agent Stark's time was running out.

Lifting his gloved hand to his goggles, he activated TEAMhome, the earpiece deep in his ear canal and his direct link to Alex Stewart. "Touchdown, Boss. ETA in five to six hours if the weather holds."

"Copy that," Alex replied easily, no doubt wearing his TEAMhome earpiece twenty-four-seven since he had other agents on ops scattered across the world. "Be advised your weather pattern's changing. You've got a low front shifting down from the northwest. The jet stream will bring it straight to you. You guys may need to hunker down and wait it out. Keep safe. Stay warm. I'll be waiting."

Ky signed off. Alex had meant what he said. The man didn't seem to understand the concept of quitting time, not if his wife's frequent late-night visits to the office with dinner were any indicator.

The quiet, feminine voice of TEAMshield spoke a "warning" deep inside Ky's ear canal. His heads-up display flashed a lime-green caution in the lower-right corner of his goggles. TEAMshield had honed in on Stark's downed Cessna's locator beacon, only now, there were two signals: one pinging directly east where Eden should be, if she'd been wise and stayed with her downed aircraft; two more pinging loud and clear, south-by-southwest. Behind his and Tate's position. Ky rolled the instant tweak of aggravation out of his neck. Didn't it figure? Easy day was over. They had company.

Grunt. Groan. ARGH! Oh, snap.

Eden's arms were beyond tired and every strand of muscle in her lithe, five-foot-five frame screamed to be loosed from its cumbersome burden. She couldn't rest yet, though. Couldn't waste the sunlight. Not yet. Maybe in twenty, thirty yards. *After* she was done. *After* she'd conquered the small incline. *After* she'd arrived at that one bare patch of ground in the whole frozen country.

Er-r-r. She dug the toes of her hiking boots into the crunchy snow on the forest floor and threw herself into her chore. Pulling. Dragging. Cussing, too. Anything to keep the awkwardly wrapped bundle moving forward over the crusty snow between the crashed Cessna at her rear and the shadowy trees ahead.

This thankless chore had to be completed before the light left the sky, and the sun was well on its way down. Her head ached and her vision blurred, but she shrugged it off. Now was not the time to get one of those migraines that had plagued her since Hawaii. God, they were annoying and some days, nearly crippling, but she had enough trouble. A migraine had to wait its turn.

The bungee cords she'd used to secure her package caught on every hidden limb or root buried beneath the snow. And there were plenty, because these were the deep woods of the frozen north.

What I wouldn't give for a hot shower right now. With my brand new bottle of Almond Suede body wash. My just-out-of-the-dryer fluffy, and oh, so fresh-smelling bath sheets. My bungalow in Maryland. My bed. My clean sheets. Six or eight ibuprofen. A glass of sweet Moscato and my pillow!

Grunting at the injustice of the day, she threw her weight into the task, sweating up a storm beneath her brand new, down-filled quilted parka. Ralph Lauren. Shearling trim. One hundred percent Canada goose down. The one she'd had to buy in Anchorage because she wasn't on a beach in Hawaii like she should've been. It was a little tight across her backside, because, well, she had a backside. Hips to match. Ralph Lauren had better live up to its claim of maximum warmth in sub-zero temps and cover those curvy assets of hers. She meant to put it to the test, day and night, if that was how long it took someone to rescue her.

She switched ends of the burden, pushing it uphill instead of pulling, needing to work different muscles in her poor body, to rest her screaming, shaking calves and hamstrings. No go. Dropping to her butt, she blew her long bangs out of her eyes and rested for five.

As cold as this part of Canada was, she hadn't expected she'd need to shed her jacket, but she had no choice. Ralph Lauren *was* warm. She was sweating. Go figure.

Unzipping the jacket, she shrugged out of it and left it on the trail she'd just made. She didn't need to freeze because she'd overworked her ass off. She'd be back.

When pushing didn't work any better, she reverted to dragging. Her load seemed heavier with each step. More cumbersome. Her legs trembled. The pain behind her eyes grew into a dull throb that engulfed her whole brain instead of just one quadrant. Not usually prone to migraines, the ferocity of this one spelled trouble. She would've attributed it to a head injury from the plane crash, except she'd had a headache to one degree or another since she'd hurriedly left the tropical beaches, the ones she hadn't spent a single second enjoying.

More grunting. More groaning. The hill she and her burden had to crest wasn't much of a hill at all, but the slightest incline required more strength, and she was on her last reserves. Still, it had to be done.

The cold solved her perspiration problem. She shivered, but didn't stop struggling with each step.

Still pulling. Still—argh. My arms are killing me. "I. Can. Do. This!"

Her voice sounded shrill and slightly hysterical in the whisper of the quiet pines. So be it. She'd been slightly hysterical before. Certain times required hysteria, maybe dementia. Maybe even outright crazy, the way this day had gone. Surely the day you fell out of the sky demanded a scream at all the crazy gods who let it happen, right?

But screaming would only burn energy she couldn't afford to waste, and she knew better. Besides, it reminded her of the day her father had left. Make that, deserted. She'd screamed plenty when that happened, her heart torn out of her at Drake Franklin's ultimate betrayal to his child. What good had screaming, *'Daddy. Don't go. Daddy, please. Don't leave me!'* done?

Nothing. Drake Franklin hadn't even looked back—just said he'd had enough of all the bullshit and walked out of her life. Left Casey Franklin and her seven-year-old daughter, Eden, without a car or a dollar to their names.

Eden grew up fast, believing every word her mother taught her. Who wouldn't believe the woman who worked her heart out to support her child? The wise woman who taught her: *Where there's a will, there's a way. Never give up. Work your heart out and your heart will steer you true.* Stuff like: *I do believe. I do believe. I do. I do. I do.*

Young Eden became a positive-thinker out of necessity— a glass is half-full kind of a girl. She believed in the inherent goodness of people. It worked until the day an illegal immigrant had broadsided her mother's rattletrap of a twenty-year-old Honda Prelude in rush-hour traffic in the middle of Podunk Boise, Idaho, and left her dead at the scene. How a guy with no insurance and no driver's license got released from jail on his own recognizance in time to flee south of the border made no sense to a fifteen-year-old girl without a friend or a relative in the world.

One of her mother's girlfriends took her in. Eden legally rejected her father when he didn't step forward to claim her. She assumed her mother's maiden name, Stark. Life went on.

But nothing had hurt as bad as standing alone at Casey's grave telling her mother goodbye for the last time. Unless you factored in Eden's dumb-butt, seventeen-year-old boyfriend, Stan's, betrayal with that hooker waitress at Denny's the day after the funeral. Stan claimed he only hooked up with her because *he* was lonely. The ass didn't have a clue what lonely was. The one day that Eden could've used a real friend, all she got was another rude awakening. Guys lie. Guys cheat. Guys only think about themselves and that puny, little thing dangling between their legs.

"I sure know how to pick 'em," she told the bundle sliding quietly along behind her.

Night threatened in black and blue shadows at the edge of the sky she could no longer see. Too many tall, bushy trees obstructed her view. Pines, every last one of them. She used to love the lacy, elegant Noble pines when decorated with snow and glistening icicles the way these were. Pines always reminded her of tinsel and Christmas, one of the few good holidays left in the world. Not anymore. These *Nutcracker Suite* bad boys just might be the death of her, which could be a good thing in the long run. Freezing to death seemed a better way to go than a double tap to the cranium, her brains spilled out for the wildlife to sample. An Eden buffet. Hmmm.

She blew out a deep breath of frosty air and staggered on. Even gliding over snow-covered ground, her load was a heavy one. Ten feet to go. Then five. *Then I can rest and maybe this headache will stop.*

At last Eden dropped to her knees, sure she'd done the best she could. This was the only bare patch of earth within dragging distance, sheltered beneath the fanlike branches of a densely packed stand of evergreens. It almost seemed serene, this spot. Serene and surreal. A little reverent. Sacred even. But mostly—diggable, if that was even a word.

Yes. It would do. A single shaft of the weak winter sunlight fell across her snow-dusted boots. A brave little bird flitted in the chilly branches overhead, but it didn't sing. Didn't even chirp. What the heck did birds have to sing about in the frozen north?

She took a moment to catch her breath, but ended the break before her limbs had the chance to seize from exhaustion or her backside from the cold. This next chore would be harder. She still had to bury the body.

Chapter Two

"I'll be back first thing in the morning," she promised through chattering teeth.

Eden brushed the back of her hand over her sweaty forehead, panting short bursts of over-heated air out while she sucked in the cold. Her lungs hurt, but Charlie Sweets was finally planted, his grave in the frozen ground shallow, but good enough. The collapsible shovel she'd found in the plane wasn't nearly enough help, but after enough effort and swearing, it had worked.

She paused, hating to leave Charlie behind and alone in the dark. Yes, he was dead, but he'd been a friendly port in a sea of measured indifference and calculated cruelty. To make it up to the congenial pilot of the Cessna 185, she'd scrounged the nearby area for downed branches and rocks, both difficult to locate in the snow and the waning light of what would be a frigid night. He now lay beneath layers of fragrant pine—lots of them, if you counted the trees over his head.

Charlie Sweets might have expired the moment he'd crash-landed, but he'd skillfully guided the wingless bird until his final breath. The Cessna had suffered nose damage and loss of both wings when it plowed through the forest, but somehow, its cabin had maintained structural integrity. Eden worried for him now. He deserved more than a shoddy burial, or worse, to be left in the open for animals.

Shivering, she scrubbed her palms up and down her biceps, her gaze fastened to the shallow grave. "Don't go anywhere."

Ha. Funny, Eden. Go find your jacket. Hypothermia's setting in. You're losing your mind.

She retraced her tracks and shuddered into her new best bud, Ralph Lauren, her fingers so stiff she could barely work the zipper. When it finally slid into place under her chin, she flipped her collar up and ducked into the chilly goose down. The first tentacles of warmth invaded her lightly frosted skin, then sunk deeper into her stiff muscles. Ralph Lauren *had* created a comfy jacket, one she wished extended over her denim-encased legs more than it did.

Darkness fell silently and completely. She'd barely reached the plane wreckage when the last glimmer of light slipped into shadow. If there were stars in the sky, she couldn't see them. She didn't look. Climbing inside the plane, she felt in the dark for the door latch and hurriedly locked herself in.

The night promised to be long, dark, and miserable. Trembling, she retrieved a penlight flashlight from her inside jacket pocket to view her new digs. The LED beam cast a stark light over her slim chance of survival. At take-off, she'd shared her getaway plane with a stack of boxes secured to the floor with nets and bungee cords. A rolled up sleeping bag had been stashed behind her chair. Various ropes. A fire extinguisher on the wall. An ice chest beside her seat.

Everything lay in a tumbled mess now, most of it forced forward into the cockpit from the crash. Some boxes had broken apart. An ice pick from out of nowhere had joined the mess. A fishing pole. A couple of blankets. Charlie's red-and-black checkered hat. Broken glass from which window, Eden didn't know. The mangled wreck would keep her safe from wildlife and snow, but not the cold.

She dragged the sleeping bag to her seat, unzipped it, and folded herself and Ralph Lauren inside before she zipped it again. A drink would've been nice, but the bottle of water she'd brought from Anchorage was nowhere in sight. Probably frozen anyway. Food would have to wait, too. She needed warmth more than anything else, so she pulled the sleeping bag tighter and wondered where her single piece of luggage had gone. Her backpack. She needed her lip balm. Her Vicks. A wet wipe wouldn't hurt, either.

But there was nothing she needed badly enough to freeze for. Snuggling into her cover, she crossed her arms over her chilled breasts and faced the music. *Never in a gazillion years did I think the plane would crash in the middle of all these trees. Where no one will ever—EVER—find me. Why me? Why now?*

She knew darned well why.

Simple. Eden was not only one of the most elite of the elite within the covert ranks of the Federal Bureau of Investigation, but she'd been born with a genetic birth defect unlike any other. It was both a blessing and a curse. Second sight. Just like her mother's.

Since she'd gone to work for the FBI, neurologists all over the world had examined her, studied her, tested her, but in the end they were mystified as to how her gift worked. They couldn't explain her uncanny talent any more than her mother had been able to, except that it did work. Eden could sense bad things before they happened—sometimes.

Like the way Charlie's right ventricle had spasmed before the crash, an extraordinarily odd coincidence given that he looked athletically fit.

Like the way the Cessna had skimmed the treetops for five long minutes before it pitched forward, another odd coincidence considering the remote location she now found herself lost in.

An involuntary shudder skittered up her spine at the thought of Mika Koenig and Arthur Shields. They used to be nice guys, but were now ruthless killing machines. Hearts colder than the frozen north. Black holes where their eyes used to be.

Even huddled in the back seat of the broken Cessna like she was, Eden could accurately gauge the distance and speed at which her assassins tracked her. If she focused and let her second sight reach out to them, she could literally read them like a book, a book about mindless zombies with two identical thoughts on their scary minds: *Find her. Kill her.*

They'd chosen a rocky outcropping to the southwest for their landing zone. No doubt a stealth helicopter, a Sikorsky UH-60 Black Hawk, rested there still, ready to lift off the moment her heart ceased beating. Yes, she, FBI Special Agent, Eden Stark, Quantico's resident psychic and overly protected asset, had been set up, and her poor dead pilot with her.

Casey's motherly wisdom came back to Eden. *Keep your opinions to yourself and your mouth shut. Once people know you have this gift, you'll never have a moment's peace. Conceal it. Control it. Be very careful of the friends you choose.*

"Yes, Mom," she whispered to the frozen air.

She'd been an obedient child and had spent most of her twenty-six years keeping her talent hidden. She'd never had girlfriends, and after Stan, she'd needed no boyfriends. Eden simply excelled at reading people, at seeing hidden agendas and deceits below the lying surface. It wasn't hard. She was also good at psychological testing. Her life hadn't been the same since.

The FBI had her hunting terrorists worldwide. Saving their victims. Their marks. She didn't need to be in the same vicinity, much less the same room, as the evil men and women she hunted in order to do her job. She just had to study her target to get a *feel* for him or her, and her uncanny brain did the rest.

Do you believe that dribble about human beings only utilizing ten percent of their brains? Guess again. A brain's prime directive was to work non-stop every millisecond of a person's life to ensure that person's survival—kind of like a refrigerator, only better. Give your brain a change of scenery, and it would work harder. Give it a good night's sleep, and it would come up with impossible possibilities. Eden learned early how to task her gray matter with supposedly unsolvable problems like finding lost souls. Missing children. Hidden bodies. Evil men.

Sometimes, a vision burst to the front of her mind, striving for attention in the way of a nagging child. She'd see her victim's face, his or her mouth open in a scream, eyes wild and terrorized or squeezed tight against his or her pain. But most times, *warnings* came like a movie trailer with just enough vague information to whet her need to know more. Often, they came like a mumbled, incoherent whisper in the back of her mind. A shiver. Goose bumps. One had come to her two and a half years ago with actual words. *God, just let me die...*

She still thought about that poor man, but all she knew was his name. Ky. And sometimes late at night, she wondered, why him? Where was he now? She was fairly certain he'd survived. Did he ever think about her? Probably not.

Eden drew in a deep sigh. Usually, she'd delegate the psychic warnings to her extraordinary brain and let it do what it did best. Profile. Search. Reach out. Touch that victim with some kind of psychic message. At which time, she'd turn her findings over to her boss, FBI Special Agent Matt Hartigen. He took it from there, because he commanded the resources for assault, recovery, and extraction. He also commanded respect. People jumped when he spoke.

That was what she probably should've done with Ky, but she hadn't. Not once did she bring Matt into the loop—she'd just stayed with Ky until the end. Until she knew he was safe and rescued. Until those other soldiers came back for him and took him to Camp Eggers. Then the connection broke and that was that. Still, she wondered.

Most of the Bureau didn't know about her. The FBI kept Eden and her extraordinary talent a thing of legend and rumor in the deepest, blackest backrooms of their clandestine world. No one knew their finest sometimes relied on what others would sarcastically term a *nut job*. Psychics were frauds and scammers, weren't they?

She chuckled into her sleeve at the world's opinion. Eden knew better. She'd accurately predicted and prevented the U. S. embassy bombing in Tokyo, Japan, just months earlier. The State Department *borrowed* her services when masked gunmen had kidnapped the Secretary of State, Royce Hammond, in broad daylight, off a street in Kazakhstan. Locating him had taken longer than she'd expected, but the nation's best *did* arrive in time, and they *were* able to prevent his beheading. The esteemed Secretary Hammond never knew he'd been given a second chance to live a long life with his wife of twenty years, all because of a *nut job*. He had no need to know.

The Federal Bureau of Investigation considered her one of their prime assets. They'd secretively deployed her to various U. S. embassies around the world when trouble struck. She did her thing, saved what or whom others couldn't, then went home until her skills were needed again. So why was she in the middle of Canada fighting to survive when she had the power to keep Americans safe abroad? Simple. Because she, Special Agent, Eden Stark, was now a target.

Enter Dr. Abraham Zaroyin, the neurosurgeon who used to be in charge of the Central Intelligence Agency's research and development. The whack job who thought he had the right to twist human nature through the experimental use of cybernetics. The madman whose defense plan for the nation included chipping every able-bodied sailor, airman, soldier, and marine with a device in their brains to subdue the primal instinct of fight or flight, and replace it with enhanced logic. In effect, he planned to turn America's active-duty military into programmable minions.

His argument stressed there would be no more friendly-fire mishaps, no more fog of battle blunders. War could be controlled at a remote site by someone smarter than the military experts on the ground, someone not caught up in the heat of battle. Like politicians. Or the president.

The scary part of the nightmare was that Zaroyin had strong congressional backing. And a lot of nerve. She'd been briefing Matt on her latest successful vision concerning the German ambassador's fifteen-year-old son who'd gone missing months earlier during spring break. She'd finally located him. In Chile. On a beach. The spoiled little shit.

Matt had just finished saying he didn't want her to waste any more talent or time on *Doogie Hauser*. In walked the madman. The second Eden had looked at Zaroyin, her blood had run cold. She'd seen past his friendly, lying eyes to the ruthless scheming predator beneath. He didn't want national security. He wanted power, and unlimited funding to accomplish his goal to get that power. He was there to enlist the FBI's support in convincing the CIA, but most of all, he was there because he needed her, Eden Stark, to make his plan work. He'd needed to meet her, face-to-face. She didn't understand why, only saw the evil intent darkening the genius of his brilliant mind.

She'd shared her suspicions with Matt. Sure enough, after a little FBI covert work, Matt had uncovered Zaroyin's insidious plan to build an army of drone soldiers. Matt had briefed his boss, Zachary Strong, the national director of the Bureau. He'd met with the CIA. Instead of granting Zaroyin additional funding for his bizarre plan, the CIA cut what funding they'd already budgeted to him and escorted him off Quantico.

And for a month, Eden had thought herself safe. She went to work and gave her country her best—until Matt's heart gave way in the middle of a Homeland Security briefing at the White House. Right ventricle. Her worst fears had come true. Zaroyin had already created his programmable soldiers. Eden had run for her life.

The question at the back of her mind was always the same. Who had outed her to the mad doctor in the first place? Who told him she had significant and reliable psychic skills? It wasn't common knowledge. Less than a handful of the Bureau's finest knew: Director Strong, Matt, and Dr. Penn, her physician.

When she hadn't been able to answer her own question, she locked her artfully decorated office at D.C. headquarters and disappeared. The FBI field office across country in San Francisco had seemed safest, until Zaroyin tracked her there. Then she'd run for the field office in Hawaii. No safety there, either. He'd arrived in less than a week. Next, she'd opted for Anchorage, Alaska, not wanting to flee the borders of her homeland for the likes of a madman. She knew three of the trusted agents in Anchorage. She should've been safe with them, right?

Wrong again. Her second sight had failed her, and another good friend in the Anchorage field office had died of a mysterious heart attack. Worse, Zaroyin had hit town in less than forty-eight hours. Eden literally came unglued when she caught sight of him stepping off the Alaskan Air Jetway. Three-piece brown suit. Black tie. Dressed for success and ready to conquer the world instead of hunting or fishing like the other passengers.

She'd been waiting for him, stalking the airport terminal. Backed into a corner, she knew then that she needed help. If anyone could save her, it had to be the director of the Bureau, right? Eden had called Director Strong, but he'd been out of his office. Didn't it figure? She'd left a hurried message on his voicemail and hopped a random ride with the nearest bush pilot she could find, Charlie Sweets. Lied. Told him her abusive ex-husband was after her, that she needed to disappear in order to survive, which was kind of true.

Charlie'd said climb aboard; he could make it happen. He knew a place. Was already on his way east to Greenland with supplies for some trophy fishermen. No one would ever find her there. Now there she was, alone in the middle of nowhere with two cyborg-type killer FBI agents out of a weird sci-fi movie on her trail.

"Let 'em come," she growled to the dark. Let 'em find out the hard way. Eden Stark was no simpering female, crying for some white knight to drop out of the sky and rescue her. Heck, no. She might've run before, but she had skills, and she meant to use every last one of her FBI talents to survive. Besides her inherently peculiar and sometimes spooky mental prowess, she'd been trained by the country's elite anti-terrorist team. Not many could best the Bureau when it came to training its agents. To shoot. To kill. To survive.

Okay, so it was mostly target practice at the indoor range at Quantico, but she never doubted herself. Mika Koenig and Arthur Shields might find her, they might even hurt her, but they would not take her back alive. She carried another FBI asset under her arm—her Glock pistol, loaded and perfectly fitted to her smaller grip. If all else failed, she meant to go out in a hail of fire.

She wrapped up tight inside Charlie's sleeping bag, content and self-assured. Kind of. True survivors were those who made up their minds to be self-reliant, and that was what she was. True survivors faced what the world threw at them, and they fortified themselves to do it alone. She'd made that decision to be a survivor years ago at the edge of a lonely grave. Alone worked better in the long run, both personally and professionally. It brooked fewer complications. Why change?

The moment her eyelids flickered shut, words she could not clearly decipher soothed even as they worried. They seemed to whisper *I'm coming for you,* but not in a frightening way. Not as a threat at all. More like a promise. Eden stiffened in her molded seat. She tilted forward, striving to see past the shattered windshield when she couldn't. Sometimes, the simple act of thinking she could allowed more second sight. More vision.

The farthest edge of her peripheral wavered, as if flexing its far-sighted muscles. Eden stilled as her psychic sight struggled with a glimmer of light, and on its heels, a particularly sensual premonition. The distinct shape of a man stepped forward from the pre-dawn murk. No definite facial features identified him enough to make him recognizable, yet she sensed he searched deliberately for her, though not as a predator. More as a—protector?

Ha. That would be the day. A man coming to her aid? She knew better. Only Matt Hartigen had ever acted on her behalf, and he was dead and buried. She shook the vision out of her head. Zaroyin's mindless drones were the only men coming after her now, and they weren't protectors. If she wasn't careful, she'd be dead by morning.

The image persisted. This man was different. He wasn't a predator, but she was definitely linked with him. Her tongue didn't cringe from the sympathetic, coppery taste of his victims' blood. No sense of terror from the sins at his hands assaulted her with the overwhelming need to run. No stifling fear of those he'd buried alive pervaded the space between, suffocating her. All the psychic, telling signs and empathic signals she'd come to rely on when seeking out assassins, terrorists, or kidnappers remained oddly silent.

Then who are you? she silently asked the far-off messenger in the inky night.

Eden had come to equate auras, the energy a person expelled back into the universe, with good and evil. The hues surrounding Koenig and Shields were gray-black smudges, like smoke from a funeral pyre. They were harbingers of Death. But this guy? The one with amber eyes? The one whose pulse she could detect throbbing at his throat, each beat of his heart a vibration on the cosmic web of life? This guy was comfortably familiar in a weird, psychic way. The air around his soul shimmered with the barest hint of crystal blue, the spiritual color of intelligence, loyalty, and—love.

The warmth of those honey-rich amber eyes reached out to her. It was like a shot of single-barrel whiskey to her soul, to be gulped, not sipped. Inhaled, not swallowed. The sensation warmed her down to her toes. It burned into the secret sight of her innermost eye, lulled her with a familiar sensation she couldn't pin down—not yet.

It had been years since this delicious warmth in her belly had reached out for her. It took a full minute before she recognized it came from that same man who'd reached out to her and begged *God, let me die.*

She gulped, daring to believe. *Are you... are you him?*

The whiskey-flavored spirit stayed just beyond her reach. He didn't answer, but a delicious shiver raced up her body, sparking goose bumps on the insides of her legs and up her spine, an unlikely pleasurable sensation given her very precarious predicament. The vision faded, robbing the last of her strength along with her sight of the tender visitor. Most visions left her anxious for her victims or angry with their oppressors. Some energized, but this one left her calm and drowsy. Feeling—lucky?

She ducked her head into the depths of Ralph Lauren's finest. Lucky was the last thing she'd ever be. Pegged by her harrowing day, Eden closed her eyes. This latest warning, if that was truly what the man with amber eyes was, needed further scrutiny. To do that, her brain needed to solve the problem while she slept. If she could sleep.

Her breathing slowed. She allowed her body to relax and embrace what heat her over-priced down-filled cocoon offered. She had time. If they ran all night, which was unlikely even for cybernetically-enhanced soldiers, it would take her assassins hours to reach her.

She pushed one final thought out to Koenig and Shields. *You guys should be worried. Not me.*

Ontario wasn't known for steep mountains, but the current landscape offered just enough pitch that Ky's high-tech snow boots slid over the thickly crusted surface like skates on ice. It was well after dark by the time he and Tate approached ground zero, the site of the crash.

They hadn't seen the wolf again—not that it mattered. Both Ky and Tate carried bear spray, a powerful deterrent to most large predators. Alex had a hard and fast rule about collateral damage, even for man-eating carnivores. If a worst-case scenario presented itself, and the bear spray failed, they could always fall back on the twin Ruger pistols tucked under both agents' arms. The sniper's first rule: *Better safe than sorry.*

As much as Ky and Tate pushed forward, the guys coming at them south-by-southwest pressed faster. They'd closed in quickly. Too quickly. They had to be using some kind of motorized device to travel, but in these woods? Odd. Really odd.

Ky stopped just short of the Cessna wreck half hidden in the trees. He needed to confront these two unknown quantities bearing down on his ass before he risked making contact with Agent Stark and her pilot, especially if they were injured. These two jokers on his butt had gotten annoying real fast. Enough was enough.

"Intercept," he muttered to his partner via their TEAMshield link.

"Copy that," Tate returned the perfunctory response.

Both Ky and he dropped belly to the ground, facing their adversaries. Ky tuned his goggles to night vision. Those following them were instantly lit up in lime-green display amongst the black pillars of lodge-pole pines. Dark stripes of bandoliers crisscrossed their chests. No snowmobile engine noise broke the eerie silence, though. Odd. These guys were on foot. Despite the knee-deep snow, both men were still on a dead run. They hadn't slowed or hesitated. Just. Kept. Coming.

"Why the fun run?" Ky wondered, referencing the Corps' demanding habit of early-morning fitness runs that were anything but fun. He looked closer, but the lime-green-tinted dark didn't reveal many more details. Both men were helmeted. No insignia visible. No rank. Just two guys in hot pursuit. Of who? Him and Tate? FBI Special Agent Stark? Why?

Pulling a flashlight up from one of his many pockets, Ky lifted to one knee. "Time to meet and greet. Let's see who these jokers are. Could be search and rescue."

"Doubt it. They act more like black ops."

"Let's find out. State your business," Ky called to the advancing duo, the beam of his light in their goggle-covered eyes.

Without one go-to-hell, the guys dropped to their knees, compact rifles drawn, and opened fire, peppering Ky and Tate with a hail of pine bark and needles.

Not exactly what Ky had expected. He dropped his flashlight to give the shooters something to aim at while he and Tate rolled in opposite directions away from it. Once out of the line of fire, Ky zeroed in on the shooter nearest him, took careful aim, and *thud*, hit the guy in the upper thigh. Joker One didn't slow, much less drop like he should've. But he did pivot and fire on Ky's new position. What the hell? Joker One responded as if that hot round in his thigh didn't hurt like a mother. Like he didn't feel it. Who the hell were these guys indeed?

The fresh fragrance of shredded evergreen filled the air as the onslaught continued. Ky burrowed into the snow bank between him and Joker One. He assumed Tate had made the same mistake, thinking he would only have to wound these guys and not kill them. That day was done.

"Take 'em out," Ky ordered via TEAMshield.

Tate's grunt of agreement came back instantly through his link.

It took two more rounds—one to Joker One's groin since the one to his helmet had glanced off. At last the men dropped and the forest silenced.

Tate, breathing hard, pushed up from beneath a downed tree a few yards from Ky.

"You good?" Ky asked, drawing in a lungful of the overwhelming evergreen scent.

"'Course." Tate brushed snow, woodchips, and needles off his jacket. He straightened his goggles and headed straight to the assailants, his weapon drawn and ready to kill if either man so much as wheezed.

Ky scrambled out of the snow bank, his ears ringing despite his protective earmuffs. He rolled his neck, searching for the reason for his lingering unease. His goggles detected no other lime-green assassins on his butt. The wolf hadn't shown, either. Only the Cessna's locator beacon pinged steadily on his heads-up display. But why was his sniper spidey-sense tingling up his spine like an electric wire? Why the extra shot of acid in his gut?

He held his position beside the wide trunk of a mighty evergreen, his whole body on high alert. Someone else was still out there.

And watching...

Chapter Three

Eden shifted her right foot, flattening her sole to the tree trunk behind her while she studied the grisly scene. Steady shooting had awakened her from a dead-to-the-world sleep she'd succumbed to. More like it had scared the heck out of her. Tumbling face-first out of the Cessna, she thought she'd been found and was fast on her way to being dead. But now that she was fully awake and had ten years scared off her, yes, she had been found, but no. She wasn't dead. Not yet.

Two men in what looked like tactical snow gear, stood between her and the men they'd just murdered. *If* it was murder she'd witnessed. She hadn't seen who'd fired first, but she was pretty certain those two dead guys were the rogue agents who'd been sent to kill her.

If they knew it or not, these strangers had just saved her the trouble of having to put down her FBI brethren. Her second sight wasn't responding to validate that, so she delayed the welcome wagon greeting. Eden needed to know who these guys were before she exposed her position. They could be more cyborg types, though she didn't get that kind of a reading from either of them.

Her heart still pounded like a greenhorn, which, she reminded herself, she wasn't. *First thing's first.* She took a deep breath and steadied the hefty Glock in her palm while she scanned the strangers. Her pistol's sight employed the wonders of thermal imaging plus laser accuracy. She could literally bring her target up close enough to count his eyelashes or the freckles on his nose. Unfortunately, these guys were both in winter gear with collars up, heads covered with knitted beanies, and faces hidden behind some kind of high-tech goggles. She couldn't see much more than their bulky shapes.

Both carried some impressive gear. Custom-made short-stocks were slung over their shoulders. Sat phones dangled on holsters at their hips.

Eden trembled from head to toe. Lying on her belly did not exactly make her invisible, not with her over-sized *girls* squeezed into her jacket like they were. She'd never been one of those tiny waifs that could fit in a size two.

Oddly, that thought led back to the weapon in her palm. She always knew she might eventually have to shoot someone someday, but now that the moment had arrived, it took her last nerve just to hold the weapon steady. Keeping her fingers off the trigger, she zeroed in on Sniper Standing, the one as still as a shadow near the big tree. And there he was, a living, breathing, flesh-and-blood man in her sights, not some paper target on the range. This was real. Her heart rate kicked up. Could she do it? *God, I hope I don't have to.*

No adrenaline brightened his aura, normally a significant tell. Interesting. Either he had some serious control over his emotions or he was a psychopath on duty, one who killed without remorse, anger or empathy. He turned and faced in her direction, as if he'd heard her thought.

She ducked, flattening those plump girls of hers against the ground. *Snap. Does he know I'm here?*

Risking a glimpse, she lifted her head just enough to target him again. Sniper Standing hadn't moved, just stood there as still as the trees around him, as if he were waiting. *Oh my heck! He used a pistol to take Koenig and Shields out? Just a pistol? Against what sounded like submachine gun fire? Is he flaming stupid? Like me? I'm using a pistol, too. Oh, yeah.* Eden gulped her condemnation down. She wasn't much brighter than he was, not lying in the snow with only her Glock and its six rounds against two men who appeared to be trained soldiers.

She forced herself to focus and mentally stripped Sniper Standing's winter gear away. In seconds, he dropped one hundred pounds to a trim one hundred and fifty, maybe less. Tall. Six-foot-something. Lean, but wide-shouldered. Muscled biceps and pecs, the bulging kind that stretched his winter cammies like hidden coiled nautical ropes, the kind that secured ships to docks and tugs to cargo barges. He definitely worked out.

He was ex-military, if she was a guessing woman. But wary. The guy hadn't holstered his pistol yet, only lowered his hood and left a knitted beanie covering his head. No longer panting, he'd slowed his breathing and expelled regular puffs of wintery vapor, still facing in her direction like he knew where she was.

Summoning her tough chick, federal agent persona, she opted for the darned-straight, over-confidence that came with it. *Let him look. Let him worry. I'm in charge here. This is my crash scene.*

Which is why I'm cowering on my belly in the dark?

To regain some semblance of false confidence, she pivoted her weapon to his partner, the guy kneeling over the bodies. Sniper Praying. Same military get-up. Shorter. Thicker at the waist. Darker complexion. He'd lowered his goggles. Shaggy black brows hung off a wide forehead, shadowing his eyes. The guy was methodical. Quick. He'd already searched pockets the way she would've if she'd killed Koenig and Shields.

Her scope scrolled back to Sniper Standing like it had a mind of its own. *Look at me*, she commanded mentally, knowing full well he couldn't hear her.

Guess again.

Sniper Standing took a step in her direction as if he *had* heard. As if he knew right where she lay hidden and had caught every word.

She ducked back out of sight. *Oh, heck, no. He didn't.*

Oh yes, he sure did. He cocked his arm, one hand lifted to the side of his head. A flashlight flickered on. The bright beam danced over the tree trunks between them. "Who's out there? Show yourself," he ordered.

Snap? How's he doing that? But he couldn't have heard her. She hadn't spoken out loud. Only one other person had ever responded so completely to her mental suggestions, and he'd gone silent for years. Two years, six months, and seven days to be precise. *It can't be him. Not Ky Winchester. Not here. No way.*

Breathing hard, she buried her pistol beneath her so nothing reflective showed. She maintained her prone position, her second sight oddly unreliable. She'd seen Koenig and Shields clearly when they were still miles away. Why not these guys? Who were they? Zaroyin's latest and greatest drones? Someone better? Or worse? Could Sniper Standing possibly be that delicious whiskey-flavored shadow?

"Shit. Get over here," Sniper Praying muttered to his buddy. "These guys are FBI. Look at their creds."

Sniper Standing stomped through the snow to crouch near his partner, his wrists limp and his hands between his knees, but his gaze still zeroed in on Eden's position.

Sniper Praying was on his hands and knees, peering closer at one of the bodies. "Look. This guy's wired. Shit, it's... The damned thing runs straight down his chest and... what the hell? It goes all the way into his pants." He lifted his gaze to his buddy as he unbuckled the dead man's belt and unzipped his trousers. "Are you seeing this? It's stuck in his..."

Eden couldn't detect the rest of Sniper Praying's words. He'd spoken too low. Sniper Standing wasn't speaking any louder. *Oh, come on, guys. Stop whispering. What did you find? Just spit it out. What's going on? Is it a bomb?*

Couldn't be. They weren't running. They didn't even look worried, just puzzled.

Sniper Standing produced a knife from his boot and sliced the wire. "Now I've seen everything. See if the other one's wired, too. They could be transmitting their coordinates, for all we know."

Sniper Praying obeyed. In seconds, he'd confirmed both were wired. Interesting and troublesome. Zaroyin wired his drones? Why? Apprehension scuttled up and over every last vertebra in Eden's spinal column, as if her enemy had stuck a pin in a map of the world and said, *'There you are, my pretty.'*

"The boss needs in on this shit, Ky," Sniper Praying growled.

Ky? It is him. Eden couldn't draw a breath. Her heart kicked up a noisy roar inside her head. This was the same man who'd reached out to her all those years ago. She couldn't believe it.

"He's already seen everything we have," Ky said as he pushed to his feet, "but you're right. We need to report in."

Sniper Praying rolled the body over and face down, still searching pockets. "You call it in. I've got to get these guys wrapped and up in the trees. I'm not in the mood to fight off that black wolf and his buddies."

Ky didn't argue, just stood staring into the dark like he knew right where she lay hidden, as if he could hear her heart beating. Frustrated, she unleashed her second sight one more time, needing to be absolutely sure, to know if his body carried the scars. The last time she'd been in touch with him—if this guy really was the same man—he'd been nearly beaten to death. She'd seen the USMC tattoo on his chest and what they did to him, the methodical knife cuts, the burns, the kicks and beatings with canes and rods. Ky had to have scars all over his body. On his face. His chest. Even... there.

Eden blushed at her audacious nerve to see beneath her victim's clothing. She never understood her psychic ability to examine the physical health and wellbeing of her subjects, either. She only knew that she'd done it plenty of times in the past. Her unique aptitude served the Bureau well. There was no reason to risk sending a SEAL team to rescue a dead victim.

But this was also why her father had left all those years ago. Casey hadn't been able to control her own sight, and Eden was just learning. Drake refused to have two women inside his head every hour of every day, so he'd walked. Funny. Neither Casey nor Eden had searched for him. Eden hadn't even considered it. She wondered now *why not?*

She tried another method to shake Ky's self-control. Projecting an image of the brutal cell he'd been trapped in, she baited him. Lured him to react. To over-react. To do something to see if Ky really was that man.

Once again, he didn't do what she'd expected. Didn't groan. Didn't shake his head to expel the demonic suggestion. Didn't even cry out. Instead, he lowered his goggles and snagged the cap off his head. Very slowly, he rotated his head from right to left and lifted his face to the night sky. His chest expanded. Breathing in. Breathing out. He repeated the simple stress-reducing exercise, then ended with the same stare in her direction. Like she didn't worry him in the least. As if he had all the time in the world.

Eden lay there mesmerized at his self-control. *Darn. If this is the same Ky, he's good.* All along she'd thought her second sight had located him two and a half years earlier, but now she wondered *why only him?* Why not everyone in the world who suffered? It was time to find out.

Eden lifted to her knees, her pistol still trained on Ky. Her weapon's laser sights confirmed his body mass. Her visual confirmed everything else about his physique, like that was hard, umm, difficult to do.

I see you, Ky Whoever-You-Are. Gentle man, not predator. Military training, yes. Mercenary, no. Heartless, never. Physically hot. Umm, I mean, excellent bone structure, yes. Ex-cell-lent. If—you really are the same guy.

Heat flamed up her neck at the errant way her brilliant mind worked, but her lips curled into a genuine smile. She squelched it. This was no happy reunion. This was work. Might even be war. She steadied her nerve to take the first shot if needed. Make that her first shot *ever*. Her hands trembled at the thought. She swallowed hard. She'd trained all right. Just never executed.

Wrong again. He lowered his pistol to his thigh when he sighted her. Gave up right then and there like he knew she was safe when she really meant to look lethal and intimidating.

"It's about time," he said, his gloved right hand extended in friendly greeting despite the weapon trained on him. "I've been looking for you."

What'd he mean by that? I've been looking for you? Not we?

Darned if a smile didn't tug the corners of his lips. Full lips, not thin and hard, not scarred or distorted, either, but ample as if he'd never been slapped around or beaten. Kissable, and she, the FBI's only psychic, was completely in the dark as to why the handsome smile, or why she cared, or why her heart kicked up a staccato dance tune. She sure as heck didn't return the cordial greeting. Her weapon trained on his full body mass didn't seem to worry him, either. *You should be scared of me. Why aren't you? Do you remember me?*

This Ky person couldn't be the same guy from Afghanistan. Torture victims took years to recover. Some never did. Too many devolved into drug addicts or alcoholics and unless they had a strong support system, they self-medicated themselves to death. It simply couldn't be him.

"Who are you?" she barked, her elbow locked and her left hand gripped under her right to keep it from shaking. *Please tell me you served in Afghanistan.*

"Agent Ky Winchester at your service, ma'am. My buddy, Agent Tate Higgins." He nodded at Sniper Praying. "Director Strong asked us to come get you since the Bureau's *persona non grata* is in Canada at the moment. You are Special Agent Eden Stark, right?"

Who else would I be? She hesitated. This was too much of a coincidence. Maybe there were two Ky Winchesters? She nodded curtly, still trying to exert one shred of FBI superiority over a common federal contractor who should be worried, darn it. "Did you serve in Afghanistan?" Okay, so it was a stupid question to lead with, but she needed to know.

A shy grin just added to Agent Winchester's boyish charm, the charm she needed to ignore at all cost. This guy was seriously getting under her skin, and it had to stop. He was good-looking in a gentle, rugged kind of way. So? Lots of guys were cute. None of them affected her like he did, and why was her heart pounding so loud in her ears?

Just answer the question.

The riddle of his first contact shivered up her spine. If this was the same man, there was a link already between them. No name. No title or rank. Just a prayer tossed into the universe for almighty help. A prayer she'd caught somehow in her psychic web and rushed to answer.

"Yes, ma'am. I'm not sure what that has to do with anything, but me and Tate both did." He winked. The jerk had the nerve to wink and—gah! She could've kissed him right then and there. Her heart turned into a cheerleader in her chest screaming, *Yes! Yes! Sis. Boom. Bah. It's him!*

Striving for that whole law-and-order thing, she holstered her weapon, nodding curtly toward the deceased, still acting tough and testing the air for a lie. "Who are they?"

"You ought to know. They're FBI," Agent Higgins grumbled. "They had submachine guns with custom-made eighty-round sticks and enough ammo to end you. You want to tell us why?"

Do I tell? Should I tell him? The implications of pulling outsiders into obvious FBI intrigue did not escape Eden. Her loyalty to the Bureau ran deep, but they'd blundered before. Their dirty laundry had been national news way too often, but this was Ky. *That* Ky. And his friend. *They* were there, not anyone else. Not her federal brothers or sisters. *They* had put their lives at risk saving her from two rogue agents. *They* deserved to know something. Maybe the truth.

Ky crossed his arms over his chest, that relaxed and completely unintimidating smile testing his lips, taunting her as if he had something on his mind. Maybe a—kiss?

Flustered at the way her second sight wasn't working while her hormones seemed to be overly stimulated, she went for broke, striving to stay on task. "Yeah, I know who they were. You guys just took down FBI Agents Mika Koenig and Arthur Shields. You're right. They were sent to kill me, but not by Director Strong. Sorry about the gun, guys. I needed to be sure you were safe." Eden meant what she said and she put every last ounce of her not-so-tough persona into it.

Agent Winchester studied her, his lips pursed and his smiling eyes sparkling. She couldn't help but notice they'd literally skated down the front of her goose down jacket to her knocking knees, taking in every shred of her false bravado like he could see right through her. Maybe like he could see through Ralph Lauren, too, and all the way to her... gah! The way her mind was working!

"You're holding back. Where's the pilot? What's really going on?" he asked, his tone rife with suspicion and something else that vibrated the air molecules between them with genuine concern and tension. Sexual tension. Lots of it.

No, I'm not holding anything back. Well, okay. Maybe I am. A little. Darn. You're good.

"Charlie Sweets is dead. I buried him." Eden blew out a deep breath, shaken that she was so close to losing her composure to this man. Agent Higgins didn't frazzle her in the least, but Agent Winchester? It took all her concentration to retain a hint of professional decorum.

This wasn't her. She might have grown close to her victims before those missions ended, but not once had she gotten this emotionally involved, and never on first sight. Whatever connection started between them two and a half years ago had just sprung back to life with a vengeance. She wanted to climb into Ky's muscular arms like a little girl, to cover his handsome face with kisses while she ripped that jacket off his broad shoulders and proved he was the same man from Kabul. She wanted to trace her fingertips over that USMC tattoo on his chest and the scars, and kiss everything better. She wanted to comfort him now the way she'd comforted him then, but in person.

Instead, Eden drew in a deep breath of FBI control and nodded toward the bodies like she did this kind of thing every day. Like she wasn't hyperventilating and sweating up a storm in Ralph Lauren. She growled in her deepest voice. Darned if it didn't come out breathy and seductive instead of threatening. "If I'm right, these guys were duped into volunteering for Dr. Zaroyin's twisted idea of national security. His cybernetic enhancement trials. Once he got hold of them, they lost all control. All freedom to choose. Everything."

Agent Winchester cocked his head, maybe not yet believing, but still smiling.

How could she fight that coaxing, little-boy charisma? Eden gave up the fight for superiority. "You see, Agent Winchester, it's like this."

Chapter Four

Ky let her talk. Make that, he needed her to talk. The moment she'd stepped forward, his soul seemed to reach out to her in recognition. To zero itself. All she'd rattled on about was her pilot and the crash and what sounded like a bizarre *007* movie premise, something about a mad CIA scientist and his plan to take over the world, yet Ky's heart had stilled, and he could only focus on one thing—the sultry melody dripping off her sexy lips. His hunger for a woman's mouth awakened for the first time in years. FBI bullshit had never sounded so good.

He couldn't place where he'd met this charming woman in a fluffy fur cap before, but there was something damned familiar about the inflection to her voice. Something kindred. He'd heard it once before, just couldn't place precisely where or when. She harbored a western accent without the annoying twang. Maybe West Coast? A lilt of some ethnicity he couldn't nail down lent a musical quality to her words, like the wind chimes on his mother's porch that rang out the tones to "Pachelbel's Canon." It was rich and deep. Not grating. Not squeaky. If anything, her voice tended toward masculine. Throaty. Hearty.

He'd never felt such a potent reaction to a woman's voice before. She enticed a strong physical response in him that reminded him of—something. Warmth and comfort. Satin sheets and sweaty bodies. His and—hers. Heat surged under his skin, lighting every last damned male receptor. All of them. Even the dormant ones that hadn't lit up in years. Yes, even *that one.*

Like a good red wine, he wanted to roll the taste of Agent Stark around in his mouth and savor her until the bottle was dry. Until he licked the rim and tasted every last drop of—

God. I'm losing my mind. Where'd these asinine thoughts come from?

But wasn't she the pretty thing? Agent Stark had nerve approaching two armed men right after one helluva shootout. Sure, he'd smiled and offered his hand. That shaky pistol in her gloved grip might have accidentally gone off if he'd done anything else. He estimated her at five-three, a little on the plush and plump side of feminine if that padded jacket stretched tight across her chest and hips was any indicator. Either that, or she had something hidden in her bra. *Maybe I should frisk her. Handle her—it. Them.*

He kept his hands to himself and continued watching. With every word, she projected a 'tough chick' attitude—just not very well. There was no way this little thing was the FBI's finest black operator. Her pretty eyes were too soft, too wide, and too innocent. Eden Stark might be professionally trained, but Ky pegged her as an innocent caught up in something FBI-related. Maybe a secretary or a file clerk. Definitely not a regular field agent. No way. She wasn't dangerous enough.

"Trust me. They won't be the last," she ended her monologue with a self-righteous chin lift that did something to his manhood, to that white-knight complex that tended to get him into trouble. The need to serve others had helped him get his life back together, but the inherent need to rescue those who needed rescuing also took a hard toll on a guy. He had the scars to prove it.

Her eyes flashed with annoyance just as his brain switched back to I-should've-been-listening mode. "Excuse me?" he asked lamely.

Damn Tate for noticing and grunting.

Agent Stark took a half-step forward and glared up at Ky. Her dainty brows furrowed with disapproval, her hands on her hips. Tangled blond hair slipped from her fur cap. Frost crystals clung to this wannabe-tough little gal's lashes. She scrunched her nose, and he was ten kinds of smitten and way over his head.

Hell, what was a guy to do? Agent Stark couldn't weigh more than a hundred twenty pounds dripping wet, but she'd turned into an ice princess with a temper. Cutest thing ever. Maybe it was the simple fact that he outweighed her, but the urge to throw her over his shoulder and test her sass flared to life.

Everything about her incited the sexual side of him that had been asleep for years. He'd come back to work, but he'd been damned careful not to get involved with any woman, on the job or off. The men and women on The TEAM were his family. They understood. They got him. And until now... that had been enough.

"Haven't you heard anything I've said?" she asked, her voice sharpened like a shard of ice with a sizzling-hot edge. "Zaroyin followed me to Hawaii. Then he followed me to Alaska. I think he knows where I am right now. I don't know why he's doing it, but—" Her eyes widened, her gloved hands fluttering up the back of her neck. "That bastard. I'll kill him if he... he wouldn't!"

Ky guessed that he did. "He wouldn't what?"

"Yearly physical. Bureau policy. But I didn't go to him for mine. I went to Dr. Penn, only..." She tossed her fur cap to the ground. Billowing dark-blond hair coursed over her shoulders, lighting up those pesky male receptors again and taking his breath. Ky's heart kicked into second gear. *What is it about long, silky hair that stirs a guy's soul right down to his cock?*

"He did something to me. That bastard! I can feel it." She peeled off her gloves and they hit the snow next. She'd no more than raked her fingers up and over the back of her head when she stamped one booted foot, also hot-damned cute. Petulant, but sexy. But then her eyes rolled back and... *oomph*. Down she went. Out cold.

Ky rushed to catch her before she hit the snow. "What the hell?"

"Check her over. See what's broke," Tate suggested, seemingly unaffected by the charms of the fainting female in their midst. "Probably just a concussion."

Ky's throat went dry the second she'd landed in his arms. Panic at holding a delicately built woman for the first time in years kicked his blood pressure up through the roof of his skull. Either that or he really was seeing stars—the last thing he needed.

He'd known he'd probably have to do some triage on this trip, that both victims might need serious medical assistance, and he'd brought enough gloves in case he had to handle people. He was prepared for that, but a fainting woman? All of her? In his arms, the cushion of her breasts pressed against his chest? If not for the padding between them, he'd have set her on the ground and backed away from Agent Stark. Holding this woman was really—nice.

He gathered her in closer to get her better situated on his lap and off the frozen ground. It was a lucky catch. Kind of. She did have some seriously gorgeous hair—not what he'd expected from a Fed. She puffed tiny frozen breaths into the air, drawing his attention to the perfect bow of her lips. To his compulsion to taste those lips. Just once...

Ky shook off his intense reaction and deferred to his training. *Assess. Stabilize. Extract. And always keep your damned gloves on and your hands to yourself.* That last rule was purely a Winchester add-on, but he had no choice. Not tonight. He'd have to make physical contact to assess this woman's medical status. Tate was watching.

Swallowing hard, he manned up. He bit the tip of his gloved index finger and pulled the leather glove off, letting it drop onto Stark's jacket. On her breasts. Okay, so they were tucked nice and tight beneath her zipper and a lot of padding, but still...

He was a man. He knew right where they were.

Tate grunted. Ky stalled. His greatest fear and his greatest desire rolled into one eternal torment. Touching another person. A woman. Skin to skin.

Agent Stark sighed one of those breathy, whimpering female sighs, and...

Oh, for hell's sake. How tough could it be? Ky swallowed hard, forcing his customary reactions to run in the opposite direction and into man-up mode. This FBI asset was not the depraved Taliban banker known as Nizari. She hadn't tortured anyone—neither was she one of Nizari's depraved soldiers. Honest to God, she was a little thing, and she couldn't hurt him if she tried.

Ky still struggled with his predicament. This would be the first time in years he'd laid a finger on a female gender. What if she moaned when he handled her? What if she sighed? Worse—what if he liked it? His pulse raced. Rapid breathing kicked in. His body turned clammy with sweat.

This is really stupid, his logical mind insisted.

I know, his irrational fear snarled back like it always did, because Nizari's despicable shadow still hulked over him. He'd followed Ky home, damn him, and some days, the bastard of Kabul still won.

Ky gritted his teeth. He had to get this done before he lost control or before Tate took over her care, and that just plain was not going to happen.

A familiar whiff from long ago drifted up into his flared nostrils. He lowered his head to Stark's breath and sniffed again, wanting more. Make that needing more. There it was again, that soothing scent of menthol and camphor, and what the hell? It came from her? Nah, it couldn't be her, the angel of his dreams. Could it? Nah. It had to be all that evergreen scent from the chewed up trees. That made better sense, and yet his pulse slowed the same as it had years ago. His rising panic lost out to calm—just like two and a half years ago.

"Well?" Tate asked grumpily, his top lip lifted in his perpetual half-sneer.

"Don't rush me," Ky retorted a little too quickly, still trying to catch his balance around the little gal in his lap. He got down to business. He ran his bare fingertips over her forehead. Oddly, that contact didn't sting or burn. It didn't create panic. He didn't need to run. He could breathe.

Ky drew in a deeper breath. He tunneled his bare fingers beneath the silky tresses spilling across his arm and knee like a river of liquid gold. Gently, he probed her scalp for swelling or a goose egg. A concussion would explain her fainting.

The white knight in him rose to the surface. Instead of a cut, the pads of his fingertips encountered something beneath her skin behind her right ear. The bump had nothing to do with the Cessna falling out of the sky, not with the distinct edges and what felt like a small cut to the side of it. He lifted the swatch of her hair out of his way, peering into the shadowy depths.

"Found something, but I can't see what it is. Let's make camp and get her out of the cold. Start a fire. We can report in then, too."

Tate grunted, pointing into the dark. "I'll put the tent up by the wreck."

"Sounds good." Now that he had a good hold on Stark, Ky lifted her hood over her head. She was still out cold, huffing in short breaths, a good sign.

He tucked her face under his chin, needing to keep her warm and liking the rare feel of a woman up close and personal. The simple contact of her lips on his bare skin soothed him, as if she'd lit an ember inside a stone-cold wood-burning stove. Something flamed to life way down deep in his gut, something warm and irresistible.

As usual, Tate didn't let him down. The genius of a man raised in the tough Alaskan wilderness by his outdoorsman father always amazed Ky. There wasn't much to the tent he set up but telescoping fiberglass poles and enough nylon for a domed-ceiling over four guys. Once a person's body heat warmed the interior, it would still be cold, but semi-comfortable. A couple of bodies crammed in during a snowstorm could keep it livable for a short time. A good layer of snow around and over the top of it would add insulation, and the MREs that Ky and Tate both carried would keep a guy alive during remote ops like this one. Wishing he didn't have to choke them down, maybe, but alive.

"Check the plane. Bring over whatever's usable," Ky suggested as he climbed into their home-away-from-home, still cradling Agent Stark. She had yet to stir, and he wasn't uncaring enough to risk her body temp dropping by setting her on the cold ground. No. He could stand holding her a little while longer. It actually felt—good. Really good.

"I'll hunt at daybreak if the weather holds. Need meat." Yeah, that was Tate for you. Half-caveman. Half-ex-Army Ranger.

"Water first. Let's get some snow melted. She may just be dehydrated."

Another grunt, and Ky stopped worrying. Tate was on the job. He'd make certain the necessities were taken care of.

Soon, the soft glow of a crackling fire lit the outside walls of the tent. With his companion agent rummaging through the wreck and setting up camp, Ky settled down to phone home. It'd be good to hear one of the guys again. Maybe Lee. If he worshipped anyone or anything, it was Lee Hart, the Marine who'd single-handedly rescued him from that hellhole outside of Kabul. Imagine Ky's surprise when he'd met Lee the second time at the hospital and got to look into his green eyes. If that wasn't unsettling after all the snuggling Ky had done with his green-eyed angel, nothing was.

It gave a man pause was what it did. Ky wondered who he'd imagined that night he was rescued, but he knew better. Lee might have the same eye color, but he was not the same angel. The hue was completely different. Ky's green-eyed angel's eyes were different, more the clear green of a mountain stream running over moss on a wintery morning. Lee's voice wasn't the same, either, and there'd been no hint of mentholatum when Lee had introduced himself. Only cinnamon, thank God.

Lee had come to the hospital for a long visit with Ky and a job offer from one, Alex Stewart, another of Ky's heroes. The man he hadn't even known had reached out to him, a stranger, and based solely on Lee's recommendation, Alex gave Ky a good job despite his debilitating PTSD, and the fact he was still in the hospital and had months of therapy ahead of him.

Nizari had done his damnedest to break Ky, but Alex was a natural at cutting through the bullshit in a guy's screwed up head. He had a way, a gruff way, mind you, but a definite way of inspiring and leading. What the Veteran's Hospital failed at, Alex provided in the guise of high expectations and a boatload of profanity.

He honed in on what a guy could do instead of what he couldn't. He'd taken a broken, confused piece-of-shit Marine, and made Ky feel like a man again. Gave him a tough job. Told him to do it right, and expected he'd get it done. Demanded that deadlines be adhered to. Chewed his ass when things went wrong. Brooked no excuses. Rarely praised. Made Ky toe the line. Made him nearly normal again, too.

But mostly, the tough-as-nails guy cared. Alex might never admit it, but he should've gone into psychology or some related field. After all the anti-depressants, the well-intended group therapy, and a near miss at alcohol poisoning, *thank you very much, Wild Turkey,* Alex had cornered Ky in the emergency room one especially dark and dreary night. It wouldn't have been hard for the older man, not with Ky flat on his back with an IV hooked into his right arm and feeling like ten layers of shit. He'd asked the nurse-on-duty to call his emergency contact, Lee, but Alex had shown up instead. Not good.

Ky'd been fighting the darkest depression. Felt useless. Powerless against what Nizari had done to him. He'd truly wanted to end himself when he'd started slugging the booze out of sheer self-pity early that day. Couldn't remember how he'd got himself to the ER. Couldn't have walked. But he sure as hell remembered Alex showing up, all full of piss and vinegar and mad as a wolverine with one leg in a steel trap.

"Why the hell are you in here?" Alex had all but spat in Ky's face, leaned over the hospital bed rail like he was. "This is the last time you do this shit, you hear me, Winchester? I hired a damned good sniper, not a clown."

Ky had had no answer. He'd turned away, not able to meet this blue-eyed bastard come to rip him a new one. He was not that *damned good sniper* Alex thought he'd hired. He was nobody, a screwed up wreck, and Alex should've been a helluva lot smarter than to hire a mess like him. Whose fault was that, huh?

But Alex had never let up. Never backed down. Just kept chewing Ky's ass like he hadn't been tortured for days and nights over in dog-shit Afghanistan, like he didn't deserve *special* treatment for his *special* situation. Like he wasn't a victim, damn it.

Alex let him have it. "You think you're scared, Winchester? You think you're a loser? Guess again. I don't hire losers! Pull your head out of your ass and stop feeling sorry for yourself. Nizari was the bastard—not you. He's the one who's dead, isn't he? Lee ended him, didn't he? Knock off the world's-shit-all-over-me routine. Grow a pair!"

Now that you put it like that...

All Ky had been able to offer at that very astute observation was an embarrassed nod. Alex had a way of clearing a man's head, the same way he probably cleaned his rifle—with a good reaming.

The light dawned. Ky turned a corner that night. He'd rolled off the bed and peeled the IV out of his arm, mostly to get the hell away from Alex. But then he'd spent the rest of the night under the benevolent duress of his hard-charging boss at a Denny's Restaurant across the Potomac in Crystal City, Virginia. Some of what Alex said got stuck in Ky's head.

Stop thinking about what went down yesterday.

Keep on moving, damn it.

Leave it in the past.

Live, for Christ's sake. Most guys don't get a second chance. You did. Do something with it.

Man up!

By the time Alex was through with him, Ky was a survivor, not a victim. The way seemed clearer. He wised up. He committed himself to cleaner living. Meditation. Working his guts out for his belligerent boss and the guys and gals on The TEAM. He decided surviving wasn't enough. He wanted to live every last second he had left. Hadn't had a drink since. Still smoked Marlboro Reds, but hey—a guy needed one good vice.

Chapter Five

Fast forward to frozen Kenora, Ontario Province.

Ky slipped his goggles to the top of his head. Alex didn't need to see that he'd kept Agent Stark on his lap, only to keep her warm, mind you, while he activated TEAMhome and told it to "phone home."

"Dialing Mr. Stewart," TEAMhome's pleasant female voice responded in his ear. "Please hold."

"It's about damned time," Alex muttered at the first ring, despite the late hour. It had to have been well after midnight.

"Morning, Boss," Ky spoke quietly. "As you know, we've made contact with Agent Stark. Also neutralized two assailants intent on killing her."

"Saw that. Who the hell were they?" Alex barked, always the proverbial mad dog when his agents encountered trouble.

"That's where it gets interesting," Ky whispered, his head low and his mouth close enough to kiss the sleeping beauty in his arms. He moistened his lips. She looked temptingly delicious and the seam of her lips was still close enough to taste. "They're both FBI. Agent Stark believes they were under some kind of mind control, though. You know anything about a Dr. Zaroyin who worked for the CIA? Has some kind of experimental cybernetic program he's trying to get congressional funding for?"

"No, but I'm damned sure going to find out. Hold on."

Ky gave his boss sufficient time to bark an order for more info at Mother, another TEAM member who spent far too much time working late. Whether she was just that smart or had a network of friends in all the right places, she could put her manicured fingernails on the darnedest trivia about any federal investigation on the planet.

It also gave Ky the opportunity to appreciate the warmth emanating from the feminine body curled into his body like she belonged there. Agent Stark pressed her face into his chest, and it didn't feel all that bad knowing that a good-looking woman had turned toward him. So what if she was unconscious? She almost looked willing, as if she wanted to be there. He didn't mind holding her. She smelled good in a refreshing, menthol kind of way, too. Oddly refreshing. Totally comforting. Like something he'd walked away from in a distant life and had rediscovered.

Was it in any way possible this FBI Agent could be his angel? He took another deep breath, wishing she'd open her eyes and that those pretty eyes would be green. The right green.

Tate pushed through the tent flap with a sleeping bag, a fur wrap, and a battery-operated lantern in his arms. "You good?" he asked as he stuffed the bag into one corner and lit the tent interior with the soft glow of the portable light in another.

Ky pulled the small fur wrap out of his arms and drifted it over Stark's body. "Yeah. I'm on hold. Take a load off."

"Can't. Plane's full of canned foods. Fishing gear. Household stuff. I'm scavenging what I can before it's frozen solid."

"Any medical supplies? Stark might need more first-aid than what we brought," Ky whispered, not wanting to wake his sleeping beauty.

"Not that I found," Tate replied, keeping his voice low. "I'm only grabbing what we need to make it through the rest of the night. You want stew or chili? This guy was hauling cases of it."

"Stew," Ky answered quickly. Not chili. He'd bivouacked with enough guys before. Chili beans in an enclosed tent full of men did *not* make for a decent night's rest. "I'll help haul as soon as I can get away."

Tate's gaze zeroed in on Stark's limp body. "Looks to me like you've got your hands full."

"I couldn't just drop her on the ground and let her freeze, could I?" Ky wanted to slap himself for the way he'd worded that peculiar question. It made him sound defensive or something, and he wasn't. Not really. So what if she'd snuggled farther into his jacket and breathed more evenly? So what if he cradled her extra carefully, or that she had his jacket clenched in her curled fingers? So what if she clutched his jacket like she needed someone to hold onto? It didn't mean a damned thing.

Tate backed out of the tent with his signature grunt.

"Stark might be right. Zaroyin's on the run," Alex returned with the latest. "The FBI wants to question him further about his experiment. He's got strong congressional backing, but the bastard's also implicated in the disappearance of several agents."

"Like Mika Koenig and Arthur Shields? Those are the guys we took out."

Alex growled to himself. Papers ruffled. "Yes. Koenig and..." More rustling. "Son-of-a-bitch. They're both on the list. Twenty others, too. Damn it. What does she think Zaroyin wants her for?"

Why indeed. Ky hadn't been able to take his eyes off of her since Tate left. He relayed what he knew. "She's got some kind of psychic abilities. Zaroyin wants to exploit her, turn her into one of his six-million-dollar soldiers. He may already have. She's got an implant behind her ear the size of a three-volt lithium battery. As soon as she comes to—"

"She's unconscious? When were you going to tell me that?"

It was hard to be impatient with a man who hid his emotions behind a mask of fake gruffness. Ky smiled it off. He should've replaced his tell-all goggles instead of just his earpiece. The continual transmission would've kept Alex visually informed, and he wouldn't be having this showdown, but honestly? His boss didn't need to know everything, and besides, all this micro-managing was not like Alex. He preferred to bark orders and let a guy handle his own operation. This latest gamble into high-tech Never Never Land had to be Mother's doing.

"Sorry, Boss. She fainted. That's the thing. She thinks Zaroyin's been one step behind her since she left the East Coast. That might be what's under her skin—some kind of miniature tracking device. I'll keep you advised."

"Do," Alex snapped. "And Ky?"

Here it comes. "Yes, Boss?"

"Do whatever you have to, but keep her safe. Understood?"

Ky smiled into drowsy green eyes, not sure how long Stark had been awake and peering up at him. Same green eyes. Same strange menthol perfume. Same everything. Stark had to be his angel.

"Don't worry. I intend to," he said smoothly, despite the extra beat in his heart.

"And Ky?"

Ky sighed. Alex never let anything slide. "Yeah, Boss?"

"Keep your damned goggles on." Alex disconnected the call.

We'll see about that.

The pink tip of Agent Stark's tongue flicked out to moisten her chapped lips. "You intend to what?"

Ky could've jumped for joy, but he didn't want to scare Stark. "I intend to get you something to drink. Tate's been melting snow while you've been sleeping. You thirsty?"

Her head bobbed, but she didn't make any effort to move, just sighed and snuggled in closer, her gloved hand in the middle of his chest. He looked down at her hand. It shouldn't have meant anything, not with all the layers of TEAMwear in the way, but it did. Agent Stark was not some savvy FBI agent with a self-righteous stick up her butt. She seemed to trust him. It didn't hurt that she was a luscious armful, either. But oddest of all, he liked the warm sensation of her gloved hand on his chest. He placed his bare hand over hers, so damned glad to come face to face with the woman who, along with Lee Hart, had saved his life.

"My bottle of water froze, and then you guys showed up and then..." she gulped. "Yes, please. I am thirsty."

"I'll bet you're hungry, too. Tate's heating a couple cans of stew. Our midnight snack should be ready soon." God, he wanted to ask if she really was the woman in that cell with him, and how did she do it, how did she come to him? How did she know where he was, who he was? That he needed someone like her to help him hold on? How was he able to see her even though his eyes were pretty much too swollen and cut to see anything? It all seemed far-fetched, crazy. How did one begin to ask so many bizarre questions of a woman he'd never met before?

Slowly, she eased out of Ky's arms and settled alongside him, but he wished she hadn't. Two bodies mashed together like they'd been produced an incredible amount of heat. Especially with her backside against his lap. Oh hell, all of her. A definite chill replaced her warmth and he wanted her back.

"Br-r-r. Did I pass out?" she asked, her hand at the back of her head. "Now I remember. Can you tell me what this is? Can you see it?" She tilted forward on her knees, one palm to the floor of the tent, the other hand lifting her hair out of her hood and over one shoulder. "Look. Is this a knot or something? It feels like—"

Ky could no longer hear a word she said. Blood rushed out of his brain at the tempting sight. She might have been wearing a quilted winter jacket, and more than likely, she had a thick pair of long woolen underwear under those denim jeans, but hot damn. She'd just assumed one helluva *Playboy* pose. On her knees. Her tempting butt turned to him. All that hair spilled over her shoulder like a silky waterfall, and that ass...

His eyeballs fell instinctively to her nicely stretched jeans before the thought registered to stop acting like a complete jerk. He swallowed hard, raised the lantern, and leaned forward to view the implant under her scalp, and only the implant. Not like getting in closer to her helped his overheated and all-male body settle down.

What was it about the nape of a woman's neck, especially when exposed like Stark's was? Ivory white. Tender. A delicate column of femininity that any man in his right mind wanted to run his tongue over. Or bury his nose against and sniff. Or sink his teeth into and nibble while his hands roamed the rest of her soft body. The tent had suddenly gotten smaller and grown warmer. A helluva lot warmer.

Running just the tip of his bare index finger over the device nestled under her scalp—*and just the device, mind you*—he forced himself to concentrate on anything but the skin she'd willingly exposed. Or the flowery scent drifting up from all that hair. Or the jut of her plump but taut rear end. The seam of those jeans delineated two perfect butt cheeks and the way to heaven.

"It's an implant," he said hoarsely, struggling for the first time in forever to keep his hands to himself. He hadn't wanted to touch a woman in a long time, but this woman was already his. He just needed to be careful how he revealed that really weird news—that he remembered her from his torture chamber. He didn't want to make it sound any crazier than it was. "It's got to come out. After you eat, we'll do a little minor surgery. I've got a good hunting knife. Shouldn't be too hard to pop—"

She cocked her head and glanced back at him, a bemused glint in her eyes, and her hair still the sleekest come-on he'd ever *not* been offered. "Do all guys like to play with their knives?"

Ky shrugged, avoiding her sultry question as much as the blatant innuendo. Play nothing. The vibes rolling off this woman had created one helluva stranglehold beneath his zipper. He couldn't help that his gaze flickered to the pleasant curve of her denim-covered rump again.

He hadn't been with a woman in a long time. He'd actually thought that part of his body had died in Hasim Nizari's chamber of horrors along with parts of his mind. Until now.

Turned out *that part* was very much alive. It might not have been all that it used to be, but it was damned happy to see Agent Stark's ass, too. Or maybe it was just that this woman was—her. His angel.

The tight-quartered tent and the audacious woman in it set his blood to thrumming, racing through his veins like molten lava. His fingers physically ached to smooth over that tempting rump. Caress the bare skin beneath her jeans instead of just looking at her denim pockets. Listen to her squeal. Or moan. *Oh, shit. I'm screwed. At least I want to be.*

He dropped his hand, clenched his fingers, and kept this physical examination professional. "I've done some triage in my time," he declared through a voice turned tight and hoarse and too damned achy sounding. "Plugged a few bullet holes. Set a broken arm once. Removing this little thing shouldn't be a problem."

She sniffed the air, still on her knees and still as tantalizing as hell. Did she have a clue how she affected him? "I'm quite lucky, aren't I? I've been saved by a chef and a cute doctor." Her eyes widened. She gulped like she wanted to call that word back. "I mean, umm, oh snap. I didn't really say that, did I?"

He grinned, flustering her more. Her lashes lowered. Twin wrinkles converged over her knitted brow. Damn, she was—cute. It wasn't often a professional sniper got called *cute*, especially not by an FBI agent who, by all rights, should've been as lethal as he was. Yeah. She might look tough, but he got the feeling that Agent Stark was as unskilled at this sexual game playing as he was. And who said 'oh, snap' anymore?

He let her off the hook, mostly to save face. His. "Food's on. Let's eat and drink. Then I'll cut that thing out."

Chapter Six

"Don't hurt me," Eden ordered, sitting with her back to Agent Winchester, her head tilted forward. The battery-operated lantern from the Cessna lit the interior of the tent. She'd loosened her jacket over her shoulders and stretched her sweater away from her neck just enough for this minor surgery. It shouldn't take long, and she didn't want to get any colder.

Ky had placed a call for retrieval, but the pilot couldn't return until morning and then, he wasn't sure of the weather. For now, they were on hold.

She knew now why she'd passed out before. No brainer. She'd been dehydrated and famished, literally running on empty after she'd survived the rollercoaster ride out of the sky, then buried Charlie. Anyone would've fainted after that kind of a day.

But now, with one bowl of hot stew and two bottles of melted snow in her stomach, she was back to normal. Confident. An expert in her field. Having these two guys from Alex Stewart's TEAM in camp with her didn't hurt, either.

Stewart was an anomaly in the world of covert surveillance. An ex-USMC scout sniper, he actually knew how to run a successful business and not just kill things. The man was a hard ass, but he took on the tough jobs no one else wanted, and amazingly, his men seemed to love him. They seemed ready to follow him anywhere. Her own director,

Zachary Strong, respected him. Some of her fellow FBI agents didn't, but Eden had no quarrel with the guy. She'd only met him once, but he seemed to know how to hire good guys and get the tough jobs done.

Like Agent Winchester. Coming to in his arms hadn't been so bad. Embarrassing, maybe, but she'd been deliciously warm for the first time since she'd literally, hit Canada. The guy radiated heat like a toaster, and he smelled good. A little sweaty, but mostly of wind, snow, and the great outdoors mingled with a musky hint of aftershave. For the first time since she left D.C., she'd felt safe, so she willingly held her hair in a loose ponytail to give him room to play with that six-inch knife of his.

"Did you really think I'd really use my hunting knife on you, Agent Stark?" he asked slyly.

"Umm, yeah." *What else?* She tossed a quick glance over her shoulder. He'd made such a production of sharpening the blade before he'd set it to glowing over the campfire, like he couldn't wait to start carving on her.

He'd taken his goggles off. At his right lay a small white cloth the size of a large napkin, along with a couple of medical instruments wrapped in sterile plastic wrap. A scalpel. An already threaded suture needle. Good to know. Like she said, Stewart's TEAM was comprised of anomalies. The man was prepared to do this right. "Are you a medic?"

"No, ma'am, just a Marine who's seen his fair share of crap. Rest easy. I've got this."

Rest easy? How? Not with him sitting cross-legged behind her, so close the hairs on the back of her neck stood up in anticipation of his touch. He flustered the heck out of her, mostly because he hadn't touched her yet, and she very much wanted him to. Only that wasn't going to happen. Intimacy with a stranger was completely out of character for the highly decorated FBI special agent she was. Completely. She avoided relationships. Didn't need them. Didn't go looking for them, not girlfriends or boyfriends. Nada. Zip. Just plain no.

But maybe... after all this was Ky. Her Ky.

He chuckled as he straightened one leg and stuffed a sterile cloth into her shirt collar. "This will catch any blood that gets away from me. There. Are you ready now?" he murmured, his voice deep and low and bedroom-easy on her virgin ears.

Prickles of desire lifted her neck hairs up higher. Goose bumps lifted up with them. "Sure, why not?" She mustered an indifferent tone. He was a professional, the same as her. This little procedure should be done in no time. She had nothing to fear.

Agent Higgins still rummaged through the Cessna, and why that popped into her mind at that precise moment annoyed Eden. She didn't care if Higgins crawled into the tent and watched Winchester operate. Not at all. Why should she? Let the whole world watch. Nothing was going on in this tent. Absolutely nothing.

Winchester's latex-gloved hand gripped her sweater-covered shoulder like he needed to steady her before she bolted. She wanted to, but not out of fear. More out of shock that it felt so good having this particular man reconnect with her and take firm hold of her. This man. The same man she'd dreamed of and yearned for since the first day she'd *seen* him all those years ago.

She closed her eyes and savored the electrifying sensation of this first physical contact. It seemed different from waking up in his arms, though that had been pretty hot, too. She liked the way Agent Winchester had held her. Tight, but not too tight. Like she was delicate or something, which she wasn't.

Heat surged up the inside of her thighs at the notion of being breakable in his big, manly hands. Of being manhandled. Heat throbbed where it had no business throbbing. Want to or not, she licked her bottom lip and trembled. She tried hard to be stern, but her stomach muscles clenched, and she ended up whispering a breathy, "Tell me when."

"Don't worry, I will. I'll make tiny stitches when I'm done carving on you, and I won't leave a scar. Promise."

That was another thing. This guy was a walking supply cabinet. He carried a first-aid kit in one of his many pockets, along with hand sanitizer, sterile gloves, and no doubt, a grenade or two. She hadn't seen them yet, but they had to be in there somewhere.

His fingers worked through her hair and over her scalp with firm strokes. A woman could get used to being handled like this. He parted her locks and dabbed an alcohol wipe over the site of the implant. "There's another bump back here and a small cut. Some blood. You must've cracked your head during the crash landing. I'm surprised you don't have a killer headache by now."

"That might explain my migraines." Only it didn't. The headache had started when she left Hawaii.

Agent Winchester didn't respond, just kept up a running circle around the implant, probing for what she didn't know. "I need to shave a one-inch square, maybe more so I can see what I'm doing. Hold still, okay?"

He took hold of her clenched hand, the one holding her ponytail, completely dwarfing her grip inside of his and... *Oh.*

My. God. If you keep touching me like that, I'm going to need a cigarette and a cold shower.

"Umm, sure. It's just hair." She trembled. Latex or not, having a big male hand in charge of her smaller one heightened the ache in her belly. She swore she could feel the whorl of his fingertips through the surgical gloves. The lifeline running down the inside of his palm to his wrist. The echo of his pulse in time with hers.

Using her hand and hair like a handle, he tilted her head, exposing more of her neck, but—gah! This little nothing-operation morphed into a living, breathing thing with him sitting so close to her ass and handling her body like he did. The man oozed confidence. He didn't hesitate. Didn't seem to need to think first. Just did. While he cut a small swatch of hair, then traded his scissors for a razor, she was fast losing her grip.

Just. *Gah.*

A small puff of his breath whispered across her neck, like an intimate secret that only he and she shared. *Oh, I wish.* He'd turned her into putty, and the dumb jock probably didn't realize he was the reason for her shivering, not arctic Canada. A frantic bevy of butterflies beat their wings against her ribs and she Could. Not. Think.

"Tiny cut," he breathed in warning, his breath warm on her neck.

Before she could offer one more speck of false FBI bravado, he'd made his incision, and—snap! That did hurt. He swapped the scalpel for a handful of cotton packing. Still in control and gripping her ponytail handle, he swabbed then pinched the incision, then pinched a little harder. She winced, but kept her mouth closed.

"So why you?" he asked.

"Why me, what?"

"Why's this nut job after you?"

Eden sighed. "I already told you. I have some, umm, abilities Zaroyin thinks he can capitalize on."

"Be more specific. Like?"

A tiny giggle escaped. She knew it. Agent Winchester hadn't heard a thing she'd said earlier.

"What's so funny?" *Oh, snap it to heck and back.* He let her ponytail loose and unfolded his other leg, but only to pull her closer. His hand on her hip. Her backside to his, umm, front side. Not good, but at the same time, so-o-o good.

A lightning-fast sizzle fried the last circuit working to her FBI logic card. The synapses in her brain quit passing logical messages. An image flashed to her dizzy mind of her on her knees in front of him with him leaning his full weight into her and...

Maybe I did hit my head when I crashed.

Agent Winchester retrieved his *handle*—her hand and ponytail—like he owned her. "What kind of abilities?" he prompted.

Once again, his words fell onto her overly stimulated neck. Darn, it had been a long time since a man had been tender and firm with her at the same time. Okay, so make that never. Stan hadn't been into gentleness the few times they'd snuggled. Not that this was snuggling, but he'd never tarried over her needs. Only his.

And why am I thinking about snuggling and my needs? The warmest shiver raced up her spine. *Because I do have needs, that's why. Unmet and probably unrealistic needs, and maybe never-to-be-met needs, but yes, I have needs enough to last a lifetime.*

"Hey, did you fall asleep? Are you dozing off on me?"

She blinked, tempted to doze off *on him,* but trying to remember what he'd asked. "I'm sorry. What'd you say?" She'd been sitting with her legs flat to the ground and out in front of her, but she crossed them now, needed them closed as tight as her eyelids to contain the fire creeping through her veins. Opening every nerve ending. Every pore. Teasing the chilled, forgotten tinder inside her inexperienced body into bright, brilliant, crackling life.

Her body had never been so revved up for sex like it was. Or so wet. If this wasn't the same Ky... Never mind that foolish notion. It had to be him. Why would she be so drawn to him if he wasn't?

"You were saying Zaroyin wants you for your abilities and..." He drew out his words, waiting on her.

"I'm psychic, okay? I can see things. He wants to capitalize on my second sight. He says it's for the good of the nation, but he's lying."

"Psychic, huh?" Ky murmured as if he wasn't really listening this time, either. The man was obviously not great at multi-tasking. Good thing, too. Revealing her second sight never failed to make her sound like a crazy lady with a house full of cats, one who read tarot cards and smoked clove cigars.

"Hmmm. I thought I could express this thing from under your scalp by just exerting pressure, but it's not moving. Am I hurting you?" he asked, his face tilted to the side to look at her better, his tone filled with genuine care, and the subject of her crazy abilities off the table for the moment.

She couldn't risk looking at him, couldn't risk him seeing the heat on her cheeks, so she kept her face lowered. "Umm, yes. A little, but it's okay. Don't stop."

"Good. I couldn't stop now if I wanted to—not with you bleeding like this."

Did his voice just drop an octave into incredibly sexy? Her brain filled with fog, steamy fog. It must have come from the inferno bubbling to life in her nether regions, because bleeding or not, she knew he'd take care of her. Good care.

What the heck is going on with me? He's just a guy. He's performing the minorest kind of surgery. It's not like we're necking or petting or—

His gloved-hand slid to her bare neck. A tingle galloped away with her last best rationalization. *Oh, snap. Maybe we are petting. At least, he is.*

He pinched her scalp a third time. Despite the tiny stab of pain, a delightful shudder overwhelmed Eden. No man had come this close to her body in a very long time. No one at work had dared. She was the ultimate hands-off FBI asset. Her management kept close watch on her, and until then, she hadn't minded the over-protected lifestyle.

"This is odd," he murmured, his breath whispering over the curl of her ear, the one with goose bumps popping up around it like popcorn.

She tipped her head farther to the left, exposing more of her neck. *Oh honey, it's not odd. It's so-o-o nice. Do it again.*

"I can see most of the device. It's dime-sized and flat, shiny, but it's got silvery threads extending from it. Like spider legs, only flat and thin. Eight of them. I'm not sure how long they are or how deep they go."

Eden blinked at that bucket of cold water splashed on her libido. *A spider? Under my skin? Who the heck put it there?* It had to have been inserted during her last physical, but she had no recollection of Dr. Penn touching her head, much less sticking anything sharp under her scalp. "I don't care. Pull it out."

Winchester hesitated. "I'm not sure I should, Agent Stark. This thing looks like it was surgically installed. I'm not seeing stitches, but there's a definite puncture mark where it went under your scalp. I don't want to hurt you if I don't have to."

"Will you stop it already? I think we're past rank and protocol. Call me Eden, okay, Ky?"

"Sure thing, but pulling this device out may not be the best solution. These tentacle things are still moving and—"

Ewww. Tentacles? Still moving? Why did it have to be spider-like? She quivered. Spiders reduced her to squeamish. No, make that *scream*-ish. Just the thought! Her quiver turned into a full-on shiver that made her legs and butt wiggle—like that helped, pressed against him like she was and wanting to press closer. "Get it out of me," she bit out, hating that she sounded like a petulant little girl.

"Hey, settle down. I won't hurt you," he soothed.

"It's not that. It's... oh, I don't care. You've already cut me open and I'm bleeding. What if it is a tracking device? Go on. Pull it out and stitch me up."

She could feel his hesitation, the way his thumb massaged circles at the nape of her neck as if he wanted her to calm down. It didn't work. That creepy thing had to go before she climbed out of her skin.

"Well, okay." He paused. "Hold on to something."

He didn't wait for her to grab anything, just ripped it out like... *ouch. Shit!* A *Band-Aid*. A really deep *Band-Aid*. It felt as if he'd pulled a handful of her hair out by the roots. How long were those tentacles anyway?

"Got it. You okay?"

She nodded quickly because she couldn't risk speaking.

"See what I was talking about?" He presented his findings at the end of the tweezers, the large kind that looked more like a pair of pliers holding a thin, bloody disc in their pinchers. Tinsel-thin wires, some as long as three inches, dangled from a dime-shaped device.

Not like she cared at the moment. She was too busy summoning her tough persona, blinking her tears away, not going to fall apart in front of this guy. Real FBI agents didn't do that. "Great. I'll study it after you stitch me up," she murmured in her deepest, more serious FBI voice.

He set the pliers and device on the napkin, then tipped her head and smoothed another antiseptic wipe over her scalp and down her neck. It must look like a bloody mess. Eden cringed, wanting this procedure done so she could gather her courage again. Her foolish, romantic side had left her high, dry, and chilled.

"Tiny prick," he warned while the first stitch pierced her scalp. For a private contractor, Ky had a great bedside manner. She'd expected more of a Wyatt Earp, shoot-'em-up-ride-'em-cowboy kind of a guy. But Ky seemed—level. Real. Just like the man she remembered.

She didn't even flinch, not once during the five or so stitches he sewed. She just held very still, hating that when this encounter ended, Ky Winchester would be done touching her, and her chance to bear her soul would be gone. He'd go back to being just another agent. Like her. They'd do their jobs. He'd get her back home and—then what? Too tired to think, she let a sigh escape and the moment pass.

"Hey. You good?" he asked, his voice hoarse and gravelly. "Don't go passing out on me."

She could only nod. He didn't have a clue that they'd met in a psychic sort of way more than two years ago. That their minds had linked, how, she couldn't explain. That she'd been there through all he'd suffered at Nizari's hands. That she'd suffered with him. But that was then and this was now, and Eden Stark was on the verge of exhaustion. Or tears. It had been a heckuva long, hard day. She hadn't broken down since her mother had passed away, but she felt close to it now.

Darn, she hadn't been able to read Ky since he'd shown up, and she didn't understand why not. How could Mother Nature allow her nearly full access to his heart, mind, and soul at a distance of what? Several thousand miles? But not now when he sat inches away? When he was finally within touching distance? Nothing. She couldn't validate what her heart kept telling her. Unfair!

Quietly, he finished his work and released her ponytail. "Just one second more," he said as he pressed an antiseptic Band-Aid gently to her scalp and smoothed it in place with his fingertips. "There you go. Good as new."

She moved out of the sizzling hot hearth of his masculine body, pulled her sweater's collar up and gathered her jacket. Shaking her head, she tossed her over-abundance of dishwater-blond ringlets and frizzy tangles to cover the incision as much as to hide her vulnerability. Her one-and-only elastic had disappeared during her very hectic day. She occupied herself taming her messy curls. Taming her messy emotions, too.

"You must be tired," he said softly as he peeled out of his gloves and tossed them onto the napkin, "and you're cold. Come on. I can't let you go without warming you up."

Dragging the fur wrap back around her, he overlapped the edges under her chin. And it happened. Agent Ky Winchester breached the unspoken rules of fraternization between federal agents and private contractors. He tugged her slowly backward onto his warm lap and against the comfort of his broad, muscular chest. He circled her inside the steel bands of his arms and held her, his chin on her other trembling shoulder like he knew she needed a hug after her less-than-harrowing surgery. "Are you okay?"

Eden gave in to his offer. She didn't think where this simple gesture might lead, just tipped her head against his jaw and murmured, "Yes, thanks."

What could've been the beginning of an intimate encounter—wasn't. He pulled away from the simple contact. "Remind me what your pilot's name was again? We can't leave him on ground level."

How terribly unromantic. A whimper lifted up her throat at her foolish and thoroughly unrealized expectations. This wasn't her long-lost friend hugging her. This was just an impersonal man making sure his impersonal patient was strong enough to travel so he could complete his impersonal task and go home. He didn't have a clue who she really was in his life, or how much she'd suffered with him.

Oh, snap. I am so dumb. Was he married? Did he have kids? She gulped at the depth of her stupidity. Of course he was married. That had to be why she'd lost track of him after Afghanistan. He'd probably gone straight home and married the childhood sweetheart who'd been waiting for him, the woman who'd nursed him back to health. He'd probably fathered three kids by then. Why wouldn't he have? She was the one without a life, not him.

"Charlie Sweets," she murmured, sucking up her pride. "His name was Charlie Sweets. He was a father and a grandfather and... a very nice man. He cared about people, and he cared about me. I buried him in a shallow grave just west of here. I need to notify his wife and sons."

"Shh. I'll take care of that," Ky soothed, his voice rumbling low in her ear again. "My boss employs enough people. One of them can make the notification. Don't worry."

Eden closed her eyes. The butterflies in her heart sprang back to life at the contact of her forehead with the scruff on his bare chin. With his breath. His body seemed warmer than hers. Broader. Harder. She couldn't miss the effect she had on him, not with the way he had readjusted his, umm, gear. Was there really a Mrs. Winchester in his life? God, she hoped not.

"I'm safe with you, aren't I?" She wanted to look into his eyes, but he was too close and he had a tight grip on her. She could barely turn. *Please tell me you're not married.*

"Yes, you're safe with me, Eden Stark, but I've got to ask. Do I know you from somewhere? Every time I look at you, I get the crazy feeling we've met... in some other lifetime." He hesitated, like he was as unsure as she was.

She twisted in his arms to at least make eye contact. A hint of concern furrowed his brows, but his eyes, his intense *amber* eyes, the darkest honey rimmed with deep brown cocoa. Filled with glints of golden light. Confirmation hit her hard. She didn't need to see his scars anymore. *It is him. I'm sure.*

"Are you married?" she blurted out instead of, '*Are you hitting on me now? Please say no. I mean yes.*'

He shook his head. "Hell, no. You?"

"Ah, no, I, umm, I'm too busy." *And I'm the dumbest woman ever. Nice job, Eden. Just ask, why don't you? Blurt it right out. Embarrass him, and put yourself out there like you're the ugliest, most desperate wallflower at the prom instead of an intelligent agent in the middle of Frozen, Nowhere.*

She held her breath. The tender moment begged clarity, but she had none to give. As much as she wanted to tell Ky how she knew him, he must never know the extent of her psychic abilities. This handsome agent wasn't meant to be a part of her world. It had to be enough that she'd saved his life in that other reality, and that he'd helped her tonight in this one. There could be nothing more.

Swallowing hard, she wiggled one arm out of his grasp and cupped his jaw, her thumb beneath his chin and her fingers along the scruff of his cheek. She shouldn't have done that. The second she touched him skin to skin, their psychic link had other plans. Eden became the tortured one. Suddenly, she was the one hanging from an iron chain in a far-off cell, her body on fire with stinging welts, her blood dripping to the filthy floor below her swinging bare feet, the concrete already stained with other crimes.

Eden choked back a cry, suffocating the need to scream. Empathy for all he'd endured at those wicked men's hands scorched through her. She felt everything. The stabbing. The cutting. The slicing away of his skin with the USMC tattoo and the layers of pectoral muscles beneath it. Blackest despair swirled up from the floor and wound its clinging tentacles around her neck, strangling the light out of her. The knives cut razor sharp. They went too deep. Into her soul. Her heart. Cringing into herself to escape the pain, she slipped into a spinning, whirling vortex of inky, oily fog.

"Eden! Eden!" Ky's faraway voice reached for her, pulled her back into the light, away from the grasping clutches of his nightmare, now hers. The scales of filth and blood fell away.

She found herself turned and tucked under his chin, breathing heart-stoppingly hard, listening to the kettledrum of his matching panic beneath her ear. With his bare hand pressed tight against the back of her head, she could smell his fear for her through his jacket. It smelled as strong as hers.

"Eden. What just happened?" His fingers were strong and gentle at the same time, splayed protectively through her hair, holding her to him. Caressing her. The thunderous pounding of his heartbeat calmed the ugliness of the vision away. For one moment, Eden felt in sync with him. Her pulse slowed. She could breathe.

Eden swallowed hard past the dry knot fading in her throat, letting her panic go. It had been a long time since anyone cared enough to be scared for her or to hold her like Ky was. She closed her eyes and absorbed the moment even as she lied, her voice more air than words. "I'm okay. Just another dizzy spell."

She licked her lips, sick and tired of feeling out of control. Like her fainting spell, this episode made her look mentally weak, which she wasn't. What had happened to her usually reliable second sight and the strength it gave her? Everything seemed scrambled since the crash. She clung tightly to Ky's jacket, holding on for just a second longer to catch her breath and her balance.

"You freaked the hell out of me," he murmured, his lips moist and warm on her forehead, "and you're lying. I can tell."

You're right, she thought. *But I can't tell. Not everything. Not now.*

Without thinking, she sank her forehead to his chin. Wrong move again. She should've stopped the second he leaned away from her. She should've quit while she was ahead. Before his body went rigid. Before he flinched under her touch and released her. Before he all but shoved her out of his arms and scrambled to his feet.

"Hey, listen. I've got a set of TEAMwear for you," he said too quickly, the hands that had just soothed her now deep inside his backpack and pulling out a plastic-wrapped package. "It'll keep you warm. It goes over your clothes. I'll leave while you dress. Hurry. Put it on."

"Ky, wait. What's going on?" she asked, but there was no answer.

He'd already gone.

Chapter Seven

I can't breathe!

Ky climbed out of the tent, needing distance from the very volatile situation he couldn't begin to resist, but couldn't endure. One called Eden Stark.

She shouldn't have touched him. The first time shocked the hell out of him. He'd honestly thought she'd gone into some kind of a seizure, but the second time she made skin-to-skin contact just plain freaked him out. The instant the satin smooth skin of her forehead touched him, he knew he'd overstepped his own preset boundaries. He'd touched her first, but she shouldn't have touched him back. Not like she did. Not so damned—nice. Like she cared. Like she wanted a whole lot more than a messed up man like him could offer a smart lady like her. Like there really was hope for him.

There was no way to explain how messed up his mind could get, to be so close to his angel but so scared it really was her. That he wasn't worthy of her. That he'd come this far for nothing!

At least Tate was too busy examining the wreck to have noticed. Ky brushed the sensation of her dainty fingers off his chin. Butterfly wings and angel kisses—they'd shot a fifty-caliber round of potent sexual heat to his groin. How would that ever, in a million years, work, something as sweet as her mixed up with something so wicked as him? Something so damaged and mutilated and ugly? Something no woman wanted to look at, certainly not in her bed?

He scrubbed one hand down his thigh, surprised at the raging hard-on that refused to settle down. The world spun around him. His carefully crafted self-control crumbled around the edges. The first panic attack in months lurked at his peripheral. Yeah. There was no way he could tell her he'd dreamed her up in the middle of being tortured. Wouldn't that be the line from hell? *Hey Babe. Haven't I seen you somewhere before? Oh yeah. I remember now. You were in that sweltering concrete cell while I was hanging like a side-of-beef about to get barbecued, weren't you? Good times... not!*

He squeezed his eyes shut, swallowed hard, and drew in a long, slow breath. David Tao, another TEAM agent, had taught him how to control these attacks. *Breathe in. Breathe out. The slower the better. Cast your mind into the universe. Focus on that silent place deep within. Rotate your head. Relax. Do it again. And again. Keep moving.*

Ky summoned every last self-preservation technique he'd ever learned. He looked up, the same as he'd done during those days and nights in Nizari's prison. The sky always seemed the direction from where help would come, either from the hand of God or a ground-to-air missile. There was a time when he would've gladly taken either. He drew in a long slow breath along with the soothing memory of menthol and green eyes, the comfort of what had worked then. The real-life comfort he'd just run away from.

Brushing his hand over his forehead, his fingers came away damp with sweat. He tugged his gloves from his rear pocket and encased his hands once more. The awful truth was that he craved human contact—just couldn't stand it. The paradox of having survived torture at the hands of psychopaths.

Even Lee Hart knew better than to clap a hand to Ky's shoulder or to do any of that guy-smacking, chest-bumping bullshit during one of their games of jungle ball at the local gym. Lee had endured his own stay in Nizari's company. Twice. Hell, he had his own demons to deal with, but the fear of human touch didn't seem to be one of them. He had Tess, his sassy wife. A baby on the way. Ky had nothing but this out-of-control paranoia and a hard job to get lost in.

This operation into Ontario was just supposed to be one of those hard jobs, damn it!

He sucked in another lungful of frigid relief. Until now, he'd been content with his lot in life. He'd had to be. Women complicated everything, and he plain wasn't ready to deal with another round of psychobabble, bullshit counseling, no matter how lonely he was. Yeah, counseling helped. So what? It hurt, too. All those carefully constructed trips down memory lane brought every last ugly moment of his past to the surface again. The last thing he needed. Ky avoided counseling as much as the opposite sex.

Isn't this just great? Along comes my angel, and I run away like a friggin' coward?

Ky locked his heart up and tamped his panic down to manageable. Survival kicked in once more. His breathing leveled out. It seemed ironic. He'd conquered most of the fears and phobias from his time served, just not the one he wanted most to conquer. The one he truly needed resolved in order to do more than just survive. To live. To be with a woman. To be handled without the imagined pain his mixed-up brain dished out.

Goddamned Nizari.

Pushing off the ground, Ky looked over his shoulder at the tent flap behind him. Despite the roaring panic attack, this encounter had felt—different. Eden's touch hadn't burned like other accidental touches had. Not really. In fact, it hadn't hurt at all. Embarrassment flooded his gut at the very real possibility his mixed-up brain might've just jumped to the wrong conclusion. That he might have over-reacted. That this might be one of those bizarre once-in-a-lifetime unrealized expectations that actually turned out to be a good thing.

"What the hell are you doing?" Tate grunted under an armload of branches as he stalked out from the shadows. "Taking another break?"

Ky blew out a cleansing breath, needing to throw out a distraction before his buddy asked him what was wrong. Nothing slipped past Tate. He was perceptive like that, but Ky didn't want him in his business. The guy already knew too much. "Something like that. Where'd you put the dead guys?"

Tate pointed up, one bushy brow lifted in curiosity. "In the trees where they'll keep."

Ky glanced into the branches overhead, still fighting for composure. Tate wasn't wearing his goggles, either—probably because he'd been busy wrapping three dead bodies in plastic and rope, and Alex didn't need to see that, either. They swung between the branches as if a really big spider had cocooned them. Three bodies dangling head-down from the high branches made for a scene out of a horror flick. Damned spooky was what it was. "Did you have to put them so close to camp?"

Tate shrugged. "Didn't figure you'd care. It's not like we're staying here long. How'd it go with Stark?"

"Eden's tough. She's a trooper, but whiplash will catch up with her tomorrow. Wait and see."

Tate grunted, "Eden, huh. You two on a first-name basis now?"

Ky released a slow, measured sigh, not going to discuss his close encounter. "Might as well. We're here, aren't we?"

"Is Alex good?"

"You know Alex. He's pissed that things went wrong, as usual. He had Mother do some checking. Stark wasn't lying. Zaroyin's the real thing. He's coming for her, and get this—twenty more FBI agents are missing. They might be in league with him and coming for her, too."

"So? We can take 'em." Tate's calm assurance righted Ky's attitude. "Where is she?"

"Changing into the extra set of TEAMwear we brought for her. Hope it fits. She's smaller than I expected. At least she'll be warm."

Tate offered a scant scowl. "Let's see it."

Ky pulled the mechanical spider out of his pocket and uncurled his gloved hand, fighting the tremors in it. The device that had once rested against Eden's skull now flexed in the center of his shaky palm like an insect, alive, its eight legs curling and uncurling. Twitching.

Tate presented his open palm. The same kind of thing flexed there.

"Where'd you get that one?" Ky asked, surprised.

"I figured since she had one, I'd better double-check her pilot, Sweets. Took it out of his head, right behind his right ear. I would've checked Koenig and Shields, too, but they were up in the trees by then." Tate pulled a piece of wire out of his jacket pocket. "Sweets was wired, too."

Things kept going from bad to worse. "Like Koenig and Shields? Chest to groin? Are you sure?"

Tate grunted. "One of us may need to check your lady friend a little better. She might be wired, too."

"She can do it herself," Ky shot that notion down. Neither he nor Tate needed to get any friendlier with Agent Stark. The TEAM and the FBI had never mixed well before in TEAM history. They didn't need to now.

He glanced back at the womanly shadow playing across the tent wall. It had to be tough pulling on a suit of TEAMwear in a small tent without enough room to stand up straight. He could understand that she'd missed the implant behind her ear. It was small enough and unnoticeable, tangled up in all that hair, but if she had the same kind of wire running down the center of her body as those other guys—well, a person couldn't miss something like that.

Tate pulled two evidence bags out of his pocket and dropped the spider he'd found inside one. He handed the other off to Ky. "I thought the wires might lead to a locating device, but now I'm not so sure. The one in Sweets ended at a solid lump in his groin, the same as the FBI guys'. It might be one of those drug-dispenser things. You know, the kind a person can activate when they need a dose of medicine."

"You mean a CADD pump?"

Tate glowered at the acronym, disdainful as ever when he couldn't come up with the right technical terminology. The guy was blue-collar all the way to his toes. Give him a wrench and he could fix any car made before the eighties. Just don't give him a computer and expect him to thank you for it. "If that's what you call it, yeah."

"A CADD pump is a continuous automatic drug delivery pump, Tate, if that's what you're thinking. My grandfather had one for morphine before he passed, only it wasn't in his groin." Ky secured the arachnid-like device he'd removed from Eden inside the evidence bag and handed it back to Tate. "You might be right, but the way this clung to Eden's skull was weird. I felt bad hurting her when I pulled it out. It was anchored tight, and look at it. Those tentacles are still moving. Did you feel the spider legs on it? They look smooth, but they're not. They're rough. Like sandpaper."

Tate grunted. "Like it's supposed to dig its way into her skull?"

"Not sure, but it could be how Zaroyin tracks and controls his drones."

"Didn't look like he was controlling Stark."

"Maybe it's got to be dug in deeper to work. That might be why it was still moving after I removed it. Hmm." Ky extended his index finger like a gun, flicking his thumb as if he'd just taken a shot. "I'll bet once it's inside a guy's brain, the device shocks Zaroyin's soldiers or something, and bang, resistance is futile."

"Do you think the devices in their groins are for global positioning then? Locators? But why run the antennae up the length of a guy's body? Why implant a mechanical device in a guy's groin in the first place? That's just plain weird."

Ky shrugged. He honestly didn't know which device did what, and he didn't have the time or the energy to waste thinking on it. One guess was as good as another, but he meant to be on his way home with his client before any of it mattered. "Either way, Zaroyin now knows we've intercepted and disabled Koenig and Shields. Sweets, too. He might even know we've interrupted his control over Eden if that spider thing had a sending device attached to it."

"Which means we could have company in a couple of hours to a couple of days. Did you happen to notice both of those guys stunk, and not just because we shot them?" Tate's nose wrinkled. "They were both saturated with sweat, Ky. Did you see how fast it froze on their chests when I tore their shirts open? And it smelled—different. Rank. Like they hadn't bathed in a while."

Ky nodded. "It did look like they'd been running a long time."

"In the dark, too," Tate hissed. "Like robots. Until their blood mingled with their sweat. What the hell's going on? What kind of a man runs in deep snow like that?"

"A cybernetic one, if Eden's right." Ky kept his tone low. "Maybe once Zaroyin turns them on, they run until they drop dead."

"Then he really is a mad man. Should I crush these things?" Tate asked, the evidence bags still in his hands. "They could be pinging our location to Zaroyin right now for all we know."

"Not until Eden takes a good look at them. Maybe she knows what they do. If she doesn't, Mother needs to see them, Alex for sure. This op smells like there's collusion inside the Bureau. Big time."

"Do you think she might be in on this, whatever this is?" Tate raised a spiked brow.

Ky's gaze scrolled back to the tent. "What? And risk her life in a plane crash to establish an alibi? What the hell are you smoking?"

Grunt. "You and me both know things aren't always what they seem."

"No. Not Eden," Ky said adamantly. "She's the victim here."

"Or she's one helluva covert analyst, and she's leading you into Zaroyin's trap."

"Why? What could he want with me?"

Tate shrugged, so Ky changed the subject. "Do you really think we can take on twenty running drones, just you and me? You saw Koenig and Shields. They were decked out in full body armor and packing powerful heat. They didn't falter once. Koenig didn't even fall down when I hit him the first time, and I hit him solid. If we're right, the next wave will be coming at us with more firepower. We won't get a chance to surprise them."

Tate grunted. "Then we need to find Zaroyin's weak spot and hit him before he finds us."

"No, that's the boss's job." Ky looked into the high branches overhead. "All we need to do is get Eden stateside. I'm calling flyboy for a pick-up at first light. Eden's FBI. She'll have a weapon. She can help hold Zaroyin's men off if they show before then."

Tate followed Ky's gaze. "Storm's coming, Ky. Snow. Silver Wolf may not be able to get to us before it gets here. Stupid name."

Ky agreed. Their Canadian counterparts had chosen their mission monikers, naming themselves as alpha to The TEAM's beta, a definite declaration of who owned these woods—not that it mattered. Silver Wolf, ha! A tough name for a guy sitting on his ass in a warm hotel room. "Then we move now. Once Eden's done, stow the tent and get us ready to roll."

Tate's eyeballs scrolled beyond Ky's right shoulder, enough of a hint for him to shut his mouth.

"Br-r-r," Eden murmured behind him, slapping her biceps. "Thanks for the extra snowsuit, guys, but no matter how many layers I put on, I'm still freezing."

Ky lifted to his feet. Damned if she didn't offer a shy smile instead of a cold shoulder as he'd expected after his less-than-cavalier departure from the tent. His lips automatically returned the smile. Despite how he'd made a fool of himself, she thought he cared. It was easy to read in the soft glow of firelight dancing in her eyes. The problem was that he did care. A lot. And this psychic woman knew it.

She shook her head, those sleek tresses tucked up inside her fur cap again. "What's the plan, Ky?"

He ignored the familiarity. "Pack up. We're leaving. What do you need to take with you?"

She glanced to the downed Cessna at her right. Caught in the confines of several massive tree trunks and a net of splintered pine boughs, it resembled a giant dragonfly in a trap. Tate's foraging had all but turned it inside out. "My bag, if I can find it."

"What's in it?"

"Clothes. Makeup." She ticked her inventory off on her gloved fingers. "Sunscreen. Stuff."

"Sunscreen?" He had to ask.

She shrugged. "I was going to Hawaii. Ended up here. Remember?"

Ky shook his head, wishing he hadn't gotten wrapped up in this woman so fast. She was going to be a problem. "No stuff, sorry. Dump the bag. Bring all the food you can carry. Tate thinks there's a storm moving in. If we can't hook up with our chopper pilot, we'll have to find some place to hunker down until it passes."

"Storm?" She lifted her pretty eyes heavenward, her palms spread wide. "I don't see any—oh, God! Look! Something's over there. In the trees."

Ky took a step toward her, his palms forward. "Shhhhh, it's okay. Don't worry. Tate put the bodies up where predators can't reach them. That's all."

"Charlie too? He dug Charlie up and hung him in a tree? But I just buried him." And there it was again, sympathy for the man she'd thought was a friend.

Ky nodded. "Charlie wasn't who he said he was, Eden. Show her, Tate."

Tate pushed off the ground and pulled the evidence bags out of his pocket. "Your buddy was a snitch for Zaroyin, same as Koenig and Shields. See for yourself."

"Sweets had the same kind of thing I dug out of your head. Do you know what it is?" Ky asked.

Eden's brows lifted as she studied the two devices in Tate's open palm. "I've never seen anything like them before. He had one in his head, too? He lied to me?" Her voice caught. "But I thought—" Those pretty green eyes widened in shock.

"It gets worse. Both your FBI buddies had some kind of wires embedded in their groins. Sweets did, too. Do you?" Ky couldn't take his eyes off Eden. A fierce trumpet call to protect this woman had just lifted up strong and clear inside his head. This was no experienced black operator. What was Zach Strong thinking to send them on a wild goose chase looking for one, when he had to have known this agent was as vulnerable as a newborn babe in the woods?

Those lovely green eyes widened with indignation. She stiffened her neck and tossed the bag at Tate. "Of course not. I would've noticed something like that."

"You didn't know about the spider-thing in your head," Ky lowered his voice, his tone stern. "You need to be sure you're not wired before we head out. Go back into the tent and undress if you have to. Check yourself thoroughly. Do it now. We need to know for sure what we're dealing with."

"I'll be right back, but you'll see. I'm not wired." Her cocky chin lift caught him by surprise. This woman had backbone.

"I will?" He couldn't resist the taunt.

She blinked. "You will what?"

A genuine smile curved his lips at the tease. He couldn't resist taking a step inside her comfort zone, daring her. "You said *I'll see*. Does that mean you'll show me you're not wired?"

Eden coughed, swallowed hard, and coughed again. Her cheeks darkened in the dim light. Her lashes fluttered, and he couldn't believe what an easy mark she was, what a refreshing change from the other FBI agents he'd worked with. "N-no. It means…" she stammered, taking a step backward. "Oh, never mind. You'll just have to take my word for it. I'll be right back." With a self-righteous pivot on the ball of her boot, she stomped back to the tent, all that shimmering hair drizzled down her back and her backside twitching.

"Make it quick," Ky warned, secretly pleased he'd gotten to her. Secretly pleased with the view of her walking away. Something about this woman drew him in, and it was more than his male attraction to her good looks. Understand it or not, her presence calmed him. If only his reactionary brain could let her in.

Eden wasn't gone long. Her countenance said it all when she returned. Ky didn't ask. Didn't have to. Judging by the size of her eyes, she'd found something, and she wasn't happy about it. "I'm sorry. You're right. I... I don't know how I missed it."

Ky grabbed hold of her forearm and drew her into the firelight. "Where is it?"

Eden pointed her gloved fingers to her breastbone and trailed a line to her navel. "Here. It ends inside the crease of my, umm, thigh. You're right. Zaroyin's got me wired like he already owns me."

"Does he?" Ky snapped, hoping to hell Tate wasn't right, that she wasn't in league with the devil.

"No, I..." She lurched forward, but stopped short of bumping into Ky. Eden bowed her head. Her cap slid to the snow. A silken blond cascade tumbled over his arms and wrists. "Oh, snap, no-o-o."

"What the hell's going on?" he asked, fighting the urge to pull her into his side again.

She sucked in a deep breath. "Run, Ky. They're coming!"

Chapter Eight

"Run? Like hell. What's going on?"

Eden dropped to her knees at his feet and pressed her fingertips to her temples, focused on the gray-black smudges in the distance. "Six. I see six."

"Six what? Shit, talk to me, Eden."

"Six men. Six FBI agents. I don't know. Three miles to the east. Coming fast." *To me.* Her second sight shimmered and changed from light to murky shadows. No black smudges materialized like before, but she could sense that someone besides the drones was out there, too. Two others. She couldn't decide how close they were, only that they were also coming for her.

The strength of the competing visions turned her second sight into a warzone, both flashing images so quickly she couldn't read one before the other collided with it, ripping up the inside of her brain, tearing her apart. Pain thundered like a jackhammer out of control inside her skull. "It hurts like an ice pick," she muttered, her eyes squeezed tight and her control slipping. "The pain's never been like this before."

Ky knelt with her, his hand gentle on her knee. "Where?" His tone changed. Not panic. Not fear. More like calm authority in the middle of mayhem. It grounded her.

"My head. My eyes. I can't see both warnings. They're... they're too much."

"I meant where are the men?"

Oh, duh. Of course he meant the men. She sucked up her whining embarrassment. "Six from the east, but more from the south, from Thunder Bay. I don't know how many though. I can't see them clearly. Maybe two. They're blurry. It's as if they're running in fog."

"Anything else?"

Worry eked out of her. "Yes. I can't see like I used to. My second sight's damaged or something. I'm missing things. Like this wire imbedded in my body. I want it gone, Ky, but why didn't I see it until now? How could I have missed something like that? I mean, really? It's not like a piece of gum stuck to the bottom of my shoe. It's not a tiny bug someone could've slipped inside my pocket. It's a long wire, Ky, and it's taped to me, and the end of it is inside of *me*. Me! It's inside my *body*. Somebody surgically implanted something in a very intimate location. That person violated me, Ky. Darn it, why can't I remember?"

He pulled her to her feet and into his side, and honestly, she didn't understand this guy. One second he pushed her away, but the next he wanted her close. She accepted the shelter of his hard body, but kept her hands to herself this time. His arm around her immediately eased the pain in her head, but touching him seemed to have triggered rejection last time. She wouldn't do that again.

"I'm no rocket scientist, Eden, but maybe that thing in your head was meant to control you so you wouldn't see the wire. Maybe you were hypnotized. Maybe Zaroyin used subliminal suggestion—hell, I don't know. We'll figure it out later when we have more time. Tate," he snapped. "Remember Morocco?"

"You're thinking riverbank? Here?" Tate's bushy brows met in the middle.

"No. I'm thinking we need a solid wall behind us. How close to the nearest one?"

"There's a place to the north. Sheer granite. Three miles or so. It oughta work."

"Let's move," Ky ordered, his fingers still circling Eden's wrist. "Tate, stow the tent. Leave no trace. Zaroyin may be tracking Agent Stark, but unless he's got some kind of a video feed I'm not seeing, he has no clue we're with her. Let's save that surprise. Move out in five. Go get your bag, Eden."

She nodded. "I'll hurry."

Hurry, heck. She flew to the Cessna, her heart on fire with this different version of Ky in command. He meant her to obey, and she meant to do it. She never thought twice, just jerked the door open, and there it was. Her over-the-shoulder bag, sitting on her seat. Tate must have located it in all his digging. No doubt he'd searched it—not like Eden cared if he had or not. She had nothing to hide.

Tate had thoroughly ransacked the plane. Much of what he'd gone through lay in disarray outside the door, but if he didn't need it, she didn't either. She focused on restocking her bag with necessities. Ammo. Lip balm. Sunscreen. Her knife. Toilet paper. Wet wipes. Her jar of Vicks. A long-stemmed lighter and a bundle of nylon rope. The TEAMwear outfit Ky gave her warmed her enough that she discarded all of her clothes except one extra pair of jeans, another pullover sweater, clean underwear, and socks.

What else? Her gaze pinged over the inside of the cockpit, coming to rest on the ax beside the pilot's seat. It went into her bag. She didn't look back, just turned her face toward Ky and put the betrayer, Charlie Sweets, out of her mind.

"I'm ready," she announced at what had been the site of the tent. Only a flat depression in the snow remained. Both Ky and Tate were packed, their heavy backpacks strapped over their shoulders. She shouldered hers as well, intent on proving that FBI agents were just as strong and capable as Alex Stewart's men.

Ky nodded at her to come stand between them, so Eden took her place. The tables had turned. She needed Ky to keep her alive now as much as she'd kept him alive two years earlier.

"We're going due north. Stay close. If Tate's recollection of this terrain's correct, we're four miles south of an outcropping of granite. I called for air support, but it's dicey. Our pilot said he'd try to get to us at first light, but he may have to wait out the storm."

"Okay," Eden replied breathlessly. They were on the run. She got it. She might not have gone through the extensive training most FBI agents did, but she was physically fit. She could keep up.

Ky stared at her, his face devoid of gentleness. "Be honest with me, Eden. Exactly what do you do for the FBI? Are you even remotely involved in black ops? How many active ops have you been on?"

She gulped, but confessed her weakness. He might as well know everything. "I'm an advisor, not, umm, a real agent. I never trained at Quantico. I only go where my handler tells me to go, and then I travel with a contingent of agents." *Real FBI agents. The kind who used to protect me.*

"What's your official job title?"

She stalled. "I'm in, umm, intelligence. I don't have a job title, but I'm sure not in black ops."

"You said you were a psychic before. What's that mean? Exactly?"

"It means that I can get inside people's minds in order to locate victims or persuade assailants. I can see things others can't. Like that jagged scar on your back below your left shoulder blade." She couldn't really see it at the moment, not with her second sight compromised like it was, but she knew it was there, and she needed him to believe her. His tormentor in Afghanistan had delighted in skewering his victims with something akin to a switch. He'd left a small blade in their backs, something he simply had to pluck to get their attention.

Ky winced, possibly convinced, possibly mortified that she'd outed him. One eyelid narrowed. One brow lifted. "Go on."

"I can't see everything, but I can get inside missing children's heads or kidnapped victims' minds. I can transfer mental images and suggestions. Sometimes. I can encourage them to hold on until help arrives." *Just like I did with you.*

He cocked his head, those amber eyes wide and rimmed dark cocoa with intensity. "You can do that?" He caught himself, cleared his throat and asked, "Who's your handler?"

"Was. Special Agent Matt Hartigen." She let his previous question slide. *Yes, Ky, I can do that and more.*

"What happened to him?"

"He dropped dead in the middle of a briefing. Heart attack. Just like my pilot before he crashed."

"Let me get this straight. Your pilot and handler died of the same mysterious heart attack? You've got some kind of weird psychic abilities, yet you've been surgically compromised, only you don't remember how or when. Someone *did* insert a possible tracking and a mind-control device into your body that you honestly have no recollection of, and were not aware of until..." His final word hung in the air as if he expected her to make it sound better than it did.

She swallowed hard. "Right. I get it. I know how it sounds, but on my mother's grave, I didn't notice the wire taped to my body until you told me to go check myself. I'm not lying, Ky. I'm wired, and I did have that spider-thing under my scalp, but I don't know how it got there, either. My second sight's been erratic since Hawaii, and, umm..." She paused, wishing she sounded less like a Tuesday-night TV drama.

"We don't have time for this. Damn, Tate's already taken the tent down. The wire comes out as soon as we camp again," he said with conviction. "You hear me?"

"Okay, sure." That sounded good in a scary, *who's-going-to-be-operating-on-me-now* kind of way. The wire didn't scare her, but that oblong lump deep inside her groin certainly did. God, some maniac could've planted a bomb in her. How would she know that he hadn't? Whatever it was, she wanted it gone.

"If we're not defending an impossible position by then," Tate cut in, the tent rolled and under his arm. "If she's right, and she's really seeing things, Zaroyin's already got his goons on our trail. We need to move."

She bit her lip rather than plead for credibility. *I am* right. *Six more drones are coming for me. Stop talking already. Let's go!*

Ky nodded, his stare probing for what Eden didn't know. A crystal blue aura glowed around him, calming her. Tate's aura had faded to more gray than blue, his doubt apparent. But

Ky believed her. She opened her mouth to accept responsibility for placing them in harm's way.

"Shut up," Ky snapped before she could get a word out. "Don't even think it."

"Think what? I didn't say anything." *Not verbally. I just thought it.* How did he know she meant to tell them to leave her behind?

Ky nodded his chin at her, challenging. "Yeah, right. You were going to tell me to beat it, that you could take care of yourself out here, weren't you?"

Gulp. How's he doing that? "Umm, yeah."

"Not going to happen, Agent Stark. Do you at least know how to shoot?"

She bobbed her head on her way to disappointing him again. "Yes, I'm a dead-eye with paper targets that don't move. Preferably the kind with big, round circles."

"Jesus H. Christ." He turned into the dark and ran a hand over his head before he faced her again, a definite twinkle in his eye. "What are you carrying? You do have a real gun, don't you? One that shoots bullets?"

The nerve of the sarcastic guy! "Glock 42, .380 auto,'" she answered proudly, needing him to know she was not completely defenseless.

"Single stack or double?"

The jerk. Who'd he think she was, testing her like that? A total idiot? She set him straight. "It doesn't come in a double, Agent Winchester." *And you darned well know it.*

He rolled his eyes. Okay, so her weapon of choice was still the smallest subcompact pistol Glock had ever produced. Get over it. It fit snugly in her hand, and she liked it.

"You've never used it on anyone though, have you? You've never killed a guy?"

He certainly got right to the point. What could she say? "I would if I had to." *I think.*

Ky shot Tate a raised eyebrow. "Looks like it's all on us, buddy. Stay sharp."

Tate grunted, and Eden wasn't sure if that was a positive sign or not. His primary language seemed to be comprised of grunts of all sizes when she was around. She couldn't wrap her brain around Ky's uncanny ability to read her, though. What was that about?

His gaze scrolled to the ax handle sticking out of the bag on her shoulder. "What do you have there?"

"An ax." It seemed a good idea at the time. "We might need it."

He glowered at her. "Give it up. It's too big for you."

She twisted to her side, intent on doing her share of the heavy lifting. Whatever they could do, she could do, too. "No, it's okay. I can carry it."

Ky brooked no argument, just relieved her of the ax. Handing it to Tate, he shook his head. "What am I going to do with you?"

She squared her chin and resettled her gear, insulted he'd decided she couldn't carry her own weight. "You're going to shut up and start walking, that's what you're going to do."

A smile shifted over his face before he stepped out and took point. She followed while Tate assumed the rear position.

Tate was right. The weak early morning sunlight dimmed when snow commenced falling. The world hushed. Wherever Ky led, she stayed close, her head down, following in his tracks with Tate on her heels. Only the steady crunch of boots through the snow marred the silence.

Eden projected her second sight to the east, needing a better sense of the six men headed in her direction. Sure enough, they'd altered course to intersect with her new projected path. She threw her focus to the south, striving to see how many more stalked her from that direction. Nothing. Just the two. Just the eerie sensation that more of Zaroyin's game pieces were in motion. Had he gotten that good? Had he improved the cybernetic implants enough that she could no longer detect his newest drones?

She alerted Ky. "I still can't see for certain how many are coming up from Thunder Bay, but the six from the east changed direction. They mean to intercept me."

"Us, Eden. Not just you. Tate, ETA to our stone fortress?" he stated clearly without turning around.

"Another hour at this rate," Tate grumbled.

Eden took his surly answer for a hint and walked faster, nearly tripping on Ky's boot heels. She was a burden and a possible threat to everyone with that device implanted in her body. If it was a GPS-locating device, Zaroyin's men wouldn't have any trouble catching up with her, but how had she not seen it until Ky told her to look for it? It made no sense. The wire wasn't even beneath her skin, not until it sank into the crease of her thigh. She should've at least noticed the tape when she'd showered the day she left Alaska.

That was what worried her. That device in her groin had been inserted orthoscopically, in the proximity of her femoral artery. Or in it. She couldn't tell. She'd been so flustered when she found it. And angry. That mad man had violated her, but she had no idea when he'd done it. Ky had to be right. Maybe she'd been mind-controlled this whole time. Maybe that was why she'd fallen for Charlie Sweets and his fatherly act.

Zaroyin seemed one step ahead. How long could that spider thing have been inside of her body? What had it been doing there? Digging into her skull to get down to her brain? Was that how he created his drones? Did he transmit commands over some kind of electrical stimulus through a neuropath? Was that what those eight spider legs really were— conductors? Transmitters? Or worse, some kind of det cord? Was she carrying an internal explosive that made her a walking bomb? *Why?*

She cringed, instantly walking more carefully to not rub or disturb that thing in her groin. The notion that she'd been manipulated like a puppet on a tinsel string irked the heck out of her, but that wasn't the worst of it. A full-on body shiver struck her hard. Had Zaroyin purposefully driven her into the darkest forests of Canada for a reason? Did he want her in this exact spot at this exact time?

She could barely breathe at the notion of that mad man in control of so many aspects of her life, but it didn't seem likely Zaroyin would've done his own dirty work. Eden scanned through each day since she'd first seen him, searching for a likely suspect, someone who would've aided and abetted, but all she could come up with were FBI agents, men and women she'd trusted. They couldn't all have been on his payroll. It was too much.

But someone had to have helped him. Eden did what she usually did with insurmountable problems. She delegated them to her brain and let it do its subconscious thing while she focused on keeping up with Ky and surviving her nagging migraine.

The terrain had grown steeper as the trees thinned. Fewer trees meant more snow, drifted and deep. Walking became progressively harder. Eden struggled on, determined she wouldn't drag this team down any further.

The wind scoured the ground, blowing the loose snow and creating the worst dilemma for anyone on foot—a whiteout. She couldn't tell north from south, and lost all depth perception. Eden tucked her chin into her jacket collar and focused on Ky's boots. He kept marching. She leaned into the wind, her head down, but with all the drifting snow, it was easy to miss the tree stump.

Eden tripped and fell, her hands forward. Her face would've biffed the ground, holding her bag over her shoulder like she was, but Ky turned and caught her as she tumbled.

"Thanks," she muttered, embarrassed she'd nearly landed at his feet.

"No problem." He dusted the snow off her knees and made sure she was steady on her feet before he let her go. "We'll be there soon. You good?"

She nodded. Good and cold was more like it. She wasn't about to complain, but how'd he do that? How had he just anticipated her tripping? Precisely then? The stump was hidden beneath a good foot of snow. He'd been facing away from her, walking uphill, and yet he'd turned and caught her in time? Weird. Ky's intuition was another problem for her exceptionally efficient brain to resolve if it ever got a moment's rest.

After an hour of steady plodding, Tate took the lead while she and Ky walked side by side behind him. "So what's the plan once we get there?" she asked, breathing hard. "Put the tent up again?"

Ky shook his head. "Tate's our survival specialist. He'll know what to do."

The terrain got steeper and the climbing got tougher. When she nearly fell again, Ky lifted the bag off her shoulders. "Here. Let me take that."

She would've protested if she hadn't been thrilled at the offer. Her bag had gotten heavier. Her thin driving gloves weren't intended for the bitter cold, either. She shivered. Her fingers were numb, but Eden was no quitter. She brought both hands up to her mouth and breathed into them for warmth.

The vision burst into her mind. Six dark shadows. Running through the snow. Growling like trolls. Sweat running in their bloodshot eyes. Short-stock rifles lifted. Ready to kill all who stood in their way.

She dropped to her knees, her heart blocking her throat. "Ky! They'll kill you! Run!"

Chapter Nine

Damned woman. Again, she wants me to run? Like hell.

Ky couldn't see her, not in the blizzard. It hit hard, full of snow and a bitter chill that slithered through his TEAMwear. Where the hell did she go? Eden couldn't have just dropped off the face of the earth. Holy shit, how much trouble could one woman be? She'd been right at his side a minute ago, but he couldn't see a thing in this whiteout. He stretched both arms into the swirling void, needing to save her from herself again it seemed, and hoping his goggles detected her before she got too far away.

"Eden," he called, his voice immediately tossed back in his face by wind and snow.

"Danger," TEAMshield warned. "Imminent contact with Agent Eden Stark at your right."

He froze in his tracks and reached for the missing FBI agent, not feeling anything to his right, not until he lowered his expectations to ground level. He crouched over the lifeless woman at his fingertips.

"I'm at the wall. Ten yards at your six," Tate informed Ky via their TEAMshield link. "Where are you? I thought you were right behind me."

"Coming," Ky muttered, lifting to his feet with a passed out woman in his arms. He cursed himself for not thinking ahead like he should have. He'd planned on keeping Eden warm and alive once he'd located her, Sweets too. That was why he'd brought the extra sets of TEAMwear. Why hadn't he thought of extra goggles, too? She needed the benefits of TEAMshield as much as the warmer clothing, especially in this storm. Then she could've seen that thing she'd just tripped over.

He made an abrupt about-face, no longer certain which way was north in the whiteout. "I can't see a thing. Ten yards?"

"Walk straight ahead. The path is clear. You can't miss me."

Ky folded Eden under his chin and advanced carefully and slowly. The blizzard consumed them. His high-tech goggles allowed for depth perception and eye protection when a man could actually see. Not now.

One misstep could send him sliding down the incline, never to be heard from again. Like Tate, he'd studied the terrain prior to this mission. Between the stretches of alpine forest, sheets of solid granite lay beneath the snow, a slippery death trap if conditions were right. Not good when a guy was carrying deadweight. Not that Eden was heavy. Hardly.

At last, a dark and shadowy shape materialized. *Tate.* The stone fortress solidified out of the blizzard behind him. It was nothing special and certainly not warm, but it offered what Ky wanted: a battlefield with one front to defend.

He'd have to outlast the storm to get a better lay of the land, but the incline he'd just climbed made the wall a favorable position. The six guys tracking Eden had to come uphill to get at her, the perfect ambush for a sniper on his belly with a damned good rifle and scope. Ky intended to be that guy.

"Sit. Stay. Take a load off," Tate commanded. "I'll tell you when to move out."

Ky sank, his back to the wall and Eden once more on his lap. He bowed his body over hers while Tate disappeared into the whiteout. "What the hell are you doing?"

"You'll see," Tate growled. "Give me five, will you?"

Ky encapsulated Eden from the bitter wind, sheltering her head with his shoulders and arms. He cupped his gloves to the side of her face. Their breaths mingled in that limited space between them while snowflakes drifted through the cracks. He stilled, listening to her breathing while the storm raged around them, the small sound of her huffing barely audible, but sweet. Feminine. What was God thinking to have created this gender so fragile, yet endowing it with the toughest job of all—the ability to co-create and nurture something as precious as a newborn's life? The resilience and sheer strength of women never ceased to amaze Ky.

He'd puzzled over many of God's miracles in the past, but right then, Eden was the loveliest of them all. She had none of the ruggedness of most of the female agents he'd worked with, none of the muscular build. No brawn. No muscle. Her body was softer. More lush. Curvier. She sported no tats that he'd seen—not that he'd seen yet anyway—just a lot of nerve to have made it this far from home without all that supposed FBI security she'd been promised. Where were they now, all those tough guys who'd been assigned to have her back? The Bureau had failed her. Big time.

This particular woman had been part of the pre-op intel he'd studied, but having her in his arms made him think. He'd been around men most of his military service. Alex had a couple female agents on The TEAM, but it wasn't often Ky came this close to truly, delightful feminine company. He'd missed it. Something deep inside of him missed it, too.

His life was sparse and downright utilitarian. He worked hard, hit the gym and worked harder. Play had become a thing of his past, but this woman brought him a different kind of energy. It was as if she'd opened a window into the darkest parts of his soul and let her sun shine. On him. In him.

He studied her better, wanting to memorize every last detail while he had the chance, like her long eyelashes. Thick. Curled against her cheeks like the wings of butterflies ready to lift up and fly away on a warm spring day. Dark brown, they were the same color as the streaks in her blond hair and the freckles scattered across her upturned nose and over her cheeks, a dusting of tiny chocolate chips.

The bow of her full lips drew his gaze to her mouth, parted in a gentle sigh. He should've kissed those lips when she'd offered them earlier, but no. The terror of human touch got the best of him every damned time. He truly wished it didn't control him the way it did. *If it still did.*

He honestly wasn't sure any more. Had he truly had a panic attack before, or had he only anticipated having one like he usually did? He leaned his nose to hers, testing his theory until they touched. See? It didn't hurt. Not one bit. The tension in his gut unclenched. There might be hope for him.

But that was the dilemma. He could touch her. She just couldn't touch him. That was why the gloves. Gloves discouraged displays of affection and gratitude, the touching that went with it. It made no sense, but his mixed-up memories jerked him through a knothole every damned time a person got too close or too friendly. *Or did it?*

He took a deep breath. There it was again, that menthol fragrance drifting up from her delicious, warm body. It didn't come from her breath, though. It wasn't a cough drop, though it smelled similar. He nosed over her cheek and into her ear. Her neck. That was where it was strongest. He inhaled another whiff, relishing the instant calm that came with it.

He couldn't place the scent, only remembered it from the depths of his own personal hell. Part menthol. Part dust. Part sweat and blood, but one hundred percent hope. It comforted him now as much as it had before, but what was it? Why did it surround her like it did? He inhaled another nose full and let it seep into his soul, more convinced she was the woman he remembered.

"Get off your butt and take a sharp left," Tate barked in his ear. "In ten or twelve feet, the ground levels out. Stay low. The wall's got a natural corner. I put the tent up. It isn't much, but it'll get us out of the wind. Look for the green glow."

Ky lifted up from the drift with Eden, his pack and hers. By then his entire right side was covered with snow. "Can do."

Tate was a godsend on an op like this. He'd snapped a chemglow light stick to guide Ky in. Locating the tent was no trouble once Ky got close enough. He ducked low at the open flap to transfer Eden into Tate's open arms. With her safe inside the domed-refuge and safe, Ky dusted as much snow off his jacket as he could, kicked more of the powdery stuff off his boots, and climbed in behind her.

The wind had turned wicked, howling along the face of the granite wall and pushing at the nylon walls of the tent. Tate settled Eden on the far side of the tent, nearest the granite wall. She lay on her side facing inward, an opened sleeping bag beneath her. Tate covered her with the fur wrap, a considerate item he'd brought along.

Her gray pallor startled Ky. He pulled off his goggles and crawled on all fours to her side. "What's going on now?"

Tate joined him just as she opened her eyes. "Are they here?" she asked weakly.

"Nobody can get through this storm," Tate muttered. "They've probably—"

"No!" She pushed to one elbow. "Please. They are coming. You can't kill them."

Chapter Ten

Tate dropped to his haunches with an exasperated huff, annoyed. "What do you mean, I can't kill them? You bet your sweet ass I can kill them, and I will. You want me to start a boy's camp for wayward mercenaries, do you? While they're taking pot shots at us?"

Eden straightened, facing him. *My sweet ass?* "But this is different. Believe me, I can see things you can't, Agent Higgins. This blizzard hasn't slowed them down because they no longer feel the cold. They've been programmed to act like robots. Their decision-making ability is compromised. They'll run until they drop or die from exposure—or until you kill them. They can't be held accountable—"

"But they *will* kill you, Eden," Ky interrupted, "and they won't think twice about it. I don't care if they're blind, drunk, or walking on water by the time they get here. I won't let them hurt you."

"But you do care," she declared. "I know you do. You care about everyone." *That's your greatest asset and your worst flaw.*

Ky stopped arguing, his amber eyes searching hers for what seemed like minutes. He swallowed hard, looking right through her. She'd said too much, but she hadn't said it out loud. She'd picked up on it all the way from Nizari's dark cell. Ky's compassion for others ran deep. It got him into trouble.

That was what had gotten him captured in Kabul. He'd charged into a blind alley to protect a fellow Marine, his RTO, and his supposed friendlies, the few traitorous soldiers in the Afghan National Army.

Ky needed to understand. Each black smudge in the distance, each one of those six guys still held a tiny red glow at his core. Zaroyin hadn't created the perfect killing machines. Not yet. These guys had feelings, maybe consciences. They should be saved, not killed. They needed to be helped, not murdered.

Tate pushed past Ky on his way into the weather. "Now might be a good time to get that wire out of her before she decides she wants steak and lobster for dinner. That ain't gonna happen, neither."

Ky hadn't taken his gaze off Eden to acknowledge his partner. "What's going on? You're gray. You said you had a migraine. How bad is it?"

"You don't understand," she whispered, the hammering pain in her skull fierce. Her second sight seemed crippled with the overload of those six men marching to her. Empathy for all they were going through reduced her to a trembling radar dish tuned into their suffering. "I can feel them, Ky. Every single one of them. Zaroyin's still got control, but they're fighting the implants. I'm sure of it. They don't want to kill me any more than you do. And they're exhausted from marching in this weather. They're like me."

"We'll talk about this later." He pushed her flat to the sleeping bag, and Eden went willingly. She hadn't the strength to argue. She closed her eyes as his gloved fingers skimmed over her forehead. "I don't have a fever."

"No, but your head hurts, right? You're dizzy? Both signs you're dehydrated. Let's get more water into you. More food, too. Tate's right. That wire needs to come out, but for now we need to get you stabilized. Drink," he ordered, his hand beneath her neck while he tilted her forward to the lip of a water bottle. "More. Drink it all if you can."

Eden did as she was told, then wiped her lips. "They're dehydrated, too, only worse. Please. You have to listen to—"

"Agent Stark!" Her name snapped out of him, a whip in the wind. "I can't do anything until they get here, now, can I? Do as you're told. Drink."

Despite his order, that sounded more encouraging, like he was at least considering her opinion even though he was irritated with her. She settled for the small victory. She had no fight in her anyway. "Where'd you get warm water?"

He winked down at her, an oddly calming gesture given the wind howling outside their flimsy sanctuary from the storm. "From my armpit." He followed that disgusting revelation with, "You can't eat enough snow to keep hydrated on winter operations, and you wouldn't want to if you could. Ingesting snow lowers your body temp, the last thing you need. I packed a bottle with snow when you went for your bag. My body heat melted it on the climb up. That's all. Do you want more?"

"No, umm, okay. Sure." Eden sat up straighter to drink, not so much because she was thirsty, more because of Ky leaning over her with all that male heat rolling off of him. The close proximity of his body did crazy things to her heart. It set to pounding, which in turn made the ache in her head that much worse. But it also spiked a flood of female hormones she couldn't fight. From the tops of her toes to the tips of her tingling, swollen breasts, he just plain overpowered and overwhelmed her with all that raw male power. If he was any more alpha, she'd melt along with the snow in his water bottle. "I should've thought of doing that," she offered meekly.

He handed her the half-full bottle with a cute little-boy shrug. "It's just Survival 101. Keep hydrated. Keep warm. Stay dry. I melted another bottle for myself. Knowing Tate, he's probably got five or six on him. The guy's a survivalist to the core."

But it was a big deal. Ky seemed determined to take care of her first and foremost, a marked difference from the previous men in her life. "Where'd Tate go?"

"Out. Don't worry. He'll do what needs to be done. That's why we're here. To get you home safely."

Eden caught his meaning. Tate would kill the first man who fired at him, and she couldn't blame him. She had no right to dictate impossible terms to the men sent to rescue her. "Tate should shoot Zaroyin, not those FBI agents."

"Nothing in life is fair." Ky kept his voice low and somber, a warning. "What do you want to eat? I know you're still hungry. Spicy corn chowder, baked potato and bacon soup, or cheese and broccoli Alfredo?"

He seemed determined to distract her, so she let him. "MREs?"

"Not exactly. Alex buys a better quality than the Army." He scrunched his nose, another adorable gesture. "Each pouch makes an eight-cup serving. We'll share. What'll it be?"

This was a serious decision. She didn't want to alienate Ky's partner more than she already had, not even over a dehydrated meal. "What would Tate like?"

"Don't worry about him. He can make his own. He's probably out hunting caribou anyway."

Eden offered a weak smile, her heart on those other agents caught in Zaroyin's drone snare. She needed Tate on her side. "The potato soup. It's got bacon. He'll like that, huh?"

"He will if there's any left when he gets back." Ky tugged a foil bag out of his backpack, ripped off the top and poured water from his bottle into it.

Eden arranged herself cross-legged while he prepared their meal. Now that she was upright, he seemed happier. He plopped their rehydrated dinner on the tent floor between them and made a production of producing two plastic forks sealed in cellophane from yet another pocket. Still trying to distract her. "Ladies first."

"Not bad. It's thicker than I expected," she mumbled around the chunky spoonful.

He grinned. "It's only soup with enough hot water."

"What happened in Morocco?"

A dimple tweaked his left cheek as he stuffed a heaping fork into his mouth. "You heard that, huh?"

"Sure. I was listening." Eden liked watching him eat. Ky took big, man-sized mouthfuls. He ate with relish, licking his lips. His Adam's apple bobbed when he chewed and swallowed, and the scruff shadowing the hard lines of his face was just plain sexy. Tinted green from the glow-stick, but sexy.

"It's funny now, but it wasn't then. My boss sent Tate and me over to retrieve a certain federal official. He'd gotten into a delicate situation with a married woman in Casablanca. Long story short, her husband also happened to be the local police chief. By the time we got there, Mr. Dumbass was in a bad way. The police chief challenged him to a duel, but he had his whole force backing him up. There were only the two of us. We got our guy all right, but by the time the Moroccan Royal Gendarmerie took over, Tate and I had our backs to some cliffs overlooking the Atlantic Ocean. Believe me, I was ready to hand our idiot diplomat over to the police chief and let him whip his ass."

"The Moroccans let you take him with you when you left?"

Ky took another heaped mouthful. "Let us, nothing," he mumbled around chunky potato and bacon soup. "They gave us twenty-four hours to get off Moroccan soil, so we did. No big deal. Guess all's well that ends well. Dumbass is running for office again."

"He's a congressman?"

"Senator." Ky held up three gloved fingers. "Three terms."

"He sounds like a creep."

"He's a piece of work, all right. Get this. We're on an Air Force chopper out of there, and he's bragging himself up like we didn't just risk our lives saving his sorry ass. He wanted Tate and me to quit Alex and go work for him. Said he had a lucrative deal in Sierra Leone. Said he needed good men like us on his side."

"I went to Morocco once," Eden murmured, another fork lifted to her lips. The bacon was still crunchy, but good. "Was he into conflict diamonds?"

"He might have been, but we'll never know. Tate and I didn't want any part of that lunatic or his big ideas. His one-time good deal ended when we dropped him at the U. S. Consulate. I see the guy once in a while on the office TV, but bam. I have a remote for that."

Eden couldn't stop thinking about how well she already knew Ky. Still she hedged. "Was it hard being a soldier?"

A shadow ebbed within the deepest amber of his eyes. "I wasn't a soldier, Eden. Soldiers are Army. Marines are Marines. Jarheads. Leathernecks. And no, being in the Corps wasn't hard. It was the best thing I've ever done. Now what say we take care of that wire if we can get to it?"

She bowed her head, willing to accept his version of the truth, but wishing he'd reveal the tiniest hint of what he'd survived, just enough so she could reveal her true identity. Maybe later.

"Are you sure you want to do it now?" Her gaze drifted to the tent flap Tate had zipped closed. The storm still buffeted the overlap, and he could come back at any time.

"It has to be done, Eden," Ky said sternly. "You and I both need to know precisely what that wire leads to. It could be more dangerous than we suspect. Do you want to see if you can get it out yourself? Should I leave?"

"No. Stay." She looked him in the eye, her heart caught on those six puppets still dangling out there in the weather on Zaroyin's string.

Ky zipped what was left of their chilly soup and set breakfast aside. His expression gentled. "Listen, I know you're worried about those men. I agree with you. Koenig and Shields were obviously under duress by the time we encountered them, but their programming, if that's what controlled them, gave us no choice. I'm sorry if this isn't what you want to hear, but these next six guys will kill you unless Tate and I stop them. You were there. You saw. Koenig and Shields didn't waste words. They didn't even ask who we were before they opened fire on Tate and me. These men aren't coming to talk, either. They mean to kill you, and I won't let that happen."

It was odd how much they thought alike. Eden braced her fingers to her forehead to cover her eyes, on the verge of tears she wouldn't let fall. "It's not fair. There has to be a way to save them."

Ky huffed through his nose, obviously exasperated. Possibly conflicted. "I'd rather not kill them, either. What would you suggest Tate and I do?"

"I really don't know." One tear rolled out of her eyelid and trickled down her cheek, giving her away. The unnecessary sacrifice of six innocent men galled her, but Ky was right. In the end, it would come down to self-defense. Kill or be killed.

He reached for her wrists, the barrier of his ever-present gloves once again between them. "Let me talk with Tate. There might be a way, but I'm not promising anything."

"Okay." She changed the subject before she broke down. "What if this wire was implanted inside my femoral artery? What do we do then?"

He leaned forward with a conspiratorial whisper. "Trust me. We'll cross that bridge when we come to it."

Time to start. She lifted to her knees, not fond of the notion that she had to bare parts of her already chilled anatomy to the bitter cold again. "Br-r-r. Then let's do this fast before I change my mind."

He rolled to his butt and turned toward the tent flap, his broad back to her and his elbows on his knees. "Tell me when."

Snap. The second she took her gloves off, her fingers were numb. She shivered as she unzipped her TEAMwear jacket, then her trusty Ralph Lauren. Lifting the front of her sweater, she clamped the edge of it under her chin and raised her layers of shirts. Finally down to her bra, she pulled it up over her ample breasts, not willing to reveal more skin than she had to.

She was already on her way to hyperthermia, shivering and blowing puffs of frozen vapor while she fumbled with the end of the surgical tape some jerk had had the nerve to stick between her breasts. She peeled the wire very carefully away. Her poor nipples hardened from the chilly air. Breathing on them while she worked didn't help, but down and off went that strip of tape.

Silently, she cussed with every inch of the wire revealed. Someone had handled her without her knowledge. Intimately! Who would've done that? When? Why? Could Zaroyin be powerful enough to have men everywhere? Already? Being the one and only FBI psychic was bizarre enough, but this whole drone thing spooked her. In less than two weeks, her life had devolved into a scene out of the *Body Snatchers*.

Folding the taped wire into a roll upon itself kept the sticky side in. Eden readjusted her bra, warmed her nipples with a quick squeeze, and pulled her layers back down. The TEAMwear top was a welcome article of clothing. Considering she was in the middle of a raging winter snowstorm, she was fairly comfortable—in a chilly, shivering sort of way.

Now the scary part. She unzipped the TEAMwear bottoms, then her jeans. Straightening her legs, she slipped far enough out of her pants to give her room to work. Pulling the front of her underwear down, she tugged the lowest reach of the wire away from her skin and out of that patch of secret, curly hairs.

Anger flared at the nerve of the despicable man who'd done this to her all over again. He could've raped her. How would she know if he had or hadn't? Eden pushed her underwear farther down. Little by little she could see better. This was so much worse than she thought. Whoever had done this had shaved a narrow line to the implant in her right groin. Her body! For all she knew, some woman could've done this! Sudden tears blurred her vision. The thought of betrayal by her own gender felt so much worse.

A childish whine nearly escaped before she caught herself. She'd only come into contact with fellow FBI agents since she'd left D.C. behind. There simply was no one she could trust any more, but darn. She was so tired of running. Of fighting the world alone.

The insertion point was still red and tender. Whoever did this to her had done it recently. "Darn you, Zaroyin."

Chapter Eleven

Until that muttered attempt at a cuss word, Eden had been way too quiet. "You need my help yet?" Ky asked without turning around. He'd hoped that implant could be expressed out through the same hole it had gone in, but it didn't sound like that was happening.

"No. I'm just so... so mad."

"Can you get it out? Will it move?" He hoped. If she could work it out, he was home free. If not... more touching.

Eden whined. "No, and I'm just making myself sore. It's, umm, really stuck."

Stuck nothing. She'd been violated, plain and simple, and he wanted to kill the guy who'd done it. "Don't pull on it. If it is inside your femoral, you don't want to break it out of there."

"Yes, I do. I'll show him. He can't do this to me and get away with it."

Ky turned to keep her from doing something stupid. The loveliest sight met his eyes. Eden, half-dressed with her chin tucked on her chest to keep her shirt out of her way. Sitting sideways with her legs straight, her pants peeled down, and her bare ass on the sleeping bag. Her lovely white hips showing. The rounded curve of her bottom, too. She'd pulled her shred of black underwear down and sat hunched over, peering at the crease of her thigh, her hair cascading around her. Her lips were pursed tight, her jaw squared off. Teardrops glistened on her lush, thick lashes. His heart melted at the sight. She was frightened and trembling, but she held the wire at a tight right-angle to her body, like a fisherman with a trophy salmon on his line. Only this fish was damned dangerous.

"Don't do that," he cautioned as he crawled to her side. "You'll hurt yourself. Stop it."

She grabbed the edge of her coat to cover her exposed lap. "Ky! Don't look! You're supposed to be over there. Not here."

"I need to see it," he insisted. "It's got to come out, Eden. If you can't do it yourself, I'll—"

"But I don't want you to, umm, look." Scarlet crept over her cheeks.

"Come on. Let me help." Ky opted for his most professional manner to set her at ease. He wouldn't look. Much. And he'd be touching her, not the other way around. If she kept her hands to herself, this could work. He stepped out on the limb, needing to set the one and only ground rule before things got more serious. "You can't touch me while I do this, okay?"

Her brows furrowed and her nose wrinkled. He'd hurt her feelings—not what he was going for. "Why not? You touch me."

Way to go, Winchester.

"You just can't, okay? It's not you. It's me. Honest." *Shit, I sound like I'm in junior high.*

Eden reached across the cramped space between them and placed her hand on his jacket sleeve. "Okay. I trust you. Now what?"

Those three words. The right words. *I trust you.* They nearly did him in. How could she trust him after what some other guy had done to her? Yet there she was, her soft green eyes aglow. Eden offered the barest glimmer of a smile. "After all, I'm the one sitting here with my pants down, aren't I? Either I trust you or I'm crazy." But then her façade crumbled. Her lower lip quivered. "He could've raped me, Ky. Whoever did this, he might've done terrible things to me. How do I know he didn't?" A sob caught in her throat. "I mean r-r-really? I didn't know about this wire. W-what else did he… they do to me?"

That shivering question stalled everything. Ky pressed a palm to her shoulder, at a loss as to how to comfort a woman who might've been assaulted. He'd endured a world of hurt in his life, some of it perverse and beyond humiliating. In a bizarre turn of events, his savior, Lee Hart, had returned for the wicked Nizari and ended him, but not one day passed that Ky didn't wish he'd been the one who'd killed the bastard. Slowly. Over a bed of hot coals. Skewered. Drawn and quartered. Bled. Hanged. Dragged through the streets and...

Ky shook off the sickness in his soul that the evil name always brought with it. He stilled until his heart rate calmed. Eden needed that same definite closure he'd experienced, but Ky couldn't give it to her. He offered what he could. "I know how you feel, Eden. You may never have all the answers. Once we're stateside, I'll help you figure it out, but for now, let's just worry about this wire." He vowed right then and there that whoever had violated her would die at his hand.

She sniffed, looking like a little girl who'd been pacified for the moment. "Thanks."

"So show me the point of insertion. How bad is it?" He let his gaze scroll down to her lap. Damn. Not the best thing to say when a guy was so close to a woman's real *point of insertion* that he could scent her. He tamped down his growing attraction to this petite blonde and focused on helping her. "Where is it?"

"Right here." Eden leaned back, one palm splayed behind her to hold her weight. Pointing to the crease of her thigh, she handed over the rolled tape. Cocking one knee at an angle, she exposed the insertion point while she kept herself covered. Mostly. "I thought if I tugged hard enough, the tip might break through the skin, and I could pull it out, but it's not moving. I've just made it sore."

Sore, yes, but she'd also displayed too much silky feminine skin for a monk like Ky to handle. He'd been on a self-imposed abstinence mission since he'd come home from Kabul. Kneeling so close to her with that lovely, warm feminine scent filling the tiny space between them created a steady thrumming in his blood. His heart thudded like a dummy SCUD over Iraq even as his nostrils flared to draw more of her in. Menthol and Eden and a musky dose of lust. Hmmm.

He forced his focus on the real problem. The incision looked red and raw. It hadn't had time to heal. He stopped thinking about sex. Kind of. At least, he pushed sex to the back of his mind. Kind of. "Where were you two days ago?" he asked, not that it mattered. This cut looked to be fairly recent.

Eden seemed not to notice his hesitation. "I was in Hawaii. That's when he showed up, so I checked out and flew to Alaska."

"Who? Zaroyin?"

She nodded.

"So someone in Hawaii drugged you, assaulted you without your knowledge before he even got there, then topped it off with hypnosis or something so you'd be oblivious to what he did?"

"I think so. That's the only thing that makes sense. I wasn't in Alaska long enough."

Ky pulled the wire taut with one hand and pinched the long, thin shape tucked inside her body between the first two fingers of his other hand. The device resembled half of a ballpoint pen, narrowed at one end where the wire connected, flat at the other. Solid, not malleable, the thing refused to budge. It didn't even tilt upward toward its point of insertion when he tugged. "Am I hurting you?" he asked.

"No. I'm good."

"How'd you know when Zaroyin showed up in Hawaii? What'd you do, stalk the airport?"

"One of my friends in the Bureau notified me he was on his way."

"Let me guess. The same guy who told you to go to Anchorage?"

Eden swallowed hard enough that Ky heard her gulp. "Um, yeah. Why?"

Because he just might be in league with Zaroyin. "He a doctor?"

"Uh-uh. Matt's friend, Cameron Levine. I met him in D.C. He's FBI, one of the good guys."

Like hell. "You go to dinner with this friend while you were in Hawaii? Have any drinks?"

She nodded, not meeting his eyes.

How could she not see what was right in front of her nose? "Ten to one your friend slipped you a roofie. That's why you don't remember getting these implants."

She shook her head, spilling those lovely gold tresses over her shoulders. "Uh-uh. No way. Cameron's a good guy. He wouldn't do that."

Well, someone sure as hell did. "How much did you have to drink?"

Her lips narrowed. "Two glasses of white wine. I did get sleepy, but I'd been on edge until then. So what? I needed something to help me relax. He walked me back to my room, but it's not what you think, Ky. He said goodbye at the door. I'm sure of it. I remember."

"And then what? You woke up in bed, but don't recall getting into your pajamas?"

She blinked three times as if the puzzles pieces had just fallen into place. "Um, maybe."

Levine, you son-of-a-bitch. I am going to rip your fucking head off.

"Bottom line, this thing still has to come out. Listen, I have a surgical kit, and I can do it, but I don't have any anesthetic. It'll hurt. I'm sorry." He shook his head at what she'd have to endure if he made a mistake and nicked her femoral.

"Then do it," she declared, her chin lift hard to miss. "Now. Let's get this over with before Tate gets back."

Ky handed her the fur wrap Tate had salvaged from the Cessna. "Lie down and cover up. You don't need to undress, but you will need to slip your pants farther down. I'll need more room to work." *Now there's a line for the history books. Slip your pants down. Give me room to work.*

Silently, she obeyed. Eden eased to her elbows on the sleeping bag while Ky prepared his surgical area. At the same time, he wondered why Alex hadn't selected Junior Agent Eric Reynolds for this op. The resident USMC medic would've been the perfect guy for this assignment. He knew how to operate in the field, and he could've done it without risking Eden's life. Instead, she was getting a minimally trained jarhead. Brave, but stupid. Untouchable, but a hands-on kind of a guy. With gloves. *Weird.*

Ky was just in the wrong place at the wrong time. And worried. He needed to report in and ask Alex to search out every last person Eden had spoken with since she'd left the Bureau's protection, especially that Agent Cameron Levine. It didn't make sense that she'd run straight into Zaroyin's trap like she had. If it wasn't Levine, someone else had to have steered her along the way, dropped a hint or given her what sounded like good, free advice.

Time to begin.

Ky reached across the crowded tent for the portable lantern. After he set it where it was out of the way but still bright enough, he retrieved his one and only surgical kit. It was rarely needed, but one of those items he and Tate took turns hauling along on missions. He placed it on Eden's chest to give her something to do. "Here. Hold this for me."

She latched onto the edges of it, her fingers trembling. Wrapped in plastic, the kit was nothing but a tray of the minimal tools needed for a quick patch-up job. Sterile gloves. One surgical mask. Scalpel. Scissors. Forceps. Two locking curved hemostats. Already threaded suture needles. Betadine. Antiseptic wash for him. Antiseptic wipes for her. A clotting agent. A stack of white, sterile gauze he didn't want reddened with her blood. Some other good stuff a real surgeon might need. He gulped, his mouth gone dry now that the time had come to put his money where his previous bravado was. *Shit. I'm no doctor.*

Nonetheless, he removed his gloves and scrubbed.

Eden had grown quiet. Poor thing. First the spider-like thing in her head, now this.

Ky wiped his hands and wrists and handed her one of the two surgical drapes. "Slide this under your hip. Just in case I... never mind. Just do it."

She arched her back and maneuvered the paper cloth under the right side of her butt, holding the tray steady as she did. "Okay. I get it. Don't get blood on the sleeping bag."

He tugged the surgical mask firmly over his mouth and nose. The latex gloves went next. He snapped the cuffs at his wrists and asked, "You ready?"

"No, but I want his power over me gone. Go ahead. Do it."

Her words struck him hard. She wanted Zaroyin out of her life. He wanted Nizari out of his. She might understand what he was going through after all.

"Let's get to work then," he said, mustering false bravado to put her at ease. "Pull the blanket back just enough to let me take a good look. I don't want you freezing to death while I'm saving your life."

She chuckled weakly and bared her right hip. "Me neither."

Angling her leg to the side, she revealed more creamy bare skin, so soft and tender. His first inclination was to whip Cameron Levine to a pulp for laying a hand on someone as sweet as Eden. The jerk must've undressed her in order to tape that wire between her breasts all the way down her abdomen to her leg. He'd stripped her and intimately assaulted her. It didn't have to be rape. Just the fact that he had to have removed her bra and panties chapped Ky's hide. What purpose did that long of a lead wire serve anyway? Was it an antenna? Was it meant to prove that Zaroyin had ultimate control over his drones? Intimidation? The threat that he could get to the men and women in his power any time he wanted? Zaroyin needed to pay as much as Levine. Worse...

Ky sucked in a deep breath of barely controlled rage. Had Levine put his mouth on Eden? Had he taken more liberties with her while she lay unconscious at his mercy? Played with her? Kissed her? Fucked her? The son-of-a-bitch.

Ky snorted out a deep breath, struggling for calm. Most doctors didn't have to operate on their knees, but there Ky was, mad as hell and hunched over Eden like he knew what he was doing. He took hold of the wire again, sizing up his next move, imagining this wire wrapped tightly around Levine's neck.

When his rage translated into trembling fingers, he shook it off. Eden came first. Then Levine. Ky took a deep breath. He honestly didn't think the device was inside her femoral artery, or he'd never have considered operating in the first place. But it had been implanted close enough to that artery to scare the hell out of him. People died when surgeons failed, and *oh yeah, I'm not a surgeon.*

He selected the disposable scalpel from his handy-dandy tray like he knew what he was doing. Lifting it between his two fingers, Ky shouldn't have risked looking at her, but he did.

Her pretty green eyes blinked, full of tears. "Do you know why I trust you, Ky Winchester?"

"Because you're crazier than me?" He opted for a touch of humor in the middle of what could very well be her last minute of life if he slipped. If he let her die.

She didn't crack the smile he'd hoped for. "No. I trust you because I've known you for two and a half years. I saw you in that despicable cell in Afghanistan. I came to you psychically, and you need to know I really was there. I know it was hard, but I wouldn't trade that time in my life for anything." Eden rested one hand on his forearm. "But most of all, I know your heart, Ky Winchester. You're the noblest man I've ever met. I know you can do this. Now get that thing the hell out of me."

The universe shifted. His suspicions were spot-on. Her green eyes. Her visions. The sensation that he'd known her before. "You are my angel then," he stated it; he didn't ask. "That really was you I saw in Kabul?"

She nodded.

That should've rattled him more than it did, but it didn't. Confidence surged up his spine. Calm assurance gave him energy. It was past time to return the favor she'd done for him. "Hang on, Eden. This may hurt."

Chapter Twelve

May hurt, nothing. It hurt like heck.

Eden forsook the tray on her chest and dug her fingernails into the sleeping bag, her eyes squeezed tight, but determined not to cry. Okay, forget that. Crying like a baby, but without the blubbering, whiny sound she would've made if she'd been alone. The tears she couldn't stop, but her big mouth she could control. Kind of. A little whimper did squeak out right after he'd made the incision. More when he stuck some of the gauze into the cut. It felt like he jammed a roll of sandpaper inside of her.

He peered closely at his work, and he was so focused. So serious. His brows furrowed. Surgery near a femoral artery was not like popping a pimple or squeezing a sliver out of your thumb. This could go scarily bad.

Adrenaline swarmed through her like a hive of energetic bees on their way to the last flower on earth. She shook, as in shook, rattled. If she'd been on an operating table, she would've rolled off the edge and hit the floor. "I'm s-s-sorry. I can't seem to hold s-s-still."

"Don't worry. You're very brave. I've already made the incision. I can see the device clearly now, and it's not inside your artery, so that's good. I'm fairly sure it's a GPS locator, like we thought. Still not real clear why the wire, though."

Oh, thank God! Pain crawled up her hip and radiated outward in all directions. Her stomach clenched along with every other muscle in her body at whatever he was doing to her. She couldn't hold her head still. Brave, nothing. She needed this over.

"Whoever did this to you threaded the wire around your femoral artery. Bastard," he hissed. "Probably because he meant his drones to die if they succeeded in pulling it out. I'll kill him."

She should've been more appalled at that scary declaration, but a warm glow lit inside of her heart. Ky was in ultimate protector mode, an unusual trait for the men in her past life. Even Matt had kept a professional distance, but Ky sounded like he cared enough to fight for her.

His tongue peeked out between his lips. A sheen of sweat glistened on his wrinkled forehead, and Eden wished she were the nurse instead of the patient, just to dab that manly sweat away. To assist him instead of crying like a baby. Maybe bump elbows with him like people who worked closely together did. Or hips. Oh, heck. She wanted to bump more than hips with this handsome guy operating on her.

"Hold real still. I've got to snip this wire, but first..." He dug into the incision with those shiny silver clamp thingies. Both of them. Eden tried to keep her body still, but snap! Her eyes watered and she flinched. Those two things stung like heck, and he had his nose nearly in the incision. He had to have all ten fingers in there. *How long is that cut?*

"There. Got it. Whew." He tipped back to his butt, the device dangling at the bloody end of his forceps. "Say goodbye to Zaroyin's last hold on you."

He sounded proud of himself, but all Eden could do was bob her head and mumble, "Uh-huh." *So stitch me up already.*

A smile crinkled the corners of his eyes. Laugh lines. Of all the unlikely guys on earth to have laugh lines, this torture survivor certainly had them. Handsome, etched rays of genuine delight radiated out from the corners of his amber eyes. The man looked like he'd swallowed the sun. "Let's get you stitched and bandaged, shall we?"

She couldn't speak. Not yet. He'd done the impossible under primitive conditions, and he had every right to be proud that he hadn't nicked her femoral artery. She was, too. It was no small thing. A burst of warmth swelled up from her stomach filling her heart with gratitude for this guy who'd literally dropped out of the sky to save her. He'd called her his angel, but it was the other way around. Ky Winchester was her badassed archangel with brimstone in his eyes and fire in his heart. Geared-up, amped-up, and one of Stewart's snipers, he was still the gentlest man she'd ever known.

"You okay?"

"Yes," she whispered. *I am now.*

"Tiny stitches," he murmured, leaning over her hip again. "Hang tight. I'm almost done."

"Am I bleeding?"

"Not much. Sorry I hurt you, but I had to clamp your artery with both hemostats while I cut the wire. Just in case."

Oh, yeah. That was what they were called. Hemostats, not clamp thingies. She held on tight while he finished closing her up. Snap it to heck. She'd survived an airplane crash with just a bump on her head, yet there she was, shaking like a leaf in the middle of what felt like a full-on body earthquake. She could not control the tremors.

At last, he smoothed a clean, white bandage over the incision, straightened, and peeled his mask and gloves off. "There. All done. Good as new."

"Th-th-thanks." She meant to be quick about pulling her pants back up, but being operated on twice in one day had left her weak. She lifted to her palms, shifting under the fur wrap, but failing miserably at her 'tough FBI agent' routine. Another tear got away from her.

"Here, let me help," Ky offered. If that didn't present her with a mess of conflicting emotions, nothing would. A handsome and very capable guy pulling her pants *up* instead of down? What was the world coming to? She endured the assist, exhausted to her core and on the verge of falling apart.

Ky didn't seem to notice, just kept helping with her zipper. The TEAMwear outfit. The incision he'd made didn't hurt much now that he'd bandaged it, but her pride was a little ragged around the edges. Eden was used to being the one who reached out to others. This was a first—someone helping her every time she turned around.

This gentle man's kindness overwhelmed her, and she very much wanted to touch Ky in a more personal way than just holding onto his forearms while he dressed her. These continual close encounters made her very aware of his sheer mass, and more than a little susceptible to the alpha male in this small tent with her. Those were some muscular arms.

He breathed in her face as he tucked her TEAMwear jacket over her pants. At last, he had her upright, but then Ky did the unexpected again. He wrapped her inside that faux-fur blanket and pulled her up off the sleeping bag and onto his lap the same way he had before. "Let's get you warmed up."

Too, too much!

Eden couldn't help it. She turned her face into his shoulder and cried like a little girl. Not cool. Not even very nice, the way she was sobbing and drenching his jacket, but he never said a word. Just held her tight and tipped her back and forth like she was a helpless baby. Yeah. Not cool at all. Worse, he could hold her, but she couldn't hold him. Not with her arms trapped at her sides again. The guy had some serious control issues, and she was way past tired. *Wah!*

"There, there," he murmured into the side of her head. "That thing wasn't in your artery, Eden, just tucked beside it. You'll be okay. Trust me. I'd tell you if you were in trouble. There was a single strand of wire around the femoral—that's why I used both hemostats. If by some weird accident I nicked that big old artery, I wanted to be able to seal it before you bled out. You're going to be fine. You're a free woman."

"Uh-huh," was all she could reply. Never—as in never—had she felt more loved than she did in this man's arms. Right then. Right there. Did he feel it, too? Did he care? She sure did. She had for years. Two and a half long years.

"You're that girl from my dreams," Ky murmured. "You're the one who stayed with me over there, aren't you? You're the one I thought I imagined."

"Uh-huh." *God, I sound so dumb.*

The improbable happened. He cupped her soggy cheek with one gloveless, warm hand and tipped her face upward. His amber eyes filled with tenderness. What was that man thinking? She hadn't a clue. Of kissing her? Hardly. She was a mess. Besides, he couldn't stand to touch her.

And yet he was...

He leaned to his right and grabbed up a handful of the unused gauze. Gently, he wiped her face. Her nose. At last, she was half-presentable.

"I looked for you when I got home," he said quietly, peering into her eyes, "but I didn't know your name. I never thought to ask. Wish I had. Searching for you was the most futile, frustrating thing I've ever done. Do you know why?"

She shook her head, sniffling back more tears. Darned if a hiccup didn't escape, making her appear more inept. What else could possibly go wrong?

"Because I wanted to thank you personally, Eden Stark, for helping me hold on when I had no reason to. When I had nothing left to give. I had no chance of surviving that hellhole until you showed up. You gave me hope. How'd you do it? How'd you know I was there? There were other guys being tortured in that prison, too. Why me?"

She shrugged. "I honestly don't know. It happened one night after work. It had been a long day. You just showed up in my mind, and you were hurt and bleeding and... and..." she bit her lip, "and you were covered in blood and sweat and tears, and I was a million miles away with no way to physically help you endure what you had to go through. I just wanted to help, but all I could do was sit on my kitchen floor as long as the vision lasted, Ky, and I... I just stayed with you the only way I could. That's all." *And I cried an ocean of tears. You were so, so hurt. I fell in love with you then. I couldn't have left you if I'd tried.*

"You saw everything?" he asked, his tone soft and hesitant.

"Only the last three days. I called in sick. I couldn't leave you there by yourself. It was such an awful place." She avoided his real question. Yes, those men had been brutal with him. They all deserved to die for what they did.

A soft growl rumbled from deep inside of his throat. "Shit. I only remember you there at the end, but if you were there three days. Shit," he growled again, "you saw the worst. I didn't think I'd get out of there alive."

"Me neither," she murmured. Yes, she'd seen more than seventy-two hours of those ruthless men at their barbaric idea of sport. "I reached out to Corporal Hart and I—"

"Wait. Lee Hart?" Ky startled. "You sent him to save me?"

"Not exactly. I, umm, *encouraged* him to believe that he could overcome his own desperate situation. I don't know exactly how or why my second sight works, Ky, but sometimes, I can influence others if they're susceptible. I can plant ideas, like maybe to turn left instead of going right. *Look here. Look there. Try harder.* Small things like that."

"Hmm." His breath warmed the top of her head. "I would've died if Lee hadn't interrupted that Taliban bastard when he did. Asshole had a propane torch, and he meant to use it on me."

"I know. I was there." Eden shuddered at the thought, her hand on the plane of his broad chest.

"That explains a helluva lot. Wow. Okay. So, it's my turn. You might as well know. I hate to be touched. It's because of all the shit that happened over there, Eden. I'm trying to overcome it, but there's this big ol' speed bump inside my head, and I just can't bear the sensation of human contact. Skin on skin. It's really not you. It's me. I've wanted to kiss you since you made the first move, but damn it, I just can't."

"I understand." She leaned against him, touching nothing more than the layers and layers between them, but making genuine contact with her heart.

Little by little, the tension left his body. His arms softened around her. Ky lowered his head. Parting her hair with his chin, he pressed a warm, moist kiss to the nape of her ticklish neck, one that sparked a tidal wave of shivers down her spine. "You taste good," he breathed, his mouth still romancing her neck. "I have to ask. What is that perfume you're wearing? It's... different."

Oh, snap. He's touching me. She scrunched her neck into her shoulders at this playful side of Ky. Perfume? Eden nearly giggled. She'd never worn perfume. It messed with her asthma. "Do you mean my Vicks?"

He drew in a deep breath. "What the hell is Vicks?"

She lifted both shoulders, embarrassed. "It's a mentholated rub. Before my dad left, he used to smear it on my neck when I had asthma attacks. It helped me breathe. I outgrew the asthma, but I keep a small jar of it with me. I know it's probably stupid, but the smell reminds me of him."

Eden wanted to point out they'd been very much in physical contact, but Ky inhaled a deep breath, inciting another rash of goose bumps and wiggles from her. "Don't ever stop wearing it. I like it."

It happened slowly, this trusting thing. This touching thing.

She twisted on his lap and circled one arm around his neck, careful not to run her hands over his cheek the way she craved to do. "Kiss me," she ordered bravely. *Please, Ky. You can do it. I know you can. Take a chance. Kiss the heck out of me. Want me for more than my brain. Really, truly want me. Just me.*

He stiffened and shook his head, but darn it, he needed this as much as she did. Any fool could see that. Eden placed both palms on his jacket-covered shoulders. "I won't kiss you back. It will be just you kissing me. I promise. No tongue. Just lips, and I'll keep my hands to myself."

Ky didn't answer—not unless short, hard panting was considered a response. The way his pulse throbbed at his throat looked like a definite *no* was coming.

Eden froze, not willing to terrorize this survivor any more, which was exactly what she'd done. Good intentions or not, in his best interest or not, she'd shoved his face into his worst nightmare and demanded he overcome his phobia just because she said so. He shuddered, and she wished she could go back in time and keep her big mouth shut. Talk about being unfair. "Never mind. That was stupid of me to think. I—"

"No. I'll try. With you. Only don't be upset if I..." Before he finished his thought, he lifted his thighs and propelled her up into his face. His mouth covered hers in a rush of moist heat and whiskers.

Eagerly, she parted her lips and let him enter. Their tongues collided. Their teeth. She inhaled his breath and tried not to respond to his frenzied exploration of her mouth. Gripping his jacket, she held on tightly as his hand found purchase on her hip while his other cupped her jaw, his thumb under her chin holding her head still as he probed everywhere.

This kiss! Hot. Wet. Full of whisker burn and pent-up desire. Ky seemed almost frantic. He trembled, breathing hard, but not once did he stop mauling her mouth. For a man who didn't want to be touched, he certainly had no trouble touching her.

A dangerous passion flared hot and strong and so-o-o good. His. Hers. Longing. Needing. Finally, truly connecting. Until he lurched backward, his head bowed to the side, shaking. "No. Just, God, no."

Chapter Thirteen

BLAM!

Before Ky could make a break for it, the report of a damned close weapon roared outside the tent. Tate pushed his goggle-covered face through the flap. "Get out here, Ky. Now!"

"They're here," Eden cried. "It's them."

Let them come. Ky rolled to his knees, still shaken from the passion of that kiss. In her innocence, Eden had touched a part of him he'd buried, a part he wasn't certain he wanted resurrected. Coming back to life would mean the reawakening of so much pain, and he'd had enough. "Stay inside," he ordered gruffly as he wiped the back of his hand over his mouth. "I'll be back."

He saw it clearly, the disappointment in her eyes that he'd wiped her kiss away. God, he wanted to please her. What guy wouldn't? She still had that 'just kissed' look, her lips swollen and pleasantly red from his mouth, her eyes bright. But she meant more than a thousand rogue FBI agents, and he had a job to do.

"I can't let them hurt you," he declared angrily. She had to get that through her hard head. She came first, and it didn't matter how many protection orders his boss signed. A man would die protecting his own, and Eden Stark had become just that. Hell, in a few hours, she'd become everything. Only it hadn't been just hours. She'd truly been a part of him for years. Ky got that now, and he wouldn't lose her again, damn it.

Donning his goggles, he pulled his jacket zipper up to his chin and joined his partner. The wind had settled, something Ky hadn't noticed until he'd come outside. He'd been too wrapped up in Eden, a nice reprieve. But this drone thing wasn't over yet.

"What's up?"

Tate laid on his belly facing downhill, his goggles in place. "We've got three coming at us from the east. Three more climbing up from the south. Look into the fog. You'll see 'em. They're not smart enough to hide."

Ky adjusted his goggles to pierce the gray mist that had settled over the landscape. It made for an eerie scene. Pine trees coated thick with wintry snow, their lower trunks lost in shifting fog. The tent frosted in a thick layer of the same. No sun broke the gray overhead, just the dimmest gray light through the swirling flakes

Ky dropped to his belly and took position at Tate's left. He switched his goggles to thermal and zeroed in on the heat signature of Zaroyin's nearest drone. Big guy. Square-body build. Headgear, helmet, and goggles. Tactical armor strapped over winter cammies. He advanced with purpose, climbing steadily.

But worse was the bolt-action weapon snugged to his chest. These guys weren't carrying the same weapons as their other two buddies had been. Hell no. These bad boys were toting Omni-9000s. Ky had only seen this experimental weapon once at a gun show, but never gave owning it a second thought. Made in Switzerland, the high-tech weapon cost more than twenty-seven thousand U.S. dollars a piece, a hefty price tag for everyone except for the U.S. Department of Defense.

That four-barrel scope on the top rack was no ordinary scope, either. More like the genius behind the computerized rifle system, it provided the shooter with a dynamic heads-up display that all but fired the weapon for him. A soldier had only to laser paint his designated target, and the specially made, precision-guided ordnance followed it home. Bingo. No collateral damage unless the operator was a total idiot. No trace of the target, either.

Ky huffed a snort through his nostrils. Eden wouldn't have stood a chance on her own.

"You see what he's toting?" he asked to be sure Tate understood what had to go down.

"Yeah. The latest smart gun. Don't mean shit if we end 'em first."

Ky weighed Tate's overconfidence against their options—like there were any. Eden was right. These drones were mind-controlled victims. He empathized with them. He'd been caught in an evil man's snare himself. He knew the mental despair that went along with physical incarceration and total, ruthless domination. But Tate was also right. Mind-controlled or not, these FBI agents meant to murder whoever got in their way. Because of Zaroyin, Ky and Tate would soon be forced to kill innocent men before those innocent men killed Eden.

The vow he'd taken when he joined the Corps came back to him in a flash. Yes. He was still one of those rough men standing ready in the dark to protect his country, and the woman he—loved? The notion hit home like a shot of single-barrel bourbon in the pit of his belly. *I love Eden.* It felt too soon, but it also felt right.

Ky rolled to his left and took rapid stock of the other three assailants climbing the east face. Killing was not his forte. There was no easy choice in warfare, only the one a guy had to make. Eden and Tate came first. He shook off the moral dilemma of blowing innocent men away. It messed with his head, and there simply wasn't time for it. Once a Marine, always a Marine. He gave the hard order. "Take the ones climbing up from the south. I'll take east, Tate. Make every shot count."

The customary grunt acknowledged that his message had been received. Ky slammed his one-hundred-round magazine home, tucked the butt stock of his own custom-made automatic rifle into his shoulder, and took careful aim. One left-to-right sweep ought to end this ugly chore.

It was sound strategy until Eden yelled behind him, "Ky, there's more!"

"Stay down!" he bellowed, angry that she'd put herself in harm's way. *More where? Here?*

Damn her second sight and its inconvenient timing, but damned if things didn't go bat-shit crazy, too. Crossfire lit up the shadows to Ky's left. Tate swore, "Son-of-a-bitch," and commenced firing downhill.

What had just happened? The three FBI drones in Ky's sights dropped to their knees to return fire, but not at him. Their barrels pointed to their right as a rocket-propelled grenade dropped out of the sky and landed between two of the three and blew them backwards. The fog cleared out of the way. Dark crimson patches stained the snow where they'd landed, never to rise again.

Bile crept up the back of Ky's throat, but he swallowed it down. The law of the jungle was ruthless. End of story. He wasn't sure who'd killed them, but the drones were dead. The firing ceased. Tate's firing, too.

"You see who did it?" Tate growled quietly.

"Not yet," Ky murmured, his every hair on end.

"You gonna keep shooting that fancy rifle of yours or are you ready to listen to reason?" a man's rugged voice called up from the misty fog below.

Drones who talked before they fired? That was new.

"Show yourself first," Ky barked back, his rifle aimed and ready. "Hands in the air where I can see them."

"Don't listen to them," Tate muttered, still aiming downhill at what had become someone else's kill zone. "Could be a trap."

"Could be," Ky agreed, glancing over his right shoulder to Eden. She'd dropped to her belly and buried her face in the snow when the firing broke loose. Her hair draped over her cheeks, her butt lifted high behind her. It would've made for a cute sight if she weren't still covering her ears while blowing the snow and her hair off her nose. If she didn't have that scared-to-death fear in her eyes. He motioned for her to stay down.

She didn't listen for shit, but crawled straight to his side like a hyperactive toddler on too much sugar. He cupped her ass the moment she drew near enough and leveled her hips flat to ground level. "I said stay down, damn it."

She folded her hands under her chin. "I know these guys."

"You knew Koenig and Shields, too," Tate muttered.

"I'm telling you these men are different. I can tell," Eden insisted. "Don't kill them."

"That's the problem," Ky said. "I didn't kill anyone yet. Did you take out any of your targets, Tate?"

"Didn't get the chance. Someone else did it for me."

Her jaw dropped. "Who? The other guys?"

"Maybe." Ky had no answer. Whoever called out to him had yet to move into the open. Either that or the bastard was already in too close and had the drop on Ky and Tate.

Ky didn't like the silence—not one bit. He scanned to his far left. Nothing but gray fog and shifting mist, the perfect cover for an ambush. Then he looked to his right and into Tate's kill zone, where the three bodies that Tate *hadn't* killed lay dead and sprawled. He adjusted his goggles. Thermal imaging added bleak realism to the scene, but still no one moved. Who the hell was out there? What were they waiting for?

"Let me try," Eden urged. "If these guys are who I think they are, they're safe."

"Heard that before," Tate grumbled.

"Ky. Please. Trust me."

"Then call to them," he snapped, every nerve stretched taut, "but keep your head down until I tell you different. Keep your ass down, too."

She nodded quickly, but smoothed both hands over that delicious backside. Ky couldn't help but take a quick glance at it. God, this woman was going to be the death of him. He adjusted his position again because he had to, damn it. Every move she made got his body's attention, and he was hard as a rock. He didn't need Alex to chew him out for fraternization with a client. The guy was nearly as psychic as Eden, which was why Ky kept his goggles loose on his neck more than strapped to his face. Except for now. Alex needed to see the combat.

Eden rolled to her back and cupped both hands to her mouth. "Tucker Chase. Is that you?"

"Might be," a gruff voice replied. "Who's up there with you, Eden? Anyone I need to kill?"

"No. These guys work for Alex Stewart," she answered. "Ky Winch—"

"Shit, don't give 'em our names," Tate barked. "God, woman. How stupid are you?"

"Son-of-a-bitch," the same man spoke below. "Stewart's men? Are you sure?"

Eden turned to face Ky when she answered. "I'm sure. Come on up. They're safe."

"Hell, I don't know if I want to now. How many did you say?" that Tucker guy asked. "You got names?"

She told Ky, "That's Agent Tucker Chase. He's worked with Alex before. Should I tell him there's just two of you?"

"Two," Ky called out for her. "How many with you, Agent Chase?"

"Just me and my good friend, Sam Becker. Lower that piece-of-shit machine gun of yours. Then I'll come in."

"I don't think so. You're FBI. You'll come in first, then we'll lower our weapons," Tate threw back at him. "Now get your asses out in the open where we can see you."

Ky adjusted his thermal imaging, still trying to detect either of Eden's friends. Whoever they were, they were good at keeping out of sight, and the last thing he needed to deal with. The Bureau hadn't helped her much so far. Why should he trust them now?

At last, a dark shadow drifted from behind a truck-high, snow-covered slab of rocks. A stocky guy stood, decked out in tactical winter gear from head to foot. He lifted his knees high as he climbed out of the drift circling the rocks, his hand gripping the barrel shroud of the assault weapon over his head. "Don't shoot, you assholes. I'm coming out."

Ky grunted. Not a smart move, calling the guy who could end you an ignorant name. "Drop your other gun," he ordered.

Agent Chase came to a dead stop. He shoved his goggles under his chin and pulled a long-barreled rifle out from the holster strapped to his back. If he were smart, he would've dropped it. "I don't care what you say, I'm not tossing my weapons in the snow," he yelled. "It ain't good for them and you know it."

"Drop it or I'll wing you, I swear," Ky ordered. *Who's the asshole now, Chase?*

Chase hesitated, his lip lifted into a sneer. He stomped the snow at his feet into a compressed pad before he laid his rifles down. "You happy now? My top-of-the-line, and very expensive, weaponry is getting wet for no reason other than you're too stupid to know a good guy from an asshole."

"I haven't seen a good guy yet. The pistols, too. Drop 'em."

"Shit," Chase hissed, but unloaded his thigh holsters, then reached inside his jacket and pulled out another pistol. Nothing special. Regular FBI-issue piece-of-crap.

This guy had a lot of nerve. Ky knew the type. Over-inflated opinion of himself and loaded with every kind of concealable weapon ever made. Probably thought he was God's gift to women, too. Must have been a Navy SEAL. He'd followed instructions like one. "I said all of them, Agent Chase. You're not coming into my camp with that belly gun up your sleeve."

Chase glared uphill for a long minute before he divested himself of not one, but two revolvers, one tucked up each sleeve. He dropped both to the growing arsenal at his feet and planted his hands to his hips, a definite sneer on his ugly face. "There, you son-of-a-bitch. Now I'm pissed off and damned near naked. Ice is pouring out of the sky. My weapons are turning to rust. Is that good enough, or do you need to see the cheeks of my lily-white ass, too?"

Eden clapped her hand over her mouth, giggling. "He'll freeze to death if he you make him drop his pants."

"Let him freeze his balls off," Tate growled. "Serves the prick right."

Ky lifted to his knees, his sights still set on Agent Chase. "The knife, too, Chase," he deadpanned, but whispered out of the corner of his mouth to Tate, "Where's the other guy? You got him in your sights yet?"

"He's lying face-up in the snow to my right. He thinks I don't see him, but I do. Want me to blow one of his pinkie fingers off? I could do it."

Ky chuckled. Tate wasn't kidding. Disarming these guys went a long way toward them proving they were who they said they were. When Chase pulled one damned long blade out of his right boot sheath and dropped it to join his arsenal in the snow, Ky lifted his rifle barrel skyward and stood down. "I'd make you strip to your skivvies, Chase, just so you could pull the weapon out of your ass, but that'll do for now. Tate, ease off Becker. Let him come in, too."

Damned if Eden's other friend didn't sit straight up out of the snow and look around, his rifle lifted over his head. "You knew I was here?" he asked as he peeled his fancy goggles off.

"It ain't hard to smell horseshit when it's blowing upwind," Tate responded easily.

Becker scrambled to his feet. "Funny. That's what led us to you guys only it was blowing downwind then."

"What? Followed the stench of your FBI drone buddies?"

Becker chuckled. "Can we dispense with the name-calling while I join the party, or do you want to see my hairy ass, too? You know I'm just gonna pick up every weapon I lay down. It doesn't seem too smart to disarm the only help you've got within miles."

"Then get your candy ass up here. Move slow so I don't have to kill you," Tate growled. He lifted to his feet, his scope still on their newest arrival.

Ky felt Eden's hand the moment she'd rested it between his shoulder blades. He calmed, knowing she'd chosen his protection over these supposed friends, but wasn't that interesting? She knew these guys, but didn't seem to trust them.

The men collected their gear and trudged uphill. One Secret Service Agent Sam Becker. Tall. Shaggy, dark hair. Coffee brown eyes, black, no cream. Moustache and a definite five o'clock shadow. Older than Ky, maybe by five years. Maybe more.

One badass FBI agent, Tucker Chase. Same approximate age as Sam. Same height as Ky. Beefy build. Muscular. Clean-shaven. Dark hair under a black beanie. Ornery blue eyes. Same tactical gear as Becker. Standard FBI issue. Lowest bidder crap, the kind the Feds bought. Nothing like the state-of-the-art gear Alex invested in for his people.

Chase veered to Becker's right. Both men moved with tactical practice, Ky had to give them that, not the robotic gait of the guys that would soon be hanging by their boots in the trees. That was another point in these guys' favor. But if they were so damned good, where were they yesterday when Eden could've used their help the most?

"Cut her loose. She's going with us, asshole," Agent Chase growled between huffing and puffing from the uphill climb. "Come on, Stark. Get your stuff. Move out."

Eden made no effort to greet these guys, and Ky's calmness evaporated. He trusted her more than he did them. "She goes nowhere."

"And I said—"

Ky snapped his piece back into action. "And I said no! Look around, Chase. You just killed six of your own men. Why the hell would I let her go with anyone wearing an FBI badge? Just because you and your secret agent friend said so? Take a hike."

Chase's weapon zeroed in on Ky, a stupid shot since Eden stood right behind him. True, he'd aimed at Ky's head, high enough he wouldn't hit Eden. Like that made any difference. Eden was going nowhere, not with some jerk who had more guts than brains. "Back off, or so help me I'll—"

Wrong move, Chase. Ky snapped his rifle into his shoulder, sure as hell going to blow this asshole out of his boots if that was what it took.

Tate bumped elbows with Ky, forming a wall that blocked Eden from Chase's view. Her head thudded between Ky's shoulder blades. She snaked her arms around his waist. Something was wrong. He twisted over his shoulder to risk a quick glimpse. Eden had gone white. Perspiration beaded above her top lip.

"Help me, Ky," she whispered, sliding down his thigh to her knees in the snow.

"You son-of-a-bitch!" Chase roared. "So help me God, if you've hurt her, I'll—"

Tate fired a warning shot over Tucker's hard head.

Ky barely had time to catch Eden before she fainted.

Chapter Fourteen

"Why's she keep doing that?" The annoyed question came from Tate, but the warm, bare fingers checking her pulse at her neck belonged to Ky. So did the breath in her face. Eden inhaled, pulling more of him into her soul.

"Because something's wrong," Ky murmured, "and she just had surgery."

"She may have another implant." That worried baritone belonged to Tucker Chase. "Did you smart boys ever think of that?"

Eden opened her eyes to four very worried men, all bent over her and in her face. Heat and way too much testosterone filled the crowded tent. Its designer surely didn't have these massive guys in mind when he designed this tent.

"Sorry," she whispered, her elbow cocked behind her to lift herself up, like that was possible in this confined space. "I don't know why I keep doing that."

"Lie still," Ky ordered, his hand to her shoulder pushing her flat to her back. "You've got to be seriously injured or you wouldn't keep fainting every time you turn around."

"But I'm not hurt," she argued. "It's like vertigo. All of a sudden the world goes wonky on me, and I'm on the Titanic, and it's sinking, and I'm..." The sensation buzzed inside her head. Sinking didn't begin to describe the vicious cold that swept over her this time. Two dark holes bore down on her as if they were—eyes? No way. They couldn't be. But they were. Black eyes. Sinister black eyes.

"Wonky?" Ky teased gently.

The vision cleared. Sam elbowed forward. "We need to check you, honey. Winchester's right. Something's got to be going on inside that pretty head of yours for you to keep passing out like he says you've been doing."

"No, I'm fine." Eden looked past Ky to Sam Becker, sure the bizarre fainting spells explained her second sight's failure to engage properly.

Sam looked as good as ever. He'd resigned from the Bureau to join the Secret Service some time back. A twinkle glistened in his chocolate brown eyes. Sexy in an older man kind of a way, Sam always had considered himself a lady's man. The everlasting alpha. Taking charge. Over-confident to a fault. He ought to be. The ex-Navy SEAL had certainly survived enough harrowing deployments to make him believe he was bulletproof. Just not her type.

Eden shot him down. "Zaroyin's two devices are out of me. Ky made sure."

Two sets of bushy brows lifted in surprise. "He did?" Sam asked. "When the hell did he have time to do that?"

"You operated on her, you bastard?" Tucker hissed. "You cut her open?"

Another alpha. Also ex-SEAL. Also tall, dark, and handsome, but close-cut. Tough as they came. Thirty-something. A definite potty mouth that got him into trouble on the job as much as off. The man seemed to live for bar fights and backtalk. His take-all-comers attitude attracted trouble. He had a chip on his shoulders the size of Texas. Yeah. Both shoulders.

"I'm fine," she assured the men now crammed into her life. Tate seemed to be the only one who believed her. He backed out of the tent and slapped the flap closed without argument.

"We have to check you again, sweetheart," Sam said smoothly. "At least one of us will. We need to make sure there aren't any more implants."

"Go check yourself," she replied quickly. "Look for a wire strapped to your chest, why don't you? That's where mine was, and I didn't know it was there. You could have one, too."

Sam nodded. "Okay. Sure. You might be right." With a cocky, lopsided grin, he unzipped his jacket and jerked a couple of layers of shirts up to reveal his very muscular and nicely tanned chest. He passed one big hand over the barest dusting of curly chest hairs, then lifted his shaggy head and winked at her, the big flirt. "You see any wires on me, darlin'? Any implants? Anything that doesn't look like it belongs there? I sure don't. It's not me Zaroyin wants. It's you. Now be a good girl and—"

"I'm not your good, little girl," she snapped, then turned on Tucker, "and I'm not your sweetheart, either. Shut up, Becker, and put your shirt down. Did you guys come up from Thunder Bay?"

Sam tucked his shirt back in his pants. "We did. Why?"

She closed her eyes, trying to understand what went wrong with her second sight. It had never been more unreliable. "Because I should've seen you coming, but I couldn't. All I saw was shadows."

Ky took hold of her hand. "But you did see the other six. That's what's important."

"I know, but I couldn't see these two guys clearly, and I don't feel good," she said as emotionlessly as possible, not easy when you really did feel like a little girl with three hulking brutes hovering over you, all of them alpha wolves who were ready and willing to jump into her life and fix her problems. "My head hurts all the time, Ky. And I'm dizzy." She shot a look at Tucker, surprised he hadn't made a smart alec comment like she expected. "Dizzier."

Instantly, Ky's bare fingers tunneled into her hair and against her scalp, smoothing over her skull. "Let me take another look. It could be the after-effects of that mind-control device I removed. It did have long roots. I might have hurt you when I pulled it out like I did."

Tucker growled, his arms over his chest. His over-protective posture and his glare wasn't helpful. She ignored him and closed her eyes, gripping Ky's biceps as he carefully searched her scalp, parting chunk by chunk of her hair and letting it fall over her face as he went. Maybe she did need a thorough examination. Maybe she'd missed another implant. How many could there be? Nausea lifted up her throat at the very real molestation inflicted upon her. She'd never felt more helpless. "You guys have got to get out," she told Sam and Tucker wearily. "I don't need an audience."

Tucker jerked his big chin toward the tent flap. "You heard her, Winchester. Get your ass out in the cold. Move it."

"Not Ky," Eden corrected, a whip of frustration in her tone. "He stays. Just you two. Get out. Please. I can't breathe with all of you in this tent. You're too big. There's no air."

Tucker shot Ky a dirty look, his head lowered. "If you hurt her, I'll—"

"God, Tucker, will you stop? He isn't hurting me. He's helping, He's saved my life three times now, which is more than I can say for you."

Poor Tucker's lower lip puckered. "We would've been here sooner, but our pilot refused to fly any farther north in this weather."

"I know. Please go," she insisted. "I'm sorry. I don't mean to be sharp, but if I do have another implant, Ky will find it. He'll take it out. I'll be okay. You'll see."

A gentle smile tweaked Ky's lips as he smoothed the last chunk of her hair over her ear. "Nothing up here but silk," he murmured, winking, his back to her FBI behemoth friends, and his warm breath on her face. That small, intimate comment soothed her ragged edge. Yes, he was the man she wanted checking her body out, not two agents she'd have to work with the rest of her career. Ky might not like that she'd selected him, but with his touching fetish, but that should actually make Tucker happy. Ky would be done with this examination in no time.

"Fine," Tucker muttered, his feelings obviously hurt and his dander up, "but we'll be right outside if you need anything. Call me. Do you hear?"

She shook her head at his perpetual obstinance. Honestly. The man could make the Pope swear. "I will, now out."

"I'm coming back in ten minutes if—"

"Tucker! Get out!"

"Fine," he growled, mumbling under his breath. Sam nodded once at her, his bushy brows narrowed before he followed Tucker's surly butt into the wintry weather.

"Finally," Eden blew out between pursed lips, exasperated with the world of bossy men. She glared at Ky. "Now you. Do your thing before I change my mind and ask Tate to search me. Get every last device out and off me, darn it. I can't work like this."

"Are you sure you want me doing this?" he asked. "I mean, before, when I... When we..."

"Ky. I get it. You can't tolerate human touch. It was wrong of me to push you before. Forget it. Let's just get this over with."

"Yes, ma'am," Ky muttered, a definite hint of worry in his tone.

Sudden tears brimmed at his about-face. One minute, he seemed playful—the next, all too serious. She got it. He was obviously struggling with that darned phobia, but God, what a day. Eden stiffened her emotions. She'd never felt more rejected in her life, and now she'd turned into a hormonal mess. Darn Zaroyin. This was all his fault.

Carefully, and probably reluctantly, Ky rolled back to his knees and began. He wasn't using gloves, though. Eden would've found that encouraging before their kiss. Not now. He'd made his intentions clear, and she meant to hold him to them. *Get over it, Winchester. This isn't touching, remember? It's just one agent searching another agent for implants. That's all.*

Feeling sorry for herself, she sat stiffly while his fingers probed every inch of her neck, twisting her head gently from side to side as he combed her hair out of his way. He peered inside her ears, then commenced examining her throat, smoothing his fingertips from collarbone to jaw, his thumbs sliding over her trachea. He made her open her mouth in case one of her teeth was false. He smoothed both of this thumbs down her trachea to her collarbones, and her angst evaporated. His touch was light and easy. Warm.

"Find anything yet?" she asked at the gentle massage. He did have a light touch. Warm. Careful.

He nodded, that same lazy smile back on his lips. "Oh, yeah."

"I mean anything that shouldn't be there?" she snapped. He needed to know she wouldn't be trifled with. *Stop smiling, Ky. I can't bear another letdown. I've had enough.*

He leaned away from her, the smile gone and a tender light radiating out from beneath his brows. "Are you sure you want me doing this? You found the wire all by yourself."

"No, I mean yes," she relented, "I mean, I'm sorry I snapped. I guess I'm tired."

"You're way past tired, Eden. You're exhausted, and you've just survived a couple serious attacks on your life." He settled to his butt, his elbows on his knees. "This can wait."

"But it can't, can it?" She refused to cry in front of him. "I don't want to be under Zaroyin's control, and I can't reach some places. I don't trust myself even if I could. Just do it. Give me a thorough once over. Make it quick."

He hesitated. "I don't know. I might have to get personal."

"Like you already haven't? Who else should I ask then? I can't and I won't let Sam or Tucker do this. Tate couldn't care less. I guess that leaves you." Her snarkiest tone knifed out at poor Ky. He might not have deserved it, but it served her purpose. He'd keep his touch clinical and quick. "Besides, I don't need Sam and Tucker knowing what Zaroyin or Levine might've done or... never mind. Just get it over with."

"Okay," he said softly. "Then let's get this over with."

Ky dropped the smile and kept going, his callused hands sliding up inside her jackets and beneath her layered shirts, feeling over her shoulder, sliding over more and more bare skin. Her stomach. Her rib cage. Like it or not, energy sizzled between them, jumping like little flames from his big, manly hands to her, lapping up her spine, peaking her nipples. Darned if the tent didn't turn into a steamy sauna. He hovered low and close on his knees, breathing hard, his palms so darned warm and—

Ky slipped one inside the right cup of her bra. Then the left. Quickly. Clinically. It didn't matter. He was still touching her, and her heart reacted along with her body. Thrumming and throbbing for more. Eden closed her eyes, no longer able to breathe. Everything he did, he did gently—almost reverently. The rough pad of his thumb brushed over her nipple, and snap. Her libido sprang to life. She arched into his hand, a total involuntary reaction.

Stop it, she commanded her traitorous body. *Settle down. Relax. He's just a guy. This is just what has to be done. It means nothing. Pretend he's a doctor. Or a plumber.*

"No implants here," he murmured, more bass to his soft voice, more heat to his palms.

A surge of heat rushed her, shoving her common sense out the door with Tucker and Sam. Flustered under its wake, Eden sat up straighter and leaned into Ky to keep her balance, her cheek against the chest pocket of his jacket. She let him smooth those big, wide, warm palms of his over her bare back and shoulder blades because... *It means nothing. It just has to be done.*

Ky pulled her close, bunching her layers of shirts out of his way and smoothing his fingers up her spinal column, one vertebra at a time. Slowly. Methodically. He breathed hard. She breathed hard. Any other time, this would've been quite the prelude to one heck of a romantic evening, but not in a tent in the middle of Canada with two father bears lurking outside and no doubt growling up a storm.

Her poor head pounded along with her heart. The migraine was back, and her control was slipping. She clung to Ky's massive biceps while his hands eased her clothing out of his way, still keeping her mostly covered while they slid lower to her waist. Then her hips. *Lower.*

Modesty was no longer a viable option. She needed any remaining implants found and destroyed, but snap. This was the most erotic examination she'd ever—*ever*—had. A blazing inferno sprang to life when he slid his hands into her pants and carefully cupped the cheeks of her ass. A low rumble lifted up from deep inside his throat. "I'm only doing this because I need to be thorough, so these dizzy spells stop once and for all. Honest. I'm not trying to molest you."

"I know," she said hoarsely. If he was really thorough, his fingers would soon slide closer to the place where no man had been before. He couldn't afford to not search—there. She swallowed hard. Wouldn't that be the perfect hiding place? *Darn you, Zaroyin.*

Ky already knew she was no real FBI agent, but she dared herself to suck it up and be brave like one. "Go ahead," she whispered breathlessly. "I'm a consenting adult. I agreed to this examination, and I know what you have to do next. Do it already. I can take it." *I think.*

He bumped her head with his chin, forcing her eyes up. "I'm not sure that's a good idea, Eden. I know you want to be out from under Zaroyin's control, but you're trembling. I don't want to hurt you, not after what Levine might have done. This examination can wait until we get out of here. You need a real doctor in a clean, private setting, not some guy you're stuck with in the wilds of Canada. Certainly not with me."

Her heart stalled at the genuine tenderness glowing deep in those pools of melted amber. Smoldering heat spilled into her like warm molasses, filling the holes in her soul left by her father and Stan, softening the blows dealt to her by life. By all the deaths around her. By the evil perpetrated against her.

A different facet to this diamond-in-the-rough named Ky, this warrior who was more scarred and more damaged than she was, emerged. He was larger than life. A gentle hero who'd been through the depravities of hell, yet retained the finer sensibilities of a good and decent man.

Despite her consent, he was giving her the choice and control over her body. He was offering her a reasonable alternative in the middle of the chaos her life had turned into instead of taking advantage of her. He was protecting her virtue. Respecting her. Restoring her confidence in herself. And in his quiet, resolute way, he was giving her what he needed. He was giving her—himself. She didn't feel quite so alone any more.

The truth came softly, spilling out before she allowed any thoughts of repercussions or second guesses. "You're not just some guy. You're Ky Winchester, my long lost friend." Eden swallowed hard, needing him to believe her. "I stood by you then, and I want you to do this now. I need to be free from Zaroyin. You're the only one who can do that for me."

The real question lay before them now. Was he willing to take that final step, to close the chasm between them? To take down the walls he'd erected to protect himself? Was he willing to trust the man he was? The tender hero he'd always been?

Ky blinked, his forehead crinkled, and his brows slanted sharply together as if he was no longer certain what they were talking about. "Are you absolutely sure?"

Eden nodded quickly. She'd never been more positive. "I trust you, Ky. Only you. I think somehow, you trust me, too. You have for years." She shackled the jacket sleeve at his wrist, needing the connection in case he panicked. "It's like we've always known each other. As if every single thing that's happened to both of us until now has put us here, at this exact point in time."

He nodded as if he understood, but she knew she'd made him nervous. She'd put him on the spot simply because he believed himself less of a man. An undesirable because of what others had done to him. *Oh, please.* If he was any more desirable, she'd melt in his hands. She'd never wanted a man more than this one.

"I'll be quick and careful, Eden. I won't hurt you. I promise," he said, his voice husky.

"I know," She was going for resolute, but her voice came out small and scared. Breathy.

With a curt nod, Ky circled her inside one muscular arm, pressing her cheek against his chest as he eased her pants down and very slowly slid one hand between her legs. She widened her knees without trembling. He smoothed his palms inside her thighs, but when the ex-Marine's breath caught at the first contact of his fingertips with her most erogenous zone, her heart stopped.

Eden buried her face in his jacket and circled one arm around his waist to keep from shivering. She'd never been this far before. Tongues of liquid fire poured out of her. The scent of her sex filled the space around them. Ky had to have noticed that her body transformed into a clenching, wiggling mass of overheated muscles she couldn't begin to control, but had to. Somehow. She squeezed her eyes shut at the physical response he incited in her. Her heart back-flipped while her belly ached with need.

"You are so taking me out to dinner after this mission's over," she mumbled, going for casual when this encounter was anything but.

The man didn't flinch or pull back as she'd expected. "I'm thinking more than just dinner."

She squeezed her eyes tight even though her heart leapt up at that word. That tempting *more,* but how the heck could there be more with a man she couldn't touch?

"Hold on to me, Eden," he murmured hoarsely. "This next part might hurt a little if Levine did what we're afraid he did."

She buried her nose in his jacket, pulling every stray male pheromone of Ky into her soul. Every last scent. The exercise only heightened her already strung-tight nerves. Want to or not, her most intimate feminine muscles clenched around his fingers. He definitely noticed. His breath hitched. "Levine might not have taken advantage of you, honey. There's nothing here."

Bet me there's nothing there. Then why is your heart jackhammering like mine? Why are you holding onto me so tight?

"Don't stop," she murmured to his chest, knowing full well that Ky had found something he needed inside of her female body. Something he desperately needed to release the inhibited male he'd transformed himself into in an attempt to protect his heart. *Please, Ky. Do it. Go all the way. Take me in your arms. Lay me down and make love to me.*

But she knew better. He wouldn't because he couldn't, and she, FBI Agent Eden Stark, was an idiot to think otherwise. This was nothing but an impersonal examination that she couldn't trust herself to accomplish, not after the way she'd been mind-controlled.

No sooner had she settled for rejection when he dipped her backward in his arm, his lips frantic on her mouth, and his fingers right where she wanted them to stay. Inside her. Eden clamped a hand to the covered muscles of his shoulder, wanting that elusive *more*. Right. Darned. Now.

The passion of his kiss took on a life of its own. His tongue slid over the seam of her lips, asking permission even as his fingers teased her senseless.

Eden gave in, combusting in the frozen woods of Canada with the man of her dreams pouring the most delightful accelerant all over her body. She stroked the tip of his tongue with hers, melting into this gentle warrior who needed her as much as she needed him. Did he know that yet? How could he not?

His fingers stayed where they were, tempting her body and soul with this heady new experience. Urging her to let go and fall over the edge of passion. To fly. Could a person go insane with passion? Could they toss all caution to the wind and hope their reckless run off a cliff proved the best decision in the end? Would Ky truly catch her like she knew she would most assuredly catch him?

Her stomach clenched. She breathed hard into his neck and threw the last of her restraint away. Prepared to fly. Prepared to trust this one man with all her heart, to finally let go.

"Give it up to me, Eden," he growled softly, his fingers gentle and warm.

Oh, I wish!

She writhed in his arms, dying and daring. So close to the edge.

"Come for me, Eden. Give it all to me." He plunged deeper, and yes—yes—oh, my God, *yes!* She felt the blood rushing through his veins, through her heart. She let herself soar. She flew. Make that she fell. Into Ky. Into the safety of his strong arms. Into the depths of his heart and the sanctuary of his soul.

His mouth covered hers, devouring her lips and tongue and chin. Greedily tasting. Sucking and nipping as if he hadn't eaten in years. Waves of blistering heat radiated off of him, blanketing her with intense feelings she'd not known before. *So this is what I've been missing. This endless oneness. This feeling of being found and eaten alive. Savored. Treasured.*

Shuddering under the sensational and very sensual onslaught of her first orgasm, her heart morphed into a throbbing beast in her chest. Tilting her head back, she gave him access to her neck. *What have I done?* Eden thought, but her mouth said, "Do that again, Ky."

He had the good grace to smile against her throat. She felt his lips crinkle. She heard his sigh. At last, he eased his fingers out of her and bowed his face into her neck, sweating and panting. "You're too much."

"Is that a good thing?"

A sexy rumble escaped his throat. "Oh, yes-s-s."

Eden couldn't hold back the smile. This was what had been missing in her life. This was the who. The one. This glorious alpha male who struggled with his own ungodly demon— himself. They were an odd pairing: a psychic very much alone in the world and a wounded warrior who'd done his best to save the world.

The air in that cramped little tent filled with the sultry fragrance of her sex and the sense of having committed a wonderfully foolish indiscretion. She held him close, her eyes filled with tears at the amazing gift he'd just given her. She would never forget this moment.

Until then, life had been a cloistered role she'd played for everyone else. She'd been a good girl, obeyed her mother when she was still alive. Eden had simply loved Casey, and poor Casey'd had her hands full being a single mom. She hadn't needed a selfish, willful daughter on top of everything else, so Eden had always strived to be that one, bright spot in her mother's fourteen-hour day.

Eden served her country. She'd worked her duty hours and every mission required. But there she was in the middle of winter, half-naked and so in love she would've gladly given Ky access to the rest of her body. A painfully intense surge of emotions lifted up from her heart, flooding her until it hurt.

Ky tugged her panties back into place. Then her jeans. "I think I owe you more than just dinner and a dance after this."

Her poor heart stalled. What a stupid thing to say. Would he now desert her like every other male in her life had? Would he shove her away like yesterday's trash? Like he did before? *Here it comes again. Another brush-off. Another ending.*

She pushed his hand away, her eyes already filled with tears he'd never see fall, darn him. He needed to run away and join Tucker and Sam, the sooner the better. "No. I'm fine. Just leave."

"Hey," he whispered, his palm cupping her cheek, lifting her chin and making her meet his eyes. "Did I hurt you?"

"I said I'm fine," she lied, giving him no more than a fleeting glance. "Now go. Leave me alone." *I don't need you, either!*

"Eden. Look at me."

Why should I?

"Eden."

She gulped and met his tender gaze. "Wh-what?" she asked in her most defiant tone, blinking fast and furious through her emotional meltdown. It had come out of nowhere, but men were men, darn it. They were all the same. They always let her down. *What was I thinking?*

Without a word, Ky encapsulated her inside of his muscular arms, under his chin and against his still pounding heart. "I'm afraid that I—"

"Stop, Ky. It's over. It meant nothing. Really. You didn't find anything and... and... just go." She twisted away, fighting his embrace.

He held her until she stilled, until she stopped running away from him. With a feathery soft kiss to her forehead, he whispered, "It meant something to me."

Eden stopped trying to be resilient and unbreakable and all those other stupid FBI traits, and she just listened. She stopped feeling sorry for herself, and throwing up her brand of barriers at Ky. She let him into her heart the way she wanted to be inside of his.

"I'm sorry about before, Eden, honest I am," he said to the top of her head. "I've been a jerk. You deserve so much better than me, but if you're willing, I'd like a do-over."

"A w-what-over?"

Chapter Fifteen

"A do-over, Eden. A second chance. Another this..." He nudged her forehead with his nose, and she took the hint, lifting her chin to stare him down, but he had his eyes closed and his lips pursed. He meant to kiss her again, and God, she should've had the good sense to reject him first, but she couldn't. Didn't even try.

Eden succumbed once again to this gentle, damaged man. Instead of smoothing her fingers into his scalp, instead of nibbling a trail of temptation to the hollow of his neck, she thrust her TEAMwear-covered body against his.

Intoxicated and probably out of her ever-loving mind, she let her trembling fingers dance over his broad shoulders. Now was not the time to push for more, but push she did, and as much as she dared. Her body slipped into a purely instinctual response, bucking against his solid frame as her insatiable hunger clutched at this second chance.

Groaning into her mouth, he obeyed her implied command, his hands suddenly under her sweater, shoving her bra up and out of his way. Palming her breast, the pad of his thumb scraped over a tightly knotted peak, and Eden nearly was very close to losing her slim hold on Ky's number one and very stupid rule. *Don't touch.*

Her fingers twitched to tunnel through his hair, to rub through the scruff on his chin, to trace the fine lines of his cheekbones and his brows. To ease the care from the edges of his eyes.

The feel of his callused hands skimming over her tender breasts, hot and heavy with a hunger for his mouth, lulled her with a delicious addiction she had no resistance to. She couldn't get enough of this man. This now. She didn't want to stop. Couldn't begin to slow this freight train of desire down.

Her breasts ached for more pressure. More squeezing. He tugged and pinched one nipple, and she wanted his head under her shirt and his mouth sucking that tender nipple until he consumed it. She knew biology, but this was so much more intense. A fierce need drove her off the ground and against him.

His fingers lit a path straight to her core. A fire had begun that she couldn't put out. She wanted it to run its course, to burn the loneliness out of her until only his smoldering touch remained, until he'd branded every last inch of her. Maybe by then, it would scorch the bad memories out of him, too. Maybe he'd finally relish her touch as much as she craved his.

Their passion roared in her ears.

The tent was too small!

She wanted him. Growling with need, she tugged at his jacket, but he caught her wrist. "Don't touch."

Oh yeah. That. "But you're touching me," she whined breathlessly, her emotions all over the board. How could she not touch this glorious male? This tender beast who needed petting in all the best ways? Who even now pressed his extraordinary hardness against her aching softness?

"Pull your hair out of my way," he muttered hoarsely.

Eagerly, she complied, tugging her tangles aside to let him have any part of her he wanted. "Like this?"

Ky answered by dipping his face into her exposed neck. Breathing hard, his mouth worked a molten path of lava from her earlobe to her collarbone, and ahh...

She shivered, her body aflame while he licked and slathered more accelerant on her than she could bear. He nibbled tiny love bites that burned sparks wherever his mouth met her flesh. Any part he touched, he claimed until she was a hot writhing mess beneath him, desperate to return the sensual stimulation. To lay him flat to his back and climb on board those manly hips grinding against hers. To rip his clothes off and impale her body, heart, and soul to his mast.

He started again, the moist heat of his open mouth skimming up her neck, and she was lost in a flash fire called Ky. A man whose heart and soul had been seared to hers during the worst of times, and now the best of times.

He swept the last of her senses away with his very skilled mouth, devouring every patch of skin he came in contact with. Resistance never entered her mind. Not this time. She groaned for release, needing the manly heat of his body on the rest of her, wanting out of her clothes and every last inch of him inside of her. But this man had extraordinary control. Ky hadn't loosened his grip, just wound her one hand behind his head and hooked it to the back of his neck.

She smiled against his cheek at this very positive development. He'd placed her bare fingers on his bare skin. He wanted her to touch him, and she wanted to. But with her heart pounding loud and clear, and her bare cheek against his bare cheek, she didn't dare clutch. She didn't squeeze. Eden didn't let her fingers wander up into his scalp or brush through his hair. As difficult as it was to refrain, she simply let this moment be exactly what it was. A very tiny first step.

"Ky," she whimpered, her lips almost on his ear, so close she had to fight to keep from licking him. Tasting him. Inhaling deeply, she took what she could, his manly, spicy scent. Her cheek melded with the warmth of his. Her tongue ached to trace the curl of that manly ear. To make him shiver as he'd made her shiver.

He grunted, one hand holding her head still as his mouth found hers again. "Yes?" he answered hotly, just before he made extraordinarily warm, wet love to her tongue and her lips and her teeth and... *Ahh. Just ahh..*

Eden gave herself up to the storm of sexual pleasure pounding at her. She forgot what she wanted to say. Something about... reminding him about...

Oh, snap. Whatever.

Her bones turned fluid. Every last FBI resolve faded. She would've given all if he'd pressed her for it, but he didn't. After another round of soul-shattering kisses that curled her toes and left her breathless, he licked her lips and gave her just enough distance to try and catch her breath. She couldn't. Didn't even try. Just kept gulping in the air he exhaled. Kept savoring the distinctly male taste of his lips and tongue. Kept her opened palm exactly where he'd left it.

At last, he bowed his head, his heated breath pouring into the hollow of her neck. She stilled, ready to slip out of her clothes at the slightest hint.

Just say the word. One word. Any word. A grunt will do.

He had only to tug at her bra strap and she could've burned the frozen north down. Or whisper. Heck, all he had to do was keep breathing hard. Oh, so hard. This man wanted her as badly as she wanted him. A wiggle hinted at her eagerness to go one step farther.

She, the ultimate loner in the universe, wanted this tender warrior in every imaginable way. Only a lifetime of rejections and betrayals kept her from opening her big mouth and telling him she loved him.

Ky lifted his head, his eyes filled with the same fire that had consumed her. Or was it stars? Unadulterated lust? Eden couldn't decide. A lazy smile twitched at his still wet lips, the lips she'd just licked and tasted and wanted more of.

"Damn it, Eden Stark," he grumbled. "You're not very good at *not* kissing back."

Oh, yeah. About that. She could only scrunch her shoulders. It did take two to *not* kiss. Surely he knew that. "But I'm only touching you where you let me."

The poor guy closed his eyes, a pleasant euphoria brightening his countenance. "It's strange, but physical contact... burns. Try and figure that one out. Those bastards never lit me up, but my head's hyper-vigilant. It still thinks they will. Any second now."

Not exactly what she wanted to hear. Eden pulled back, but Ky flattened his hand to hold her in place. "No. Don't move. Your touch doesn't feel the same. It's just a crazy time-warp thing my brain does. It's a rut. A pattern I'm kind of stuck in. I don't know how to get over it yet. But I will."

His conviction pleased and bothered her. "I don't want to hurt you."

The saddest smile stretched his lips. He cupped her bare hand, touching her, but not allowing her to touch him. And yet they were. The very act of not touching was—touching.

"You're not them. I really do know that, and I know your lips were touching mine when we kissed. It's kind of unavoidable when two people go crazy on each other, but I'm sorry. I want to, but I can't handle you touching me as much as I'd like. Not yet."

She smiled despite the rebuff, content to let him hold her however he could. There was still a lot of little boy inside this manly body, and that little boy wanted to be free to play with her. What was it Confucius said? That the journey of a thousand miles began with one small step? Well, today was the day for that one small step, and Ky Winchester had invited her to take it with him. In person this time.

His eyes narrowed, and she wanted nothing more than to trace the arch of his furrowed brows and erase every one of those bad memories that struggled to keep him in check.

"Lee gave me a knife," he began hesitantly. "A rusty knife. When he left. Must have been the one he'd been stabbed with because I'm pretty sure he was bleeding when he found me. I was all beat to hell, and my nose was broke, but I could smell it on him." Ky leaned back onto his elbow, pointing to his bicep. "I think he'd been stabbed here. The damned guy should've run for his life, but there he was, wasting time, saving me. Some guy named Jack showed up after Lee took off. It's kind of funny now, but he knocked when he opened my cell, and he whispered 'hello' like I might have fallen to sleep in that rat hole. He kept telling me not to stab him, that he was there to take me home. You'd disappeared by then, and I've got to tell you. I honest to God thought I'd lost my mind, only..."

She held her breath and waited.

"They put me under, you know, to stitch me up and stuff, but I kept smelling that Vicks of yours. I thought you'd come back for me, and sometimes when I was laying there in the hospital during the night..." He pressed his lips tight as he forced a hard swallow. "Sometimes when I can't sleep... I still smell it. You're the one place I withdraw to when all that crap comes back."

Oh wow. "Was that what you were doing at the crash site? You know, with that whole neck-rolling thing? You were remembering my Vicks?"

He frowned. "Yes. I had an ugly thought. When Lee gets a panic attack, he's got this specific mental exercise he does of a little boy throwing fallen stars back up into the sky. It works for him, but me? I summon menthol and green eyes. That's the only thing that gets me through."

Aww. Her heart melted. "You summon… me?" She had to make sure she'd heard right. Eden couldn't imagine hearing anything more perfect than that he'd relied on her all these missing years.

"Yeah, after I stopped drinking myself to death, I turned to meditation, and I learned how to summon you instead of a fifth of Jack. You're the quiet place I go to where I catch my balance, and... wait a minute. Did you put that ugly memory in my head last night?"

She ducked her head into her shoulders. "I did. I thought you were you," she admitted, "but you were so calm. It was a test. I wanted to be sure."

"You little shit," he said with a devilish grin. "Damn. So there I was thinking of you while you were screwing with me?"

And wishing I was screwing you. She changed the subject. "But you are a good kisser."

That produced the barest amber twinkle. "With you. I haven't been with a woman since I got home, Eden."

If ever two people were on the same wavelength, it was them. She saw it in his eyes. He wanted something more, but she also saw the hesitation. The fear. He wasn't ready to take more than that first step, and a kiss was just a kiss.

God, how embarrassing. She blinked hard, woefully inexperienced and totally head-over-heels in love. She spilled her secret along with her tears. "I'm a... I'm a..."

"You're a virgin," he finished, a tender smile on his lips. "Oh, honey, I know. I can tell. I'm sorry I went so far, but I needed to be sure Zaroyin or Levine hadn't taken advantage of you, and, well, once I got started..." He rolled his eyes. "I'm a horny bastard. I'm sorry."

"Don't," she squeaked. "Don't... spoil it."

He had the good grace to pull her against his chest again, and for a moment, all was right with the world. But she'd been wrong before, and she didn't want to appear as needy as she felt. She gave him the chance to retreat. "Let's stay close, okay? Always?"

The Chemstick glow on his handsome face faded into dark green shadow. His gentle brows narrowed to a *V*. "Close?"

Frightened at how this pleasant but so unrealistic dream might end, she ordered him to, "Check my feet, Agent Winchester. Hurry. I'm cold, and I want to be sure Zaroyin didn't stick anything else on me."

"So now I'm Agent Winchester? Okay... if that's how you want to play this," he murmured as he untied one of her hiking boots and slid it off. He pinched the toe of her sock and tugged it off to reveal her bright-pink painted toenails. "Hmmm. I like pink. On girls."

His words made her smile. She struggled for distance and composure while he ran his thumb down her instep and cupped her heel, visually checking her foot and ankles with those honey-warm eyes. With exquisite slowness, he lifted her toes to his mouth and blessed the rounded bottom of each with a warm, wet, whiskered kiss. "Just close?" he teased seductively, his voice deep and rumbling as he planted another kiss. "Like this?"

"Uh-huh." *Oh, God, yes.*

She arched toward him, a marionette on an invisible string, tingling from one end to the other. Every hair on the back of her neck stood on end. Who would've thought that feet and ankles were connected to that other needy place, the one weeping for his attention? That with one word Ky could command every last feminine muscle and nerve in her tightly strung body? That her traitorous self would be ready to jump off that edge again? So soon? Snap, even her nipples hardened into wanton little beggars for his touch.

"Find anything else?" she asked hoarsely, smoldering, out of control.

"I found you, didn't I?" he murmured, his tone husky and low, full of seductive promise. There it was again—that hint of permanence from his lips. The insinuation that this was no one-time operation for him. That he wanted her. Did she dare believe? Did she dare take the same risk she had demanded of him?

He smoothed one manly hand up her calf inside her pant leg. His brows spiked. "Sorry. Pants all the way off. I found something, and I need to see what it is."

She gulped, but dragged her leg out of her multiple layers, all except her underwear. They had to stay on or she'd turn into one big, gooey puddle.

Ky twisted her ankle to his right, then lifted her leg straight up in the air while he examined the underside of her right calf. With her foot imprisoned in his big hand and her pink toenails pointed at the ceiling, he had an unlimited view of her ass and very nearly everything else. Hyperventilation ramped up. Her pulse spiked through the nylon tent ceiling. *Here we go again...*

Unabashedly, he looked her up and down. Mostly down. A sexy smile tweaked his lips when his gaze slithered to her backside. "You're gorgeous. Every last inch of you."

"What did you find?" she asked, her voice thin. There was no way to get control of this situation. Not anymore. He owned her, and he seemed to know it.

He zeroed in on the back of her calf and peeled something off her skin. "Did you apply this?" he asked, lifting a square bandage into view.

She squinted to get a better look at it through her overly dilated, steamy eyes. "No. What is it?"

He turned it over. "Looks like some kind of drug patch. Are you on the pill?"

"No," she answered, her hackles up. "I don't smoke, and why would I need the pill?" *I'm a virgin, remember?*

He winked. "Now, don't get your panties in a bunch. Sometimes women take the pill to regulate their monthly cycle. It doesn't mean you're sleeping around."

"My panties are not in a bunch, Agent Winchester, and for your information, I don't sleep around." He needed to understand that one thing about her. She could wait forever for the right man, and she had, darn it.

"Hey, calm down. I'm just asking because it looks like the one I'm wearing."

"You're on hormones?" Snap, she wanted to kick herself at that stupid question. *Of course, he's not on hormones, silly.*

"No, but I'm trying to quit smoking, so I'm wearing a nicotine patch." Ky lowered her leg, his eyes hooded and his hands curled around both ankles. "How close?" he asked pointedly as he settled his knees between her feet. "I mean, how close do you want us to stay when this op's over? Pen pals? Distant friends? Roommates?"

Us? There's an us? She could not think with this glorious man handling her nearly naked, shivering self.

His gaze drifted between her legs, but if this was just about sex, she wanted nothing to do with it. Besides, FBI agents didn't dare hope for long-term relationships. The job was a divorce waiting to happen. Everyone knew that. She swallowed wrong at that lie and nearly choked. Who was she kidding? She wanted anything this guy offered. Casual sex. Committed sex. Sex in the tent. The whole nine yards.

"Umm, friends?" she squeaked, pathetically at his mercy. Rational conversation was impossible. *Utterly impossible.*

"For starters." He lowered her leg and eased his body into a careful push-up over hers until she was trapped by his arms and legs. He was eye-to-eye and nose-to-nose with her. "I'm not Agent Winchester, damn it. I'm Ky and you're Eden. We're just us, understood? Two people who found each other, got it?"

She gulped her crazy heart back down where it belonged. The hysterical little thing kept bouncing up her throat like it wanted to do the talking for her. Like it wanted to blurt out that it loved him, that she loved him. Always would. "But I'm FBI," she said weakly, like that had anything to do with—anything.

He eased back, his knees between hers, his eyes filled with the tender light of love, his voice low and raspy. "It's okay, Eden. Like I said, I smoke. We all have our faults."

A giggle escaped. "No, I mean that whole fraternization thing. I shouldn't—"

He peered into her eyes, one brow spiked devilishly. "Are you breaking up with me?"

Ha! He almost made her giggle out loud with his serious, funny face. Eden honestly couldn't speak, afraid she'd scare him off. Afraid she'd jumped the gun like she did when she'd asked if he was married. She refused to be one of those pushy women who wanted a kiss and a ring and, in a year, a divorce because they'd chased a man down until he'd caved.

Ky seemed to understand her reluctance. "The way I look at it, *Agent Stark,* you and me need to get to know each other better before we take this relationship forward. We need to take long walks and spend a lot of time together. Would you at least let me buy you a cup of coffee or something once this op is over?"

"Or something, Ky," she murmured his name through the knot in her throat.

He covered her with his body again, jumpstarting her heart, but he only planted a tiny kiss on the tip of her nose. "Then it's settled, *Eden.* I'll pick you up at 1800 hours the day after we get back to—"

"Kiss me," she whispered. "Shut up and kiss me."

Chapter Sixteen

Tate was missing, as usual, by the time Ky stopped kissing Eden and crawled out of the tent. Chase and Becker both shot him dark looks—not like he cared what they thought. At least they'd had the common sense to park their asses a healthy distance from the tent. They'd arranged a decent fire pit, too. Both were elbows to knees, crouched near a crackling fire.

Before he left her, Ky had given Eden a minor sedative to help her sleep. The poor thing needed rest in order to heal from all she'd been through, and he couldn't seem to rein in that over-protective streak of his. He'd tucked her in with his jacket and several packets of hand- and foot-warmers. It was either them or him, and he knew where climbing under that fur wrap with Eden would lead. He'd be tucked deep inside her curvaceous body and all the way to heaven.

Chase and Becker wouldn't like that, either.

He slapped the tent flap closed, shocked at what he'd just done with Eden. What he'd just said to that lady with drowsy green eyes. His feelings for her had happened fast, but each encounter with her had gotten more intimate, and a man could only resist a woman the likes of her for so long.

She was everything. His light. His air. He had to wonder though. Eden was intelligent and capable, a caring woman. What did she see in him? Because whatever it was, he knew different. She might think she had an in with that psychic link of hers, but she couldn't see what could hurt her. Too many ghosts still hung over his shoulders. Too many nightmares.

He had his support system in The TEAM and good parents back in Montana who worried and loved him, but the night still won sometimes. The dark still dripped off the ceiling. The cloying stink of Nizari's sandalwood oozed up from the floorboards and suffocated every last good thought and mantra. Ky hadn't had a drink since that night in the ER, but he kept Lee's number on speed dial, just in case, just to talk ops and training and the latest smart gun on the market in the middle of the night sometimes. Stuff like that. Guy stuff. Just to talk with someone who'd been there and knew the sound of an American voice could save the day. Or the night...

Brushing a hand over his head to roust out the beanie-hair thing he had going on, Ky worried. *I damned near asked her to marry me. What was I thinking?*

But he knew what he'd been thinking. Of never letting Eden go. Of telling her he loved her and making damned sure she knew he'd loved her since she'd come for him in that hall of horrors. Since she'd stayed…

Marriage seemed more honorable than throwing her over his shoulder and hauling her off to his man-cave for hours and hours of mind-blowing sex. A sneaky combination of lust and over-protectiveness had detonated out of his big mouth the second he'd gotten too close to her fire. Close nothing. Nothing smelled better than the sweet fragrance of this pure woman in heat.

Did she know how hot-damned hot she was? That he had no defense against her? That he'd been starving for the taste of her for years? That he'd move heaven and hell if she so much as hinted they were out of alignment in the universe? Ky not only wanted her physically, he needed every last beat of her heart. Every last stretch of her perfect soul. Her life.

Funny thing. The notion of marriage didn't feel so bad. His hard head rephrased it. *Will you marry me, Eden Stark? Would you ever consider doing such a foolish thing?* Would she say yes? Should she? Hell no—not if she knew what was good for her. She needed someone better, a whole man. He'd left too much behind in Kabul, and yet...

Eden Stark was a fire in his blood to stay.

"You done playing around with federal property that ain't yours, asshole?" Chase growled from the shadows, interrupting Ky's tender euphoria.

He swallowed hard and scrubbed one hand over his stupid face. "Found something."

"I'll just bet you did." On his feet now, Chase punched one fist into a cupped palm.

Ky downplayed the taunt before it got the best of him. This FBI agent seemed driven to challenge or denigrate at every turn, like he needed to pick a fight. Like he needed to prove something.

"Let's see what you found," Becker interceded calmly.

Ky joined them at the fire and handed Becker the patch he'd removed from the back of Eden's sexy bare leg. Just thinking about her flat on her back with one leg straight up in the air sent another wave of lust to his groin. At least he'd been smart and kept his bulkier frame between Eden and this side of the tent. No shadows.

Becker still hunkered near the fire. He turned the patch over before he passed it off to Chase. "Looks almost like a bandage. How'd you find it?"

Chase lifted the patch close to his nose and sniffed it, the bastard. His eyes glittered. "How else? He felt her up and—"

"You got a problem with me?" Ky barked, ready to dish out as much whoop-ass as it took to back Tucker off once and for all

Chase squared his shoulders and stuck out that big chin of his, begging to be punched. He had the nerve to walk into Ky's space before he lanced a hard finger into Ky's chest. "I got a problem with anyone who fucks with my family, jarhead. You're damaged goods, and you goddamned know it. Keep your hands to yourself. Stark ain't yours to play with, you hear me?"

Ky batted Chase's hand away, wanting very much to twist it backward and snap it off. The creepy shadow he usually suppressed at the back of his mind jumped to the forefront, ready to knock the shit out of this belligerent asshole and stomp Chase into oblivion. "You think she's yours?"

It had been a long time since his ugliest demon had surfaced in daylight, but Chase sure knew how to tap into it and rile it up. It ruled the dark, like Ky explained to Eden. He just hadn't told her everything. She didn't need to know how many times he'd awakened in a sweat with his clothes torn to hell, his room, too. Sometimes his entire apartment, if the nightmare won that round.

He swallowed hard. *What have I done?* Folks had no idea how bad a panic attack could get, how deep into hell those two words took a guy. No one knew, not until you lay alone in your room, afraid to close your eyes. Afraid that when you woke up, you'd be dangling at the end of a chain again, that being rescued was the dream—eternal torment the reality.

Chase might be a pain in the ass, but he was right to protect Eden. Ky *was* damaged goods. He had no business toying with her, thinking they could ever have a normal life together.

He looked back at the tent full of heaven. Remorse lifted its ugly head and made him think twice about that innocent cup of coffee.

"Where was it?" Becker asked, breaking the rant inside Ky's head.

Now why was that a need-to-know? "Why's that important?"

"Because my wife wears a patch like this one for birth control, but there's nicotine patches, too. I'm hoping you found this—"

"I know. I wear a nicotine patch, but this was on her calf." Ky glanced back at the tent where his woman lay resting. *My woman.* God, it felt good to think of her that way. A guy could almost believe he was worthy. But birth control? What the hell was Zaroyin up to? Ky's fists curled into two hammers. "It's not a nicotine patch. She doesn't smoke."

"No, she doesn't. She's as pure as the driven snow," Tucker declared, an edge to his voice. "Least she was."

Ky whirled on the son-of-a-bitch. "Knock it off. We're all here to save Eden Stark, so quit already."

Chase pointed to the east, the whip of command in his voice "Our being here voids your contract, dirtbag. Go home. Get the hell out of here. Let us do our job."

Ky forced slow, even breaths. "Then why don't you ring up Alex Stewart and tell him what you think, like he gives a rat's ass? Hell, play it on speaker so we can all get a laugh. I'd love to hear the end of that short and meaningless conversation."

Chase rolled his eyes at the dare, but Ky saw the hesitation. If he'd really worked with Alex like he said he had, Chase knew damned well how that phone call to Alexandria would end. Alex said what Alex meant to say, and people jumped when he did, or they got the hell out of his way. Or he knocked them down and ran over them.

Ky dragged his sat phone up from his pants pocket, daring Chase to make a bigger fool of himself than he already had. Alex would surely do it for him.

"Let it go, Tucker," Sam said quietly.

Chase never broke eye contact, but Ky backed off. A fistfight would wake Eden, and Chase wasn't worth it. Ky put the phone away and opted for a side run instead of the frontal assault he and Chase always seemed to end up in. "When did you guys work with my boss? In the service?"

"Nope. Remember that helicopter crash on the White House lawn a couple years back?" Becker replied evenly. "I was there. So was Stewart. We worked the same undercover sting. He's not the kind of a guy to back down from a fight. Trust me, I know. I got my ass kicked after that op, good. The man means what he says. He told me to stay the hell away from his wife, and by God, he meant it. My jaw still hurts, and I was just trying to be nice. There's no sense calling Stewart or Strong. We'll be glad to work with you, right, Tucker?"

Chase slapped his fist into his open palm again, but growled, "Yeah. Shit. Why not?"

He seemed full of more attitude than Becker. Less of a diplomat. Always ready to fight. The man seemed to have unresolved issues eating at him, and honestly, Ky understood. He could write a book on unresolved issues, but he and Chase needed to find common ground before they came to blows, and it wasn't going to be Eden.

Once again, Ky tried to breach the chasm between him and Chase. "So how do you know Alex?"

"Undercover op in northern Cali. He lost a good agent. I ran a little recon for him afterward. Got the bastard we were both after. No big deal."

Ky breathed a sigh of relief. These guys weren't so bad. Neither of them. He rolled the kink out of his neck and went for broke. "You have feelings for Eden, don't you?"

Icy blue eyes zeroed in on Ky. Damn. He had the same killer look as Alex on a bad day. "She's a good kid. I'd like to keep her that way if it's all the same with you."

Ky let it go. He knew Eden, and because he did, he understood Chase better. They were on the same side. This big blowhard was her brother, not her lover. If anything, his feelings for her were overly protective, ready to get down and nasty if that kept her safe.

"Your friend showed us the implants he dug out of our guys," Becker said, unruffled by the near showdown. "You're right. The wired-in device was definitely a tracking locator. I've never seen one implanted, though, not with an antennae wire. The eight-legged thing? That's new. Could be just what Tate said it was—a mind-control device. It makes sense, since it was under her scalp."

"Where's Tate?"

Chase chin-nodded to the east. "He said he had a date with a moose or something. Took a hank of rope with him."

Good. Ky noticed Tate had retrieved all the rope he could carry from the downed Cessna. That meant fresh, red meat for dinner, and maybe that the six dead men would soon be trussed up high in the trees. Ky looked eastward. Burgeoning gray clouds rolled overhead, drifting low and skimming the treetops. Snow clouds. He wondered if Tate needed help wrangling those bodies or hunting. He'd never ask for it, and Ky doubted he'd accept it. That was Tate for you, a loner through and through.

"She doing okay?" Chase asked, his tone softer.

"She's tougher than she looks," Ky answered. "How much ammo are you two packing?"

"Enough." Chase instantly reverted to his mind-your-damned-business tone. A look Ky couldn't decipher passed between him and Sam. What was really going on?

"We brought enough to take down a couple dozen more drones if we need to," Sam interjected before Ky had time to dwell on his uneasy feeling, "unless your buddy brings back the Omni 9000s the last six guys were carrying, or we get out of here before anyone else shows up. You got a flight plan?"

"Did. Not now. Our pilot's stranded in Thunder Bay until this weather clears."

"Ours too." Sam cocked his head to the east. "Your buddy doesn't say much, does he?"

Ky nodded. "Tate's quiet like that." He glanced back at his tent and brushed the first of many flakes off his shoulders. "I've got MREs to go with whatever dinner Tate brings back."

"It's not like he's going to find anything with this storm coming in anyway," Chase groused. "Big game lies down when the weather's bad. A real hunter would know that. You guys got any drinking water?"

Ky ignored Chase's opinion on Tate's hunting prowess and offered his remaining bottle of melted snow. The jerk never gave anyone a chance. "Always. You thirsty?"

"Yes," Chase admitted as he lifted the bottle to his lips and drained it. Wiping his mouth with the back of his gloved hand, he grunted and returned the empty bottle with an exasperated, "We've been humping since we touched down. Couldn't waste time to melt snow to drink. Had to get here before Zaroyin's men."

That explained a lot. Hungry *and* dehydrated were not a good combination in the freezing temperatures. Neither was stupidity. Chase should've taken the time to melt snow and keep himself hydrated. "Why are you guys here? I thought the FBI couldn't operate up north."

"I don't give a shit about protocol, Canadian or U.S.," Sam drawled. "Eden saved my life a couple years back. I owe her."

"If you must know, we're officially off the books," Chase piped up. "At least you're on contract. Strong will fire me when he finds out I'm here."

Tucker Chase had just climbed up a few notches in Ky's esteem. "What'd she do for you?"

"None of your son-of-a-bitchin' business. I'm here to keep her safe. From *everyone*, asshole."

God, the man took one step forward and ten back. Whatever Eden had done for him must've left a powerful impression. "Do you have any idea how many more of these drones are after her?" Ky asked, trying like hell to keep the conversation on neutral territory.

"That's the thing," Sam muttered, his voice low. "Zaroyin's got dozens of these young bucks signed up to his drone program, maybe more. Poor bastards had no idea what they were getting into. Bick funded him, and—"

"Senator Bick?" Ky asked, just to be sure he'd heard right.

"Yeah. Bick tacked a line of pure pork belly onto the latest appropriation bill before it went to Congress," Sam replied.

"Pork nothing. It was pure bullshit legislation is what it is," Chase replied. "The president should've vetoed it. Why? You know him?"

A dirty fingernail slithered up Ky's spinal column. This whole Dr. Zaroyin debacle had just gotten a hell of a lot worse. Bick came from old money. He had friends in high places, and he wanted power. His wife, a movie star straight out of Hollywood's liberal agenda, was a gold-digger of the brightest magnitude. She detested the military, said the men and women who kept her sorry ass free made America look bad. His blood boiled just thinking about Cassandra Bick.

"Yeah. I know him all right," Ky admitted. "Tate and I saved his ass in Morocco a year ago. I can't prove it, but he said some things on our way out of the country. I'm pretty certain he's into the illegal diamond trade."

"Figures you'd do something stupid like that. You should've left him there, dumbass," Chase hissed. "He's on Strong's list of possible traitors. We're watching him."

"He's suspected of dealing with Al Qaida, but we can't prove it," Sam rumbled. "Who asked you to go get him, Ky?"

"Strong. He wanted Bick on U.S. soil. Alex made it happen." Ky looked back at the tent where hopefully, Eden lay sleeping. Tate's words came back to him. *Let 'em come.*

Chapter Seventeen

Eden stretched languidly, or as languidly as she could under the deep layer of blankets. She pulled Ky's jacket to her nose and inhaled the rich, musky scent of him off the collar. Sweat and aftershave. Cool spice and musky man scent. She'd been wrapped up in him and finally slept decently. Best men's cologne ever.

Being rescued did have its merits, and Ky certainly was one of them. Better yet, he'd allowed her touch during their last encounter—not like he'd had a choice once his self-control had evaporated along with hers. Maybe that was all he needed—to want someone so badly that his deep-seated compulsion took a back seat to pleasure and passion. To love.

Because that was what it was. Like it or not, she knew this man. He might have some monsters to tame, but who didn't? He was a keeper, and she meant to keep him now that she'd found him again.

Her muscles still ached for him in all the best places. Scrambling to her feet, she folded Ky's TEAMwear jacket over her arm. They'd gotten intimate darned fast, but the memory of his powerful hands roaming over her bare skin sent shivers rocketing up the back of her neck. Right on cue, a smile stretched across her face and love filled her heart. Handsome Ky Winchester was with her in the flesh, not thousands of miles away in some Afghanistan cell. Now they just needed to survive Zaroyin.

Out she went into the wintry weather, rested and her heart light. For the first time in a couple of days, no headache squeezed her tired brain. It had yet to come up with answers to all of her questions, but she wasn't worried, not with her two best agent friends in camp. They'd help her figure it out. Tate wasn't so bad, either. He didn't like her much, but she could see it in his eyes. He was coming around.

It had gotten dark. Snowflakes fell steadily except over the fire. Someone had rigged a nylon tarp at an angle up in the trees to prevent the snow from dousing the flames. Her nose picked up a lovely scent. She lifted her face and sniffed again, drawing the delicious aroma in. A slab of actual meat sizzled over the flame. Tiny tendrils of white smoke and the most delectable flavor sensation lifted up through the steady falling snow. While Tate turned a makeshift spit, Eden licked her lips and joined Ky in the chilly circle. Her stomach growled. "What time is it?"

"Dinnertime. How'd you sleep?" Ky asked, his eyes on the fire.

She returned a knowing smile, wishing he'd caught it. "Good. My headache's finally gone. Here's your jacket. Where'd you get, umm, the beef?"

Ky nodded toward Tate as he shrugged into his TEAMwear. "Courtesy of Tate. It's yearling moose, not beef. Nearly done burning, too."

Tucker muttered too low for Eden to catch what he'd said, but she let it go. She dropped next to Ky. "Thanks, Tate. That was thoughtful. Where's the rest of it?"

He grunted. "Up in a tree. Where else?"

Enough said. Eden glanced shyly at Ky, but he had yet to meet her eyes, and she wanted him to. "Those heat things were a good idea, Ky. I slept like a baby."

"Good. You needed a decent rest after what you've been through. Look what else Tate rigged up while you were sleeping." He jerked his head back at the tent, still avoiding eye contact.

No wonder she'd been comfortable and warm. A pine bough structure and a thick layer of snow now covered the tent. "Did you do that for me?" she asked Tate.

He grunted as usual, but she was getting used to his standard, non-answer kind of answers.

She patted his forearm, more determined than ever to get to the bottom of his anti-social vibes. "I mean it, Tate. I'd be a mess without you. Thanks."

He looked away, so she let it go. Some men were just like that. Recalcitrant. Grumpy. Loners, like her. But she did notice the reddish creep of color over his bronzed cheeks. Yeah. He was coming around, but what had happened to Ky? Why the cold shoulder? She tucked her fingers into the crook of his arm and leaned into him, determined he was not getting away from her. "Hi there," she murmured.

He turned to meet her gaze. Melting amber poured its golden light down on her. His bigger hand cupped hers on his arm. "Hey," was all he said, and that was enough. He pulled her snug against his hip. A woman didn't have to be clairvoyant to know something was bothering him.

"You feel like talking?" Sam asked, his eyes on the meal roasting over the flame. "The guys and I have questions."

"Sure. What do you want to know?"

"Why you, for starters?" he asked quietly. "What does Zaroyin really want? I get that you're psychic, that you have abilities most of us don't, but what's he hope to gain by capturing you? What can you do for him?"

She shrugged, still trying to figure that answer out herself. "I think he needs someone to control his army, someone who already has psychic skills. Think about it. Internet signals are lost all the time. Satellite signals, too. Even the best cell providers can't reach the entire planet, but someone with psychic abilities could. That person, if they were good enough, would have a direct link to every FBI drone on the planet, and not need any infrastructure to maintain it. Zaroyin could be anywhere he wanted to if he controlled that person. He and his drones would be unstoppable."

"So you think you might be the key to his plan for military domination?"

"I just know the impression I got the first time we met, Sam. He thought he was selling Matt on the premise of no more friendly fire, but my second sight kicked in. All I saw was a crazy guy intent on bringing his dream of cybernetic soldiers to reality at any cost, but he hadn't figured out how to control them yet."

"Uh-huh," Sam drawled. "Seems obvious. Straightforward. You might be right."

She caught his doubt. *I might be right*? "But..." She drew out the word so he'd spill his suspicions.

"But what if it's not so obvious, Eden?" Tucker asked, his eyes also on the fire. "What if he planted that idea in your head as a misdirect? What if he already has another psychic in his control, and he doesn't need you? What if this whole mess is just him testing the capability of his drones and his psychic prototype? His protégé?"

"His what?" Her hand went to the zippered collar under her chin. She sucked in a breath of cold air at the thought that Zaroyin might have pitted one psychic against another. "But that would mean... oh, snap. I never thought about that. You think he's using someone else to locate me? Why? To kill me? That doesn't make sense. I'm harmless."

"No, you're not," Ky muttered, his voice as low as Sam's and Tucker's had been. The steel in his arm tightened around her. "If Sam's right, you're in Zaroyin's way. That might be why he's led you up here away from the Bureau's protection. He needs you dead. Think about it. You already got him kicked out of Quantico. Then he lost his congressional funding until Senator Bick and his rich wife showed up. Only you can reach out and stop his other psychic, if that's what's really going on. Only you can influence him or her to turn on Zaroyin, and, as you've just pointed out, you could do it without electricity, Internet, or satellite. He knows that. If he can't have you, Zaroyin at least needs you out of his way. He wants to make sure no one else has you, either."

Her throat closed at Ky's very logical argument. *Oh shit. I have to die.*

Ky's arm squeezed as if he'd just read her mind.

"But why kill Charlie? That makes no sense." A tear eked out of her eye. She brushed it away before anyone noticed it. It wasn't so much for Charlie as for Ky. Now she knew why he'd seemed withdrawn. These guys had been doing a lot of talking and if they had, Tucker and Sam had no doubt warned him to stay clear of her.

She turned to look closely at Ky, saddened he could be so easily bullied. *'What?'* he mouthed as he smoothed a big palm over her well-padded hip. That simple gesture of obvious male dominance helped, but she could see it in his eyes. Something was definitely bothering him.

"Sure it makes sense, darlin'," Tucker added gently. "Look around. Zaroyin's running the ugliest black op we've ever been up against. Do you see anyone providing triage or medical care to these drones once they're hit? No, and do you know why? Those poor guys have no backup and no logistics tail. They've got no support and no supply line. Zaroyin doesn't care if they live or die. He has no use for his own men once they fail or fall, and because he doesn't, this idea will never fly. No one on the Hill will ever fund throwaway soldiers. The decent people in America won't stand for it, which is why he turned to Senator Ruston Bick. Zaroyin doesn't need appropriated funding now that he's got his hands on Bick's blood diamond money."

"Senator Bick?" Her head pivoted to Ky. "Wasn't he your dumbass in Morocco?"

Ky's brows arched. "How'd you know?"

"Because you and I are linked. Mentally." She tapped her forehead. "The second you said Morocco I knew he was the man you'd saved. His wife's an actress." *And if these two megalomaniacs are behind this madness, hanging around me is going to get you killed.*

Ky's eyes narrowed. "Knock it off, Eden. I'm not leaving you, so shut it."

"Excuse me?" He'd done it again—read her mind. Ky was getting good at that. "But I—"

"Shut. Up." He slapped her hip with his open palm. "Don't give me any of your noble bullshit about protecting me. Like it or not, you and I are joined at the hip. You're not leaving me, and no, being with you doesn't make me a target."

A chuckle lifted up her throat. He *was* reading her mind! "Sheesh. Would you let me speak?"

Another playful slap landed on her hip and stayed there. "I'm right, though, aren't I?"

"Yes, but, it's really aggravating when you tell me what I'm going to say before I say it," she shot back at him, not so much annoyed as needing to set boundaries. "You need to rein that mental reach of yours in. I don't like having other people in my head." *So this is how my father felt. How annoying.*

"Wait a minute. You two can read each other's minds?" Tucker asked. "For real?"

"Yes," she admitted excitedly at the same time as Ky grumbled, "Hell, no. It's easy to read Eden. Her emotions are written all over her face."

"They are not." She wiped a gloved hand over said face. "Even if they are, explain how you knew I was going to trip over that tree stump before?"

Ky tapped the goggles hanging around his neck. "Easy. TEAMshield warned me. I saw it coming. You didn't. Problem solved. I'm no psychic, Eden. I'm just a regular guy."

She squinted at his logical explanation. It covered everything. Almost. Everything except how he'd reached out to her from Afghanistan years ago. That had nothing to do with high-tech goggles or her emotions. That was all on him. So was his mind reading. "Okay, but if you're anywhere near me, you're still going to be a target."

"And if you're on your own, you're dead. Cut the crap, Eden. It's my job. I'm here. I stay."

"And I stay," Tucker growled.

"I'm in," Sam muttered.

When Tate added his version of loyalty with his customary grunt, her heart flooded with warmth. "So what do we do now, Tucker? Run for our lives like we have been?"

"That may be difficult with this storm front hovering over us," he replied. "Hey. You burned that moose enough yet, Higgins?"

Tate pointed wordlessly at the spit. Enough said. Well, *unsaid*.

Tucker lanced the roast with his SEAL knife and jerked it off the spit. He dropped the steaming slab onto a nearby tin plate. The man was always prepared. And hungry. He doused the meat with a bag of seasonings he'd pulled out of his pocket, and, with three deft cuts, the moose buffet was parceled out into five thick, steaming slices. Dinner was served.

Ky handed Eden a paper plate for her portion, along with a plastic knife and a fork. The others went primitive. No one spoke. Eden wiped the juices dripping off her chin. The tender meat disappeared amongst a few moans and a lot of lip smacking. Sam wiped his moustache. Tucker burped like a water buffalo.

Eden noticed the pine lean-to against the vertical wall of the granite mountain opposite the tent. It was well-camouflaged with all the snow. "Who made that?"

Tucker stabbed his knife at Tate. "Sam and I started one, but he showed up and made it stronger. Now it's waterproof. We ought to be comfortable."

"Said he took care of the drone bodies," Sam muttered, the last of his portion of moose meat at the tip of his knife. He snapped it down with relish, still chewing. "The man's a damned workhorse. He should've joined the Bureau or the Secret Service. We could use a guy like—"

"Never," Tate growled. The mood around the campfire fizzled.

"Oh, come on, Higgins. Give us brothers-in-arms a chance. We're not that bad," Sam persisted, pointing his knife at Tate. "Come on over from the dark side and—"

Tate pushed up from the ground. "Don't wait up," he grumbled at Ky as he walked into the dark.

Sam's bushy brows lifted in surprise. "Was it something I said?"

Ky exhaled though his nostrils. "Leave it alone, Becker."

Eden followed his cue, but immediately sicced her second sight on the odd man out, hoping it worked, for a change. She wasn't sure why, but if anyone needed saving, it was Tate.

She stood to follow, but Ky waved her off with a curt, "All of you. Leave him the hell alone."

Chapter Eighteen

Ky lifted to his feet the second Tate stepped away. The quiet man could only take so much stupid banter before he'd had his fill and needed breathing space. Even in the office, Tate struggled with the nuisance of camaraderie. The man just plain didn't like people. Ky got that. Most days he could do without folks, too, but he also recognized that Tate was lonely. Maybe the loneliest agent on The TEAM.

TEAMshield employed simple walkie-talkie technology without having to engage with Alexandria. Good thing, too. Ky activated them and asked, "You with me, buddy?"

Tate's signature grunt sounded deep inside his ear.

"Copy that," Ky replied. He didn't offer platitudes or hints, didn't suggest Tate stay close to camp or watch his back, either. No sense in it. No black operator appreciated being told what he already knew. Tate just needed space and time to himself. He'd be back when he was ready.

Ky got Tate like no one else did. Lee came close to understanding him, but for whatever reason, Tate had never connected with Lee like he did Ky. Ky didn't know what the big guy's story was, and he'd never asked. Still wouldn't. The day Tate came to grips with his demons was strictly his business. Until then, Ky contented himself to be like Eden— maybe not as pretty, but an angel in the shadows nonetheless.

After the heated exchange with Chase, Ky wasn't certain where he stood with her. Reasonable second thoughts dug into his hard head. Chase had been right. Ky was damaged goods, damn it. Things between them had gotten carried away. She deserved better, there was no doubt about that, but the notion of her being with another man pitched acid up his throat. He'd never wanted to stake his claim on a woman like he did Eden, but did he have a right to drag her into his nightmares? His torments?

Damned if TEAMshield didn't beep an incoming-call warning. "What the hell's going on that you can't keep me better informed?" Alex hissed without preamble.

Shit. Just what Ky needed, a butt-chewing from a guy sitting in his air-conditioned office in comfy, far-off Virginia. "A blizzard for one, Boss. Performing minor surgery on Eden Stark, for another," Ky replied evenly, picturing his hard-driving boss at his desk, coffee in one hand, piss and vinegar in the other. Alex wasn't mad, just impatient and no doubt hyped-up on caffeine.

"Surgery?"

"Two, actually." Ky explained about the implants and wires, the six drones, and Becker and Chase's arrival.

The blatant hostility pinging all the way from sunny Virginia was hard to miss. "Why's Becker there?"

"He and Chase are hell-bent on getting Agent Stark home safe."

"That's *your* job. Tell those guys to take off. You don't need them."

"It's not that easy, Boss. They took out six of their own men to protect Eden, and Sam's sure more of Zaroyin's drones are on the way. I'd like him and Chase to hang around until this thing's over."

Alex growled, a sure sign he considered Ky's opinion, but reluctantly. Otherwise, he'd have sworn a blue streak Becker and Chase could've heard from their seats by the fire. "When?"

Ky rolled his eyes at Alex's curt question. *When what?* He didn't have ESP. He forged ahead with what he thought Alex needed to know. "As soon as I have an ETD out of here, I'll let you know."

"Is it still snowing?"

Ky scanned his goggles over the camp to give Alex a glimpse. "That would be a roger. It's primitive here, but we'll be warm enough. What's the weatherman say?"

"You might be snowed in for days. The jet stream dipped into the lower forty-eight. You guys okay?"

"As far as food and water, yeah. Zaroyin's our real problem. The drones he's sent after us are relentless. He runs them until they drop dead or until we have to kill them."

"Bastard," Alex hissed. "Mother can't locate him. I'll send Maverick and Gabe to assist; Harley and Adam, too. They can standby in Thunder Bay until the storm blows over."

"If they can get into Thunder Bay."

"Damn."

My sentiments precisely. For now, Mother Nature had the final say, not his boss nor Zaroyin. "Don't worry about us. We'll be back in the States before you know it."

"Keep your head up. One way or the other, Harley and the guys will be there. How is she?"

Ky looked to Eden at that unexpected question. "She's good," he replied in as monotone a voice as he could muster.

"You okay?" Alex asked. *Could he read minds, too?*

"Tate and I are good. Thanks, Boss."

The line disconnected. Ky placed a quick call to the RCMP pilot and requested immediate evacuation. The prognosis was grim. He couldn't fly in the current conditions. *Hang tight. We'll be there when we can. In the meantime, don't take chances. Avoid undue exposure. Keep warm and hydrated. Shit. We're on our own.*

Ky ended the call, but delayed activating his goggles. He silenced his earpiece, too. Alex didn't need to see or hear what happened next.

Chase had gotten extra-animated, leaning toward Eden as if he couldn't quite hear the story tripping off her tongue, and Ky knew the feeling. Eden's voice was soft and musical, something extra sweet that a man craved. It made him sit up and listen. But when Chase raised his face to the sky and belted out a raucous laugh, Ky'd had enough. Whatever enchanting story Eden had just shared with her FBI buddy stung Ky to the bone. He curled his fingers into fists, tired of his demons and just as tired of Tucker-Damned-Chase. Things had to change.

"Hey, Eden. Can we talk?" Ky waved her over to him.

Curious greens speared him from across the camp and Chase's side, but she shook her head. Damned if her hood didn't slip when she'd turned. She wasn't wearing her cap, so her blond spirals cascaded in a silky cape over her shoulders while other tangles pooled in the cup of her hood. She looked like a fairy princess sitting too close to a lecherous dragon. "I'm busy. Can it wait?"

What he deserved but not quite what he'd expected. "Not really," Ky offered through dry lips that might be lying.

When she turned back around and said something to Chase, Ky's blood boiled that she'd ignore him. He hadn't played this smart, and he wouldn't blame Eden for blowing him off. He deserved that for giving her the cold shoulder before, but things between them had happened awfully fast. He didn't want to pressure her any more than he already had.

Chase took her plate, a better response than laughing, but he still bugged Ky. Eden lifted to her feet, her chin clenched and one brow raised as she approached. "What?"

Ky swallowed hard, on the verge of saying something from which there would be no return. He wanted to reel her into his arms, needing her with him. Against him. Wanting desperately to be inside of her. The aromatic scent of eucalyptus drifted across the distance between them, luring him to her like a fish on a lovely hook. So why was he fighting his feelings?

He knew why.

"Sam thinks that might be a hormone patch on your leg. Tell me if you start feeling different now that it's gone. Maybe better. Happy. Sad. Anything." It was a lame beginning at best, and he knew it. His gut lurched halfway up his throat.

"Is that all?" she asked, a tease in her voice while she tucked handfuls of her silky hair away from her face and under her hood again.

"Yes," he said while he shook his head. "I mean... no. That's not all."

Her big green eyes widened. "Are you ditching me, Ky Winchester?"

She'd used his words. And there it was. He should say yes. He should be smart and let her live a better life than one with the likes of him, but... he couldn't bear the thought of letting her out of his sight. He knew what pain was, and losing her would kill him.

"No, Eden," rolled off his tongue while "never" lifted out of his heart. He swallowed hard. "I just want you to be sure."

She cocked her pretty head. "About what? Coffee?"

His heart climbed up the back of his throat and took up residence at the ledge of his stomach. "No," he croaked. "I meant about having coffee with me. There's something you need to know. I'm not..." How did a man explain that a sadist had carved on his privates? That he wasn't easy to look at, that he wasn't the whole man she needed? That he might not be able to give her babies? He swallowed hard and tried again. "Eden—"

She closed the distance between them and took hold of his shoulders, the swell of her luscious breasts pressed to his chest. There. In front of Becker and Chase.

"Ky," she said sweetly, a tender sheen in her eyes. "I was there with you, remember? There isn't anything you can tell me that will make me..." a gentle smile tugged at her lips, ". . . miss our first date."

"I can't give you what you need," he declared hoarsely. Quietly. "You have to understand that going in. I won't lie to you. I'm not who you think—"

She lifted up on her tiptoes, rubbing her nose against his neck like a cat. Scenting him. Claiming him. Touching him. "Are you sure about that?" she asked in her sultry, tease-me-crazy voice, the husky one he'd give anything to wake up to every morning for the rest of his life.

"Pretty sure. I've got scars, and those guys..." He jerked his head toward the east behind him, toward Kabul. "They worked me over pretty good. I've got—"

"You've got me," she said firmly but quietly. No more than a whisper. No more than a promise. "You've got me for the hard times and the good times. Look into these eyes, Ky Winchester, and tell me what you see there."

He couldn't look away, because, well, he saw his whole world in Eden's green eyes. His daytimes. His nighttimes. His every-heartbeat-in-between times. "Are you hypnotizing me?" He hoped so.

Eden shook her head. "Better. I've fallen in love with you, Ky."

His heart stuttered to a screeching halt before it jumped up high and somersaulted into a perfect swan dive down his throat. "Me?" he asked, like he needed to hear it again. Because he sure as hell did.

Her gaze melted into a warm green glow there in the deep woods where light was dim and a man's heart had grown cold and scared and bitter. "It's been you since that night you first came to me. Only you, Ky."

He couldn't speak, not with the tears about to breach the dam in his eyes.

She tunneled her fingers over his ears and into his shaggy hair, touching him with gentleness. Anchoring him. He didn't even wince at the brush of her satin skin over his scarred body Not once.

"I need you in my life, Ky," she vowed. "I want you where I can get my hands on you. I chose to stay with you two and a half years ago. I choose to stay with you again today. Is this why you've been quiet tonight? Is this what you've been worrying about, that you might not be man enough for me?"

If it were only that simple. Ky snaked an arm around her neck to hold her in place. With her smiling up at him from the crook of his arm and the snow falling into her eyes, he bowed his forehead to hers. "I just can't ask you to give up everything for me. You need someone better. Someone—"

Eden launched herself at him, crashing into his lips with her open mouth, growling as she licked his lips and tangled her tongue with his. The snow stopped falling. The world stopped turning. Chase's and Becker's voices faded until there was only the tip of Eden's cold nose in Ky's cheek. Her moist, warm breath in his lungs. All the pieces of his broken, damaged heart in her hands.

"I choose you, darn it," she said, nipping his lower lip and biting like she needed to get his attention, "and you'd better choose me if you know what's good for you."

And there it was. Her gift freely given, Eden style. He decided to do something smart. "I choose you, Eden Stark. I love you," he whispered raggedly into her demanding lips. "So. Damned. Much."

The woman had the nerve to grind her body against his, matching the warmth of her core to the heavy steel shaft behind his zipper, her plush breasts flattened to his chest. "You just wait, Ky Winchester," she declared hotly, all moist lips and steamy breath. "When I get you home, I'm going to rip all those winter clothes off of you, and I'm not going to stop loving you until you're covered in strawberry marks and lipstick."

His happy cock jerked to attention. The damned thing nearly climbed out of his pants. He dropped both hands to her ass, and with one tug, he hefted her boots off the ground and wrapped her delectable body around him like taffy on a stick. There was nothing else in the world. Only this woman. This now.

Damned if Chase didn't spoil the magic. "Get your asses on the ground! They've got the moose!"

The what? The moose? Ky launched Eden into the snow, covering her protectively with his body while Chase snapped off three quick rounds into the trees below camp. An animal yelped somewhere in the darkness. Chase leveled another couple of shots before he lowered his piece with a grin and stuffed it into his hip holster, the cocky bastard. "You can put your goggles on now, pretty boy."

"That's what this was about? The moose carcass? You wanted to scare us? Holy friggin' shit!" Ky tugged a panting Eden up and back into his arms. "Damn you, Chase. You could've warned us you were shooting at a wolf."

"Wouldn't have made much of an impression, would it?" Chase extended a gloved hand to Eden with a cocky, "There you go, kiddo. Tucker Chase, always at your service. I've got your back even when Junior Agent Winchester can't perform. Are you okay?"

"Th-thanks," she muttered breathlessly, his hand bracing her upright. "Wow. You scared ten years off me. Did my hair turn gray?"

He grinned, those blue eyes of his flashing nothing but charm. "No, darlin'. You're just as pretty as ever."

Ky grunted, dusting the snow off his knees. His calves clenched with the need to kick this jerk's hairy ass down the hill. Man, Chase acted like he had a permanent hard-on for Eden, one he was never going to get satisfied. Didn't seem to stop him from trying, though.

Chase cocked his elbow for Eden to accompany him back to the fire pit, now steadily sputtering from the heavier snowfall. "You'll be safer with me. Bring your friend if you have to."

Eden draped her hand over Ky's forearm instead. "Thanks, Tuck. Save a seat for me?"

Ky could've kissed her for the loyalty he didn't deserve. He pulled her in close and breathed a sigh of relief. He didn't know how, and he didn't know when, but they were going to have that cup of coffee and a whole lot more.

But wait. He jerked back around. Moose carcass? Wasn't that supposed to be up high where wolves couldn't reach it? Isn't that what Tate had said?

Chase kept flirting with Eden. "Just don't let that lowlife contractor talk you into anything you don't want to do."

"Like what?" Ky called him out, his gut still full of fight, but needing to chat with Tate.

"Like taking off after your buddy, Agent Higgins." Chase turned back around. "You ever wonder why he's so quiet? Why he's got nothing to say? You ever check into his background just a little bit, or do you guys believe every shittin' thing Stewart tells you?"

"What are you talking about?" Ky had to ask. "Tate's a decorated war hero. He's—"

"So the hell are the rest of us," Chase snarled, suddenly as deadly as he'd seemed before. "So were half of those guys I killed today. That didn't stop them from drinking the Kool-Aid, did it? It doesn't mean Higgins hasn't been in touch with Zaroyin, either. You ever think about that?"

"He what? Not Tate. No way."

"Tucker's right, Ky," Sam quietly said as he joined the standoff. "That's another reason why we were late getting here, and that's also why we're here at all. Once we heard who was with you on this mission, we had to get involved. I'm not even sure Alex knows, but Zaroyin contacted Agent Higgins three weeks ago. That's why I badgered him. I needed him pissed off enough to leave so I could talk to you alone."

"Are you sure?" Ky asked, disbelieving every last word out of Becker's and Chase's lying mouths. Not Tate. The man was true to the core. *But that moose carcass...*

Chase nodded. "It's a fact. We've been following Zaroyin's activities for months. Had a court-ordered phone tap on his phones. Matt's death was just a diversion to get you out of Virginia, Eden. Tell me who gave you the idea to run to San Francisco?"

She leaned deeper into Ky, and he didn't fail to tighten his grip. She'd chosen well, and he meant her to know it. "Matt's friend, Cameron Devine. We were talking about which field offices were safest if ours ever came under attack. I said none of them, not after McVeigh took out the Federal Building in Oklahoma City, but Levine disagreed with Matt and me. He said the San Francisco field office was actually more protected, that their security protocols were better than D.C.'s."

As Ky listened, more puzzle pieces fell into place. Devine was definitely another snake behind the scenes.

"Cameron said the only one better than San Francisco's was Hawaii because of NOAA, the National Oceanic and Atmospheric Administration. You know, because it utilizes the online Pacific Tsunami Warning Center and..." She shut her mouth then opened it again. "Only when Cameron showed up in Hawaii, he told me I'd be better off in Anchorage. That he'd had second thoughts. Hawaii was an accident waiting to happen. That it was too close to Japan and China, and... snap. Ky's right. I panicked and ran. I have been set up."

"Want to bet Levine wanted you in Hawaii just so he could plant those devices, get you rigged up so he could keep track of you?" Becker asked.

Chase nodded. "Zaroyin's got good men in high places at his bidding. We're just the riffraff dogging him."

"Director Strong?" Ky asked. "Is he in on this, too?"

"No, he's with us, but I'll be honest," Sam drawled. "He's fighting an uphill battle inside his own department. Zaroyin's idea for a highly controlled military makes sense to a lot of liberally minded folks. They don't want the Department of Defense to have the power it does. They're out to cut the balls off of the Army, Navy, and Marine Corps, once and for all. A cybernetically enhanced army controlled by an outside entity, maybe a defense contractor like Zaroyin makes sense, though I don't follow their reasoning. The last thing I'd want on my ass is a mind-controlled moron with a computerized rifle and no sense of honor."

"Shit. The Omni-9000s," Ky muttered. It made sense—all except Tate's part in Zaroyin's plan. No friggin' way was he involved.

"Exactly," Chase muttered. "Where the hell are the weapons your buddy supposedly pulled off those dead bodies? You seen 'em yet? For that matter, where are the bodies?"

Ky had no answer. He'd been with Eden while Tate was out taking care of business. A twinge of guilt flickered through his mind that he'd too easily given Tate the dirty end of the stick on this mission. Just as quickly, suspicion lifted its ugly head. *Or did Tate intend it that way?*

Sam pressed his hand hard into Ky's shoulder. "Let's go check on those bodies your buddy supposedly hung up in the trees. If they're up high and tight, I'll back off. But if not, we might have a helluva problem headed our way."

Ky shrugged Sam's grip off. "Bullshit. Tate's not like that. They'll be where he said they were." Only the moose wasn't.

"I sure wish you'd use your brain once in a while, Winchester. Your buddy was gone a helluva long time. Do you really think he had time to hunt a moose, secure six bodies in the trees, and reinforce your tent while Tucker and I barely had time to build a crappy lean-to?"

"Tate's no girly federal agent," Ky growled, bound and determined to prove his buddy's allegiance. "You guys should've confronted him with this stupid notion instead of pissing him off like you did. Let him defend himself, and we wouldn't be sneaking around behind his back. Jesus H. Christ, he's done nothing but help you guys since you showed up."

The six bodies might not be plastic-wrapped like the previous three, but they would be heads down and feet up. Tate would have a good explanation for that moose, too. Hell, maybe the wolves tore it out of the tree. If they were anything like that black fellow, they could to it.

"Couldn't take the chance," Chase replied, "not if he's confiscated one of those smart guns while he's been out hunting. Now shut up and let's get this over with before he comes back."

Ky pulled Eden along with him. "I've got news for you guys. If Tate has thrown in with Zaroyin, we're already dead. He's a helluva shot. That's why he got the moose so fast. He might not know these parts, but he knows animals and how to hunt."

Sam grunted. "Quiet. Let's find those bodies before this storm gets any worse."

"In the dark?" Eden asked.

"Have to. Stay close," Chase ordered. "No lights. Try not to lose sight of each other."

Ky tugged Eden in closer until they were nearly tripping over each other, Sam on their right, Chase to the left. Snow kept falling. Their boots squeaked in the dry powder. A dark object laid several meters downhill from the tent.

"Wolf," Chase hissed. "Good. I hit him solid. Keep your heads on a swivel. There was more than one. That moose carcass has to be around here, unless they dragged it off."

Ky's heart fought with the logical argument these guys had presented. So what if Tate didn't talk much? So what if he didn't like people? Most guys coming back from the sandbox couldn't relate to civilians. A man's silence meant nothing.

The night was too quiet. Too dark. Until six pairs of glowing eyes glowed hatefully through the snow. Chase lifted his pistol, but Ky's hand clamped on his forearm. "You don't have to shoot everything."

Chase jerked his hand free. "Bet me."

Ky left Eden behind him and stepped out in front, positive these big bad wolves were chewing on something, just not the moose carcass.

"Are all Stewart's men as stupid as you?" Tate hissed.

"Hold," was all Sam offered.

"Ky," Eden breathed. "Be careful."

He intended to be darn careful, but three steps forward and there he was, face to face with long-legged, big-footed wolves. Five silver. One black.

"You need to take off," he told the supreme alpha predator.

Six heads lowered. Menacing growls answered. Hackles lifted straight off the big guy's back.

Ky lifted his arms, making himself larger as he advanced. "There's nothing for you guys here. My kill. Not yours."

Bet me. The black wolf snarled and stepped on the carcass, claiming it while his buddies grumbled and shifted their positions from guard to attack. Paws planted. Snouts lowered to the ground. Not sniffing, though. Daring.

That didn't go as well as Ky had hoped, but something about his wild brother called him on. Ky growled back. "Leave. Now."

The whole facedown took a weird turn. Almost as if Chase had threatened them with an Omni 9000, the lead wolf ducked his head. He snarled low and steady, then bolted sideways with a yelp. His pack followed suit.

Ky took the opening and closed in on the carcass. It wasn't big enough to be a moose. Sam's flashlight beam flickered over the bizarre sight. Five fingers spread wide in the frozen air. Five chewed on, bloody stumps of fingers. The wolves weren't fighting over a moose carcass. Not one of the drones, either.

Ky knelt and dusted the snow off the body. Shit. He'd found Charlie Sweets again.

Chapter Nineteen

Sam called the meeting, but four people inside one small tent? Not good. When Tucker climbed out to stand guard, the freed up space didn't do a thing for Eden's state of mind. At least the other six drones and the moose carcass were in the trees where Tate had said they were.

But Charlie Sweets? His body being out there didn't make sense. Not one bit. Like Tate had earlier, Tucker and Sam dragged him back and hung him in a tree at the edge of camp. It took them a while getting the rope over a sturdy tree limb. Tucker cussed the whole time, but at last, Charlie was hanging high and gruesome.

Now Sam couldn't seem to shut up. "Higgins has been spying on Alex and Strong for six months now. He's met with Zaroyin twice. We've got him on video if you want to see it."

"No," Ky said woodenly, "I don't believe it."

"Shut up, Sam," Eden insisted. "You don't know what you're saying."

"Then tell me where he is if he's so decent? We've got the money trail. Zaroyin deposited one-point-five million into Higgins' savings account over the last three weeks, and there's more. He owns an Omni 9000. If we don't move before he gets back, we'll end up dead. He'll sneak back and kill us in our sleep."

"No!" Ky roared. "Not Tate. I know him. He wouldn't do this, whatever *this* is. I won't leave him behind."

Sam brushed an impatient hand through his shaggy locks. "That's just not smart. You've got no choice, son. We've got—"

"Stop with the *son* bullshit, Becker! Did you think to look at that bullet hole in Sweets' head? You should have! There's no fresh blood, only GSR and stippling from one close-up shot to a dead, frozen body. Someone dragged Sweets up here and shot him to make it look like he'd been murdered, but that someone was not Tate Higgins. So who did it, Becker? Who's still out there while you and your buddy are ready to lynch Tate?"

Sam stilled. "Shit. If Tate's not behind this—"

"Zaroyin is," Ky finished the thought. "I'll wait for Tate, but you and Tucker get Eden out of here. Go now before anything else happens."

"No." Eden glared at Ky. She was the number-one priority, and she got that, but Tate was no traitor and Eden Stark was no coward. She squared her shoulders. She meant to stay.

"Damn it to hell, Winchester. You *both* need to leave. Let me and Tucker track down Tate while you get Eden to safety. You have my word. We won't kill him."

Ky growled, his gaze on Eden. "If leaving Tate is the only way to save you, I have no choice. But I swear to God, Becker, Tate will put you and Chase down if you're not square with him. If he doesn't, I will."

Sam nodded. "Copy that. You two take off. We'll get to the bottom of this. There is one thing I've got to ask before you leave, though." He dipped his head in her direction, the way polite men did to a lady. "Sorry, Eden, but you need to step outside with Tucker for five minutes so I can make sure your boyfriend's not wired."

"Excuse me?" She could've rung Sam's neck. "Why would he be wired? He's not FBI and—"

"It's okay." Ky calmed her with just two words. "I'd be wondering the same thing if I was him. Go ahead. Join Chase. This won't take long."

"No," she argued. "There's no way you're wired. I would've seen. I mean my second sight would've seen if you were wired, too."

"That second sight of yours hasn't been very reliable lately, has it?" He winked. "Go on. Give me five. I'll be right out. Then we leave."

Eden shot Sam a dirty look, disgusted for the part he played in this—*this,* whatever it was. How dare he challenge Ky Winchester's and Tate Higgins' integrity? Who did he think he was? After all they'd done to protect her? Reluctantly, she obeyed. "You've got five minutes."

"Knock first," Sam muttered. "You know, to make sure your boyfriend's got his pants on."

Eden tossed the flap aside and climbed out of the tent. Tucker stood there on guard, his rifle snug against his chest. A wind had picked up again, kicking up snow and hitting her in the face. She stuffed her hair back into its fur cap and shivered into the weather. "No Tate yet?"

"No Zaroyin, either," he murmured, his eyes sharp on the tent, "but someone is out there. Step into the shadow with me. I can keep watch from there." Cupping her elbow, he drew her to the far side of the fire pit. "You think we're dirty dogs, don't you?"

"No, Tucker, I think this whole mess is insane. Cybernetic drones? GPS locators implanted into human beings, and now someone shoots my dead pilot to make it look like he wasn't already dead? Why?" Even she could hear the hint of hysteria creeping into her voice.

"So riddle me this." Tucker turned on the charm, his gaze still fastened to the tent. "How do you and I know that Sam, or Ky for that matter, aren't wiring each other up right now? How do we know they aren't working with Zaroyin? Your psychic skillset isn't working for shit. We can't see what they're doing, and they can't see us. Who can you trust, Eden?"

Who indeed. Truth was, she didn't know what was going on with Sam and Ky. How could she? Her second sight had been spotty at best since the crash. Maybe before. She only knew that, except for his added bulk, Ky Winchester was essentially the same man she remembered from Afghanistan. Kind to his core. Too sympathetic for his own good.

As much as he'd tried to fight it, her link with him had grown stronger. Mental, physical, or spiritual, it didn't matter. Their connection had been forged in the fires of unspeakable misery. It was built on trust and loyalty that most married couples only dreamed of.

She turned to meet Tucker's steady gaze, never more sure of this one thing. "You're right. I can't see what Ky's doing right now, but this is what I know, Agent Chase."

He stiffened at the formal title, an invisible barrier sprung up between them.

"I love Ky Winchester, and he loves me," Eden declared bravely, "and I don't need second sight to know the truth. I never filed what happened two and a half years ago on any report, so you don't know what I know. Let's just say that Ky and I went through heck together. Me? I had the privilege of standing at his side during the hardest time in his life, and what was undoubtedly one of the bleakest in mine. I couldn't physically help him, and it gutted me, but I was right where I was meant to be."

She drew in a calming breath of icy-cold confidence. "You see, it wasn't me two and a half years ago. It was him. He reached out to me from Afghanistan, not the other way around. I don't know how this crazy psychic gift works, but I do know that when his spirit searched the universe for someone to strengthen him, he chose me. He did the hard work. He wanted to live, Tucker. I only stood by him during his hours of greatest need."

Tucker's eyes softened. "I didn't mean to—"

"No, you have every right to ask. You're FBI and you're a real agent. That's what you guys do. You interrogate. You make crazy assumptions and you bully people, but understand this. I won't be bullied where Ky is concerned. There's no way to quantify what he and I have. Pull us apart or bury us alive on two different continents. Send us to opposite ends of the Earth never to see each other again. It doesn't matter what you do to us or where we go, I will always find a way back to him, and he will always find me. That man in the tent over there?" She nodded at the wind-whipped tent flap slapping up and down against the pale-blue nylon fabric. "He doesn't just own my heart. He *is* my heart."

"You sound like Melissa," Tucker said quietly.

"Melissa?"

"Yeah. Melissa McCormack. I met her on that op in Northern California. Thought I stood a chance. Thought I could show her what it's like to have a real man in her life.

She's been through so much. Lost her young husband to war injuries, only she can't seem to let him go. Doesn't matter what I do or say, she's still in love with Brady McCormack, and me? I'm still the guy she doesn't see."

Eden drew in a deep breath. Tucker was all male—all brawn and too much testosterone. The kind of guy who never planned to get in touch with his feminine side because, well, he might not have one. Other than the flaming red Challenger he drove like a maniac to work, she hadn't known much about his personal life until now. "It sounds to me like she already had a real man in her life, Tucker. Maybe you need to acknowledge the love she had for her husband instead of trying to replace him."

Tucker growled. "How the hell do I do that? The kid was a goddamned war hero. Shit, Stewart's the jarhead who saved his life. Doesn't it figure? I'm the asshole who can't do anything right, and I'm stuck between two gods who can't do anything wrong."

She scrunched her shoulders. "I don't know, Tuck, but it sounds like you care a lot about Melissa."

He dipped his head. "I do. She's the real deal. Just wish she'd see me once in a while. Wish she'd stop going to the son-of-a-bitchin' cemetery every damned day. Hell, she talks to the honor guards at Arlington more than me."

Eden hadn't a clue how to solve Tucker's problem, but she tried anyway. "Then don't ignore what Brady meant to Melissa. Listen to her when she talks about him. Heck, ask questions. Honor his life. Like it or not, he's still a part of her. You might as well acknowledge her feelings. She needs that validation. She needs to know that you see her, too. All of her."

Tucker grunted. "*If* I have a life with her. Right now, she's..." He snapped his mouth shut as if he'd said too much. "Never mind, Stark. I'll work it out."

Eden couldn't help herself. She reached for the wrist of the man so obviously in pain. "I'm sorry. I'm—"

The second she touched him, the vision snapped over her. A platinum blonde woman with too much makeup. Red, red lipstick. Humongous boobs and ample cleavage. Skinny waist. Dark, dark eyes. Definitely not Melissa. This woman's name was Nicole, and she hated Tucker. Vicious words spoken in heated anger. The red sting of five fingers on Tucker's scruffy cheek. His hands clenched tight into knotted fists. A wall of restraint on his part. A wave of ice-cold disgust on hers. Between them stood a frail little boy with Tucker's deep blue eyes and a violin in his shaking hand. The saddest word pierced Eden's second sight with a shrill, "Daddy!"

She dropped to her hands and knees in the snow, her strength sapped. Darn. Each vision took more out of her, this one in particular. She'd not only seen this time, but she'd felt the abysmal longing in this man's heart for the son lost to him.

Tucker dropped to her side, his rifle slung over his shoulder, his hand in the center of her back. "What the hell happened?"

So that was it. She lifted her head to meet his worried gaze. "You've lost custody of your son, haven't you? Your ex-wife won't let you see him, will she?"

His brows narrowed. A shadow of sadness clouded his angry blues. "No, I... She left and I... damn it. You know everything, don't you? I can't lie to you, can I?"

Eden shook her head as he lifted her to her feet and pulled her under his arm. "Not everything, Tucker—just that your heart's wrecked over the loss of your son. That you believe Nicole did it to hurt you. That you love him so much it's killing you. What'd she do? Move out of state with him?"

"Shit. The bitch took my little guy to Vietnam on business. Never came back."

"Let me guess. Vietnam has no extradition treaty with the United States?"

Tucker nodded glumly. "That and her boyfriend owns a string of textile factories there, but I still deposit a child-support check to her bank account every month. I'm trying to take care of him as best I can. I know she's spending it. God…" He sucked in a deep breath. "I'd give her everything I owned if it made a lick of difference. I just want to see my kid."

"What's his name?"

"She calls him Devlin. I call him Deuce."

Eden sobered. "You ought to hire Alex. He'd get Deuce back."

"Don't think I haven't thought about it."

"Suck up your pride, Tucker. Do it."

He eased her away to look down into her eyes. "Stop looking through me, Eden. Knock it off. I'll get my kid back in my own way and in my own time."

"Good. I'd like to meet Devlin," was all she said, but she had to smile. It didn't take a psychic to see through all that bluster, to know that this tough guy planned to contact Alex Stewart the second he got back to the States.

"You satisfied now?" Ky asked as he stepped back into his TEAMwear trousers and pulled them up over his cold ass hiding his scars as quickly as he could.

"Sorry, son. I had to be sure. Let's get out of here."

"Not so fast. It's your turn. Take 'em off."

"Excuse me?" Becker bristled. "I don't think that's necessary."

"Why not? You don't think I've got suspicions about you and Chase?"

Becker's lips turned into an upside-down smile. "Guess you're right. You already know I'm not wearing a wire. How about I just let you check my scalp for that spider-thing? That way I don't have to undress and freeze my—"

"How about you drop your pants and let me be the judge of whether you're wearing a wire or not? For all you know, someone could've taped one up the crack of your ass. You could be sending signals off the top of your bushy head and not know it. Now drop 'em."

Becker groused and grumbled, but undressed as quickly as Ky had. Neither man appreciated seeing the other's naked body, so visual inspections were fast and brief. Before Ky had himself tucked back into his jacket, Becker was pulling his pants up and his layers of shirts down.

"Crap, it's freezing," he muttered, fumbling with the snaps on his pants. "So how'd you and Eden meet? You work an op together?"

Ky shook his head, "Not exactly." Becker didn't fool Ky. He was trolling for info.

"College? Neighbors?"

"What's it matter? Let's move out."

Becker shrugged into his heavy fur-lined jacket. "I don't guess it does. Just seems the more I know about a guy, the easier he is to trust."

Talking about *those days* never ended well. Ky gulped, but supplied the missing cipher. "She came to me during a particularly bad time in Afghanistan."

"Torture?" Becker asked quietly, his hand warm and steady on Ky's shoulder. "That's why the scars. I'm sorry, son. How long? Where?"

"Five days. Just outside Kabul." *Hell, everywhere. My back. My face. Down—there.*

"Ahh. Our little psychic wonder picked up a signal from you, didn't she? What'd she do? Make one of your wardens drop dead so you could escape?"

Ky shook his head. "No. She's not like that. She just... she just stayed with me until the end. There was no way I could've escaped, not after they..." He swallowed hard, the damned tent suddenly stuffy as hell. "And then Lee Hart showed up and—"

"The same Lee Hart who works for Alex? No shit?"

"Yeah. He was stuck inside one of Nizari's cells, too. She sent him some kind of mental message. That's, umm, all." Ky blew out a deep breath, needing this confession to end.

Becker's grip tightened. "No wonder Stewart relies on you like he does. I'm damned proud to know you, son."

"Why do you keep calling me that?" Ky had to know. "I've got a good father. I don't need another." Not that Ky considered Becker father material.

"You're right," Becker said, "but I'm the oldest agent on this screwed-up op, and it's my job to make sure the rest of you make it home in one piece. Guess it's an old habit I picked up on Team Three. I'll knock it off. Let's get the hell out of here."

The wind set to howling and rattling the pine boughs over the tent. Ky slung his gear bag and his rifle over one shoulder, intent on getting Eden to safety. He slid his goggles over his head. One last time, he reached out to Tate. "Comm check. Testing. One. Two. Three."

"Hang on. I'll save you," Tate muttered in his earpiece.

"Say again?" Ky requested, not sure what that last communication meant.

Damned if a knife blade didn't pierce the far side of the tent. Just as fast, a big gloved hand reached in and jerked Ky off his feet and into the storm. He struggled, punching the arm that held him even as he slid downhill. Snow covered his face, the same hand closed over his mouth.

"Shut up," Tate hissed in his ear. "They're here, Ky. Zaroyin's men. Lots of them."

"Eden," Ky growled. "Where's Eden? Hell, where are Becker and Chase?"

Tate jerked Ky's face into his. God, the man had eyebrows from hell. "I don't know. I'm just glad you're the one I grabbed. Now shut up. Zaroyin's men are everywhere." He shoved Ky into the snow-well drifted around a big tree trunk. "It took me an hour to get back here without being seen."

Lanterns flashed. Several men tramped through the snow alongside their hiding place.

"How many?" Ky asked.

"Shit. I don't know. Maybe fifty."

"I have to get to her. Becker and Chase, too. If it is Zaroyin's—"

"Trust me. It's them." The big guy turned his back on Ky as if he'd never been missing. Like Ky still trusted him.

Ky wasn't so sure. "Tate. What have you done?"

Tate leaned onto one side and faced Ky. "What else? I ditched those GPS locators we took off your girlfriend and those first two guys. It was a mistake keeping them as long as we did."

A bright light flashed uphill, illuminating the tent. It glowed with the exception of the two shadows struggling inside. The bigger guy got in a good punch. The other man flew backward while the big guy dived out the same slit Tate had pulled Ky through.

"Becker," Ky called.

"Shut up!" Tate snapped. "You're going to get us killed." But it *was* Becker, and Tate *did* help pull the FBI agent under the same tree and into the shadow of the tree well.

Men ran through the camp that had once been a safe haven from the storm. The beam of the lantern in the tent flashed this way and that. Some guy bellowed, "Find them!"

"Holy shit," Becker hissed, his hair a mess, his nose bloodied, and his eyes wide. "Where have you been, Higgins?"

"Out," Tate grunted, an oddly comforting sound amongst the chaos.

"I have to get to Eden," Ky growled, ready to go back into the storm. "Get out of my—"

"She's gone," Tate shot back at him, his hand clamped on Ky's wrist. "Trust me. Chase has her. She was fighting him plenty, but he got her out of there in time. We're the ones you need to worry about."

Some idiot back at camp lit the pine-covered tent on fire. Black smoke billowed up from the short burst of bright orange flames.

"Shit. My gear was in there," Becker hissed.

A sickening sensation slithered up the back of Ky's neck. They had another problem.

"Where are the Omni 9000s, Tate?"

Chapter Twenty

Eden would've screamed when all those storm troopers charged into camp if Tucker hadn't clamped his big paw over her mouth and dragged her into the shadows. He kept retreating and dragging. She kept stumbling to keep up with him. Still he wouldn't release her, not until she heard rifle-fire through the trees. Not until she saw the snow-laden sky in the east glow orange. By then, the deep, dark forest lay between Eden and Ky. And her pounding heart.

Tucker dropped his hand from her mouth. "Don't scream, and for God's sake, don't call out for Ky."

She turned on her FBI buddy, elbows flying and ready to fight. "What the heck are you doing? We have to go back. We can't just leave them."

"It's too late. Zaroyin's men are already there. A little warning would've been nice, Eden. I thought you were good at that kind of psychic stuff?"

"I was. I am. I mean..." She couldn't take her eyes off the glow to the east. That tent and Ky were her safe places. Pressing her fingertips to her temples, she couldn't sense him. No blue aura. No black smudges, either. Nothing. Even the link with Ky felt—off. Muffled. Her heart kicked up a notch. Was he dead? "Ever since the crash, my sight hasn't been reliable. I have to go back."

Tucker grabbed her wrist and pulled her in the opposite direction, his rifle ready in his fist. "No way. Sam will take care of Ky. We keep moving."

She jerked out of his grasp and stabbed one finger eastward. "How can you say that? How can you just walk off and leave..."? It all came back to her. Tucker's question. *Who can you trust, Eden?* Sure as heck not him.

"What going on here, Chase? You and Sam show up out of nowhere. Suddenly, Tate Higgins is one of your suspects, and Sam's making Ky prove he's not wired. The body Tate hung up in the trees is back on the ground." She stomped one booted foot. "I am so dumb. You set this up, you and Sam, didn't you? You wanted to get me away from Ky and—"

"For Christ's sake, Eden, knock it off. Think about what you're saying. Why would Sam and I lie to you? When did we have time to stage what you just saw back there?"

"You tell me. I was out cold in the tent."

"We didn't lie. Higgins is the one in league with Zaroyin, not us. He's the one cashing in on this cybernetic nightmare. Trust me. That much I do know. Unless..." He glanced sharply over his shoulder to the diminishing glow in the east.

"Unless what?" She wanted to know.

He blew out a ragged breath of misty gray vapor. "First, you didn't see Sam or me, then you didn't see Zaroyin or his army of men. Why not? What's different between the drones and everyone else?"

Eden stared into the face of the man she thought she knew. Stripped of her second sight, she had no choice but to trust Tucker Chase. "I honestly don't know, but you're right. I've had no trouble seeing any of Zaroyin's drones."

He kept his eyes to the east. "What made them stand out? You said you couldn't detect Sam or me before we arrived, either. How the hell does your second sight work, anyway?"

"You know as well as I do that no one knows precisely what triggers it. Sometimes it's a personal belonging, but not always. There's no one-size-fits-all rule to being a psychic, and no, I didn't see Tate either. I did see Ky, but I didn't know it was him when I—"

"Wait. You saw Ky?"

She nodded quickly. "Yes, but not the same way I saw the drones. Ky's different. The drones were like clumps of ash with a faint red glow beating inside. Ky's always blue when I see him. Crystal blue. I can usually make out his entire, umm, body." And his caramel-colored eyes. That sexy smile.

Tucker stared at her like she had two heads. "*When* you see him? How often have you been *seeing* him?"

Eden stared past Tucker, recalling that first time. "I already told you. The first time he was a prisoner of war in—"

"Yeah, but what's with the crystal blue shit?"

"It's his aura. Every person emits one. It's your energy, that's all."

"What's blue mean, that he's some kind of superman? A hero?"

"No, Tuck." She gentled her tone. "Blue usually means compassion. It's Ky's greatest strength and his worst weakness. Sometimes it gets him into trouble."

Tucker's brow spiked. "What's my color?"

Ah, Tuck. It was so like him to need to compete over something as harmless as personal auras. Eden allowed a smile to tug at the corner of her mouth. "Are you serious? You really want to know if yours is bigger and better? Snap, Tucker. It's like comparing one person's soul to another's."

"So? Are you gonna tell me or not?"

Eden blew out a measured breath between her pursed lips and dutifully acquiesced. "It's no big deal. Most of the time your aura is on the darker shade of blue, just like Ky's. There, are you happy?"

"*Most* of the time? What's that mean, that I'm more compassionate?" The big jock sounded hopeful.

"Not necessarily. I've seen your aura go so dark its nearly black," she admitted, needing to get off the topic he obviously couldn't grasp, not with his male ego sucking up center stage like it was. "Are you thinking these new guys may not be Zaroyin's drones?"

"Maybe. You didn't see Sam or me coming at you, did you? The guys with Zaroyin, neither. Yet you did see Ky when he was in prison halfway around the world, and you saw all of Zaroyin's drones. Can you only sense people in pain? Is that maybe how your second sight works—it hones in on physical torment?"

She gulped, not sure of anything at the moment. Psychic powers were an unreliable science at best. He could be onto something. Tucker kept staring east. She kept going over the facts she thought she knew while the slimy tendrils of self-doubt invaded her mind. He actually made sense. Her gift did tend to zero in on people undergoing severe stress. Abducted children. Hostages. A man in the throes of torture. Men who didn't want to be drones...

Drones...

The light dawned. "Tucker! That's why I keep passing out. My second sight isn't impaired. It's overwhelmed. Think about it. Every sanctioned operation I've been on only dealt with one victim, but now, I'm bombarded with the feedback from all those drones..." She blinked at the horrible implication. "Tuck, it's Zaroyin's implant—that's what's reaching out to me. That's why I keep fainting. Oh, my God, he's created a way for all those poor men to—"

"So you're saying that crazy doctor's spider thing is what links you to the drones?"

"No. Maybe." She shook her head. "I don't really know the precise mechanics of how it works yet, but something he's done to the drones is killing my second sight. It's too much, kind of like a lightning strike blowing a fuse. His plan won't work, Tuck. If he wants one psychic to be his master controller, he's got it all wrong. I'm a level ten, but I can't handle the surge of all those conflicted emotions pouring into me."

Tucker still stared east, half listening. "Those guys hit us fast and hard. They weren't carrying the same rifles as the other drones. No Omni 9000s. Did you see a single smart gun?" he asked, not waiting for an answer. "Yeah. Me, neither. I didn't see any high-tech weaponry come to think of it, not on these new guys. Only the old—"

She caught the logic in his drift. "Twelve-gauge shotguns. Short pumps and—"

He turned to face her, his tone clipped and confident. "Those were Remington sniper rifles, Eden. Standard FBI-issue. Shotguns, too. Shit. You didn't see these guys coming because they aren't Zaroyin's drones. They're black operators. They're—"

"Us-s-s..." she hissed. "They're FBI, Tucker, the real FBI. How can they be here in Canada? Who's really behind this? Do you know?"

He nodded, his gaze still distant. "But why would he run over the top of us like this? Why not make contact and advise us that he was in transit? Why come in with guns blazing?" His breath poured out in a plume of heated vapor. "Shit, Eden. This smacks of Zaroyin, but it's not. I'm almost certain it's—"

SNAP! Eden's world exploded in a kaleidoscope of splintering pain, razor-sharp images, and the coppery taste of blood. His blood. Not Tucker's. That other guy's. He was back. The guy with black holes for eyes, with rivulets of bloody tears dripping out of those holes.

Black eyes.

Her ribs clenched tight against the pain. Her throat closed tighter, as if he'd reached across space and time and squeezed her trachea with all five fingers. The sound of her larynx cracking filled her head. The simple act of drawing air into her lungs hurt. She dropped to her knees, afraid to breathe. Afraid to move.

But he wasn't trying to kill her. His grasp was the desperate, reflexive act of a drowning man, fighting to hold on to anything that would keep him afloat. Panicked. Frenzied. His mind clenched hers tighter. She raked a hand under her cap and through her hair, spilling the cold over her neck, needing him to release his death grip.

Let me go, she ordered mentally. *You're killing me!*

A masculine vibration of disbelief rippled through her mind. *Eden? Eden Stark? You're... you're real?*

Shadows closed in. Blackness danced everywhere. "Talk to me, darlin'," Tucker pleaded from somewhere far away. "God, not you, too." His voice faded into twilight.

She couldn't answer. Could barely catch... one. Cold. Breath. Just fell...

Chapter Twenty-One

Tate never got the chance to say where the high-tech rifles were—not with Zaroyin's men too close for comfort. Ky backed away from the camp, sliding on his belly, descending into the foggy shadow with Tate and Becker alongside him.

Searchlights at the crest of the hill probed the uneven landscape in all directions, but in the midst of their impressive takeover, Zaroyin's army had created confusion. They had to be Feds. They didn't smell of sweat and fatigue like the drones had, and these guys moved with clipped precision. All in uniforms, jackets, helmets, and tactical gear. Muted gray and winter cammies. Heavy-footed and heavier-handed. Maybe fifty. Maybe more.

Ky kept his focus on the short guy nearest the flattened tent. The one barking with a definite Eastern Bloc accent at the broad-shouldered, thick-necked Pit Bull to his right. "Then where are they, McCluskey? You said they were all here."

The Pit Bull, McCluskey, obviously ex-military, obviously a dick, said, "Gone, sir. We nearly apprehended Special Agent Becker, but he—"

"You lost him?" Short Stuff shrieked.

Ky strained to pinpoint the man's country of origin. Not Russian. Czechoslovakian, maybe? Polish?

"Where's Zaroyin from?" he asked Becker out of the corner of his mouth, keeping his eye on Short Stuff. "What country?"

"He's Armenian, but he's from Chechnya. You're looking at him."

So you're him... Ky's fingers clenched with what he wanted to do with this arrogant doctor.

"He won't get far," McCluskey maintained. "We'll track him, sir. Don't worry. Shouldn't take long."

"He doesn't want Becker, you fool. He wants Stark and so do I," Zaroyin snarled. "You know what this woman means to his plans for the future. You know what she means to me."

That over-the-top rant perked Ky's ears up. *This woman? Eden? What future?*

"Let's go," Tate hissed, tugging Ky's boot.

"Not yet."

McCluskey rolled one shoulder, like he had an extreme pain in his neck. "She can't have gotten far. She's just a female, sir. I'll put everyone on it. We'll get her."

"Do," Zaroyin spat, "and tell your men not to believe everything they see. She's good. Shoot her if you have to, but don't kill her."

"Yes, sir." McCluskey didn't salute, but he might as well have. He bobbed his head plenty before he pivoted and snapped at the unfortunate lackey behind him. "Gather the men. Now!"

Ky'd heard enough. He stopped listening to the drama uphill and rolled alongside Tate. They were at the edge of the tree line, but he'd never left a guy behind, much less a woman. He wouldn't start now. He'd have to cross the clearing, and it might put him in harm's way, but he meant to find her. Pushing up off the ground, he hunkered low and headed west.

"No, Ky. We go east," Becker ordered, already on his feet and slapping the snow off his jacket and pants. "If we're lucky—"

"Go where you want," Ky growled without turning around, keeping out of the reach of those spotlights.

"Trust me. Tucker will keep her safe."

Ky whirled on Becker. "Then head east. Tate and I are going west!"

Becker groused. "You trust him more than me?"

Tate caught the jibe. "Why wouldn't he?"

"Because he thinks you're working with Zaroyin," Ky spat. The truth needed telling. "He doesn't believe you secured the six drones in the trees, either."

Becker squared his shoulders, facing Tate. "Admit it. You've been on the take for months. I've got video proof."

"Like hell you do." A shaggy line of thunderclouds descended over Tate's eyes.

"One-point-five ring a bell, Higgins? That's what's in your bank account," Becker pressed, "and I'm damned sure Stewart doesn't pay you that well. Want to explain where you stashed those six Omni 9000s from the guys Tucker and I killed while you're at it? You didn't leave them rusting in the snow, did you?"

Lightning crackled between Becker and Tate, but the big guy only jerked his head toward the trees behind him. "Go see for yourself."

Becker's jaw stuck out. "By hell, I will. You coming?" he barked at Ky. "Let's get this out in the open, once and for all. Then you can decide who to believe, him or me."

Ky stomped after him, wanting this argument over so he could go after Eden. "Make it quick."

Tate's upper lip lifted. "You don't believe me, either?"

"Course I do." Ky set that record straight. He might have wondered there for a second. Not anymore. "You heard me order you to head out with me, didn't you? Now move it. Prove you're square to this asshole, so we can get back to work, damn it."

A snort through both nostrils clouded Tate's already dark expression with a double shot of frosty attitude. He turned his back on Ky and trudged into the cover of pine trees. Zaroyin's searchlight still pierced the foggy landscape, but the big guy seemed to know his way around without getting lit up or shot at.

Ky followed his buddy, needing this evidentiary hearing to be short and sweet. He'd always trusted Tate with his life, not Becker and Tucker.

They hadn't gone far when Becker pulled his pistol and aimed it at Tate's back. "Stop right there, Higgins. Slow and steady. Let me see your hands. Both of them. I'll take it from here."

Tate raised his hands, but Ky'd had enough. He leveled his rifle at Becker. "Don't even think about it, Becker. He's clean. I goddamned know it."

Tate cast a dark glance over his shoulder, catching Ky's eye before he raked Becker. "You'd shoot me in the back?"

"I would if I had to," Becker hissed, his weapon aimed skyward and both hands raised.

Tate pointed up without taking another step. There in the trees, right where he'd said they were, in typical Tate Higgins' style, hung six male bodies, their heads down and their arms bound to their sides.

Ky sucked in a deep breath of relief and holstered his piece. "There. Do you believe him now?"

"What the hell is going on? And the guns, Higgins?" Becker asked. "Where are they? You didn't leave them behind, did you?"

Tate growled something unintelligible back at Becker, but stalked to another bundle strung between two other trees. Deftly, he jerked the line he'd tied off at shoulder level on the nearest pine, and the bundle dropped.

If it had been any other night, Ky would've laughed at the dumbfounded look on Becker's face when Tate peeled open the cavernous stomach cavity of the butchered moose. There lay all six Omni 9000s and their powerful, four-barrel scopes. Wrapped in plastic. Safe. Protected. Where no one in their right mind would've looked for them.

But not tonight. "Guys, we don't have time for this. Didn't you hear Zaroyin? He gave orders for his men to shoot Eden, to injure her if they have to. Let's go."

Becker blew out a deep breath, his hand outstretched to Tate. "I'm sorry. Ky was right. I had no business accusing you. But the money and the video? How do you explain them? I saw you shake the doctor's hand myself. I know it was you."

Tate ignored Becker's offer of reconciliation. A sneer lifted at one corner of his lip. "What are you talking about?"

Becker retrieved his hand and ran it over his thick hair. "Shit. If you're right... If this is a set-up..." He let the words hang.

"Someone's toying with us," Ky said. "Someone deliberately planted that evidence against Tate, then dragged

Sweets body out in the open. He wants us to fight each other. We're nothing but game pieces on his chess board, and the bastard's winning."

"That's not as farfetched as you might think," Becker mulled. "I've known Eden to do some mighty strange things in order to save lives. Could be Zaroyin's got a psychic on his side who's a helluva lot stronger than she is."

Ky nodded. The drift of Vicks. A few carefully spoken words in a dying man's ear. Positive reinforcement. Yeah. Eden was good at her job. His gut pitched at the distress she had to be in. "Or Zaroyin knew Director Strong would contact Alex to bring Eden home. Maybe he's got an informant inside the Bureau. Maybe inside The TEAM." Anything seemed possible.

"But how would Zaroyin have known when he planted the evidence against me that Alex would assign me to this mission?" Tate cast an evil eye at Becker. "And those guys in our camp are Feds. I smelled the drones a mile away. They stank to high heaven, but not these guys. Why the hell are they after us?"

"And why drag Charlie Sweets' dead body up here and plant it where we'd find it?" Becker asked.

Ky shook his head. "No. Stop. We're thinking about this all wrong. Shit. It's not about the evidence, guys—at least, not this evidence. All this bullshit proves is someone's trying to pit us against each other. Stop with the questions for a second. Let me think."

"What?" both Tate and Becker asked at the same time.

Ky stilled as their real dilemma hit home. "These are all misdirects manufactured to throw us off the track. God, why didn't I see this before? Remember what Bick said when we touched down in Spain?"

Tate stepped closer. "Yeah, I remember. He said he'd finally found what he wanted. He kept yammering that he'd found heaven. Dumbass was talking out of his butt."

"Only he didn't say what that heaven was, did he?"

Tate shook his head, his face stoically expressionless. "Could've been diamonds."

Ky stilled as he sorted through what had happened during the last forty-eight hours and back to Morocco. A helo had got him out of that country and a helo had dropped him into Canada. His client then was an errant and supposedly cheating husband. His client now, the purest woman Ky had ever met, a psychic with little worldly sophistication, yet filled with an almost motherly need to help others. Somehow, the two were connected. He felt it in his gut.

Ky rolled one shoulder as that creepy ride with Bick in the helo flickered to mind. The overweight bastard was suave down to his expensive, croc-skinned loafers. Dressed to kill. His hair was slicked back over a wide, sweaty forehead. The man was barely breathing hard after all the ruckus he'd caused, but not so smart that he didn't need his dumbass saved when his plans went awry. Or was he? Was there ever really a jilted husband in the mix? What intelligent woman in her right mind would want a slimy, two-timing blimp of a man like Bick? And there at the end of the trip, he kept tapping his greasy fingers on his knee, a smarmy smile on his face and jabbering about, *'Heaven. I'm in heaven...'*

Then there was Eden. What the hell connected the two?

The scent of her favorite mentholated rub drifted into Ky's thoughts like a ghostly finger, more vapor than substance.

More tease than solid clue. He pulled the coolness of it in and let it work its soothing magic. Bick had something to do with Eden. She was the connection. Hadn't she said she'd been in Morocco once, too? When? Suddenly, Ky wanted to know exactly why Bick had been there. He slid his goggles over his head and ordered TEAMshield to, "Call home."

"Stewart."

"Boss? Do you remember that op in Morocco?" Dumb question. Alex had a photographic memory and thought everyone else did, too. Ky activated the speaker to his goggles so Tate and Becker could listen in. "Why was Bick really there? Why did Director Strong want him back on U.S. soil? Did it have anything to do with blood diamonds out of Sierra Leone?"

Alex stalled. "I'm not sure Zachary wants me to divulge that intel, Ky. Why? What's happened?"

"Call him, Boss. Get clearance. I need to know if Eden Stark was in Morocco the same time Bick was."

Dead silence.

Ky blinked. Alex already knew the answer. He just didn't want to say it.

"She was, wasn't she? That's why Strong wanted Bick out of Morocco. He might have been playing around with some other woman, but that was just his fallback cover story, wasn't it? Bick was really after Eden, wasn't he? He orchestrated her being there, didn't he?" *Shit!* Ky didn't need Alex to concur or deny, but he begged to hear the words anyway. "Talk to me, Boss. Tell me I'm wrong. Shit, tell me I'm the dumbest jock on the planet and to get back to work." *Please tell me I'm wrong.*

A growl rumbled deep inside Ky's ear. "You're right. The Moroccan president requested a meeting with the elite FBI asset. Zachary needed to find out how that intel had slipped, how the president of Morocco heard about her and from whom. None of us knew she was being used as bait until we got word Bick was there, too."

Ky held his breath.

"You have to understand. Bick's an oddball. His pet project on the hill has always been paranormal research and psychic abilities. Yes, he's deep into the diamond trade in Sierra Leone, but that's just the tip of the iceberg, according to Zachary. He needed Bick stateside because Bick had already kidnapped another psychic. A young man. One Isaiah—"

"Isaiah Zaroyin," Ky hissed.

"Yes. Zaroyin's son is a level-ten psychic like Eden," Alex said. "Zachary claims he's what the experts call a precognitor."

"What exactly is a level ten? That's what that bastard who ran us out of our camp mentioned."

Alex grunted. "Yeah, I found it tough to swallow, too. In Zaroyin's son's case, he can read people's thoughts well enough to project their possible futures, or to influence them to change it if he wants a specific event to occur. He can alter the way they think, maybe even their decisions. Like an automobile accident that's really no accident because they made a wrong turn."

"Or cause a physically fit pilot to suddenly die of a heart attack at the stick?"

"I don't know if he could cause a heart attack, but in theory, yes, it's doable. You're right. The cheating scandal was Bick's cover. When he knew he'd been made, that Zachary was onto him, the bastard screamed 'save me' to the President, and

Zachary asked me to intervene. He needed you guys to retrieve Bick while his men went after Zaroyin's kid. That's why—"

"Why's Bick want Eden?"

Another stretch of dead air before Alex muttered, "Eden's number two on Bick's hit list."

"What hit list?"

Dead silence.

Shit. Shit. Shit! Ky squeezed his eyes at the danger Eden had been in. "What son-of-a-bitchin' list, Boss?"

"It's a shortlist of mates for Isaiah."

"Mates?" Ky damned near shrieked. "My Eden? A mate for that asshole's son?"

Both Tate and Becker voiced deep groans. They sounded like two bears at his admission, but Ky didn't care that his emotions had leapt off his lips like they did. *Yes. My Eden, damn it. Get used to it.*

"Possibly," Alex hedged. "Isaiah's number one on the list. Zachary thinks it's Bick's paranormal wet dream to have an untouchable army."

"To do what? Read minds?" It all made sense now. "That's why the patch on her leg. He's drugging her, isn't he? He's trying to control everyone she's come in contact with. He's controlling her body with all those implants, too. Was Hartigen with her in Morocco?" Why that question popped into Ky's head, he had no idea.

"Yes. So was Strong."

"Where's Isaiah? Tell me the FBI has him in protective custody."

Alex huffed out a deep sigh. "Zachary's men never found him. To this day, we don't know where Bick's keeping him."

"Shit, boss. I'll bet you ten to one he was never in Morocco. Bick just needed Eden out in the open. He orchestrated this whole thing. We're lucky he didn't get her, too." Ky swallowed hard. "Boss, remember what he said?"

"What the hell are you asking?"

"It's in my report, remember? He kept singing that stupid song. *'Heaven. I'm in heaven.'* He meant Eden, Boss. He's wanted her for a long time."

"Son-of-a-bitch. Where is she?"

Lying never worked with Alex. Ky looked to the gathering dark clouds in the west and said the only thing he could, "I don't know. Zaroyin's men overran our camp. Tate's with me, but Eden's with Tucker Chase."

"She's what?" Alex roared. "Goddamn it, I told you to keep her—"

"And I will!" Ky shot back across the miles. Now was not the time for one of Alex's famous butt-chewings. "Tate and I are on her trail. We'll find her."

"How many?" Alex barked.

"Zaroyin's got at least fifty men on-site. I've got Tate and Becker. I don't know where Bick is yet, but he's the only one who could've sent FBI SWAT all the way to Canada and gotten away with it."

"Son-of-a-bitch!" Alex hissed. "Screw the weather. I'm sending more help. Right damned now."

"They can't get to us fast enough," Ky argued.

"No, but they can back up the guys I've already sent. Watch your six, Winchester. Harley is on his way and he's bringing Hell with him."

The connection went dead. Ky turned to face his buddy and Agent Becker. They'd heard every word, but he would brook no argument. "I'm not waiting. I'm going to find Eden. Who's with me?"

Chapter Twenty-Two

Eden groaned at the cobwebs in her mind. Nothing made sense. One side of her felt frozen; the other warm and toasty. A band of steel held her arms to her sides. She shifted restlessly, needing to pee, but these covers were too tight and this chair too hard. Her butt had fallen asleep.

"Stay still," a deep voice rumbled in her ear. "You can't fall. I've got you."

Fall? "Tuck?" she asked weakly, her vision still blurry. "Is that you?"

"Yes, ma'am," he murmured, loosening his grip. "You're safe now. Take your time and catch your breath."

"What happened?" she asked as she took in her surroundings. Nothing but nighttime and pine branches, above, below, and all around. She found herself sitting nearly on Tucker's lap. "Sheesh. Where are we?"

"Up a tree. I had to get you out of sight so here we are. You passed out just as I was about to amaze you with my deductive reasoning skills and tell you who's behind this mess. What the hell happened back there?"

Oh, snap. Yeah. Him. Her heart rate kicked up just thinking about what her second sight had seen. "You were right. Zaroyin's got another psychic. I saw him. Then everything went blank."

"Who is it?"

"I don't know, but he's strong. Maybe stronger than me."

Tucker grunted. He nearly sounded like Tate. "No one's stronger than you, Eden."

"This guy is. He's got eyes the color of coal, and he looks like that guy in the mailroom. You know, the one with the bowl-cut."

"The one that looks like a skinny Moe?"

"Who?"

"The bossy guy on the *Three Stooges*."

Eden drew in a deep breath, hoping the extra oxygen would kick start her brain. "I've never watched the *Three Stooges*. Are they anything like *Dumb and Dumber*?"

"Better," Tucker purred. "Slapstick. You'd love them."

Somehow, Eden doubted that. She detested television as it was. Dumbing down America's entertainment hadn't made it better.

"Only, I had the strongest sensation that he was sad. Mean and sad. Maybe sad because he was mean or forced to be mean or... snap. I don't know."

"As I was saying—"

Mother Nature called again. "Sorry, Tuck. You'll have to wait. I need out of this tree so I can pee."

He chuckled deep in his throat. "Damn, you know how to hurt a guy's ego, don't you? Here. I think we're safe enough. Take my hand. I'll lower you down. There you go."

With his help, she maneuvered to ground level, a good fifteen feet or so below her perch. "How'd you get us both up there anyway? Are you a monkey or something?" she teased.

"Deer hunter. Been in a few deer hides in my time." He jumped to ground level and pointed to a fairly dense thicket to their right. "Those bushes over there ought to work. I'll turn my back. Step on it."

"Ha." She chuckled at his unintentional *faux pas* about stepping on it. "You don't seriously mean that, do you?"

He turned his back on her. "Just take care of business. Hurry up about it. We need to talk."

Eden dispensed with her poor attempt at humor and retreated behind the only available cover to relieve herself. It didn't take long to pee, not as cold and dark as it was. She quickly zipped up her multiple layers and rejoined Tucker. "You can turn around now."

He scrubbed his gloved hands together and faced her. "Now, what was I telling you when you passed out on me? Oh, yes. I think I know who's behind this whole mess. For one thing, those weren't drones back there. They were FBI SWAT."

"I know. We already discussed this. They're carrying FBI gear, remember? Man, Canada's not going to like all of you FBI guys inside their borders." She slapped some warmth back into her arms.

"They're not going to like the war that's coming their way, either."

"So who's behind the FBI takeover if not Zaroyin?"

"Senator Bick. Somehow, he's made an end run around Director Strong and got permission to come after us, and he's using legitimate resources to do it."

"But we're Americans. We haven't done anything wrong."

"So? Those guys back there don't care. They're following orders. Who knows what they've been told?"

"But why would Bick want us?"

"That, my dear, is the real question. You got a phone on you? Mine's dead."

"No," Eden replied. "We left so fast. I don't have anything with me."

He retrieved his cell from his jacket pocket and smacked it into his palm. "It was working a minute ago. Stupid thing."

"Let me see it."

Tucker handed his phone over.

Eden fiddled with it until the screen came to life in brilliant color, complete with the latest iOS technology and a gazillion apps. She sheltered the illumination with her palms in case anyone looked in their direction. "Hmm. Looks like it's working to me."

He peered over her shoulder. "Yeah, right. Don't play games with me. It's dead, damn it. No power."

She frowned and pressed the phone icon, not sure what Tucker thought he saw. She accessed his recently called list and tapped a familiar name and number. "I just called Director Strong. It's ringing."

"No shit? Great!" He grabbed the cell and pressed it to his ear. "Director Strong? Hello? Hello? Damn it, Eden. Don't jerk me around like that. It's not funny. This bullshit's serious."

"Oh, snap, don't hang up on him!" She rescued his phone before he could manhandle it any further and said loud and clear, "Director Strong? Hi. It's me. Agent Stark."

"Eden! Thank God you're safe. What the hell's Tucker Chase doing there?"

"He's here with Sam to—"

"Sam Becker?" Zachary Strong snapped. "What's going on? Why are they there in Canada? I hired Alex to bring you home quietly. He sent two agents. I know he did. They should've been there by now."

"Yes, sir, Mr. Stewart sent Agents Ky Winchester and Tate Higgins, but Zaroyin's men overran our camp. Tucker and I got separated from Ky and Tate, and—"

Suppressed anger radiated all the way from D.C. "Put Chase on."

She pressed the speaker button for Tucker to join in.

"Chase? You there? Mind telling me why you and Becker didn't think to advise me before you went into Canada?"

"Plausible deniability, sir," Tucker replied smartly. "This deal is completely on us. We didn't want you invol—"

"Damn it, I am involved! I've been involved for months! The President will have my head for this unauthorized foray onto foreign soil, not to mention what the Canadian Prime Minister will do when he finds out."

"Not if we can bring Eden safely home."

"Then do it!" Strong snapped. "Shit, Chase. Get her home now. Zaroyin's got international connec—"

"And one of them is Senator Bick," Tucker interrupted. "He's the lynchpin, sir. Look into his dealings in Sierra Leone. Connect the dots."

Silence filled the chasm between Ontario and Virginia.

"Sir? Are you there?" Tucker asked angrily. "Damn it, Eden. Did he just hang up on me?"

"Director Strong?" she asked, not quite as forcefully as her companion.

"Is there anything else *you* think *I* should be doing, Agent Chase?" Strong asked acidly. "Do you seriously think I don't know what's going on in Sierra Leone?"

Eden let Tucker answer that one. He'd started this war with their director. He could finish it. "My apologies, sir, but—"

"But nothing! This is a direct order. Bring Stark home, and do it now. Get her out of Canada and out of Zaroyin's reach. Let me take care of the bastard."

"Yes, sir." Tucker disconnected the call before Eden could get another word in edgewise. "You heard him, Stark. We're going to get Zaroyin or die trying."

Eden froze. "Excuse me? Director Strong didn't say that."

Tucker glared back, his pupils fully dilated, but not focused. He seemed to look right through her. "Bullshit. He wants Zaroyin's head on a platter. You heard him. Move out. We can still apprehend the bastard if we're quick about it."

"What's wrong with you? Director Strong said nothing of the sort."

He snorted a billow of frosty vapor. "Are you questioning my authority?"

"No, but I know what I heard and—" She took a step back from him.

He slapped an angry fist in to his open palm. "I don't have time for this, Stark. Zaroyin's on the move, damn it. Let's go."

"No," she said softly, her hackles lifted at the un-Tucker-like behavior she was witnessing. The guy she knew cared about her safety more than anything else, which was why he continually banged heads with Ky. She clenched her fingers into a fist behind her back. "What did you hear Director Strong say?"

Another snort. "The same as you, shithead. Neutralize Zaroyin with extreme prejudice. Take him out. Kill the bastard. Then his son. Now, move your dumb ass before he gets away. Let's get it done and blow this place while we still can."

Shithead? Me? Oh, snap. Eden sucked in a deep breath. Somehow, Tucker was under Zaroyin's influence. She lifted the back of her hand to her forehead and feigned a dizzy spell. "Ouch," she whispered as if she were in pain. "My head."

"Knock off the drama, asshole. Get your lazy butt in gear and do it now!"

Asshole? More proof Tucker was under someone else's influence. Who was Black Eyes that he could influence a trained FBI agent from long distance?

"I... I can't," she whimpered and dropped to her hands and knees, searching through the newly fallen snow for something solid to defend herself with. A rock. A branch. Anything.

Tucker kicked a boot full of snow into her face. "You don't kid me. I've been around. You're stalling, sailor. If you're cruising for a Section 8, you're barking up the wrong tree!"

The crusted ice crystals he kicked at Eden stung her cheeks and forehead. This guy had totally lost touch with reality. Section 8s were ancient history. Anyone who'd served in the military knew that, especially an ex-Navy SEAL. It proved her theory. Whoever was at the other end of this psychic manipulation did not know military regs. Frantically, Eden raked beneath the snow for a deterrent. Nothing!

He kicked at her, but didn't connect with anything but snow. "I said move!"

Eden rolled to her butt before she made eye contact, her elbows stuck in the snow and her fingers still searching. "Tuck. It's me. Eden. You don't want to hurt me. Zaroyin's filled your mind with lies. It's—"

"Aw, for shit's sake!" He lunged at her and knocked her flat, one hand at her throat, the other tugging the weapon from his holster. "I'm not telling you one more damned time, jerk-off," he growled, his pistol pressed to her temple. "Now you listen and listen good. Man up or so help me, I will end you right the fuck—"

BAM! She swung the thing her fingers had just located beneath the crusty snow with all her might, connecting with the side of his hard head. "Get off me!"

Tucker blinked and stopped his assault, dazed. Not good enough! She hit him again, needing this heavy male off of her hips and stomach so she could breathe, darn him!

His grip loosened. The pistol in his hand lowered to his thigh. Blood trickled down his cheek and dripped along his jawline.

Adrenaline made her do it. She landed another good, hard smack before he shifted off of her and back to his haunches. She scrambled out from under him on her hands and knees, but kept possession of the thing in her hand, whatever it was. Oh. A chunk of ice. A little bloody and a little bit pointed, but hey. It had worked.

Not until she was yards away from him did she glance over her shoulder.

Tucker growled something unintelligible. He hadn't moved, just sat on his butt in the snow with his knees spread wide and a bewildered, vacant look in his eyes. He'd developed a slow but definite list to his right. He tilted. His eyes scrolled to hers. "Eden? How'd you get all the way over there?" he asked hoarsely, right before he face-planted.

Oh snap! Did I kill him? Eden scurried back to his side, shaking from the terrible thing she'd done. This was so bad, smacking another agent. It went against all she knew to be right, but she'd needed to, and now he was hurt, and—

Get a grip, Stark. He's out cold. Not dead.

Tucker groaned, which was a good thing, but he probably couldn't breathe with his face in the snow like it was, so she rolled him to his side and then onto his back. He grunted at the not-so-gentle treatment. Too bad.

Sucking in a deep breath, she smoothed her gloved fingers over his poor, dented head. Three corner-shaped cuts bled profusely. She lifted the chunk of ice for another look. It wasn't even cracked.

"You gave me no choice," she told him in no uncertain terms. "Darn it, Tucker, you asked for it, and buddy, you're lucky I didn't have my Glock, because I would've... because I... oh, snap. I couldn't have shot you, but I would've pistol-whipped you. Why didn't you just shut up and listen? What happened to you?"

Tucker didn't answer because he was out cold, but he breathed evenly, a positive sign.

Now what? She made sure his collar was up so his cheek wasn't resting on ice or snow, then glanced up at the tree branches where he'd hidden her. Nope. Not going to happen. There was no way she could drag him to higher heights. The man was twice her size and a deadweight. So where could she put this big oaf where they'd both be hidden from view while he, umm, healed?

The line of snow-frosted pines at her six beckoned in the night breeze. What choice did she have? Eden dug her fingers into the shoulder pads of Tucker's jacket. She planted her heels, braced her weight backwards, and dug in. Little by little, she slid him into the shelter of the noble trees. Finally situated beneath the low boughs of an enormous pine, she rolled him onto his side in case he started to choke.

The wind kicked up, erasing the ruts of her journey with a dusting of snow. Inside her fragrant hideaway, stillness reigned, broken only by the sound of her hammering heart. What now?

Eden knelt at Tucker's side, scooped up a handful of snow and pressed it against his bleeding head. God, he was a mess. Head wounds bled so much. The snow was already soaked dark red beneath his head. Spattered blood stained what was once his winter-camouflaged jacket. Could things get any worse?

Eden slid her hand out of its glove. With the pad of her thumb, she peeled back his eyelid. It was hard to tell for sure, but the pupil didn't seem to be as black or as dilated as before, just the same dark eyes of one of her favorite agents. Her method of snapping him out of it might have been extreme, but it seemed to have worked. Daylight would reveal his true condition, but for now, she needed to keep him breathing and warm.

"Don't you dare die on my watch, Tuck." She gulped at her audacity and her fear.

Snap, he was a big man, broad-chested, handsome as heck, and now vulnerable with those three dents in his skull. Puffs of frozen vapor huffed out between his parted lips. His thick eyelashes twitched as if he was dreaming. She placed one palm to his sternum and drummed her fingertips, just because.

She was alone again, her one source of protection down for the count. What was a girl to do? Bawl like a baby like she'd done with Ky after he'd cut her open, not once, but twice? Her eyes replied with a blur of tears thinking about him. Not cool. Eden summoned Tuck's salty vernacular instead. Whoever that asshole with the coal-black eyes was, it was darned time for a little tit-for-tat. She was no ordinary FBI analyst. Black Eyes needed the comeuppance and the shiner he deserved for messing with Tucker's mind. And hers!

She lifted Mother Nature's icepack off Tucker's poor bludgeoned noggin and checked the bleeding. It had slowed, thankfully, but he would have scars. Three of them. Right in a row. "I got you good, huh? Frozen water. Who knew, right?" she asked, wishing he would snap out of it, sit up, and just be his usual, rowdy self again.

But no. He wasn't going anywhere, so Eden did what Eden did best. She settled into a comfortable cross-legged position, her butt against Tucker's side so she could monitor his condition while she stretched that contrary psychic muscle of hers to do the one thing only she could do.

Search out Black Eyes. Once and for all.

Chapter Twenty-Three

Ky slipped away from Zaroyin's army with Tate and Sam at his side. Tate had re-secured the Omni 9000s in the moose carcass since they didn't have the software to support them. Like shadows inside more shadows, they clung to the inky shroud beneath the trees and headed west. The wind and snow aided and abetted, but going was slow.

If not for their goggles and the incredible infrared heat signatures put off by every living thing, walking in the dark would've been impossible. At best, it was still a hit or miss. Animals were easily detected, but vegetation and rocks required the absorbed energy from the sun to be visible with night vision, and there hadn't been any of that since Ky had stepped foot in Kenora.

"I'm coming for you," he murmured to Eden on the chilly breeze. Ice and wind lashed them at every step. Logic told him to hunker down in the storm and wait it out. Never. Eden was out there somewhere.

What he wouldn't give to hear her sweet voice coming back to him over TEAMshield, but no. He'd neglected to bring along an extra pair. He had no way to know where she was.

It didn't make sense how Zaroyin had gotten his army of Feds into Kenora as fast as he had. They were equipped for the weather, yet none came with snowshoes or skis. There'd been no sign of snowmobiles, either. No winterized all-terrain vehicles. No Snow Cats or dog sleds. Fast-roping from any chopper, no matter how big, in the middle of a snow storm would've gotten most of the men killed, SWAT or not.

Zaroyin and his men had to have already been in Kenora and waiting for Eden to drop out of the sky. That bizarre notion actually felt true. A level-ten psychic might just be able to sense where Eden's plane would end up. Maybe that same psychic had guided Sweets' last desperate actions as the Cessna plummeted to earth. Hell, Isaiah Zaroyin just might be behind all of this.

An icy finger of dread tap-danced up Ky's spine. That was a helluva lot of maybes and mights, but it made sense in a weird, science fiction sort of way. If Eden could reach all the way to Afghanistan, the doctor's son could certainly get inside somebody's head in Canada.

The bastard was evil and sly. He'd muddied the playing field with one misdirect after another. The GPS locators. The spider-like mind-control devices. Charlie Sweets. Hell, even Becker's worthless evidence against Tate had kept everyone unbalanced and running around like chickens with their heads cut off.

Ky quickened his step. He wasn't sure which bastard was running the show, Bick, Zaroyin, or Isaiah, but the bottom line was the same. This was nothing more than a friggin' beta test of the drones' capability to hunt Eden. They wanted her for a breeder in their bizarre, sick plot. No. Damned. More.

"I say we stop to rest a few," Sam suggested between heavy pants, most of which Ky suspected was an act.

"No," Ky returned without so much as a glance at the guy who still seemed to think he was in charge. The guy didn't even have a pack to carry. Why was he tired?

"Tucker will take good care of her," Sam commented quietly, still trying to exert all that Navy SEAL dominance.

"Piss off." Ky underscored his answer with a burst of energy, slogging through the drifted snow and ready to go it alone if need be. Tate shut that wild notion down with a growly grunt, a good show of loyalty in what sure felt like a hopeless night with the odds stacked in Zaroyin's favor.

"Stay where you are, Eden," Ky hissed into the dark. "I'm coming."

So. Psychics. Where to begin? Better question, how to reach out and touch a specific one when you wanted him, instead of when he wanted you?

Eden cleared her mind, not sure her second sight would respond like she needed it to. With her index finger, she carved an arc in the snow around her, beginning and ending it at Tuck's body behind her. She'd never done anything like this before, but that circle seemed like it would serve as her invisible barrier should things go wrong—her last line of defense should Black Eyes prove to be more wicked than she could handle.

In her past experience, most kidnappers were easily influenced psychically. They weren't exactly rocket scientists. Most hadn't completed high school, much less gone onto college. Ignorance and greed ruled their method, motivation, and opportunity, making their actions easy to predict. But this guy? From that single second look she'd had of him, she'd sensed a higher intelligence. No. Black Eyes wouldn't go easily into the night. He might attack once he knew she was onto him.

She rested both gloved palms to her kneecaps, took a deep, slow breath in, and, exhaling it just as slowly, she let her second sight venture forth on a cloud of her frozen breath. It didn't really work like that, but sometimes, the visual seemed to stimulate her unique abilities. The whole *"if you see it, you can be it"* philosophy. Whoever thought up that mantra was pure genius.

Oddly, her second sight obeyed. She wiggled her backside at that simple achievement. With nothing but the shroud of this ice-cold Canadian winter wrapped around her, and Tucker's heat behind her, she drew in another deep lungful of wintery air, closed her eyes, and projected her energy beyond the arc. This was her element. Her genius.

Most people didn't understand psychic channeling. They equated psychics with magic and witches. Worse, Hollywood made psychics out to be con artists or liars. The truth lay somewhere in between. Most people were born with some degree of sensitivity for the unseen. Intuition. A sixth sense. Dreams. Others called it a gut feeling. It was nothing more than the innate observation skills all living things developed in order to survive. Watch people, truly watch them, and you'd be surprised at what lay beneath the surface.

So much of a psychic's skill began with simple observations. Eden employed no cons or sleight of hand, just cared enough to look deeper into her victims and their oppressors. To really see the reason behind why they did what they did. To truly listen to the dreams of their heart and the sorrows of their past. Their hopes for their future.

Sometimes handling an object they'd owned helped. Sometimes it didn't.

She drew in another breath and focused on the snowflakes drifting through the evergreen canopy. The delightful fragrance of crushed pine lifted into her nose and filled her half-circle with its natural energy. The world changed into hues of blues and whites, shadowy blacks, pewter grays with the softest violet borders, and greens that changed from darkest forest shades to limes to yellows.

Black Eyes, she called silently. *Are you sad? Talk to me. Come to me.*

Empathy. Her best and worst talent. It drew her into the most horrific situations, but combined with her gift of clairvoyance and the small dab of her mother's specialty, the psychometrist's ability to 'read' objects, it also allowed her to save people. Better yet, now that Black Eyes had revealed himself, she could mentally follow his psychic trail back to him.

The audacious man. Or child. That first impression of him had left her unsure how old he was, only that he'd suffered becoming who he was today. That he might not have wanted to hurt her like he had.

Uncertainty clouded the way between him and her. She swallowed hard and lifted her face to the branches overhead. Awareness of her current location faded as she kept her eyes closed and projected her second sight forward and beyond into the distance between.

"Black Eyes," she whispered again. "We really need to talk."

Three auras with shades of blue glowed nearby. Had to be Ky, Sam, and Tate on their way to rescue her. Of course. She smiled to see Ky so close and so intent on finding her. Warmth flooded her insides.

She pushed forward. More like she aimed her second sight forward, thankful it cooperated and moved beyond the scene of her would-be rescuers. She needed to locate Black Eyes before Ky arrived. Her second sight would grow quiet upon his arrival, but only because he commanded every beat of her heart. When he was near, she really did have eyes only for him.

It's easier to see when your body is clean of foreign agendas, her mind whispered.

"Yes," she whispered back, willing to talk with herself if it helped.

Anything was possible in a world so misunderstood and unexplained by science, a world full of telepaths who really could read minds. Intuitives who could grasp the intimate emotions and feelings of others without the burdensome need for spoken words. Psychic surgeons who healed the invisible damage to the psychic consciousness all people were born with, but never realized they had. Telekinesists who moved objects with their mind.

Last, but not least, the gift Ky didn't realize he possessed: clairsensitivity, the ability to sense other psychic energies afoot in the universe. It was all his doing the day he'd reached out from far-away Afghanistan and touched Eden with a desperate mental cry for relief. That was why he'd contacted her. He had the ability to feel out other sensitives. It also explained why he was able to intuitively detect the aromatic scent of her Vicks rub half a world away.

She breathed evenly as the vision of him materialized. He'd never once cried for help, just the strength to persevere his tormentors or die trying. To not reveal what little he knew about troop movements and military intelligence. To not give in.

Just as she began to truly savor the nature of the man she'd grown to love, the vision of a small dark-haired boy edged into the scene. Friendless and alone on a narrow metal bed, he stroked a fluffy Siamese kitten on his lap. Its back rose with every caress, its tail twitching. The sweet thing mewed, lifted its bony hips and purred a definite, 'Do it again.'

The kitten loved to play almost as much as he—

Excuse me, she, *loved tuna and catnip.* Eden smiled at the psychic reprimand. Yes. She was that kind of sensitive. Eden could read the wishes of animals, too, even though the memory might be years old.

Ah, the grace of furry pets exuded its own degree of sympathetic energy. The universe retained that psychic energy footprint, and only level tens could see it. She paused in her psychic journey and let the comfort of the years old memory work its magic. Hope lifted in her heart for the man she knew only as Black Eyes. Any man who had loved a kitten as much as he'd loved this one couldn't be all bad. His eyes had to be black for a reason other than evil.

The vision faded. She hovered between the warmth of Tucker's body behind her and the chill of the blizzard before her, for a moment unsure where Black Eyes might be. Her second sight detected no black smudges as it had during Koenig's and Shields' approach. No blue aura, either. No faint glow of a good heart—

Oomph! A hand close around her neck. She threw out a muffled scream even as the hand fought for a better hold. A gruff voice growled, "Got you."

Ky stopped dead in his tracks. A scream of terror had just rent the cold, dark night, close to his location. He shifted to north by northwest, his heart on fire. "Eden! Stay put. I'm coming!"

Tate and Becker followed him somewhere close behind, but they'd better damned well keep up.

Suddenly, Alex's voice burst into Ky's ear. "Do not engage."

"Bullshit," Ky hissed, obeying that stupid order the last thing on his mind.

"Ky!" Alex bellowed. "Hold up. It's too late."

Ky shut his mind to his very stupid boss and ran faster, intent on closing the distance. What did Alex know? What kind of a man would stop now? *It's never too late! Isn't that the rule? Never give up? Never stop trying?*

He blasted by dark tree trunks on his way to get to Eden. Branches whipped his goggles and jacket. He nearly fell in the drifted snow, not once, but twice, and still he forced his legs to pump faster.

A light glowed ahead. Not fire. More like the green glow of a Chemstick. He stopped at the source, his lungs on fire and his heart in his throat. The sight on the frozen ground sent a shock wave through him.

"Hold your position," Alex ordered, as if Ky could've done anything else.

Tucker Chase lay there. Dead. A bloody hole in his head. Dark blotches of blood on the snow. His eyes open. His arms stretched wide.

"Son-of-a-bitch," Alex hissed at what TEAMshield had just visually relayed to Virginia.

"We're too late," Tate muttered. "She's gone. Chase is down."

"Goddamnit." Becker dropped to Chase's side, "Not you, buddy. Not you."

Ky scanned the darkness, searching for one glint of a scope, one shadow of the bastard who'd done this. Eden had to be nearby. He'd just heard her. Tate scouted the immediate vicinity, his shoulders hunched, his rifle tucked into his chest and ready to engage. Ky stumbled onward. *Where is she?*

"Mother picked up a satellite transmission," Alex explained firmly. "I'm sending new coordinates via TEAMshield. Go north, Ky. There's an underground complex. You'll find Agent Stark there. Let Becker stabilize Chase. Call me—"

"He's dead, Boss." Ky panned to the bleak scene behind him.

"Think, damn it!" Alex roared. "If he's so dead, why's he spiking orange and red on your TID?"

Ky switched his goggles over to thermal imaging display, the TID his goggles virtually shared with Alexandria. Sure enough. Chase's heart glowed strong and red, but another item glittered on the display. Ky dropped to one knee to retrieve his only link to Eden.

Something blue.

Something round.

Her jar of Vicks.

Chapter Twenty-Four

Eden could barely move her little finger on her right hand. But she did. Gradually, the sensation of swimming in heavy concrete subsided. She flicked her wrist, not sure why she was weighted down like she was. Even drawing in a breath took effort. She labored to wake up. Her other hand tingled with the stabbing numbness of a cramped limb. Flexing, she exorcised the pain along with the stiffness.

Movement became more bearable. The simple act of breathing, too. She rolled her neck and stretched as, little by little, the oppressive sensation released the rest of her limbs. Sleep clouded her groggy mind, but the terror of having been abducted dictated wakefulness, something she struggled to achieve.

Warmth rewarded her first full breath, a pleasant change from all she'd endured since the Cessna went down. The fresh scent of evergreens was absent—a sure sign she was either dreaming or no longer in Canada.

Eden took a chance and opened both eyes. Somewhat dizzy, she lifted onto her elbows and found herself covered with a pale blue blanket on a narrow bed in an expansive white room. No leafy, emerald branches laden with snow overhead. No leaden clouds. No drifting snow.

No Tucker.

Instead, soft light poured from wall panels behind her. Metal rails lined her bed, one up, the other down. A single shiny silver stool with a black padded seat stood at her bedside. Apprehension slithered across her shoulders. More disconcerting, a full bag of fluid hung off the IV tree at her bedside. She lifted both arms into view, needing to understand what had happened to her while she'd slept.

Someone had inserted a line into her forearm, only it wasn't attached to the drip bag on the tree. The sealed end of it had been taped to her bicep. This was no ordinary IV. It was a PICC line, a peripherally inserted central catheter. Cancer patients needed PICC lines. Not her!

She cast the blanket aside, angry at yet another intimate violation. Who'd authorized this procedure anyway? *Sure as heck not me.*

Her bare feet hit the gray ceramic tiles stretched below from wall to wall. Not good. A dizzying wave of shadows swarmed her poor head. She plopped gracelessly back onto the bed as the door opposite her bed opened. A short, slight man in gray scrubs the same color as the tiled floor entered, his feet covered in surgical booties. "Ah. You're awake."

It was him. Dr. Zaroyin. Same Eastern Bloc accent. Same wire spectacles. A surgical mask covered his face while a matching paper cap covered his shorn head, leaving just his bushy brows and dark eyes visible. "It's okay, Miss Stark. You're safe and warm now. No need to panic."

"I was safe before, and I'm not panicked," she lied, her heart pounding at the sight of him. "Why the heck am I in a hospital, and how'd I get here? What's this PICC line for? Where's Ky? Where's Tucker Chase?"

Dr. Zaroyin approached slowly while she struggled with the cobwebs messing with her mind. "You're not in a hospital. You're actually quite safe for the moment. I'm sorry about all the cat-and-mouse games. Trust me. They were necessary. As far as your friends, I really don't know where they are."

"Overrunning our camp was more than a game." She wanted answers, not the run-around, but she also wanted to stay upright for longer than half a second at a time. The room kept dancing, spinning her in circles. "You had someone drug me so you could stick that spider-thing in my head! But that wasn't good enough, was it? Then you implant some kind of a locater inside my body. What'd you do, hypnotize me? Give me some of your mind-control drugs? God, what kind of a pervert are you?"

He lifted his palms forward as if to placate her. "I'm not the monster you believe me to be, Agent Stark. All will be revealed in—"

She borrowed Tucker's belligerence to disguise her fright. "Bullshit! You're behind everything that's happened to me, and everyone who's died. Start talking."

"May I sit?" he asked softly.

"It's your darned stool," she growled, feeling behind her ear for another creepy spider implant. That would be just Zaroyin's style. Stick things into her body while she lay drugged and unable to fight back. Her fingertips encountered nothing but the tender line where Ky had worked his first surgery—like that eased her suspicions. She had no recollection of being implanted before, either.

As discreetly as possible, she smoothed her right hand down her thigh, her thumb feeling for the incision along the crease of her leg. No implant there, either. "I want my clothes. Where's my stuff? I'm out of here."

Instead of answering one single question, he pressed his palm to the wall behind her bed. A door-sized panel slid open with a soft whoosh. "You're right. We do need to leave. The sooner the better."

Oh. A closet. Darned nice to know, only those weren't her clothes hanging there. Neither was that stunning floor-length fur coat with what looked like a silver fox collar or those darling red leather hiking boots with three-inch heels. Or the black jeans. Or the Henley knit shirt splashed with glitter.

"I said *my* clothes," she set him straight. "I'm not walking out of here looking like, like *that*." Sheesh! Did he think she was some brainless bimbo from Hollywood?

He lifted both shoulders, not reacting to her rudeness as he came to the bedside again. "These are clean, and they're your size. You may wear them or the hospital gown. Your choice."

Eden crossed her arms over her chest to conceal her quivering breasts under her thin excuse for clothing. He knew she wouldn't choose partial nudity, but where was the nice, warm TEAM outfit Ky had given her? And her fluffy fur cap? Where was Ralph Lauren when she needed him?

Dressing in Zaroyin's gaudy but very glamorous winter wear felt like betrayal, not only to herself but to Ky, too. Still, those were the only clothes in the closet. They would keep a respectable distance between her and the mad man. *Okay, fine.*

"So talk. Where are we going?"

He lowered to the stool, his hands on his knees. "I'm taking you back to America where you belong."

That was no answer. "Where in America? Why?"

"Because like it or not, you, Miss Stark, are about to make history."

"Bullshit!" Tucker would be so proud of her. "This is abduction, not history. It's breaking the law, but you already know that. You've done it enough."

Zaroyin tugged the mask under his chin. "Unfortunately, sometimes to advance historically and scientifically, the rights of the many must outweigh the rights of the few."

"Why are you doing this to me?" she demanded to know, a sudden knot in her throat. She didn't want to make history. She just wanted Ky.

"Get dressed. I'll explain when we're in the air."

"Are you crazy? We can't go anywhere in this weather." Unless she'd been unconscious for so long the weather front had changed and the skies were clear. Panic crept up her throat at the black holes in her memory. "How long have I been under?"

He lifted both palms, placating her. "Only hours. Calm down. You really have nothing to be afraid of here. I won't hurt you."

"You already did," she spat at him, her jaw tight, her fists clenched, needing a moment to compose her tough FBI persona. There she was, alone and fighting the world all by herself again. Ky had to be frantic. Tucker and Sam, too. Maybe even Tate. "Then get out while I change."

Zaroyin nodded once. "I will leave you to your toiletry. Press your palm to the panel on the other side of your bed to reveal a water closet. You have fifteen minutes to freshen up and change, but know this, Miss Stark. There are two armed guards outside your door who'll be more than happy to assist you with your attire."

"More drones?" she quipped as sarcastically as she could, her throat gone dry at his threat. "What? Are they going to shoot me with one of their smart guns?" The scary question welled up in her heart. "Did... did you rape me?"

He narrowed his brows, nearly squinting. "I expected better of you. Your virtue has never been compromised. Why would you think that?"

"B-but all those implants..." Her eyes brimmed. Everything she'd survived during the last forty-eight hours had caught up with her, making her sound weak and emotional. "You kept chasing me."

He nodded, his lips pursed in a thoughtful way. This mad scientist was not the brash, coldhearted man she remembered from her first and only encounter. "Believe it or not, Eden, your psychic skills are world-renowned. The FBI tried to keep you a secret, but we've known for years where you were. More people sing your praises than you'll ever know. Please don't disappoint me after all I've done to acquire you. There'll be time for further explanations later."

Zaroyin's East European accent seemed more pronounced than she remembered, but his shoulders sagged and that was enough of a clue. He'd even used her name, a clever ploy to establish a link between abuser and victim. She got that. She'd done it enough in the middle of life-and-death rescues, but something was off with the guy. Zaroyin seemed different. Subdued. Perhaps his association with Bick had exacted a greater toll on him than he'd expected. Well good. He and Bick deserved each other.

Eden dropped off the edge of the bad, instantly dizzy again. When he grasped her wrist to keep her from falling, the vision rolled over her in a wave. She saw it all. The man strapped to a metal platform in a dark, dark room. His arms, wrists, and ankles manacled. A solitary bright light glared overhead. Sweat dripped from his short, black hair, running in rivulets down his brow and temples. He groaned, but turned toward her.

He would've had a beautifully sculpted face if not for the lines of torment stretched out from the corners of his eyes and his mouth, or the thin streams of blood running from his delicate, straight nose. His aristocratic brows were thin and drawn.

It was him. *Black Eyes.*

Awareness dawned. That was no examination table he was on, not with the perforated stainless steel panels beneath him and the metal buckets on the floor. Not with the matching stainless steel splashback to his left. Faucets with quick-access triggers instead of handles. A woven, metal hose looped over a metal hook at his right. A sink next to his head. Levers to raise and lower the incline of the table.

Oh God! Her heart jumped to her throat. The poor man was laid out on an autopsy table. Across the distance, she took stock of his mental and physical condition. Weak pulse. Barely breathing. Desperate, but alive. He didn't open his eyes, but she swore she heard her name breathed out from his parched lips. *Eden? You came?*

She nodded, fully aware that Dr. Zaroyin had moved in much too close and that he still gripped her wrist. *What are they doing to you?* she asked mentally. *Where are you?*

Don't... come, Black Eyes murmured into her mind. *It's... a trap.*

Her empathy for all things living took over. She breathed her message of hope back to him. *Don't give up. I have friends who can save you.*

N-no. S-stay where you are. It's hopeless.

There is always hope.

His shallow breathing all but stopped. Slowly, he opened his eyes. The blackest, saddest gaze lasered straight into her. Eden's heart dropped to the floor of that distant prison. This was the little boy who'd loved kittens, now made to suffer alone. He wasn't mean at all. Nor evil. Just tortured. Like Ky had been.

The barest smile tugged at his lip. *Her name was Hoi-Toi. She lived to be a very old cat.*

That was all Eden needed in order to trust him. *And you loved her.*

She was my only friend.

Eden made up her mind. He wouldn't suffer alone. *I'm coming for you. I'm your friend, too.*

No. Stay with Ky.

She delved deeper into his energy. Black Eyes wanted to die, but he was more worried for someone else. *Oh, snap. Me? Why are you worried about me?*

Not you. Our child. Our perfect child.

But we don't have a child.

If you come to this place, we will.

She shifted her bare feet on the cold tile floor, uncomfortable with the implication that she and he might be together that way. *Who's doing this to you? Where are you?*

Don't worry about that; just don't come. We were never meant to be. You love Ky. Stay with him. Live for him. Be happy.

Where are you? What's your name?

The faintest grimace flickered over his beautiful, weary face. *I'll never tell.*

Chapter Twenty-Five

Ky followed Alex's coordinates, his ornery boss deep in his ear canal the entire way. He didn't stop until he and Tate were in sight of a concrete bunker built into the low-lying granite hill. It wasn't much larger than a two-story building, and thick rows of icicles draped its southern face.

"We may lose this connection the moment you step inside," Alex warned. "Jed's satellite is state-of-the-art, but it can't pierce the cloud cover."

Alex must have been relying on TEAMsky, the industrial satellite placed in orbit by NASA but owned by Alex and his close friend, the billionaire defense contractor, Jed McCormack. As much as Alex disparaged technology, he nonetheless relied on Jed's eye-in-the-sky.

Ky scanned the impregnable structure. "If I can get in."

"You've got two gun turrets topside, one at each front corner," Alex instructed like he had no doubt Ky would get in. "The best approach will be from the north. Climb the hill behind the bunker and enter through the roof. All buildings have ventilation ducts topside, but be careful. I can't detect every dirt bag at this altitude."

"There are bound to be a few," Ky muttered, still trying to catch his breath after the five-mile run. Every strand of muscle burned up his legs and down his legs. He tasted blood—not like that was any big surprise. Felt like a normal day drilling at Lejeune.

Tate pulled up alongside him, a layer of frost on his goggles. "You ready to do this?"

Ky nodded, still surveying his target. "Zaroyin's men have got to be waiting for us."

"They're just FBI. We can take them." Over-confidence, another Tate identifier.

"Alex thinks we should enter through the roof, but I'm not so—"

A burst of rifle-fire coming from the bunker resolved that question. Ky and Tate dropped to their bellies and dug in. They weren't going anywhere.

"I could light them up," Alex muttered a long way from Kenora, "if I were there."

Ky barely heard him over another burst of machine-gun fire. Spotlights flashed on from the rooftop, illuminating the fog. He bobbed his head up over his shallow snow bank for one quick look at the enemy's position.

Both rooftop gun turrets were lit up, the FBI snipers hard at work laying down suppressive fire. The gunners swept right to left, then back again instead of focusing on any specific position. Zaroyin didn't know he and Tate were out there, but something had definitely rattled the bastard.

"They're not shooting at us. They're just shooting," Tate grumbled.

"Copy that," Ky returned. Alex kept his mouth shut, a good strategy when his men were trying to stay alive on the ground.

The onslaught continued until a more ominous sound replaced it. The steady *thwack, thwack, thwack* of rotor slap in the night air. Brilliant white columns burst upward from the rooftop into the snow-laden clouds. *Landing lights.*

"Shit. They've got a chopper coming in," Ky growled.

"In this storm?" Tate barked. "Idiots. They'll get themselves killed."

"Either that or they're drones." That pilot had to be out of his mind. The wind had died down, but the steady snow would've grounded most aircrafts, and a smart pilot would have known better that to fly in poor conditions. Slowly, the craft descended.

Ky recognized the re-purposed USMC workhorse by its sheer size and the twenty-degree cant to the tail rotor. Except for the flat-black paint, the *stud*, as it was affectionately called in the field, aka the Sikorsky CH-54E Super Stallion, was the same heavy-duty, armored beast he remembered from his tours in Afghanistan. The USMC helos had a proud history in covert operations. Several CH-53s just like this one had secured Camp Rhino, the first land base in Afghanistan, in 2001. Others had dared heavy fire to rescue evacuees from the United States embassy in war-torn Somalia back in the 1990s.

This bad boy hovering just above the bunker had the capacity to haul as many as fifty-five troops and three combat gunners. If armed, and Ky had no doubt it was, it could dish out chaff, flares, and a helluva lot of hellfire from its window-mounted GAU-15A BMGs, as in the powerful Browning Machine Guns. Call it interdiction or call it eradication, Ky wouldn't take on that lethal weapon or its wicked ordnance.

Except for Eden...

"I'm going in," he told Tate, his mind made up

"Knew you'd say that. Go wide. Those dumbass gunners are kicking up enough fog they'll never spot you. I'll do what I can to keep them busy."

"Like what?" Ky hated that he might have asked his buddy to die.

"Let me worry about it. Go!"

Ky rolled to his left away from Tate. Zaroyin's paranoia had inadvertently aided and abetted. Every hot round fired into the snow raised mist and vapor, enough cover that a guy in white and gray winter cammies stood a chance if he crawled on his belly and stayed low. A loud explosion far to the right of his last position had to be Tate's diversionary tactic.

Getting in close was not the problem. Ky skirted the building until he was at the west wall. Finally able to stand, he took cover and took stock. The gunners had both focused where Tate's incendiary device blew. An occasional spray swung west, but the dozen guards at the main door stopped Ky cold. Overhead, the steady beat of that damned stud grew louder. That Sikorsky was the problem. His heart sank.

If he couldn't get inside before the helicopter took off, Eden would be lost to him.

Eden woke to the steady burst of gunfire. Groggy again. Zaroyin sat across the aisle.

"What'd you do to me?" she demanded, vaguely remembering a poke in her neck.

"I told you what would happen if you stalled."

"I wasn't stalling. I was..." What could she say that wouldn't reveal her connection to Black Eyes? Nothing. Eden played dumb.

Strapped into a harness, she could only stare out the window of what sounded like a very big helicopter. Gradually, the fog in her head lifted. She peeled the straps off her shoulders and clung to the window, her palms flat to the glass. "You're killing them! Stop it! Please!"

The chopper couldn't drown out the sounds of the battle waging below. Zaroyin's men were engaged in a gun battle, shooting down to ground level. Each staccato shot lit the dark with bursts of bright orange and white. Ky was somewhere in that maelstrom of snow, ice, and bullets below. He had to be, else why would the doctor's men keep firing in one continual pattern?

"They're laying down suppressive fire while we takeoff," he said tiredly. "It's a precaution. That's all."

"It's murder! Ky's out there. I know he is." Her eyes filled with tears. "I'm not going anywhere with you. Let me off this thing!"

Zaroyin signaled the pilot instead. The chopper's erratic flight pattern forced her to sit. It bobbed back and forth as if fighting the weather. The comfortable padded seat beneath her might as well have been ice. She couldn't take her eyes off the melee below. "I'll fight you every step of the way!"

"Do what you want. It will all be over soon."

"Where are you taking me?" she demanded again.

He turned his face to the window, the coward.

What the hell? A buzz of gunfire burst over Ky's position, headed away from him instead of at him.

"Ranger danger on your six," Senior Agent Harley Mortimer chirped affably in Ky's earpiece. "Get yer butts off the ground, boys, and join in. I didn't come all this way to take Zaroyin out by myself. Let's kick these bastards' asses."

"Copy that," Ky replied over the top of Tate's identical comeback. Eagerly, he engaged, catching the nearest enemy shooter in a crossfire as, one by one, his TEAMmates provided location and status.

"I've got you covered on your right, Ky. Keep laying it down," Adam Torrey muttered between firing. "God, I hate dictators and liars. Let's finish this."

"Coming at you front and center, buddy. Don't shoot me," the deep baritone of Maverick Carson chimed in. "I told China I'd be home for dinner. Do not make a liar of me, Winchester."

"Wouldn't dream of it." Ky aimed and squeezed off a barrage, advancing steadily instead of laying low. The FBI agents who'd flooded out of the bunker were now taking expert fire. Lots of it.

Unpleasant duty? Yes. Unnecessary? Maybe. But to be in a battle to win it? To finally have a fighting chance against Zaroyin's minions? To have the nation's best sharpshooter brothers at his back every step of the way? Best damned feeling in the world.

Ky took a half-second to scan his TEAM.

"Damn you," Gabe Cartwright hissed, his rifle aimed toward the rooftop as he squeezed off a few rounds, every fifth a tracer. "Do not shoot that shit at me one more time!"

One of Zaroyin's men pitched over the edge, never to *shoot that shit* again.

The helo hadn't taken off yet. There was still time. But it took twelve long minutes of steady payback before the enemy laid down their weapons. As senior agent in charge, Harley Mortimer assumed control of the scene.

"Get in there, Winchester," Harley ordered. "GO on. Get it done. Now. Before the Mounties show up, and we're forced to turn over jurisdiction. You too, Tate. Give him a hand. Find that woman and let's get out of here." He turned to the other men on his team. "Wrap 'em and strap 'em, guys. Tend to the wounded first. Cover the dead. RCMP is due to land in"—a troop of men in dark uniforms thundered from the trees—"right about now," he finished, the last words Ky heard as he scrambled into the bunker.

The chopper overhead had grown louder. He was running out of time.

The entry way opened to a *T*, gray walls everywhere. Ky pulled his goggles under his chin and nodded to the right. "TEAMshield won't work in here. Use your walkie-talkie. Go right. I'll go left."

"This place smells like a hospital."

"It may be one," Ky said. "Keep sharp."

Tate shrugged one shoulder. "Someone's watching. We're on camera. I can feel them."

"Copy that." Ky felt it, too, the nagging sensation that all was not well. By the time he'd reached the end of the hall, he'd encountered nothing but an open elevator at the L-shaped intersection. "You find anyone yet?" he asked Tate over his walkie-talkie.

"No. You?"

"Not yet." Ky held his position, his head cocked and listening. The sound of a door closing happened somewhere to his right. Footsteps padded away. Ky raised his rifle, ready for the target. "Got someone."

"On my way."

Too late. Ky turned the corner as another elevator door swooshed closed farther down the hall. All he caught sight of was a gray lab coat. He picked up his pace to intercept but nearly ran into Tate. "Someone was just here." He hit the stairwell next to the elevator, hoping to intercept him or her.

Holy shit didn't begin to describe the scene Ky and Tate encountered one level up. Row upon row of hospital beds, all occupied with unconscious men—or bodies—lined the expansive room. No privacy curtains. No walls. Just beds.

"What the hell?" Tate hissed.

"I think we found where they make the drones," Ky whispered, his rifle snugged into his chest, the barrel down. He approached the first row cautiously, while Tate took the second.

The bizarre scene screamed science fiction of the worst kind. The first bed held an unconscious man in a hospital gown, his eyes taped shut, his right arm strapped to a board, and various IV lines stuck in him. His stats were displayed on a nearby monitor. Various wires draped from beneath the gray blanket to another monitor. His head was shaved. A tan bandage showed behind his right ear.

"They've got implants. Just like Eden," Ky murmured, in shock at the size of this bizarre room. There had to be a hundred men laid out like corpses, the monitors quietly beeping away.

Tate moved from bed to bed on the next aisle. "All these guys are drones?"

"Sure looks like it." Ky bumped the foot of the unconscious guy on the next bed with his elbow. "They're all out cold."

Tate grunted. "Or they're dead."

"Umm, please don't do that," a nervous voice called out from behind him. "They're all recovering. They need their rest in order to heal."

Ky snapped his weapon onto the frail guy in gray scrubs standing at the elevator door and wringing his hands. "Who are you? Who are these men?"

The guy wiped a nervous palm over his brow. "I'm, umm, Thornton, and these are my surgery patients. They're... they're in recovery. You need to leave."

Ky waved the barrel of his rifle toward the expansive room, his anger barely in check. "Did you do this?"

Mr. Timid bobbed his head. "Yes. No. I mean, yes. Oh, dear. I mean we had no other choice. The drone technology failed to account for unquantifiable variants. None of these poor, poor men passed the beta test. The good doctor had to reverse the procedure. I assisted. It was the only humane thing to do."

Good doctor? Humane? Zaroyin? Those words didn't fit together. Ky took a step toward this Thornton bastard. He was obviously distraught, but Ky had no intention of making things easy on him. He lifted the business end of his rifle to the guy's face. "Which way to the roof?"

Mr. Timid backed up against the closed elevator doors, out of Ky's reach. "D-don't hurt him. The failsafe wasn't his idea. That other guy wanted proof the D781s were flawed. He did it. Not D-Dr. Zaroyin."

"What other guy? What D781s?"

"Mr. B-Bick." Thornton nodded so fast the skimpy hairs on top of his nearly bald head flopped up and down. "The mind-control things and the locators. He ordered them. Not Dr. Zaroyin."

"I don't give a shit who ordered what," Ky hissed. "How do I get to the roof?"

"You're too late. You'll never catch him."

"Where is it?" Ky bellowed, not going to wait one more second.

"Stairs. End of the hall." A trembling Thornton pointed the way.

Ky ran with Tate on his heels. There was still time. He shoved the rooftop door open. Both rooftop gunners were dead, but the powerful rotors of the helicopter whipped a frenzy of snow crystals across the roof and into Ky's face. He ducked into the wind, but the chopper had already lifted up from the landing pad.

He ran for the Sikorsky's skids, intending to grab hold and throw it off balance to keep it from gaining more altitude. He never stood a chance. The workhorse lifted vertically as easily as if no winter blizzard buffeted it. He'd never even made contact with one landing skid. Up it went into the overcast sky. Ky stood there until he lost sight of its landing lights.

Shit! He flopped to his back, sick and angry. He'd lost her. Eden was gone.

"Get off your backside, Winchester. Now. The Canadians are in control of this crime scene"—Harley barked from the stairwell —"and we need to vacate the premises. Alex is sending a Nighthawk. I brought the ballast to get you aloft. Be ready for pick-up within the hour. Can you do it?"

Ky swallowed hard. *A Nighthawk?* As in, the savvy extraction system whereby a man harnessed himself onto a fast-rising helium-filled balloon, aka the ballast, in order to escape certain capture or death at ground level?

He swallowed hard at the daring solution. Some insane engineer at McCormack Industries who'd never had to use the scary thing himself had dreamed up the latest get-out-of-jail-free device. The premise behind the Nighthawk was pure genius. It saved lives provided the UAV, the unmanned aerial vehicle designed to intercept the Nighthawk ballast, performed as planned. So far, no spec ops guy had been lost during a Nighthawk extraction, but damn. Ky'd never done one before. That meant a bone-chilling ride through one of the biggest blizzards of the century.

He kept his opinion to himself. Yeah, he could do it. He could do anything.

For Eden.

Chapter Twenty-Six

Black Eyes, Eden called out psychically. *Talk to me. I need to know you're okay.*

He hadn't spoken since their last conversation, and she'd grown more worried the farther east the helicopter flew. The co-pilot, one FBI Agent McCluskey, whom she didn't know, refused to listen. No matter how hard she tried to convince him she'd been abducted, not once did he lower the black-tinted face shield on his helmet. "Take your seat, ma'am, before I make you," he'd growled when she'd gone forward to confront him.

"Do you have any clue who this man is or the trouble he's caused? Do you realize you're acting as his accomplice?" she'd asked, pointing at Zaroyin. "He's a murderer, and you're helping him escape."

"My orders are to bring you in. Now sit."

"Which makes you as dumb as one of his mind-controlled drones," she shot back at him, her FBI attitude back in action.

McCluskey's chin clenched below the shield. His lips thinned. He pushed out of his seat and took one threatening step toward her. She didn't intend to spend what was left of her life drugged and unconscious, so she took her seat again, pissed at her stupid boots, irritated at the ridiculous high-fashion get-up she didn't remember getting into. Another violation of her privacy. But spitting mad that Zaroyin had caught her after all she'd done to stay out of his reach. Furious that she had no way to know whether Ky was dead or alive.

She gulped a tear away, not going to break down in front of this, this... What would Tucker call McCluskey? An asshole? *Yeah. That.*

Glancing cautiously at the doctor, she tapped her finely booted toes out of sheer frustration and reached across the void to another lost soul. *Black Eyes, talk to me. I can't do this without you,* she demanded.

Silence.

"Here, you'll need this." Harley tossed Ky a balaclava, a white skull painted on its face. Good enough. Wasn't that appropriate in a really sick way? Ky donned the face protection and his TEAMshield goggles. Damn, if this killed him, Alex would get a birds-eye view of his death.

"Are you ready?" Harley asked, his brows knitted as he tightened Ky's chest straps and adjusted the shoulder harness one more time. Tall and lanky with a streak of tease in him a mile wide, Harley looked more serious than Ky could remember.

"Yeah. Let's get this done."

Harley's lips pursed. "You ever done this before?"

"No." Ky's stomach pitched up his throat. *And I'm never going to be this stupid again.*

"All you've got to do is hang on. Let the Hawk do its thing." He peered intently into Ky's face. "Remember to breathe. The air will get thin. Don't panic. This is a short trip. You'll be fine."

Ky nodded, adrenaline coursing up the length of his body, pushing him into panic mode. Harley needed to shut up before it took over. The Nighthawk ballast had already been inflated. It tugged at his harness from its lofty position somewhere in the snow clouds overhead. Ky didn't waste time looking for it. He gave Harley a solid thumbs-up.

"Be safe." Harley returned a quick two-fingered salute and a final shoulder bump with his fist.

Oh, shit. Lift-off. Ky fisted both gloved hands around the hard plastic harness tethered to the innocuous-looking white balloon somewhere overhead. The second Harley released the line from its anchor, Ky's boots lifted off the ground. With his gear and rifle strapped to his chest, he was on his way into outer space.

Adam Torrey, nicknamed The TEAM's flying squirrel, loved HALO jumps. He got a kick out of jumping out of perfectly good C-130s. Ky closed his eyes. His heart thumped at the sudden acceleration of the craziest thing he'd ever done. What was Adam? Insane?

The trip would be short, but only *if* the UAV intercepted the tether that held him to the ballast as it was designed to do. One big scary *if*. If the Nighthawk drone missed, he'd be that man lost in the stars, a meteor set to fall to earth when his shallow orbit decayed. By then he'd be dead, frozen stiff and asphyxiated. *Not good.*

That Mother, Alex's nosey admin assistant, remotely controlled the UAV from somewhere deep inside the sunny state of Virginia should've made him feel better. It didn't. She was smart, maybe even a genius when it came to techie stuff in the office, but remote-controlling a military asset that she'd never seen much less used before? Damned tricky.

His gut lurched. It might not be Mother behind the controls. It could be Alex, his technologically challenged boss. *Even worse.* Ky gritted his teeth as he gained altitude and growled into the wind, "What the hell am I doing?"

Up, up, up, and holy shit! This was why he hadn't joined the Screaming Eagles, the Army's 101st Airborne Division, renowned for its air assault operations. Hell, no. Suspended from a balloon that, with the right conditions, could still run into a prickly pine tree and—*pop!* Send him to his death before he'd acquired enough altitude? *No thank you, Uncle Sam.*

Yes, Ky needed to get to Eden quickly, but br-r-r-r-r. The higher the balloon lifted, the colder the atmosphere. TEAMwear wasn't made for these frigid temps. He shivered and focused on looking up, not down. At this rate, he'd have hypothermia before interception.

If...

Yeah. There were a lot of ifs when a guy literally flew by the seat of his pants, when he was hanging on for dear life. *What was I thinking?* Ky hunkered into his safety harness and manned up. He wouldn't be hanging like an idiot at the end of a clothesline if there were any other way. *This is all about Eden, tough guy. Shut it down and get it done.*

TEAMshield interrupted his half-hysterical rant with a calm, "Intercept in five. Four. Three. Two—"

Whoosh! Precisely on schedule. The stealthy UAV somewhere overhead in all those clouds hooked Ky's tether with its extended nose-pincers and jolted him and his balloon with a rapid change in direction. Now he was really moving.

"Shit," he ground out between clenched teeth, the wicked cold of a rapid getaway tearing into him. "How long before I l-l-land?"

TEAMshield responded with the infinite patience programmed into her. "Touchdown in ten minutes, Agent Winchester. Shall I adjust the temperature of your TEAMwear until then?"

"Do it," he said.

"Will ninety-eight-point-six Fahrenheit be acceptable?"

"Yes," he hissed to the sky. Just do it. Instantly, TEAMshield activated his internal heater and warmth spread through his TEAMwear suit. He wished he'd thought of that sooner. Swallowing hard, he ceased being a pansy. This insane idea might work.

He summoned those pretty green eyes to mind. The scent of mentholatum. The taste of Eden's sweet mouth. His heart calmed. Yeah. This would work.

"Ring TEAMhome," he ordered.

"Dialing Mr. Stewart," the feminine voice replied without a hint of emotional distress. God, she could be annoying.

"Ky?" Alex barked. "Harley said you refused the oxygen. What were you thinking?"

"The tank's too heavy, Boss. They only had the one, and Chase needed it more than me." Ky's teeth chattered despite the added heat sweeping inside his suit. "He's injured, remember?"

"Son-of-a-bitch, who cares? He's got ground support. You don't. You ever hear of hypoxia?"

Ky nodded despite the miles between him and his boss. Now was not the time to argue about something he couldn't change and wouldn't if he could. Chase had been in a bad way, blue-lipped and still unconscious the last time Ky saw him. Hypoxia only mattered if this contraption gained extreme altitude, which it was not designed for. "You do know Zaroyin's headed south in a Sikorsky stud, don't you, Boss? It's fitted with super-sized sponsons for additional fuel. That bird won't land for hours."

"Yes, Harley filled me in."

"Where's Zaroyin now?"

"Still headed east. That gunship's high enough over the storm, and it's caught a good tailwind. There's no way you'll catch it, but don't worry. I've got everyone stateside working on this recovery."

"I'm not worried about me, Boss. Send someone to intercept Zaroyin before he gets away. Save Eden."

"Plan on it," Alex said. "There's a Snow-Cat waiting for you when you land, courtesy of the Mounties. They'll get you to Thunder Bay where Rory and Taylor are on stand-by. They'll accompany you home."

"Copy that. Keep me apprised."

"Will do. Fly safe." Alex disconnected.

More like fall safe. Ky's ears popped at the gradual change in altitude.

"ETA in twenty seconds," TEAMshield informed him.

Ky bent his knees as the Nighthawk drone began its descent. He braced for impact with a tree. A house. Anything that might jump out at him in the murky weather.

"Five. Four. Three. Two. One."

The articulate ruler of the midnight sky drifted parallel to the ground at a good five or six feet before it cut the ballast free and released him. While the balloon drifted skyward, he dropped to his boots and rolled, his arms and shoulders tucked in tight.

Overall, it was a smooth landing. He came to a stop on his butt, thankful to be on the ground again as he took in the snowy scene. Whoever operated the remote control had successfully deposited him alongside the runway of a one-plane town. No hangars. No terminal. Just a long stretch of concrete. So, so close. He could've ended up as one long skid mark on the tarmac if that person had so much as sneezed or miscalculated.

"Thank you for flying with the Nighthawk team, Junior Agent Winchester," Mother's disembodied voice whispered into his earpiece. "I hope you'll fly Nighthawk air with us again soon."

"Mother? I should've known it was you guiding me home," Ky replied as he climbed to his feet, unscathed. *And not Alex.* "Good landing. I owe you one. Thanks for not letting the drone miss the tether on that hot-air balloon, either."

"It's called a bladder, Ky, and it's made of one of the toughest, most resilient materials…"

Ky let her ramble without really listening. He dusted his butt and jacket, took his goggles off. She liked people to think she knew more than they did. Maybe she did. She wasn't up here in frigid Ontario, Canada, was she?

"Zaroyin's pilot just made a course correction, Ky," Mother informed. "He's headed south toward Boston and losing air speed. Ember's checking all private runways in the area. We'll have more definite intel soon. By the time you leave Thunder Bay, you'll know precisely where to go. Stand by."

"Copy that." Ember was working this op, too? Mother's topnotch techie assistant? Good deal. Things were looking up. Who didn't like Ember? The woman was easy on the eyes.

Drop-dead gorgeous. Ex-Navy and happily married to Rory Dennison, one of the two agents waiting on Ky in Thunder Bay.

He stopped thinking about home and peered through the falling snow at the hefty vehicle rumbling toward him. Snow-Cat nothing. This relic was old, diesel-driven, and a state-of-the-art godsend with four, not the standard two articulating tracks. It would get him to Thunder Bay in no time.

"Get onboard," Alex rumbled in his ear. "You've still got work to do."

"Copy that."

Chapter Twenty-Seven

It took three hours to get to the airfield in Thunder Bay. By then, Ky was fit to be tied. He joined Rory Dennison and Taylor Armstrong at the only aircraft in sight, a two-winged bush plane that had seen better days.

"You look like shit," Rory said with a lopsided grin. Man, the guy had perfect teeth.

"Feel like it," Ky acknowledged. "Haven't slept since we touched down. Who's flying this deathtrap?"

"That'd be me," a guy in brown Carhartt winter coveralls, a knitted beanie, and dark glasses replied, "and it ain't a deathtrap. This here's Bessie. Man's best friend. I'm Marlin Carter, the guy who keeps her warmed up and ready to go on a moment's notice. You're the one these guys been waiting for?"

"Yes, sir," Ky admitted, rolling his shoulder, "but before we go anywhere, I've got to ask you a favor. It's going to sound crazy, but would you mind taking your cover off?"

Rory and Taylor came to a dead stop at that bizarre request.

Marlin's nose wrinkled. "Why should I?"

Yeah, this was awkward, but Ky wouldn't take chances. "Trust me. I need to see the back of your head, maybe feel your scalp behind your ears. The last pilot I know had a device implanted under his scalp. It got him killed. He died of a heart attack. Would you mind?"

Marlin growled, but tugged his headgear off and twisted his neck so Ky could get a good look.

Ky stepped closer, searching for a dime-sized bump. Nothing. Satisfied that Marlin was not another drone under Zaroyin's evil influence, he clapped one gloved hand to the affable fellow's shoulder. "Sorry, sir. It's been a helluva few days. I just needed to be sure you were who you said you were. Thanks for cooperating."

"That's alright," the older guy muttered as he replaced his headgear. "I've seen crazier folks than you."

Taylor thumped Ky's bicep with his fist like guys were prone to do. Tall and straight as an arrow, his bronzed skin and black hair belied his Native American heritage. The guy was as stoic as Tate, but easy-going. "You ready to get out of here?"

Ky jolted to a dead standstill. He stared down where Taylor's gloved knuckles rested against his bicep. No panic. No burning sensation, either.

Taylor pulled back. "Sorry, man. It was good to see you, and shit, I forgot. My bad."

"No. I'm, umm, good," Ky answered quickly. "It's okay. Really. It felt kind of weird for a second there, but it... it didn't hurt."

"You sure?" Rory asked, his dark blue eyes bright with surprise.

Ky caught the genuine disbelief on his buddies' faces. "Yeah. Weird, huh? It's gone. I couldn't be better. I guess I've been a real ass to work with, huh?"

"No," Taylor declared, his fingers gripping Ky's forearm, pulling him close, "but this has been a long time coming, brother. Seem this op's been good for you."

Ky nodded, swamped with the peculiar sense of relief. He took in a long, deep breath. Smiled. Wiped the tear out of the corner of his eye before he made a fool of himself. Thumped Taylor's bicep a good one in return, then wiped his eye again. God, it took all he had not to bawl like a kid. He'd never thought this day would come. Nizari's hold on him was no friggin' more.

He sucked his lower lip in, biting it hard before he fell apart in front of his friends. "Let's get this done, guys," he said hoarsely, his heart swelled up in his throat. "I've got a woman to save."

"Do you know what this means, Ky?" Rory asked. "Kegger at my place when we get home. Tackle football. The whole TEAM. Plan on it."

"And Gracie can finally hug the stuffing out of you," Taylor chimed in. Gracie, his wife, was a hugger.

"Ember's been dying for this day," Rory added. Another hugger.

"Wait 'til Alex finds out." Taylor fist pumped. "You did it, Ky. You beat that rat-bastard Nizari."

"Hell, wait until Lee finds out," Rory said quietly, his hands on his hips.

Ky got stuck on the tender light in his teammates' eyes. The pride. The brotherhood. Lee *would* be proud. He'd been Ky's advocate since those first few minutes on the floor of a putrid cell a half-world away. He'd never doubted Ky would overcome the crap he'd survived at Nizari's hand. Just gave him what he'd needed to keep on keeping on. A shoulder to rest on. A knife to defend himself with. The love of a brother...

Alex, too. He'd hired a broken-down Marine sight unseen. Gave him a damned hard job and a place to belong. Gave him a hand up. Somewhere to belong. A home.

Shit. Ky squeezed the bridge of his nose and shook the tender feelings off. He had a woman to save, but damn it to hell. Emotion climbed up his throat. He'd waited a long time for this day. He was free. Nizari's hold on him was no more. And all because of a tenacious woman with pretty green eyes who'd poured love into the battered husk of a man with no hope of living. She'd given all she had to give to him, a mess of a man, until their psychic connection was lost. Eden. And now she was the lost one.

Ky took a deep breath of icy air and blew it out. He needed her there, in his arms, hugging the stuffing out of him. "Let's go, guys," he said determinedly. It was his turn to save her.

It took them a few tense moments to get the turbo-charged Beechcraft up in the air, as bad as the weather was, but Marlin did good. After the propellers lifted out of the clouds, they had nothing but sunshine smiling on them.

Like a fool, Ky craned to catch a glimpse of Zaroyin's chopper somewhere ahead. No deal. It was a stupid notion. Eden had to be miles ahead of him. They touched down to refuel a couple of times at out-of-the-way and mostly deserted airstrips, but by noon, the Atlantic lay off the nose of the plane.

Ky dialed Mother via TEAMshield. "Any news?"

"How are you feeling?"

"Fine. Any news?"

She got the point. "They stopped in Bangor, Maine, a while ago, maybe to refuel or eat. Right now, they're south of Boston, losing airspeed. I'll let you know which airfield they land at.

Senator Bick and his wife own some property in that area. A couple of warehouses."

"Why?"

"Not sure. Ember's digging into that one. One of us will ring you the second we know more."

"Thanks, Mother." Ky disconnected. If Zaroyin's drone factory was in Canada, why did a United States senator need warehouses in Boston?

McCluskey doffed his helmet and stood in the cockpit, poised for trouble. He was a redhead. Crew-cut. His right hand rested on his BFG, as in the big fucking gun nestled in his holster, its safety strap flipped open. Snap, the guy was built like a wall and ready to charge. Make that tackle. His tree trunk legs were spread, his knees bent. His hulking body filled the narrow aisle between Eden and Zaroyin's seat. What'd he need a gun for?

"Time to move, princess." He extended his gloved left hand to help her to her feet or throw her over his shoulder, Eden wasn't sure which.

She declined the offer, not wanting to touch the behemoth's ugly mitt. Her second sight might kick in at the contact, and Eden did *not* want to know what went on inside that big, square head. She slapped her coat pockets, automatically looking for her pistol that wasn't there. Old habits died hard, but something *was* in her right pocket. Something solid. Plastic-handled. Down deep where she hadn't noticed it before. Definitely not a tube of lipstick.

She slid her fingers between the folds of some poor dead animals and wrapped them around what felt like the grip of a gun. Eden borrowed one of Tucker's favorite words again. *Shit. A taser!* The safety cover on the business end was missing, which meant the weapon could be fired the second she pressed the trigger. When she did, an arc of electricity would drop tough-guy McCluskey to his knees before he knew what hit him. He'd be reduced to a drooling moron crying for his mommy.

Eden licked her bottom lip at the shift in power. She cast a furtive glance at the doctor. Had he stashed the weapon in advance or someone else? Was that why he'd wanted her dressed to the nines? Was he the one who'd ensured the safety was off? She couldn't catch his eye. He was busy brushing some miniscule piece of lint off his trench coat.

"I said move," McCluskey growled. "You go first."

"I am moving," Eden replied, intending to put on a show for this jock if only to prove her point. He only thought he was in charge. Ha.

Being dressed in this silly coat and boots didn't feel so wrong anymore. She lifted out of her seat and balanced on her ridiculously high heels. Her ankles buckled, but she righted herself. If other women could do it, so could she. Releasing her grip from the seatback in front of her, she ran a hand through her thick hair and twisted her shoulders from side to side. Men liked long hair, and she intended to give McCluskey an eyeful. He needed to be watching her when she finally let him have it.

She took a full, seductive minute and str-e-t-ch-e-d every last tired muscle in her stiff body, making sure the front of the coat fell open enough to reveal her full cleavage. Zaroyin, if he was the one behind this get-up, had chosen a tight fitting knit

Henley with tiny buttons, the top ones undone because the shirt was too small. She wiggled two her best assets, then bent forward to touch her toes. In the process, she let her long hair sweep to the floor while she made certain her backside jutted more than usual. She'd always been a bit on the too curvy, too plump side, but she knew how to use it. *There. Take that, you creep.*

Straightening with a throaty sigh and a flourish, she let he hair settle around her shoulders in a silky, tousled cascade. Eden thrust her chest forward and moaned. Right as rain, McCluskey's all-male eyeballs gave her a quick up and down, but mostly up. Those eyes were definitely glued to her breasts when the titillating tour ended. Just like she'd wanted. His upper lip twitched, as if he stood a snowball's chance in heck of getting any closer to her. *This, big boy, is all about distraction. Nothing more.*

He lifted one brow and jerked his big square head at the exit. "Get out."

Silently, she did as ordered and climbed down the ladder to the tarmac of some small-town runway, careful not to stumble on her heels. McCluskey might have acted like he was unaffected, but she'd seen him run his tongue over his bottom lip. She'd seen his eyes narrow, then drop to her cleavage. Even now, she could feel his eyes on her backside as he followed with Zaroyin right behind him. He might think he had plans for her and she was willing to light him up—just not the way he expected, the jerk.

No other planes stood parked nearby, and there was only one hangar. She sniffed and detected the pleasant fragrance of the sea in the air. "Where are we?"

"Move it," McCluskey ordered instead of answering.

"But you said you had orders to bring me in. This isn't FBI headquarters, Quantico, or Langley. Exactly where are you taking me?"

"Stop with the bullshit, Stark. You know the Bureau doesn't do all its business out in the open." He stuck that chin of his at the long, brick building opposite the hangar. "Over there. Move it."

She had no choice but to obey, to wait for the right moment to end McCluskey. Could she do it? Yes. He wouldn't die from a taser, but he would go down. That left Zaroyin. He had to have known about the taser. What was she supposed to do next? Run from him? Run to him? Trust him?

Eden stopped at the hangar door to look over her shoulder. Ky was out there somewhere. She could sense him A breeze caught her hair up in a billowing fluff. Smoothing it back behind her ear, she took what might be her final breath of freedom. Whatever happened next could be her last. She projected one last thought to the man she loved with every last breath. *I always loved you. Know that. Never doubt. Stay strong for me. Live.*

The hard tip of McCluskey's gun barrel in her back ended the reverent moment. "Stop gawking and get your ass inside."

Ky shifted in his seat again, antsy to be on the ground and engaged in whatever the hell was going on with Eden. Ember had called with the location where the chopper had landed. Alex had agents on the way, but Ky wasn't there. The few remaining miles of this long day galled him.

So much could happen in covert operations. A team might start with a foolproof plan, but by the end of the game, it always turned into shit. All those unknown unknowns. Random accidents. Equipment failures or just plain stupid human error. Friendly fire. Anything could and would happen between kickoff and touchdown. Murphy's law never took a day off.

From a combination of the warmth blasting out of the Beechcraft heater and the nearly three days without sleep, Ky drifted into a deep slumber. Sultry green eyes sparked through the haze in his exhausted brain. Eden whispered, "I always loved you, Ky."

He jolted upright, his sleep ruined by the sad tremble in her voice. *Loved? As in past tense? Not love? Not I'll always love you?*

She gulped and turned the brass knob on the hangar's wooden door. It opened easily. Eden stepped over the threshold and into a wide, empty room. Sunlight streamed through the array of windowpanes covering the entire east wall. Two doors broke the expansive brick wall across the dusty floor to the north.

Again with the gun barrel in her back. "First door on the right," McCluskey ordered, pushing her forward

With her head held high, she stepped out smartly in front of him and took her one and only shot at a high-fashion modeling career. With her left hand on her hip, she stuck her right hand deep inside her pocket. With a flounce of her head, she lifted her chin and squared her shoulders, and hoped she wouldn't fall off those darned high boot heels. Swishing her hips, she put her best foot forward. He needed to believe she'd go down easy. Well, guess again. She had no intention of finding out what lay beyond that door on the right.

Suddenly, McCluskey gurgled a hissing, "Lying son-of-a-bitch..."

Eden whirled on the desperate scene. Dr. Zaroyin, the smaller guy with a garrote wrapped tightly around McCluskey's thick neck, stood behind the big guy while McCluskey struggled on his knees, his fingers caught between the deadly wire and his trachea. He growled and sputtered, wheezed and choked, his eyes wide and bulging. Zaroyin's face contorted into a fierce mask, his brows slanted into deep spikes, but McCluskey was unable to break loose.

"Get his gun," Zaroyin hissed as the big guy twitched. Only when McCluskey slumped unconscious—or dead—did the doctor relax the wire. Blood dripped off his fingers as McCluskey fell to the dirty concrete floor.

Eden pulled her gaze from the grisly death scene to secure McCluskey's weapon, in shock at Zaroyin's abrupt about-face, but willing to go along with it. "You gave me that taser, didn't you? You're the one who stuck it in my coat pocket. What's really going on?"

"They've got my son," he declared angrily. "I'm supposed to deliver you to Bick and his wife next. The stupid clothes were her idea, but the coat was mine. I needed to give you a way to defend yourself. His wife wanted you dressed like her, but I'm not going through with the rest of his plan. I can't. Hurry! That tailwind put us in early. I don't intend to hang around here and wait for them to show."

"What plan?" She needed to know.

"The plan to kill you, Agent Stark."

"Your son is here, isn't he?" she asked, just to be clear. She couldn't detect Isaiah, but it made sense after what he'd told her about them having a child together.

"Yes. Isaiah is here." Zaroyin nodded at the ordinary-looking door stuck in the massive brick wall across the enormous empty bay. "This building belongs to Bick. There's a lab in the back. Some other... stuff. Maybe a technician or two. We must do this right. We must hurry."

He paused to really look at Eden. Taking hold of her wrists, his harsh gaze softened. "Miss Stark, you must believe me. I began my drone research only to stop the unnecessary human cost of modern warfare. The friendly-fire mistakes that kill so many good men and women. The errors in human judgment. The incorrect target coordinates. The near misses. If mankind is to survive, we must find a better way of dealing with terrorists and mad men."

For the first time, Eden glimpsed a different man behind the evil mask, the depth of the worry etched at the corners of his eyes. The gray pallor of his face. The man she'd mentally reduced to Dr. Zaroyin became Abraham. The irony of this trembling father's very Jewish first name did not escape Eden. Any man who named his boy after a heroic prophet in the Old Testament had to have been a good and decent man at one time in his life.

Abraham grasped his forehead, rubbing his fingers nervously back and forth across it. "I thought some level of carefully administered brain control would be the perfect solution, only... I was wrong. My chip is defective. It makes no allowances for individual choice. It forces a man to become a killing machine instead of a willing host. It needs further study, only I wasn't smart enough to wait. I acted rashly. I sought congressional funding long before my device was perfected or beta-tested, and I... God, I..."

He looked at the dead body on the floor, his jaw tight with disgust. "I courted a devil named Douglas Bick for the funding he promised, and now he has my only child. Hurry. We've got to go."

Eden rifled through McCluskey's pockets and relieved him of a couple of mags and another pistol, a pearl-handled snub-nosed thirty-eight special. Good enough. She was packing a weapon she could actually handle, and she was ready to engage. Eden handed the BFG off to Abraham. Together, they ran across the bay, Eden amazed she could actually run in those heels. "The chip isn't defective. The concept behind your whole mind-control idea is what's wrong. Is your son implanted, too?"

He paused at the door, his head cocked to listen as he eased it open with his gun in hand. "Oh, no. Isaiah is a gentle soul in a man's body. He doesn't belong in this world. His heart is too soft. It was because of him that I had the idea to stop warfare as we know it. No father wants to leave behind a world that will eat his child alive, yet that is precisely what I've done."

Eden smoothed one palm down the ridiculously expensive fur coat that covered her from her neck to her ankles and followed him into a dimly lit hall. "Tell me why Bick has Isaiah if he's not a drone like the other guys. Did you hand Isaiah over to Bick or—"

"Never! He kidnapped my son to get to me. To control all of my work. To bastardize my solution for world peace. To force me to do what he wants." Abraham explained as he walked brusquely down the hall. "Bick wants the cybernetic enhancements trials to succeed for all the wrong reasons. He's obsessed with total military control. That's all my hard work and research means to him."

A shudder rent the man's shoulders. "Bick doesn't need you alive for his dream to come to fruition, Miss Stark. A woman is born with a finite number of eggs and those eggs can be frozen long after she's been murdered. Bick has no qualms about killing, in fact, I think he and his wife enjoy it. He believes a child born of two level-ten psychics will be mentally stronger, more capable of controlling his perfect cybernetic army, and he'll do anything to get that child."

She could only nod in dumb agreement at the awful truth. This was a risky operation, but another truth glowed just as brightly. Dr. Abraham Zaroyin loved his son. He was prepared to die for him. It didn't take a psychic to see that. "You didn't implant that mind-control thing in my scalp, did you? You didn't hurt me."

"I did not," he said, his voice laced with genuine sorrow. "It's common procedure for the agents in my program, yes, but for no one else. Bick had to be behind it. He's been obsessed with you for years. What you called the spider thing is nothing more than a regulator. It injects miniscule amounts of a memory loss drug to prevent a volunteer from second-guessing his decision to join the program. The mind-control chips are different. They're very tiny and are implanted deep within the limbic portion of the brain, one to block strong emotions in the amygdala, the other to restrain hormonal responses that originate in the hypothalamus to outside stimuli such as temperature, thirst, and hunger."

That explained why the eight FBI drones she'd encountered ran through the snow all night. They had literally been programmed to ignore the cold and fatigue. Eden still needed to know who'd sent them after her if not Zaroyin.

This warehouse made her feel off-balance, and it wasn't just the heels. It felt more like the ghosts of all those FBI agents were reaching out to her, their long skeletal fingers demanding she acknowledge them, begging that she see them. That she save them. Spooky.

Abraham explained as they walked, oblivious to her rising angst, his feet moving faster with his words. "I found out too late that Bick has a long reach, Agent Stark, and he knows a lot of the wrong kind of people. Yes, I admit that I went behind Director Strong's back. We all did. I was obsessed with the prospect of cybernetic enhancement, and what it would mean to the world. My test subjects, too. We had a common vision, and they were so willing. What man wouldn't want to be like Superman? To be able to withstand the fear and shock that bloody battle induces? Or to rise above the effects of adrenaline when he's being shot at? But I needed funding to continue my highly technical research and—"

"By the time you spoke with Director Strong, Senator Bick already had Isaiah, didn't he?" It made sense. Take a group of testosterone-fueled egomaniacs like Tucker. Amp them up. Make them believe they could save the world. Eden saw how easily this vision could've been sold to patriotic idealists, to battle hardened warriors who knew full well the cost of war. To men who'd seen their brothers and sisters die in the deserts and jungles.

Abraham nodded, the utter torment in his voice easy to read. "I was a fool. I believed everything he and his wife told me."

"Cassandra Bick?"

"You know her?"

"I know *of* her." The thought of an innocent babe at that twisted actress's beck and call chilled Eden to her core. A freight train of maternal instinct swept through her body and soul, filling her with a crushing, feral need to protect an unborn baby she hadn't yet conceived, hadn't even thought of yet. Even her breasts tingled. How extraordinarily odd.

"She's something else entirely, Agent Stark, nothing like her husband. If he's Hitler, she's Charlie Manson. Trust me. You don't want to meet Mrs. Bick in a dark alley, much less in this place." He stopped, nearly causing her to collide with him. Turning on her, he cried, "My God what have I done bringing you here? I needed your help, but this could go terribly wrong. You need to leave."

"No way." Eden set him straight, chin nodding him forward. "You've brought me here to save Isaiah's life, that's what you've done. Now let's go get him."

He didn't move. "But this may get you killed, too."

"But it may not," she growled, a little more fiercely than she'd intended, "and what's this *too* bullshit. Neither of us is going to die." Her hackles were standing painfully on end, her motherly instincts sprung ferociously to life over the fate of an unborn child. She'd never felt more capable of killing another, especially if that person meant to hurt a baby. Her baby.

The doctor's head bobbed, his momentary guilt, or whatever it was, gone. "Yes. You're right. Isaiah. Let's get Isaiah out of here."

"Damned straight I'm right." *And now I sound just like Tucker. What's up with me?*

She shouldn't have taken another look at Abraham, though. The man's eyes brimmed with tears. "What's wrong?"

He let out a shuddering sigh. "I know it's foolish to tell you this now after what I've done to you, but I would've been proud to call you, Daughter."

Oh, snap. A stab to the heart Eden hadn't seen coming. Here stood the man she'd thought she hated. The guy she'd believed had tracked her down and threatened her life, and he wanted her as a daughter? Why? Her own father hadn't wanted her. Why this guy? Why now?

Still dealing with her newly activated and enraged motherly hormones, she shook the perplexing notion of being wanted as a daughter out of her mind. She could only handle one desperate problem at a time. "Did your son have a kitten as a child? A long-haired Siamese named—"

"Hoi-Toi. How do you know this?"

"Come on, Abraham," she ordered gently instead of explaining her visions and adding to his fears. He'd gotten caught up in his guilt and confessing when they should've been saving Isaiah. "Times a-wasting."

Chapter Twenty-Eight

Abraham eased another door open and stepped inside a long, dark corridor that seemed to lead to the opposite end of the warehouse. Eden would've preferred to lead, but he seemed to know where he was going. He also seemed competent with McCluskey's *Dirty Harry* pistol, a formidable Smith and Wesson .44 Magnum. Typical hardware for an FBI agent who'd obviously thought he was Wyatt Earp.

Like Tucker Chase. Her friend's bravado walked with her through the halls, but it was her favorite hero's calm presence gently stroking at the back of her mind that kept her steady and strong. It was Ky's touch. His love. He'd been with her every step of this insane journey.

She sighed at the rush of heated memories of their tumultuous times together. From the get-go, he'd known her. He might not have realized it that first night, but he did now. Her fingers longed to be touching him now instead of that snub-nosed revolver and taser in her pockets.

"This way," Abraham whispered, still walking steadily into the bowels of the warehouse and away from the front entry. The place was a chilly maze of dimly lit halls and closed doors, any of which could end in a death trap. He turned right into another long corridor, but stopped short at the second door on the left. Cocking his head, he leaned into the closed door. "Shhhhh."

She stilled, adrenaline surging through her veins, the thirty-eight special lifted and ready, the taser still snuggled low in her pocket. She meant to keep it out of sight for as long as possible. A lady didn't reveal all of her secrets.

"Isaiah's still in there," Abraham murmured. "I'm almost sure of it. Quiet."

Isaiah, Eden called mentally, needing to know for herself that this was not a trap. The only one she'd gotten a clear read on since the Cessna crashed was the doctor's son. Her gut instincts declared him safe, his father too, but Eden had unanswered questions.

She followed the doctor into a darkened room. A stifling combination of sweat and copper drifted into her nose. As she reached out with her second sight, Isaiah's inert form became visible, his aura grayish-white, the color of death. She called softly to him, "Isaiah. I'm here. Your father's here, too."

He didn't offer back so much as a whimper. Isaiah was taller than his father, but so gaunt. So pale. Some of the cuts inside his biceps were red, but healed. Others were fresh and still dripping as if he'd been bled recently to keep him weak. His bare chest was muscular. Chiseled. Restrained beneath a wide leather belt. A puddle of red blood lingered in the metal bucket beneath the table. Someone had tortured him recently. That someone had to be in the building. Maybe closer.

"My son!" Dr. Zaroyin hurried to the stainless-steel platform that held Isaiah "Mother of God, what have they done to you while I've been gone?" When he pressed a switch at the end of the table, a dim light flickered on beneath the narrow hood. That he knew the location of that switch shot a creepy wave of gooseflesh up Eden's neck. What else did he know?

What else had he done on a worktable like this one? Autopsies? On who? How many?

She shoved the scary suspicions away and focused on saving Isaiah, her pulse skipping frantically in her throat. The guy was a study in sculptured muscle, sweat and blood. He hadn't moved so much as a finger.

"Help me get him off this work bench. Quick," Abraham ordered, his voice tight. "We don't have time. They're supposed to check on him once every hour unless…"

Workbench. A very creepy name for a stainless steel contraption designed to hold bodies still. Dr. Zaroyin had some explaining to do.

"Unless what?" Eden asked, her nerves frayed, and her newborn faith in her doctor friend shaken. She unsnapped the padded cuffs from Isaiah's ankles while his father undid the leather straps and released his wrists. The leather band around his forehead fell aside next, and Eden was very afraid.

Until this moment, she'd left physical rescues to actual heroes: FBI SWAT, Navy SEALs, and other more qualified operators. But being there, being the one saving Isaiah's life, brought a whole new perspective to her chosen, and until now, very safe career. All of those brave men and women she'd sent in to save others had risked their lives, yet they'd done it. Every single time.

Eden swallowed hard. She understood now. She didn't want to die in this concrete tomb with its labyrinth of hallways and secrets, but neither would she leave this tortured man behind.

Abraham didn't look at her, just kept working the belts and buckles to free his son. "Unless they want something, Agent Stark. I was afraid of this. Isaiah's ethics are rock solid.

Torturing him was the only way to force him to misuse his psychic abilities. Damn them."

She gulped at the brutality, her throat dry and her fingers trembling. Isaiah was the ultimate bait, and there she was, smack in the middle of a deadly trap that would not only kill him and her, but their future children, too.

"How do you plan to get him out of here?" she asked to keep her mind focused on success.

Abraham didn't skip a beat. "I have a friend on the outside. See that gurney behind you? Bring it close so I can transfer Isaiah."

She hurried and rolled the empty gurney alongside the autopsy table. *The workbench.* "You take his shoulders. I'll grab his feet."

Abraham's head bobbed. "On one. Two. Three."

Like pros, they transferred Isaiah to his singular chance for safety. He never made a sound. Never moved. Not even when his skin stuck to the dried blood on the table. Eden could've cried at the monstrous crimes wrought on his poor body. His curly hair was soaked with sweat, his lips chapped. She suspected his tormentors had done more than just cut him. There was no IV line to replace bodily fluids. No cup for a simple glass of water. No sign that he'd eaten recently.

"God, he's so light," Abraham cried, his palms splayed over his son's chest. "My poor boy."

Eden doffed her fur coat and covered her wounded charge with it. "He'll be warm now. What's next?"

"We wait. I called my contact the minute we landed. He'll text me when he arrives, and we'll wheel my son out of the back door. We'll be free."

"You called someone?" she asked, not remembering that little news item. "Really? When?"

Dr. Zaroyin nodded emphatically. "Yes. Why do you think I let you and McCluskey step out of the chopper first? I knew we'd need help, and I didn't know if I could trust you yet."

Understatement of the year, but at least he had a plan. "How long will that take? Who is this friend?"

Isaiah's quiet groan interrupted his father. *Eden?*

She lifted his hand, intertwined her fingers with his. *Yes. It's me. I'm here.*

He arched his back, his eyes still closed. *I told you not to come.*

The abject sorrow behind those words stabbed her heart. She didn't need protecting. *Isaiah, be still. Everything's going to be okay. We're here to save you.*

I'm dying, he whispered silently. *You shouldn't have wasted your life to save mine.*

No, you're not. Your dad and I are saving you, and that's all there is to it. Now let us do that for you, okay?

My father is here?

Yes, Isaiah. Try to open your eyes. See him. Then you'll know. A good father risks everything for his child. He loves you.

Isaiah stiffened but slowly turned to face his father. "Dad?" he whispered hoarsely.

Dr. Zaroyin cradled his adult son's head inside the crook of his arm like he was a baby. With tears streaming down his face, Abraham placed a father's fervent kiss to Isaiah's sweaty cheek. "We're going home," he said, his eyes glistening as they scanned over Isaiah's desperate condition. "And look. Eden is here."

"But Dad..." Isaiah's weak voice trailed away.

"Your friend had better get here soon," Eden muttered. "Isaiah needs a hospital."

"He'll be here," Abraham insisted, his forehead pressed to his son's. "He's a good man. You'll see."

"Is it Cameron Levine?" She had to know.

Abraham stared up at her. His brows narrowed. "Who?"

"You didn't send Levine to intercept me in Hawaii?" *Then who did?*

"I don't know who you're talking about. Why would I send someone to you? I could barely keep up with you myself."

She swallowed her snappy comeback. If this so called friend was such a good man, why wasn't he already there and waiting for them when they arrived? Why hadn't he helped take McCluskey down? That would've been darned friendly. And another thing. The part of the puzzle she still hadn't figured out reached out of nowhere and slapped her in the face. If Dr. Zaroyin hadn't stuck those implants inside her body, and if he hadn't placed that hormone patch, or whatever it was, on the back of her leg, who the heck did? Was it truly Levine or— was someone else in this twisted game?

Eden could see how Levine might've manipulated her into fleeing to Hawaii, then Alaska. She was scared and trusty of her FBI brethren then, but Levine couldn't be in two places at once. No. Someone else was behind Charlie Sweets' death and the crash. If her instincts were right, Zaroyin had been forced to follow where she ran. That was why he'd shown up in San Francisco, Hawaii, then Alaska so quickly. They'd both been manipulated, she to save her life, him to capture her to save his son. She still could not explain why Levine had Zaroyin chasing after her, though. Why didn't Levine, if he truly was the nut-job behind this nightmare, have let Zaroyin catch her before she'd ever fled for her life across the Pacific? Why engage not only Charlie Sweets, but all those poor FBI agents he'd turned into drones?

The anxious need to be far, far away from this twisted scheme and Bick's insidious torture chamber skittered up her spine. Something still didn't add up. She needed time to think, darn it.

Eden cracked the door just enough to peer into the outside hall, but the doctor's cell phone buzzed, startling her. She turned to watch him read the screen with relief. "He's waiting at the rear exit with a van. Is anyone in the hall?"

Claustrophobia clutched her larynx, stopping her breath. *Who was out there?* "No, I don't like this. but something doesn't feel right."

Abraham's eyes flashed sheer panic. "What do you mean?"

"I mean I'm a level-ten psychic, and I've got a bad feeling. Are you sure you can trust this friend of yours?"

His head bobbed adamantly. "Oh, yes. He's been with me every step of the way."

"Give me a name, Doctor. Who is he?" Eden stared the older man down. Every ectoplasmic speck of her second sight had finally sprung back to life, but it was on fire. Bright red danger lights flashed in her mind, cautioning her not to take one more step. But adrenaline thundered through every vein, clamping down her lungs, demanding fight or flight. She needed a name, darn it. "Tell me who your friend is, doctor."

"Come on," he urged. "If we stay here, we're all dead."

If you leave, you will die.

Whoa. That voice came out of the blue. She froze in her tracks. *Isaiah. Was that you?*

His lips hadn't moved, and he looked closer to death, but he had definitely spoken, his mental voice less than a whisper. *Don't go. I feel the danger, too. Stay here. Please.*

A noise banged from the hallway.

"Oh, my God," the elder Zaroyin cried. "It's too late. We're caught. They're coming! We have to go. Now!"

Panic jolted Eden into action. If she believed Abraham, to stay meant certain death. To go meant risk laced with the possibility of life. There was no choice. "Let's do this."

At her words, he threw his weight behind the gurney while Eden opened the door and peered both ways down the hall. "Hurry," he hissed.

"Clear," she reported, not sure where that last noise had come from, darn it. Where were those people who supposedly checked hourly on Isaiah? Suspicion poked at her.

Angling the gurney into the hall, Zaroyin turned left. "The rear exit's this way. Whatever happens, keep moving until we clear the building."

That sounded ominous. Eden didn't like this one bit. She shrugged yet one more stab of adrenaline off her tense shoulders, guarded their rear, her weapon ready to take command at the slightest hint of either Bick's presence. Zaroyin's cell phone buzzed an incoming text. He fumbled it out of his pocket and laid it on his son's feet while he read the message. "He's right outside. Hurry. God, please hurry. He says the Bicks are on their way."

"Who is he?" Eden hurried already! She passed the flustered man and flung open the rear exit. Tucker's words sprang to her lips with a hearty, "Son-of-a-bitch!"

There stood the last person she expected to see.

Matt Hartigen.

Shots fired?!

Ky could've crawled out of his skin at that report from Mother. He gunned the gas pedal of the SUV Alex had waiting when he, Rory, and Taylor landed. Mother advised that most available TEAM agents were already on-site at Senator Bick's warehouse. Mark Houston was acting agent in charge, but on hold along with FBI SWAT and local law enforcement.

Ky jerked the SUV around a family van and broke the speed limit two times over, needing to fly. Five long miles stretched between him and the warehouse. Rory and Taylor didn't say a word.

Hang tight, he mentally commanded Eden over the distance. *Goddamnit, wait for me!*

Eden slammed the heavy door before Matt and his buddy Bick could step inside. Without asking, she relieved Zaroyin of McCluskey's piece.

"But he said—"

"He's a friggin' liar. We need a defendable position. Where else can we go in this place?"

"Nowhere, Agent Stark," Matt's voice boomed over the loudspeaker system. "Let's make this easy. Come out so I don't have to kill you when I come in."

The bastard could hear her? Could he see her, too? She peppered the rear exit with a hearty 'Hell, no!' from the very vocal Smith and Wesson in her sweating palm. Rolling the tension out of her stiff neck, she faced a father who, until that moment, she'd fully believed just wanted to rescue his child.

"What the heck is going on? Hartigen died in front of my eyes," she spat, "as least, he pretended to. He fell over dead, and I watched them bury him. You want to explain why he's on his feet and still thinks he's god?"

Someone had the balls to jiggle the rear doorknob, so Eden fired another round of *'Mind your damned business before I blow your head off!'* She meant to kill the next guy who crossed her or lied to her. Enough!

"Answer me, Doctor," she hissed. "Are you in bed with Hartigen, too?"

"No, he was my friend. I thought—"

"He put that implant in my fucking skull! They wired me like a goddamned Christmas tree and screwed with my hormones. They've been working with Bick, and you want me to believe you didn't know?" Even she heard Tucker's vitriol screaming out of her mouth, drowning out Ky's calmer influence.

"I didn't know," Abraham replied quickly, his palms splayed, no doubt attempting to placate her. "Agent Stark, as God is my witness, I—"

"Do not pull the God card on me. Not now."

He looked down at his unconscious son, blinking. Drawing in a deep breath, he rested his hands on Isaiah's forearm. "You're right to suspect me. This is all my fault. Everything. I made the mistake of trusting Matt and Doug. It's up to me to fix it. What would you have me do?" Lifting his face, he returned her gaze. "I'll talk to them if—"

"No!" snapped out of her. They were long past talking.

There seemed no way out of the warehouse or this God-awful dilemma. Breathing hard, Eden shot one quick look at the bullet-riddled exit door. Hartigen and Bick hadn't said much in the last few minutes. Either they were dead, wounded, or already inside the warehouse and sneaking up on her.

When no clear way forward presented itself, Eden opted for the least of the worst, like Ky had in Canada. She needed a defendable position, a place of ensured safety, someplace with enough explosives at her back to scare Hartigen and Bick and maybe keep them from firing at her. Plain and simple, she needed to buy time until Ky got there, because he *was* coming. She couldn't sense him at that moment, but she knew it in her heart.

"Where's the cryo-lab?"

"Back one corridor. I'll take you there."

She motioned for him to move it. Of all the bad luck, Eden had a distraught father on one side, and an unconscious torture victim and her worst nightmare on the other. Could things get any worse?

Chapter Twenty-Nine

Ky peeled out of his TEAMwear before he hit the ground running. His SUV hadn't rolled to a complete stop. Police cars, FBI vans, and officers surrounded the warehouse, as well as two TEAM vehicles. "Where is she?" he called out to Mark Houston, Alex's senior agent on-site.

"Not sure," came the answer. "SWAT won't let us pass. Rory and Taylor, gear up and take position. Ky, come with me."

Ky stifled the need to run into battle without accurate intel. "Whatcha got?" *And make it quick.*

Mark Houston. Big bruiser and a farmer's son from Ohio. Dark-haired. Usually, the easiest man to get along with on The TEAM. Not today. Not dressed in tactical gear like he was and bristling with armament. He waved Ky to the open tailgate on his SUV where an arsenal waited on the local authorities for the green light to engage. Resting his butt to the rear bumper, he crossed his arms over his broad chest and lowered his black-as-sin sunglasses, another TEAM specialty. Piercing dark brown eyes skewered Ky. "Tell me what you know and do it fast."

Ky obliged. "FBI Agent Tucker Chase and Eden escaped camp before it was overrun. Somehow, Zaroyin wrested Eden Stark away from FBI custody. He or his men shot Chase in the head and left him for dead. Stark is valuable, Mark. She's what they call a level-ten psychic, able to reach anywhere on the planet to influence people or events with her mind. She suspects Zaroyin wants her to control his drone army."

"And you know this how?"

"Because she was with me when Lee Hart pulled me out of Hasim Nizari's cell outside Kabul. I saw her as clear as day. She stood by me until the end, until Lee found me. I know it was her."

Mark tugged at his left earlobe. "But you didn't really see her, did you? If I recall your after-action report, you were in damned rough shape by the time you were airlifted out of there. You were talking out of your head, and you fought everyone who laid a hand on you."

Ky cast a sideways glance at the warehouse, every muscle in his body tuned toward that desperate woman inside before he faced Mark again. Deep dark brown eyes locked onto Ky's, boring through the bluff. "I don't have time for this, Mark. Yeah, I fought everyone, and you know why. I couldn't bear to be touched after what I went through, but it's different with Eden. Her touch is different. It—heals. Facts don't quantify what she can do. There's no way I can prove it. Either you believe me or—"

"Hold on, Junior Agent." Mark's tone mellowed. "I'm not denying you and Agent Stark have a link. What I want to know is if you can use it to our advantage? Can you communicate with her? Is it possible you're psychic, too?"

Ky grunted at the sincerity behind that ludicrous question. "Me? I'm no psychic."

"Then how do you explain her ability to reach out and touch you in that hellhole all the way from the East Coast?"

Ky shifted his stance. Truth was, he couldn't. Her finding him out of millions, suffering across the globe, had always baffled him. It still did. He hadn't had time to think about it, but it was obvious Mark had. "So what do you want me to do? Meditate or something?"

Just the thought of calming himself enough to meditate spiked more adrenaline in him. God, this was not the time or place for this conversation.

Mark shrugged. "You tell me. How'd you reach out to her before?"

Ky ran a hand through his short-cropped hair, exasperated he wasn't at that moment storming the warehouse. That was what real men did. They charged into hell, and they made a difference, damn it. "I was dying, Mark," he snapped. "I was hanging like a side of beef off a hook in Nizari's ceiling, and one of his asshole soldiers was fixing to barbeque me for the fun of it. That's what I was doing. I was hanging on a chain by my goddamned wrists, and—"

"Junior Agent," Mark murmured, a thread of gentleness in his tone, "I know exactly what you went through. There's no need to preach to the choir. Sit your ass down and focus on that woman in there, the one you love enough to die for. See if you can reach her. Find out exactly where she is and who's in there with her. Get us some intel."

Ky gulped. How did Mark know he loved Eden? Was he friggin' psychic too? Was he that good at reading his men? "What if I can't communicate with her? Can we still get inside without SWAT knowing? Is there any way to get past them?"

Mark's eyes dropped to the tailgate, his order standing, and damn it. Ky sat, his arms across his chest, wishing he held Eden safe and sound instead.

Several more gunshots rang out from within the brick building, and it was all Ky could do not to run to her. He raked a hand through his hair again, his frustration at the breaking point and his senior agent out of his friggin' mind. *I'm no psychic. Let me do my job, damn it!*

Slapping one hand to his thigh, he opted to give Mark's insane idea a try, but one try only. Then he was going in.

Eden stood between Zaroyin's cryogenics laboratory door and the man himself. His poor son still lay unconscious on the gurney, fighting for his life. Behind them against the far wall stood a row of stainless-steel, ceiling-high, barrel-wide cylinders, clearly marked: Nitrogen, refrigerated liquid. To the side of the tanks, an oblong metallic pod-type contraption rested on a table.

"Why so much element N?" Eden expected a tank or two, but five? "What'd you need it for?"

Zaroyin cocked his head as if he didn't understand.

"Don't play dumb. You heard me. Why this much liquid nitrogen, Doctor?" Other lab equipment lined the room, but Eden's gaze closed in on the pharmacy-style refrigerator alongside the wall to her right, the one with rows and rows of test tubes and bottles behind double glass doors. "What's this for? Lunch?"

"N-n-no, umm, that's where the, umm, harvested eggs will go after—"

"You bastard. You planned to build a psychic army with Bick, didn't you? You planned—"

"Yes. I already told you. I made mistakes and—"

"Oh, puh-leeze! You put too much faith in the good doctor, Agent Stark." Cassandra Bick herself stepped out from behind the farthest nitrogen cylinder, her nose crinkled as if she found the situation funny. "I'm afraid he doesn't have what it takes to be a truly great man, do you, Abraham?"

Zaroyin shifted between Cassandra and the gurney. "Stay away from my son. You can't have him. None of him."

"Oh, but that's where you're wrong. I'm going to have the very best of him." She lifted her palms to the ceiling, gesturing like some diva from a talk show and looking silly in a really sinister way in that pure white lab coat and six-inch heels. "Look around, Agent Stark. You've come to the perfect place for my little experiment. Why, it's almost as if you wanted this to happen all along, isn't it?"

"You look around. The only reason we're here is to make sure you and your jerk husband don't take a shot at us. If we go, you go, got it?" Eden shot back at the haughty woman. God, who'd painted those eyebrows on her? Pointed. Black. She looked like Cruella de Vil on steroids. Or crack.

Bick's despicable other half stalked toward Eden. "Isn't it about time we had a little girl-talk about the birds and the bees? Aren't you sick of being a nun?"

Eden lifted her lips into a snarl, her weapon now pointed directly at Mrs. Bick's long nose. "Isn't it about time you back your shit up and run for your fucking life?" She nearly choked on the words out of her mouth. *Shit! Why can't I stop channeling Tucker?*

Cassandra narrowed those stark brows, squinting as she came to a complete standstill. Her lips pinched into an absurd, little girl pout. "Why, Agent Stark. You're not the prude I was told you were. What happened? Finally got your perfect ass screwed?"

Eden aimed, the reticle of that BFG positioned precisely between Cassandra's eyes.

"Oh, come on," Cassandra huffed. "I'll be extra careful when I harvest the eggs from your cold, dead body. Honest I will. I'm trained. I promise, you won't feel a thing, and trust me. You will be cold. I know all about vitrification and how to prepare those delicate little eggs of yours for the cryo-vials, but would you care to hear the best part?" She lifted both of those gaudy brows, not waiting for an answer. "Why, that's when I get to plunge those unborn children of yours into liquid nitrogen. I get to flash-freeze your precious tiny babies into the outer darkness of one-hundred-seventy-five degrees below zero. Ah-h-h! You wouldn't believe the thrill of wasting your one and only opponent's genetic line. Nothing can surpass that."

Cassandra winked—the bitch actually winked! This woman was seriously out of her ever friggin' mind, especially with that one and only opponent dig. How could she, Eden Stark, a nobody from Idaho, ever have threatened a woman with the worldwide fame and notoriety of this demented movie harlot?

Extending a long pointed fingernail, Cassandra beckoned Eden to come closer. *As if.* "There's a good friend I want you to see before I end you. Oh, Mathew," she called over her shoulder without taking her eyes off Eden. "Be a good boy and join us girls, wouldn't you?"

"He's no friend of mine," Eden growled when Hartigen stepped into view. Still dressed professionally, he loosened the tie Eden wanted to strangle him with.

He cocked his head at the corner behind him. "Utility entrance, Stark. You didn't think we dropped these tanks through the ceiling, did you? Use that empty head of yours for a change."

"Traitor," she hissed, the BFG now trained on his smirky face instead of Cassandra's. "I thought you were my friend."

"Yeah, well, you thought a lot of stupid things, didn't you?"

Cassandra chuckled low and deep in her throat. "Only what you wanted her to think, Matt. Look at her. Dressed to kill. Ready to die for her friends. All noble and shit like that."

"She looks like a whore," Matt purred. "My kind of woman."

Douglas Bick peered around the corner. God, the man was the picture of gluttony incarnate, right down to his extra-large pleated trousers and broken-down penny loafers. His plump cheeks spread downward over his chin and jaws. He had no neck, just one puffy pillow of fleshy wrinkles. "Mind if I join the party? I mean, I'm paying for it, aren't I?"

Eden took a step back, her butt now against Isaiah's gurney and no further retreat left. The room had gotten crowded in a hurry. She needed more space between her and this bastardly threesome. Too bad there was none. "Stay back," she ordered, her tone edgy and hard. They needed to be scared of something, darn it. The gun in her hand didn't seem to worry them enough.

"Don't do this," Zaroyin said firmly. "Doug. Matt. The chip doesn't work. You both know that. I've showed you all my research. Your drone army won't survive."

Doug shook his head slowly, the cellulite in his jowls jiggling under his blotchy skin. "It's not about the chip anymore, Abe, and you know it. Yeah, those armies you were so proud of didn't pan out like we thought they would, but who needs them? Think about it." He nodded at Eden. "That little gal only came into this world with a finite number of eggs in her tubes, but with your boy's sperm, and what we now know about cryogenics, we can still get that army we wanted. Only we'll get a better one. One we can add to anytime we want. One that doesn't depend on anyone but me."

"And me," Cassandra interjected. She stepped over to her husband to run a long fingernail over the shoulder seam on his white dress shirt. "Don't forget me, big guy."

Eww, sickening. A svelte half-attractive younger woman preening to jolly old saint Bick's ego. Just plain revolting.

Bick patted his wife's butt through her lab coat and snickered. "Well of course, pumpkin pie. I get it. This way, you'll finally be able to have that little girl you always wanted." He shrugged, his eyes diverted to Isaiah then back to Eden. "Or a boy, if that's the flavor of the month. 'S all the same to me as long as you keep your brats out of my way while I'm working."

"Who do you think she'll look like?" Cassandra planted her lips on her husband's flaccid cheek. "Blonde like Agent Stark, or dark-haired like my pretty boy, Isaiah?"

"I'm sure either way she'll look just like you, Cassie." Bick stroked his wife's ego right back at her. "After all, it's about the nurture, not the nature."

Cassandra giggled like a demented sixteen-year old at that less than scientific comment. Nature had nothing to do with these freaks.

"No," Eden bellowed, her raging motherly instincts on overload. *They're my daughters. My sons. My babies!* The muzzle of her pistol aimed over Bick's head to the stainless steel tank behind him. "One more step, and so help me, I'll—"

Cassandra took a deliberate step toward her. "You'll what? Shoot the nitrogen tanks and blow this place sky-high? You'll kill Isaiah? Innocent women and children in the surrounding neighborhood?" She took another step. "I don't think so. You're too good to do something so heinous, Agent Stark. You don't kill people, do you? Well, you ought to try it. For once in your pitiful, fatherless life, you really should do something, even if it's wrong."

My fatherless life? "Really?" Eden taunted right back. "What'd you do, read up on me? Was that your plan—needle me until I break?" She grunted deep and low, and Tate would've been proud. "Newsflash. My mama was my hero. Do you want to know what she taught me?"

Eden racked the slide, something she should've thought of a heckuva lot earlier, but hey. It surprised Cassandra Bick, enough that she took a step back for a change.

Eden sucked in a deep breath of now or never. Could she do it? Dare she? You bet. The end of the barrel trembled as if she was a novice at killing, mostly because she was. The Bicks didn't need to know that. She huffed a hard breath through flared nostrils, finally faced with the moment that came to all who chose to stand for something they believed in.

"My single mother taught me to believe in myself," she declared proudly, her chin tilted and her gaze fierce. "And she taught me how to take care of a bully. Who's first?"

"Come on, Doug," Zaroyin coaxed at her side. "You don't have to do this. Let these kids go. They haven't done anything to you. This is my fault. Kill me, not—" He lunged at Matt before Matt could draw his handgun, and down both men went to the floor.

Cassandra took the opportunity and rushed Eden, forcing the BFG upward. She didn't waste time digging her long fingernails into Eden's cheek, edging toward her left eyeball. So that was the way it was going to be. *Catfight!*

Eden grabbed a hank of Cassandra's fine black hair and jerked her face down to her knee in one smooth '*Take that, bitch!*'

Snap. Crackle. Cassandra jerked backward, fire in her surprised eyes and blood streaming out of her broken nose. She muttered something unintelligible, probably, *"Ouch, you're hurting me."*

Eden caught the odd coincidence in the millisecond she had to avoid another slap. *Oh heck, Cassandra has green eyes like mine. Only mine are prettier.* She promptly forgot them. They'd soon be black and blue.

Growling and wearing a nice shade of bright red splashed all over that pristine lab coat and her ugly face, Cassandra seemed up for more calisthenics. She charged and threw her shoulder into Eden's chest, spinning her around and stealing her breath, but not her fight.

With her back to the missus, Eden stomped down hard with one stiletto-heeled boot on the tip of Cassandra's foot. Mrs. Bick squealed like an over-compensated cheerleader. Eden swung her around. It didn't take much to tip Cassandra's arrogant ass backward enough that she fell over Isaiah's gurney.

Eden snaked easily out of Cassandra's stupid attempt at a wrist hold, too. Plain and simple, the woman might think she was tough, but she had no self-defense tools in her bag-o-bitch.

But Eden did. She might not know how to kill people for a living, but she meant to beat this Bick there and then. With all her might, she cocked one arm back and planted a curled fist into Cassandra's throat when she pushed off Isaiah. Dimly aware of the ongoing struggle between Hartigen and Dr. Zaroyin, Eden paused for one fleeting moment to consider the overall problem. Abraham had better know how to fight, or kicking Cassandra's uppity ass might not be enough to win this war.

Chapter Thirty

Ky stilled, his butt on the back bumper of Mark's SUV, the rest of his entire being focused on the memory and the color of Eden's sexy eyes. The tilt of her nose. The soft-as-honey fullness to her lips. The taste of her mouth. Her breath. The tender murmurs deep in her throat when he'd first kissed her. When he'd swallowed that first spark of passion and found her not only tempting, but deliciously willing.

He smoothed both palms over his thighs, attempting to block the rampant activity swirling around him, but controlled chaos was everywhere. FBI. SWAT. An army of locals. The fire department. There was simply too much noise to sit still long enough to focus. He stuck one hand deep into his pocket, frustrated with this cockamamie notion of Mark's. It wasn't in the cards, damn it. *Me, a psychic? That'll be the day.*

His fingers curled around that jar of Eden's he'd come across when he'd found Tucker's half-dead body. Dredging it up from his pocket, he twisted the lid off and pinched a dab of the translucent ointment between his index finger and thumb.

Ky lifted it to his nose and took a deep sniff. The strong vapor of camphor and eucalyptus watered his eyes, but suddenly, Eden was there. He breathed in the unlikely signature scent of the heroine of his soul. This peculiar fragrance offered the same hope and comfort as it had two and a half years earlier. Oddly refreshing. Different than any other. Totally. Uniquely. Eden.

Ky settled his back against the side of the SUV's rear gate and studied the brick structure opposite Mark's SUV. At that moment, SWAT had everyone else pushed back beyond their bright yellow *FBI—DO NOT CROSS* tape. No one was allowed inside. Not local authorities. Not the EMTs standing by. Especially not private contractors.

The red-brick building itself looked to be three stories at the rear, with the north side possibly one large area at the front, judging by the solid walls of windows at the east and west. Typical for a large equipment bay that led to administrative offices or smaller work areas. In other words, the place looked like any other old warehouse.

Then why hadn't the FBI stormed it yet? What were they waiting for? Better question, what were they afraid of? Ky channeled a question to Eden, just in case there was any truth to this psychic theory of Mark's. *Where are you, baby?*

Instead of a mental reply from a soft-spoken woman, some loud-mouthed SWAT officer rounded the rear corner of the building, his hand cupped to his mouth. "Pull back! Shooter! We've got liquid nitrogen inside and a shooter! This place is gonna blow!"

Shit! Adrenaline spiked up Ky's ass, screaming at him to do something besides sit on it. Done deal. He grabbed the first AR within reach, slammed a full magazine home, and stuffed another in his belt. He jumped to his feet to do what he should've done to begin with. His friggin' job. His real job. *Save Eden, damn it!*

Dodging lawmen and their silly yellow tape, he headed around back of the warehouse as several heavy fire engines and a ladder truck pulled up front. This ought to be good. Now he had more authorities to contend with, not to mention Mark, who was all at once hard on his ass. He'd expected more lawmen, but none followed. Must have been scared of the nitrogen blowing. That worked.

"Where do you think you're going, Winchester?" As big as Mark was, he had no trouble sticking close to Ky's six like white on rice.

"In." Ky sprinted across the open lot to the rear loading dock. *Isn't that what we do? Run in when others run out? Aren't we dumb like that?* He slowed alongside a diesel tractor-trailer backed up to the rear loading dock.

Mark matched his position, his own weapon locked and loaded. "You sure about this? I can call the others to join us."

"No," Ky admitted, "but I'm not backing down either. Let's hold off on dragging Rory, Taylor and the guys into this."

The dock itself stood in their way, a five-foot high stumbling block that would expose Ky and Mark to FBI SWAT fire, and maybe end this daring plan before it got started.

The only way in was to climb it and hope like hell no one shot them. It wasn't likely. Not with the number of federal agents on the other side of this diesel rig. The last thing Ky wanted was Mark dead by friendly fire. How would he explain *that* to his rabid boss? Or to Mark's wife and family? Yeah, not good. Not good at all.

Shit. He wiped the sweat out of his eyes, his heart on fire to reach Eden.

"I haven't made contact with Agent Stark," Ky murmured out of the side of his mouth, *because I'm not friggin' psychic.* Yet his mind and heart screamed, *Damn it, Eden, talk to me.*

"You wouldn't happen to have the schematics for this warehouse on you?"

"In fact, I do." Mark whipped out his cell phone, swiped his thumb over a few screens and handed it over. His palm cupped Ky's shoulder, a silent signal that he was in this all the way. "Getting past SWAT will be tough, though. What's your plan? Have you tried to reach out to her yet?"

Ky looked down at Mark's hand on his shoulder. There was a day he would've come up fighting at some guy bracing his weight on him like Mark was doing, but Eden's touch had changed everything. "I tried to get through to her mentally, if that's what you're asking, but I'm no psychic, and we don't have time to play around."

"Sometimes we can't see the forest through the trees. We try too hard. Never mind. She's too busy to pick up your signal anyway." Mark just wouldn't give it up.

Ky focused on the real-world shit he was dealing with and expanded the view of the building plan in the palm of his hand. "Where are the nitro tanks?"

"There." Mark stabbed a finger at the rear wall. "See the heavy-duty power lines?"

Ky and Mark looked up at the same time from their hiding place at said power lines. If Eden was that shooter and if she'd taken refuge there, she was close to the rear dock. Two things stood in their way. Getting shot by the FBI or the building exploding.

"She's in there," Ky murmured. "She's close. I can feel her." She has to be.

"I knew you could do it. Say when," Mark urged. "We're here. We might as well try."

Ky borrowed a line from another warrior *in a galaxy far, far away*. "There is no try. Only do." With that, he hoisted one knee onto the concrete lip of the dock and scrambled aboard. Mark never missed a beat. He charged alongside Ky. Funny thing about Mark. He'd positioned himself between Ky and SWAT like a dammed linebacker running interference in an ungodly football game.

A roar of righteous FBI anger and authority went up behind Ky and Mark, but rules and Feds be damned. This was not one of those times when a man asked, 'Mother, may I?' and Ky didn't intend to apologize for anything. This was go-time. Apologies, if there need be any, would fall to Alex.

Together, Ky and Mark breached the rear door. Ky rolled to both knees, sweeping the inside of the loading bay with his scope. No tangos presented themselves. Mark had dropped to one knee, the fingertips of his left hand splayed to the concrete floor. "Listen," he hissed.

Ky heard them, too. Voices. One in particular. Eden. Screaming, "Let me go!"

Not the best thing for a man already ramped high on adrenaline to hear. He reacted. Ky punched into high gear, jumped off the floor, and bellowed, "I'm coming!"

Mrs. Bick fought dirty. The beast had concealed a pocketknife in her lab coat and adeptly used it to slash the back of Eden's shooting hand. Eden didn't release her BFG, but the blood pumping out of her arteries made the pistol grip slippery. The trigger, too.

She heard Zaroyin fighting the good fight somewhere behind her, but Bick? Where the heck had the senator slithered off to? Poor Isaiah hadn't spoken a word, and Eden was scared. The longer this stupid fight continued, the worse his chance for survival. This confrontation had to end.

Dodging the knife blade, she captured Cassandra's wrist with one hand, and finally managed to get the barrel of her pistol where it mattered—straight up against Cassandra's skinny neck and pointed into that soft spot under her chin.

"Don't shoot. Don't shoot," Cassandra whimpered on contact.

"Call your boy off," Eden commanded.

"I think it's the other way around," Douglas Bick ordered, huffing like he'd actually exercised. He certainly hadn't hung around to fight. "Drop your weapon, Agent Stark. Now."

Eden glanced at Abraham while Hartigen climbed off the floor. He looked a little worse for wear, but the doctor had been through the war. He stayed on his knees, his nose and lips bloodied. His hair stuck up off his head. His eyeglasses were gone. Worse, Bick held a pistol to his head.

Eden shoved her pistol harder into Cassandra's throat. "Stand back, Mr. Bick, or I will end your wife right here. Right now."

Hartigen shook his head as he swept his pistol off the floor. "Eden, Eden, Eden," he mocked as he stepped into her space and leveled his weapon at Isaiah. "Stop playing FBI and step back. You never were very good at it. We've got you solid. Two to one is not a standoff. It's a massacre."

"Try assassination," she hissed as she faced facts. The war was lost. Shoving Cassandra away, she lowered her pistol. She had nothing, her other weapons still in that stupid fur coat. "What now?"

Matt lifted the BFG out of her grip and tucked it in his pants. "Now we do what we intended to do all along. Cassandra. Do your thing."

The woman righted herself. Standing near the gurney, she took the time to smooth her over-sprayed hair back into place before she wiped the blood over her mouth, a dangerous glitter in her eyes. "The color of blood suits you, Agent Stark. It's a good thing we don't need you alive."

"We'll still do the procedure correctly," her husband soothed. "We'll be humane. Get her ready to move. We still need a sterile area. Abraham? May I assume you will not be offering your surgical skills for the record?"

Abraham bowed his head. "My son. My precious son."

Eden stood her ground, stalling for time. "Whose idea was it to stick those locators inside me?" she asked as Cassandra wasted more time putting herself back together, smoothing her hands over her rumpled lab jacket and skirt, tucking her blouse in, and tending to her broken nose.

Hartigen lifted a hand. "That was me. Needed you available twenty-four-seven, Stark. Fresh meat on the hoof, so to speak."

"You had your friend, Cameron Levine, do your dirty work," she hissed.

Hartigen shrugged one shoulder. "Yeah. So? You always thought you were untouchable, you prissy little bitch. Guess we showed you."

"But what about your wife? What about Melody and your kids? They think you're dead. Don't you feel anything for them?"

His eyes narrowed. "Cost of war. It all comes down to what matters most, and I promise you, in the long run, it ain't family."

"And the wife you vowed to love, honor, and obey? What is she? Collateral damage?"

"Shut it," Hartigen ground out. "That bitch is my problem, not yours. All you need to worry about is how to count backward from a hundred. You ready to go yet, Cassie?"

Oh, now it's Cassie. No wonder Matt had cast Melody aside. He had *Cassie*.

Bick shoved Zaroyin to stand near a nitro tank. "If you two are done with your lover's spat..."

Hartigen took the hint and jerked several zip-ties from his pocket. "Yeah. Let's get this thing done. Stark, hands behind your back."

"What are you going to do? Kill me? Here? With SWAT outside?"

"You just don't get it, do you?" Matt grabbed her wrists and secured the ties. "Not everything is as it seems."

She didn't understand until Cassandra strutted over to one of the nitro tanks and thumped it with the side of her fist. Darned if it didn't slide open to reveal an empty tank—and steps. Down. That was what Bick meant about getting ready to move.

Cassandra's crooked, bloody smile turned into pure evil. "You see? We planned for everything. This leads to a secure vault. Once we blow the tanks, no one will ever be the wiser. We'll leave through our escape tunnel. You'll never be seen again."

"Grab the kid," Bick ordered Matt as he waved his pistol from Eden to the fake tank. "You first. Cassie, make sure she doesn't try anything on the way down. Zaroyin, I ought to kill you right now, but I hate leaving loose ends that could lead back to me."

"But my son," Abraham ground out. "He shouldn't be moved. He's hurt."

"Don't worry, Pops." Matt wrapped the fur coat around Isaiah before he jerked him over his shoulder. "Just to prove how nice I can be, I'll keep your son warm. He's too valuable to kill anyway."

What could Eden do? She had no choice but to drop down the stairs behind Matt, and into the eerie silence ahead of Mrs. Bick. Abraham closed in behind Eden. The portly senator brought up the rear. By the time he reached the bottom step and the secret panel slid into place, he was breathing hard.

Bright lights flickered on overhead. Cassandra shoved Eden forward through another doorway into another room— Eden's worst nightmare. Two autopsy tables. Solid concrete floors, walls, and ceiling. Shiny medical instruments in rows on the side counter. She gulped past a dry throat. So this was where her journey would end—murdered in a fireproof vault where no one could hear her scream.

Cassandra shoved Eden onto one table and strapped her in while Matt dropped Isaiah like a side of beef onto the other. Senator Bick tied Dr. Zaroyin to a metal chair at the foot of his son's table. All hope was lost.

"How about you, Pops?" Matt asked Abraham as he fastened a belt around Isaiah's forehead. "You want to watch while we finish what you started? This was your idea, after all."

"The concept of a level-ten psychic controlling intelligent, thinking drones was my idea," Abraham corrected sadly. "This is nothing but cold-blooded brutality."

"You could call it that," Matt agreed. He tugged Eden's fur coat under Isaiah's chin. "Your boy's been real helpful, though. I don't mind keeping him warm until it's his turn. Between him and me, we've located all twenty-one of the known level-tens in the world. He might not have wanted to, but with a little persuasion, he got the job done. You should be proud."

"You tortured him to get that intel," Eden hissed. "That's why you've been bleeding him."

"Of course. I'm also going to milk a million swimmers out of him every day as long as he can produce. You're the one we don't need."

"You're so smart," Cassandra purred, now standing over Eden with surgical gloves on her grasping fingers and a long hypodermic needle in her right hand. She'd cleaned the blood from her face, but she'd need a good plastic surgeon for that mashed nose. She skimmed her fingernails over Eden's head. "You do have beautifully long hair. I like it. Such a pity none of your babies will get to meet their pretty, brave, heroic mother. Life is like that for many of the world's children, isn't it? At least you'll die knowing I'll be a good mother to the ones I let live."

"You're a fucking bitch," Isaiah murmured hoarsely from where he lay in restraints.

Cassandra's eyes narrowed. Her painted on brows slanted in a severe *V*. She pursed her ruby red lips. "Wait here," she whispered, her eyes bright. "I need to cut that boy's tongue out. I'll be right back."

Chapter Thirty-One

"Where is she?" Ky hissed.

They'd entered what appeared to be a laboratory from the loading bay through a utility door behind the tanks. Eden's scream had to have come from this room, but the place was empty. Except for the angry FBI rhetoric outside, it was damned quiet, too.

"Where is she, damn it?" he asked again, his weapon still poised to murder that rat bastard Zaroyin. The sterile-looking room wasn't large. How could she have gotten out of it so quickly?

Mark peered out the door opposite the nitro tanks, his short-stock rifle aimed to the ceiling. "The hall's clear, but someone was just here." He nodded to the blood splatter on the floor.

Ky reverted to the alpha hunter he was. Fresh blood on the floor. Blood on the gurney. All six senses kicked into high gear. His nose twitched. Eden was still close. The smell of menthol and eucalyptus was strong.

Hitching his weapon over his shoulder, he resorted to tactile, hands-on intel. Skimming over the walls, he searched for a pressure-sensitive panel or a pressure plate. A wall that moved. Anything. That deviant Nizari had delighted in using secret hiding places for his victims. Maybe Zaroyin did, too.

Mark opened and closed the doors on the metal cabinets opposite the bloody gurney. Nothing but medical supplies. Test tubes and more supplies lined the refrigerator shelves. Hypos. Vials of drugs. But nothing that indicated where Eden could've gone.

Ky stared at the nitrogen tank in the corner. Cylindrical, yes. Ceiling-high, bright and shiny, yes. But a few inches wider than the others. Why? The FBI would barge in soon and he'd be forced to leave. But first...

He placed both palms to the cylinder, feeling for a seam in the metal. A crack. Anything.

Mark joined him. "This tank's warmer than the others. You find the spring mechanism yet?"

"Not yet," Ky growled. But wait. He pounded his fist along the right side of the tank. The hidden panel slipped noiselessly to the left. "Found it," he whispered as he slung his short-stock back into his hands. Down he went with Mark into a well-lighted but empty room. Empty but for that hint of Vicks.

Mark clapped Ky lightly on the right shoulder, signaling him to take the lead and enter the opposing door. Ky never hesitated. Bracing for hell, he kicked the door open and pure animal rage took over. Zaroyin had strapped Eden to a stainless-steel table with belts on her ankles, arms, and head.

Only he was strapped to a chair at the end of one of the tables. It didn't make sense, but Ky didn't think twice. The fat bastard with the gun fell first, a double tap to his skull. No one raised a gun to Ky and lived to talk about it, not even an almighty senator. Mark shot the only other armed man dumb enough to offer resistance, and the fight was over as quickly as it had begun.

All except for Cassandra Bick. The witch had a hypo in the guy's neck on the other stainless-steel table. Had to be Isaiah Zaroyin, if the doctor's scream of alarm meant anything. "Stop! Don't kill him! He's all I've got."

"Put it down," Ky ordered, his rifle trained on Mrs. Bick's chest and ready to do the deed.

The woman trembled, her wide eyes popping from her dead husband to Eden and back to Ky. "You killed him," she whined. "He's all I had!"

"But I don't have to kill you." Ky mustered as much restraint as he could. If not for that needle pressed to Isaiah's neck, he'd take the shot and waste this psycho.

Mark positioned himself at Eden's side, loosening her restraints. That helped Ky settle his nerves.

"You? You're the man she loves?" Mrs. Bick sneered. "You're Ky Winchester?"

"Yes, ma'am, I sure as hell am." Now how the hell did she know that?

"Isaiah told me everything," she hissed, as if in answer to Ky's unvoiced question. "We gave him no choice. His father, either. They had to cooperate if they wanted to see each other again, but now... you've spoiled everything! I'll never have my precious babies!"

Ky lifted his rifle. *Keep talking, bitch. You don't deserve children.*

"Dr. Zaroyin saved my life, Ky. He couldn't go through with what the Bicks had planned," Eden called to Ky. "He saved me from Bick's assassin, from McCluskey. He killed for me, Ky."

That should've mattered, and it did, but right then and there, Ky only had eyes for the crazy woman in a blood-spattered lab coat. Mrs. Cassandra Bick. The lady with a death wish.

"Put it down," he commanded her. "There's no way you come out of this alive if you kill Zaroyin's son."

She snorted, her eyes dilated and her brows raised. "You think I want to live without my husband? Without Doug? Are you stupid enough to—"

A sizzling crackle filled the room. Pop. Pop. Snap!

Cassandra lifted to the tips of her toes. Her neck stretched. Her lips twisted frightfully wide open. The hypo dropped from her outstretched fingers to the floor. She screeched in what sounded like Morse code. She gasped. Growled. Drooled.

Ky pushed her away from Isaiah, intent on keeping him safe. "I've got you, buddy. You're going home now."

He whispered something back, but Ky couldn't catch what he said with all the grunting Mrs. Bick was doing. Finally, she dropped stiff as a board to the floor and just as silent.

"Say again?" Ky asked.

The words eked out of Isaiah. "Ta... ser."

A swarm of federal agents stormed the underground cryo-lab and took over the scene. Eden answered a few questions. Ky a few more. He gave up his weapons and every last piece of his tactical gear. The big guy with him did the same, but after a glowing commendation from Eden, both Ky and Mark Houston were released. Funny thing, though. Not once did Ky take those amber eyes off of her until he was told to vacate the premises. It seemed the FBI needed to secure it now that Ky and Mark had rendered it safe. The TEAM might mess up the evidence. Go figure.

Eden watched him watching her while he walked away with Mark. He wouldn't go far. Dr. Zaroyin was cuffed and directed into an FBI van. Cassandra Bick had already been transported to the nearest emergency room. Two medics attended to and rendered Isaiah emergency medical aid while the FBI medical examiner transferred Senator Bick and Hartigen into body bags.

I'd like to see you come back to life this time, Matt, you snake.

The universe seemed balanced again.

Until the FBI Director Zachary Strong showed up. Eden could feel him coming. The silver-haired man was a mighty force to be dealt with. A tidal wave of power pushed time and space out of his way as he strode into the underground den, his bright eyes taking in everything. "Agent Stark," he said crisply. "Status report."

"I'm still alive, sir," she answered meekly. That seemed important. She figured he already knew everything else.

"Out!" he barked to the room. The few FBI agents lingering left with the medics, Isaiah, and the ME.

"Director," Eden said calmly. She stood at the end of the autopsy table where she would've met her death.

"Agent Stark," he replied from his position at the door, his spine ramrod straight and his shoulders wide. "You are never, I mean never, to do that again, do you hear me, young lady?"

Young lady? So not what she'd expected. "W-what?"

"Why the hell didn't you tell me you suspected Zaroyin? Why did you run? I could've protected you, damn it. I could've prevented all this!"

"But I... I didn't know who to trust, and I couldn't risk—"

In two quick steps he was in her face. "Why the hell do you think you work for the FBI? Why do you think they've guarded you with their lives?"

"They, umm, didn't do a very good job this time," she reminded him.

"I know, God, I know, but damn it, Stark. You're worth a hundred agents. Don't run again."

"Yes, sir." Snap. He sounded like he thought he was her father.

"I mean it. I'll give you all my numbers. You will contact me at the first hint of trouble from now on, understood?"

"Yes, sir," she repeated, not sure why he didn't just put an official reprimand in her file and call it good. Eden reached one hand to his wrist and clamped on tight. It might work this time.

The vision came easily. Drake and Casey Franklin. A tow-headed girl swinging between their clasped hands, calling out, "Higher, Daddy! Higher, Mama!" Her parents in love, and lost little Eden the happiest baby girl ever.

She dropped Director Strong's wrist. "Who are you? Did you know my dad? My mom?"

He huffed through his nose, but told her, "I'm your uncle, Eden. Your father's brother."

"But why? How? His name's Franklin, isn't it?"

"Only in the witness protection program. Your mother witnessed a mob hit the year after you were born. Psychically. Not really, but when every detail panned out, and the press got hold of it, the mob went after her, and I got involved. I thought I had you safe and sound until your parents split."

"But she died," Eden whimpered. "Why didn't you, umm, come get me?"

Director Strong rubbed a hand across his forehead. "Because she left the program after Drake left her, and we couldn't track you. Honest, I had no idea Casey died until you tested at the top SAT scores in your high school. The Bureau's always looking for the best and the brightest, so I sent Matt to recruit you. Even then, I didn't realize you were Drake's daughter until I signed off on your top-secret clearance."

"Where is he? My dad?"

"He's working for General Dynamics in Crystal City. You'd be proud of him. He stopped drinking and cleaned up his act. He'd love to meet you."

"He drank?" Eden had no recollection of her father drinking, just that he'd loved her, but not enough to stay.

"He drank himself nearly to death after he left Idaho, but damn it, Eden. Your mother drove him away the same way she drove everyone else. She had this amazing gift, but she thought it made her better than everyone else. She thought it made her special, but not once did she develop it like you have."

"She never told me any of this."

"Why would she? She spent half her life trying to get lost."

"But she taught me everything I know." Eden needed to defend Casey. She'd protected her up until the accident, and she'd been the best mother ever. At least she hadn't left like Drake had.

"Why do you think the Bureau offered you the job they did when they did?" Director Strong asked, a definite tenderness to his tone. "It was the only way I could keep you close to me once I found you. I couldn't leave you in Idaho, could I? God, you would've married a potato farmer and had a dozen kids by now."

She nearly giggled. "Does anyone else know we're related?"

He shook his head. "Not until you want them to. Would you rather keep this to yourself for now?"

"No, I, umm..." God no. This was her boss—not just her boss but the director of the entire Federal Bureau of Investigation. But he was also her only living relative beside her father. Her uncle. *Wow. I have an uncle.* And a dad. "I'd like to meet him again."

Director Strong's eyes teared up. "Trust me, he'd really like that."

"Me, too," Eden said quietly. Director Strong did look like her father now that she had time to notice. He had the same brows. The same earlobes. "Are there more like me?" Maybe her whole family was psychic, if she and her mom were. Maybe it was a genetic thing like Zaroyin and Bick thought it was. Okay, it didn't make sense, not if she got her second sight from her mother, but at that moment, anything seemed possible.

Director Strong shook his head slowly. "I'm afraid not. Your mother had no living relatives and the rest of us Strongs are just regular Joes."

They stood there facing each other for a long minute.

"Snap. I don't know what else to say," he murmured, raking one hand through those silver spikes, kind of exasperated. "I know this is a lot to take in, but let's get out of here. You've got a young man waiting for you, and I've got work to do. Let me talk to Drake, and we'll go from there."

"You said snap."

He paused, his hand on the door and a crooked smile on his face. "Your grandmother used to say it all the time, young lady."

"I have a grandmother?"

He nodded. "Yes. You've got cousins, other uncles and aunts, too."

That did it. Eden rushed her Uncle Zachary, and he caught her. A quiet groan lifted up from his throat as he tucked her under his chin. He sniffed and growled, "Vicks? Drake had you using it, too? That stuff doesn't work."

Eden squeezed her uncle as tight as she could, her eyes filled with tears. She could barely speak, her heart was so full. "It worked for me."

Chapter Thirty-Two

"It took you long enough," Ky kidded from the warehouse door where he and Mark stood waiting.

Tucked under FBI Director Strong's arm like she was, Eden had a lively spring to her step and a glow on her face. She looked genuinely happy. "Ky Winchester, I'd like to introduce you to my uncle, Zachary," she said with a big smile. "Uncle Zachary, this is—"

"Yeah, I know who these guys are." Director Strong grabbed Ky's outstretched hand. "Hell, I've got their boss on speed dial. Ky. Mark. Thanks for taking care of my girl."

"Your girl?" Ky asked.

Mark slapped his back while he reached for the FBI director's hand. "Uncle, huh?"

The guy nodded. "It's a long story, one I'm sure Eden will be eager to share before the day is done. Looks like we've got this mess wrapped up. Feel free to take off. You too, Eden. I trust these guys. You couldn't be in safer hands."

Smart girl. She swapped Director Strong's arms for Ky's. He couldn't wait to get her alone, but back in his arms? Damned near heaven. He kissed the top of her head.

"Feel free to reach out to us anytime, Director," Mark quipped. "You know The TEAM. We're always here to help the good guys."

Director Strong waved them off. "Don't I know it. Tell Alex hey next time you see him. I'll be in touch."

"Will do. I'm on my way to brief him right now."

Ky and Eden walked Mark back to his TEAM SUV where Rory and Taylor stood waiting.

"I'll tell Alex you'll be in the office tomorrow," Mark said. "Where can he reach you?"

"We'll be at Ky's place," Eden replied quickly, then turned to him. "Won't we?"

He could've kissed her right then and there. "We will. You wouldn't mind giving Rory and Taylor a lift back to the office, would you, Mark? I need the rental."

"I see how it is," Rory quipped. "Dump us guys the second a pretty girl shows up."

Ky winked at him. "Absolutely."

"Take off," Mark groused. "Go on, get. See you tomorrow."

"Later," Ky said to Mark as he steered her to his rental. The drive from South Boston to his home in Silver Spring, Maryland, flew by, but with every mile, Ky worried. Eden had chosen wisely. He couldn't trust himself in her apartment or wherever she lived, that was for certain. If by chance he fell asleep, he couldn't guarantee he wouldn't wake up in the throes of a nightmare and tear her world apart. Maybe her, too.

But still...

Apprehension gnawed at him. Eden was pure and clean, a child compared to the likes of him. *What am I doing?*

His home was Ky-proofed. No lamps. No stray electrical cords. No curtains and no blinds. Nothing he could dislodge or throw in the midst of a nightmare or a panic attack. Nothing he could break or hurt himself with, either. He locked his piece up tight in The TEAM's vault before he left work at night. Never took it home. Couldn't take the chance. Even today, he'd secured his arsenal in the back of The TEAM's SUV while he'd waited on Eden to finish up with Director Strong.

Ky had also painted his bedroom window black. It made sense at the time. His job required odd shift-work. He needed to be able to sleep through the day.

His home had no carpeting, just a Turkish rug in the front room and wooden floors throughout. No comfy sofa. No cutesy dinette set. He'd given up on American Contemporary when he'd medically-retired from the Corps. It didn't agree with his new phobia, and there was no way a guy like him could ever be normal.

But there he was bringing a woman home. Why? How did a guy tell the woman he cared about that he slept on the floor? That he might wake up in the middle of the night and kill her? If he fell asleep...

It had been years since he'd trusted himself with the feminine persuasion, but now? He drummed the steering wheel as he closed in on familiar territory. In less than three blocks, he'd be home. If she thought she knew him, she was in for a shock. Playing around in the middle of the frozen north was one thing, but back home? *What the hell have I done?*

"You're quiet," she commented. Eden hadn't hugged him much after that initial snuggle, and honest to God, he'd needed one. Once he'd had her in his arms, his anxiety seemed to evaporate. She honestly was oxygen to his messed up mind. She was breath and life and light all rolled into one. But now...

"Yeah, well..." He swallowed hard. "Guess I'm just glad everything worked out as good as it did."

"As good as it did?" she mimicked. "You showed up in the nick of time, Ky. You saved my life. That makes, umm, how many times?" She held up her fingers, counting. "First, you rescued me at the crash site by taking out Koenig and Shields, then you operated on me three times, and... oh yes, you saved me from that baby-stealing bitch, Mrs. Bick. The nerve of that woman."

He relaxed enough to chuckle at Eden's vehemence. Even mad, she had a way about her that soothed his legion of devils down to a manageable crowd. Drawing in a deep breath of her scent, he focused on his calming techniques. He'd need every last one of them.

She released her seat belt and climbed over the middle console to kiss his cheek. Impulsively, he intercepted her lips while he kept his eyes on the road. "And taking Senator Bick down like you did makes six," she murmured into his mouth. "Don't forget, you owe me dinner and a dance, too. And coffee."

Yeah, about that...

"Are you hungry?" he asked, not necessarily stalling, but... stalling. There was no food at his place. Maybe this wasn't a good idea.

"Cassandra Bick meant to kill me, Ky," Eden kept talking. "She wanted my eggs and one of our children and—"

"Wait. What? Our child?"

"No. Mine and Isaiah Zaroyin's baby."

Oh no. Not going to happen, as in no-way-in-hell no. Ky shot her a look. "In-vitro fertilization?" It better not be the normal, body-slamming, one-on-one kind of reproduction.

"Yes! Can you believe the nerve of that woman?" Her head bobbed in ignorance of his growing need to kick the shit out of

Zaroyin's kid, and all those lovely blond curls tumbled onto his arm. "She said she wanted one of our daughters and maybe a son and—"

"Not going to happen," Ky snapped. *No way will Isaiah Zaroyin ever touch you. I'll kill him.*

"Well, I know that," Eden snapped back. "After all, you saved me, remember?"

Ky turned into his driveway, intent on one thing. "We're home," he said with a renewed sense of conviction. "It's not much, but it's mine and so are you."

That brought Eden up short. She faced him, those green eyes bright, and as always, seeing right through him. "I am?"

"Damned straight." He latched onto her wrist and dragged her luscious, giggling body over the console. Slamming his door, he stooped to toss her over his shoulder, one hand on the ass he meant to claim. She might as well understand and understand it fast. Isaiah Zaroyin could get his own. Ky let his fingers tap out that message on her backside. *Mine. All mine.*

"What are you doing?" she giggle-shrieked from her upside-down position, her hands snug on his waist. "What will your neighbors think?"

"That I'm home," he groused, itching to smack that sinfully soft backside. His caveman side seemed to have taken the lead, and it was about time. He'd nearly forgotten what it felt like to be a man with a woman in his arms.

Ky paused to unlock his front door, then angled Eden inside his humble home without bumping her head on the doorjamb. Funny. Once he set her on her feet, it didn't look so humble. He didn't bother turning on the lights, not with her glowing like she was.

His hesitation backed off, and he meant to show Eden who was boss, but, damn it. *She was.* She just didn't know it yet.

"I don't have much," he admitted as he locked the door behind him. "I've got no frozen pizza in the fridge and no wine coolers or beer, either. Hell, I've got no mattress in my bedroom or sheets. I sleep on the floor." She might as well know how bad it would be. He'd lived the life of a monk the past couple of years.

She seemed not to notice, just stood there, wringing her hands like she wanted to do something with them but didn't know if she should.

"Damn it, Eden. Say something."

"Kiss me," she whispered. "Like you did in Canada. Burn me down, Ky. Kiss me like you mean it."

He shook his head. This was moving fast, and as much as he wanted it, he didn't. This was that moment, that Christmas morning moment when all those lovely presents under the tree could still be all you'd ever wanted and all you ever dreamed. But the second you unwrapped them, the excitement was over. The dreams and wishes were either fulfilled and you were on cloud nine, or you were left wanting.

My God, until that intimate unwrapping took place, she still thought she loved him. She thought he'd rescued her, that he was some kind of a hero. In truth, he was more the Beast to her Beauty. His body craved hers with the single-mindedness of a heroin addict for crack. By the time this—whatever it was—was over, by the time the meager present he had to give her was unwrapped and revealed, the thrill of her expectations would be demolished. He'd have what he wanted, but she'd hate him forever for it.

The need to slow things down sneaked up on him. "Shower first?"

Some of the stars fell out of her eyes, but she had to understand who he was before they took another step. She had to see him. All of him.

He gave her no time to answer, just tugged her headlong down the hall to his equally sparse bathroom. Ushering her in first, he followed and closed the door behind him. "Strip," he ordered before he lost his nerve. It was now-or-never, and he needed it done before he had time to think. To renege.

She was a compliant little wench, wiggling out of her clothes in a split second, no questions asked. It surprised him when she stepped on them like they were rags. Almost defiantly, Eden presented her lovely, lush body with all its plump curves, her chin tilted upward, her green eyes glittering like emeralds. Her tiny waist tucked nicely to her rounded hips, and his fingers ached to latch onto her.

"How's this?" she murmured breathlessly, her hands at her sides instead of in the demure Venus pose he'd expected. She stood there in the nude, her curves and secret places revealed and offered as if he deserved one scant cell of them. As if he merited one scintillating pheromone emanating from her delicious self, and yet his greedy nostrils flared, wanting every last molecule.

The soft expanse of her blushing skin stopped him cold. The barest hint of shyness smiled on those full-as-wild-strawberries lips. He'd seen parts and pieces of Eden, and he'd loved them all, but to finally have the total picture, to be able to drink in the full hips and the steamy valley between her lush breasts, to know that a better man might deserve her, but that she'd chosen him in all of her unworldly innocence. That he would soon have his dirty, bare hands on her...

Ky nearly faltered. She'd made good on her side of the deal. The rest was up to him. He yearned to wrap her in his arms and kiss the hell out of her, to savor her first. Instead, he curved one arm over his head and jerked his shirt off. He unbuckled and unzipped his pants, kicking them aside.

The light in those timeless emeralds glistened. Her gaze drifted downward. She blinked. She murmured, "Oh, Ky."

Yeah. Oh, Ky. Now you know. This is the real Ky Winchester. What's left of him. I'm not the man you thought I was. I'm damaged goods, baby. Take it or leave it.

He swallowed hard, his throat gone dry and his heart thumping. For five long days he'd been carved on and battered by Satan's best. The divot in his upper left thigh was a solid reminder that even a dull knife could make you bleed. There was a flat and ugly, six-by-six-inch scar on his chest where once the proud USMC anchor and globe tattoo had been laboriously inked and dyed, then sadistically peeled off. He was covered in various other nicks and welts, some committed by bastards, some by doctors trying to correct the damage the bastards had left behind. All ugly. All him. But that wasn't the worst.

He breathed hard, damned sure meeting this final challenge, this final dare, head-on, Eden might not like what she saw, but she was going to see it. Every last piece of what Hasim Nizari had reduced his body to.

Ky shoved his boxers over his thighs and kicked them aside. Damned if she didn't know where to look, to that lopsided sack where one testicle had been hacked off that last day. He swallowed hard, filled with shame for being less than the full man she deserved. Angry at the thought she might run. She should. Yeah, it could've been worse. She'd said she'd seen what took place those last three days, so why was she still standing there? Why hadn't she at least taken a step back?

"Is this what you want?" he asked gruffly, pushing her away before she could push him, prepared for the rejection of his life. A guy looked plenty tough when he was camouflaged in tactical gear and toting a sniper rifle, but naked and exposed? Vulnerable. How could she love him now that she'd seen?

The smile was gone, but not the woman. Eden didn't hesitate, just surprised the hell out of him when she charged up his body like a naked linebacker tackling the quarterback, her hands on his bare shoulders and her legs wrapped around his hips. She didn't ask, just plastered her lips over his and cried, "Don't you get it? I love you, Ky. You. All of you."

He cried along with her, all right. He cried, her tears and her love the final straw. She meant more to him than she could possibly know. Hope. Love. Dreams. A woman's touch. All those things he thought he'd never have again in his friggin' desperate, celibate life.

Eden dug her fingers into his scalp, and what could he do? His number-one rule failed miserably. He grabbed onto her sweet ass and held her in place. Tight.

She didn't kiss him. This was more an assault than a kiss. She grunted and forced her tongue into his mouth like that was difficult. She devoured his lips and tongue, groaning as if she could force herself into him orally. He let her, but for the life of him, he had to ask, "What the hell do you see in me, Eden. Why me?"

"I was there, remember? I was in that dirty cell, too. I lived through the worst they did to you. God, Ky, I screamed right along with you when they cut you. You can't scare me now because I decided then if I was ever lucky enough to get my hands on you, I'd make you forget everything but me, and darn it, Ky Winchester, I'm not going to ask you again."

He honestly couldn't remember her asking a question, but he held on for every last inch of his soul to this fierce woman. His angst was gone and his mission clear. The time had come to nail this woman to his soul. But not in the bathroom. Not this way. She was that odd quirk in the universe. A miracle. A virgin falling in love with a monster. The least he could do was love her with the best he had left to offer.

"Kiss me, Ky," she ordered.

Oh. That. The shower could wait. Ky fumbled for the door with his woman attached where she wouldn't stay a virgin much longer. He marched to the only soft place in his home, the sleeping bag and pillow on the floor of what passed for his bedroom. This woman was a luscious handful of curves in all the right places, and he meant to bed her.

Crouching to his knees, he laid her on Cabela's best green-checkered flannel. She beamed up at him, her eyes gone soft and hazy, a deeper emerald than the flannel, and her arms around his neck. Smoothing her fingertips over his brow, she ended at his jaw. His mind had made a remarkable recovery. It no longer told him this was wrong, or that her sweet touch was in any way similar to the grip of those barbarians a world away.

"God, I've loved you," he whispered fervently, his forehead to hers, "so much, Eden. For years."

"I've loved you more," she murmured, her nose and tongue roaming over his chin and nose, her fingers in his hair. "I've wanted to touch you like this. To kiss you. To smell you skin to skin. To taste you. All of you."

He buried his nose in the crook of her neck, breathing in that familiar hint of Vicks and not a lick of panic creeping up on him while her nose moved over his chest and along his collarbone. "Are you smelling me?" he asked, secretly delighted.

"I love the smell of you." Her tongue came next, as she drew a moist line up his jaw and whispered into his ear, "I like the taste of you, too. I declare you healed and ready for me."

Halle-friggin-lujah!

Her open palm slid between their hot bodies to what was left of his manhood. He winced, somehow expecting pain, but all he got was the soft caress of a woman in love exploring her man. She didn't hesitate, just took hold of him and breathed hotly in his ear. "I've got what I want."

Chapter Thirty-Three

"I won't hurt you," he said tenderly as his fingers slid up to cup her breast. "I promise. I'll take it slow and easy."

Eden had to smile. The only way he could hurt her would be to push her away and leave, and that wasn't going to happen, not if his heavy breathing meant what she thought it meant. Or the honey-gold light inside the burning amber of his gaze. She drank the sight of him in. The map-work of scars over his chest, some ragged, some smooth. The hand-sized blot where once the proud globe and anchor had rested. She'd watched in horror when those evil Taliban had cut it off. Smoothing her fingertips across the gnarled skin, she ached to overcompensate for what others had done for the rest of her life. Brushing over the dark rough of chest hairs, her nostrils filled with the sweaty, manly scent of her new world.

"You've been working out," she purred, delighted with the coiled musculature beneath her palm. This naked man hovering over her quivering body was only going in deeper if she had her way.

And she intended to. He wanted her, but he'd been so tormented by devils past that he hadn't known the best way forward. But she did. She might be inexperienced, but she knew biology.

"You're so beautiful," he rumbled, his knees between hers, his body positioned and the tip of his body already tasting hers.

She trapped his hips with her legs, encouraging him with just her fingertips to do it. All of her choices had brought her to this place and this perfect time, and she wanted him. Only him. Her body wept for him, every part of her slick with anticipation. *Just. Do. It.*

Yet he dallied over her nipples, and honestly, the man knew what he was doing. Pinching. Kissing. Suckling. Tugging her into the warm hollow of his mouth, inciting a clenching ache deep in the pit of her belly. She'd perched on the verge of shattering against him when he stopped playing and took a deep breath. And there he paused, his gaze dripping sizzling sparks.

"Why'd you stop?" she whined breathlessly. "Why now?"

"Because this is a first for you," he whispered, his breath washing over her lips but his mouth not touching. "This is your first time making love, Eden, and it's my first time falling in love. I want to watch it unfold. I want to watch you blossom when I give you all of my heart. There will never be another first, and I intend to savor every last second of it. Every tiny sound when I make you come. The sparkle in your eyes. The way you scrunch your nose when you're scenting me. The way you lick your lips after you've tasted me. This perfect now. I'm gathering memories, baby, so I'll never forget one heartbeat of this once-in-a-lifetime moment with you."

Aw-w-w. Her heart stuttered even as the fire in her belly clenched with a voracious hunger for this gentle, sweet man. "I can't give what you won't take," she murmured into his mouth. "Take me, Ky. Now. Don't leave anything behind but yesterday."

He hovered, a man so strong that he'd brought evil to its knees, now on his knees to her. The quiet moment stretched, fire in the amber dark and filled with promise. Eden held her breath, the silence in his humble room more reverent than she'd ever in her wildest dreams expected.

"I honest to God love you with my whole heart," he said, the dearest smile on his handsome face.

Tears brimmed even as she pushed her hips upward, relishing the heat between them and wanting every last inch of him inside of her. "Prove it."

And he did. He barely moved, yet he moved all the way. Slowly. Carefully. Inside of her body. Inside her soul. His eyes never left hers as her world deliberately changed from empty to full. She succumbed to the tender loss of virginity, gently impaled and claimed by a deeper, greater reason to live. Wanting this man with every last throbbing beat of her life's blood.

Eden matched his rhythm, her fingernails imbedded in the muscles of his back as he branded and claimed. As he filled her up. As he sweated and took and gave. And she flew. Into a universe of pleasure and ecstasy she'd not known before. Higher. Still higher, until Ky ground out, "Come for me, Eden."

With those ragged words spoken, with the amber light of his love spilling down upon her, Eden's world exploded into warm, quivering fireworks of blues and reds and golds and whites that took her, breath by shuddering breath. She shattered. She flew. She cried. Throbbing ecstasy pushed her higher still. She grabbed him close and clung to him, a wild symphony of emotions singing through her body. Pleasure. Trust. The purest joy. Unselfish freedom.

With two strokes more, Ky joined her, and they flew together. The power of that moment burned them into one heart, melted them into one soul. Joined them forever.

She arched into him one last time and fell back to earth, their hearts pounding in sync. Two halves rejoined. Two lost souls found. She clung to him as aftershocks swarmed up her body, her cheek to his cheek, her lips to his ear. "I'm touching you," she murmured thickly. *Oh snap, am I ever touching you.*

He growled another "I love you" in her ear, and there was nothing better than their two sweating bodies clamped together in the same place at the same time. Every last measure had been given and eagerly received. Their hearts were entwined, and they were wrapped up inside each other's hands and arms and legs. This was all she'd wanted since that long-ago day. To be mated with the only one brave enough to reach through the universe for her.

Just her. Just him.

Eden lost track of time after Ky wrapped her against his hard body. She had what she wanted—his arm around her and her back to his front. So what if they were wrapped in a sleeping bag? She understood the reasoning behind his austere furnishings. The day might come when he'd explain his humble home, but what woman in her right mind cared about what didn't matter? She didn't need a fancy bed when she had the perfect man to sleep on. They'd survived so much together. Could endure anything together. That much she knew.

He breathed hotly, his nose buried at the back of her neck and tucked in her hair. He seemed to like that part of her body when he wasn't roaming over others. The man had skills. He'd taken her through three orgasms and went with her each time until they'd tired each other out. Still, the solid shaft of velvet steel pressed against her backside promised another round of pleasure in her very near future.

The Canadian operation that had started so miserably had ended in an unexpected happily-ever-after. Eden breathed a deep sigh of contentment. There would be no unborn children for Mrs. Bick to steal, no embryos for her to decide which would live and which would die. No level-ten psychic monster child to rule the world. No cybernetic terminators, either. But best of all, Eden had ended her harrowing run from terror in the protective arms of her very own Prince Charming.

He murmured a sleepy rumble. "Don't go. Stay."

No problem.

After all, claiming went both ways.

Eden rolled out of his arms and onto his hips. Straddling him, her blonde hair a silken drape to wake him with. To tease. To tantalize.

"You want more?" he asked, a cute, tired little hitch in his voice. "Already?"

"I want you," she breathed, seductively blowing a warm breath down the centerline of his sexy body. Who cared about those scars? She didn't. They weren't the real Ky. None of those scars had reached his heart. If anything, they'd made him the man he was today. The hero.

Besides, he still had all ten fingers, ten toes, and that very thick, very hard other body part that she craved. The one poking at her behind. Eden eased forward onto her knees enough to adjust her position. To take Ky back inside of her where he belonged. She moaned at the pleasant friction of a good tight match. The thrill. The crush of her internal ridges against him. The exquisite beauty and contrast of the male and female sexes. Soft against hard. Tough against gentle. The slow, sensual ride of give and take.

He groaned, a delicious rumble that vibrated all the way to his toes and spiked her need for him into overdrive. Planting her palms to the wall of his muscular chest, she began again. A sexy tango with dips and bows, mouthwatering thrusts and mind-blowing anticipation. Ky took over the lead, his fingertips digging into her backside, holding tightly to the rhythm, increasing the beat as his hips bucked into her. Castanets clacked somewhere in the distance of her steaming mind, urging her on. Driving her up.

"Open your eyes," he ordered, his hands still on her ass. "I want to watch you watching me."

She obeyed, his voice velvet magic as she teetered on the edge of another swan dive into paradise. "I love you, Ky," she breathed, needing him to know. Needing him to be sure.

He blinked once. Twice. The moment froze as a raging fire shivered up her thighs into her core, her gaze locked on Ky. He held her tight and Eden fell, even as the world vanished into night and stars exploded around her. She clenched him into her with her whole body, needing him to fly with her.

"Now," she commanded, lighting a match to his torch. No sooner said than done. Their coming together rippled through them, an incoming riptide of desperate, eager need. Of out of control desire. Of lust and love and the promise of forever in his dreamy caramel eyes.

The man beneath her looked so tired, but oh, so pleased with himself. A smug, masculine smiled tugged at his lips. "I knew you had it in you," he teased.

"I certainly do now," Eden teased him right back.

But she wanted to cry. Not every man could've survived what Ky had. She dropped to one elbow, her hair to one side while she traced the laugh lines at the corners of his eye, then the right angle scar when his orbital bone had been repaired. Even in the dim light, the tiny lines where skillfully placed stitches crossed the split skin still showed. His poor nose was a tiny bit crooked. Another scar left a dimple on one side of his chin.

Eden tipped forward and kissed every one of those scars, her heart filled to overflowing for this gentle warrior. She wasn't sure she deserved him, but she knew one thing for certain. She would spend the rest of her life loving him. Pleasing him. Living for him.

The tears came softly, running down her cheek to drop onto his neck.

"Hey, what's wrong?" he asked, pulling her into his side and under his arm. Ky wiped an index finger under her eye, catching the tears she couldn't stop.

Eden honestly didn't know. One second she was happy, the next, she was shivering with foreboding. A slither of unease slid down her bare back. "I could've lost you, Ky. Back there. Back then. They would've killed you. How could I have lived without you? Not one day," she answered her own question. "I mean it. There I was, dying along with you, only I was sitting in the middle of my nice clean kitchen while you were going through heck in that disgusting cell. I would've died right then and there with you. I knew it then. I know it now. You're my light and my life, Ky. I honestly don't think I can live without you. I don't want to. I can't. I just… can't."

He bowed his forehead to hers, kissing her cheek and breathing hard. "Oh, Eden," he said quietly. "Wow. I don't know what to say."

Eden wrapped her arms around his head, holding her to him, needing to feel his heartbeat and his breath against her skin. Suddenly aware of all she stood to lose. This man. This tremendous connection. This—now. "Don't ever leave me, Ky Winchester."

He nodded, his face in her neck. "Leaving you was never on my mind, honey. Only staying. Loving. Building a family and a real life." Ky lifted out of her stranglehold. "You probably noticed that I could use some furniture. Maybe a bed. A mattress. Sheets. A real home."

He made her smile. The irrational vision of him suffering faded. The skulking shadow on unexplained unease dissolved. Eden nodded, composing herself, not sure why she'd gotten so emotional. "Things are a little sparse around here."

Ky tangled his fingers in her hair, tilting her face upward to his. "Help me shop?"

"That I can do," she admitted, sniffing, hoping she hadn't just made too big of a fool of herself.

"Oh, Eden," he breathed, his eyes glowing with love. He molded her body to his, cradling her, one big manly hand on her ass, right where she liked it. "The world can wait. Let's buy a big bed and stay in it for a week."

She let the contentment in his voice soothe the rough edges away. Maybe she was just tired. "I can do that, too."

The gloom crept up on him. The warmth was gone. Ky was alone and fighting for his life. It was hard to breathe. The monsters were back. The Taliban. He thrashed, searching for his lifeline. For her. For Eden. Again. The nightmare took hold like it always did, strangling the life out of him. Suffocating. Until...

His sixth sense roared to threat level Delta.

"Eden!" He flung himself up from the flannel bag tangled around his head and arms. His empty home was too quiet. Too cold. He pushed the sleeping bag to his bare feet. Hell, his bare everything. He hadn't needed clothes with her, but now...

"Eden?" he called again, his heart a jackhammer climbing up his throat. *Where is she?*

He edged down the hall with full-blown panic in his veins, and his heart sank. His front door stood wide open. Not caring what the world saw, he charged naked onto his concrete steps. She wouldn't have left. Not after the love they'd just made. Not after the promises. The tears.

God, she couldn't. Could she?

The hollowness of his empty house screamed the answer at him. *She's gone!*

Chapter Thirty-Four

Three long months later

A man would do a helluva lot for his family. There was no fiercer warrior, no more dangerous beast on the planet than a man hunting for the woman who'd been ripped out of his life.

Ky Winchester was no more a junior agent working for Alex Stewart and his TEAM. He was hell incarnate, and he plain didn't have time to run covert operations for his boss, not stateside nor on foreign soil—not when he was on the toughest op of his life. Alex could take a number and wait.

It had been three long months since Eden Stark had vanished from his home after their first intimate encounter. Encounter, nothing. They'd jumped each other's bones like love-crazed bunnies until they'd collapsed at the end of a very satisfying, steamy night. He'd still had the smell of her on his fingertips, the taste of her honey in his mouth when he'd awakened to an empty house the next morning. The sucking chest wound of what he'd initially thought was abandonment followed dead on its heels.

Her leaving took everything out of him. It made sense she'd run out after she'd finally understood the half-man he was. But common sense and a slap in the face from his most annoying nemesis, Tucker Chase, set him straight later the same morning. Over hot black coffee. Tucker had called a meeting with Ky and Sam Becker to go over what they knew. It went something like this...

"She didn't leave you," Tucker hissed. "Someone took her, you moron. I know Eden. She's not petty like that."

Tucker looked a little rough after surviving what Ky had originally thought was a gunshot to the head in Canada. It turned out the younger Zaroyin had been tortured into working some mind control mumbo-jumbo on Tucker. When Tucker went off on Eden, she'd cold-cocked him with a hefty chuck of ice to the side of his hard head. No big deal. He might've lost a little blood, but that skull of his was plenty dense. He could take it.

"Then why didn't I hear anything when they took her?" Ky tried hard not to bellow. "God, I was right there."

"Because you're stupid!" Tucker had no problem raising his snarky voice. "Shit, I don't know why you didn't hear anything, Winchester. Maybe you were tired. You were a Marine, weren't you?"

Again with the nasty, sarcastic insinuation. The perpetual Navy SEAL bullshit. Of course he'd been tired. He'd barely slept on the Canada op, then made sweet love to the woman of his dreams all night. That meeting with Chase and Becker would've nearly came to blows if not for the intervention of one mad-as-hell alpha wolf named Alex Stewart.

"You called your boss?" Tucker had snarled when he'd caught sight of Alex fast-tracking toward their table.

"Why wouldn't I? He's got my back. You never did." Ky had wanted to knock the arrogant FBI agent on his ass. Tucker thought he was the smartest, toughest, baddest ass on the planet. Well, he'd gotten one thing right. He was an ass.

Alex had to have overheard the hostile volley, but you never would've guessed it the way he'd sat down and ordered a coffee, black, like he'd owned the place. Good thing he'd showed when he did. Until then, Tucker had spent more time railing on Ky about letting someone kidnap Eden than strategizing to get her back.

"Sit rep," Alex had barked, and damned if Tucker suddenly didn't straighten up, snap to, and spout off an answer before Ky could open his mouth. Maybe it was the business suit Alex had worn. Maybe it was something else.

"Agent Stark's been kidnapped, sir." Tucker had leveled an accusing glare Ky's way. "I've already contacted Director Strong. He has a team on site at Winchester's place looking for evidence and clues."

You do? That was a surprise to Ky, but good to know. Tucker *could* be helpful. Ky should've asked Tucker why he'd waited so long to share that info-byte, but time was precious in those first few hours. Ky had let a lot of shit go. The urgency to get Eden back had ruled all.

"What else?" Alex had snapped, his hands clenched on the table in front of him, his fingers locked together as his stern gaze scrolled from Tucker, to Ky, and ended at Sam.

"Sorry, Alex. No. FBI satellite surveillance was not overhead at the time of her abduction," Sam had offered calmly. He'd always seemed the yin to Tucker's yang, the calm eye in the middle of a friggin' hurricane. "No traffic cams. No home security cameras, either. Ky lives in the middle of starter-home America, where most kids don't have the money for fancy extras like security systems."

Alex jerked his cell phone up from his inner jacket pocket and stabbed his thumb to one number. Who would've thought he'd have the FBI Director on speed dial? "Zachary? Anything yet?" He'd paused and shot a dark eye to Ky. "I see. Count on it."

He'd disconnected the call, his next words only for Ky. "Zachary's men found a note in your mailbox."

The common mail receptacles at the end of the street? Ky hadn't given them a thought. "And?"

"It's not Eden's handwriting, but whoever put it there wants us to think it is." Alex pursed his lips as if he needed to couch the next words with care. He'd paused a moment too long.

"What'd it say?" Ky demanded.

"It said you're not to look for her. That last night was a mistake. That it will never happen again. That—"

"Bullshit!" Of all people, Tucker roared. "You should've seen these two in Kenora, Stewart. They couldn't keep their hot little hands off each other. Eden didn't write that crap."

Ky took a second look at Tucker than. It had almost sounded as if the arrogant FBI hotshot defended Ky's and Eden's dalliance while on a mission. As if he'd known how much they cared for each other. Yes, their coming together had happened fast, but did Tucker also know how they'd first met? Did he know where and when? Did he know about the psychic link that welded Ky to Eden in the middle of the blood, sweat, and tears of a madman's torture chamber?

"Didn't I just say it was bullshit?" Alex had retorted. Those cold blues of his had drilled Tucker with razor-sharp disdain. It seemed to be one of those alpha wolf traits. Growl before you rip a guy's jugular out.

Tucker got the hint. He'd backed off. He might have been a wolf, but the stronger alpha male ruled the pack.

Alex turned his back on Tucker and addressed Ky directly. "There's more. The note also said she could never love a man like you."

Again Tucker went off half-cocked. "Lies!"

Alex hadn't wasted a breath on him that time. "It's a poor attempt to rile you, but you need to know it was signed with a bloody thumbprint, Ky. Zachary confirmed. It's Eden's blood and her print."

"They hurt her!" And Ky hadn't been able to sit still any more. He'd jumped to his feet, needing to fight the world. Needing a cigarette. Needing Eden!

Until Alex barked a throaty command to, "Sit, Junior Agent."

Ky had taken his place, but honestly, a hive of angry hornets had just taken up residence in his head and up his butt. He couldn't focus, much less sit still enough to strategize. There he'd been with the owner of the most elite surveillance team on the East Coast, two savvy ex-Navy SEALs, and a direct line to the FBI director, but he'd never felt more useless. Shouldn't they already have Eden back if they were so smart? Why didn't they? They had all the best resources. What was the goddamned problem?

It was all he'd been able to do to wait on Alex to speak. "We will find her, Ky."

That was all? A promise? A line of BS? It wasn't enough. Ky had lifted his tired ass up off the chair in that mom-and-pop diner. Eden didn't have that kind of time, and neither did he. Furious to the bone, he'd walked away from his boss, his job, and the tough guys who thought they owned the world, but didn't know squat.

Which brought Ky right back to where he sat today. Three months later. In that same diner with Alex, Sam, and Tucker. On their third carafe of coffee. Strong and black. Back with the three men who'd stood by him through every failed effort, every dead-end over the last ninety days, and every accompanying meltdown and double shot of booze to numb the pain.

Why was Ky back at ground zero? Because a man really couldn't fight the world by himself, no matter how angry or desperate he became. Because a pack hunted better than a lone wolf, and these three arrogant alphas were his only hope. His last hope.

Director Strong had chipped in, too. He'd offered all the resources and man-hours of the FBI he could, but he had an agency to run and a president to answer to. Besides, he didn't need to know how black or how dark Operation Find Eden would get. Strong needed that fairytale myth of deniable plausibility to cover his ass. No one else bothered with it.

"Are you sure it's him?" Tucker. Always the disbeliever. The friggin' pain in the neck.

Ky nodded. "Mother and Ember sighted him again in Freetown at oh-six-hundred hours yesterday. Your man's on him, Sam. Thanks for that."

Freetown, the capital of Sierra Leone, West Africa. The heart of rampant government corruption that had led to a decade-long war that left tens of thousands dead. Impoverished as hell. One of the few countries on Earth where the life expectancy was less than fifty years. Known for its multi-million-dollar blood diamond trade. Also known for the wicked Ebola virus.

But those things meant nothing to Ky. They didn't seem to slow Alex, Sam, or Tucker down, either. They were military to the core with their intensity and attention to detail.

Sam had a confidential informant on the ground in Freetown he'd only referenced as Chappy. Who knew what his real name was? Who cared? He'd gotten close to one dirtbag, a.k.a. ex-FBI Agent Cameron Levine, after Mother and Ember found the bastard, now one of Interpol's most wanted.

"Your satellite makes how many revolutions each day?" Tucker asked curiously, the tip of his index finger running annoying squeaky circles on the rim of his empty coffee cup.

Alex shrugged. "Jed owns five, not me. Does it matter?"

"Not really. It's just interesting the difference a little money makes."

Ky plowed through the latest Tucker Chase inquisition. He never gave a man credit, just poked and prodded until said man came up swinging at the persistent insinuation. "Who's going in with me?"

Tucker nodded, Sam, too, but Alex met Ky head-on. "I've already got a man inside."

"Who?"

"Tate Higgins."

Ky caught the wink that went with the revelation. Like Sam, Alex was one step ahead of the game. He knew people the world over, too, and what was more, Tate was solid—one of Ky's tried and true friends. Maybe this would be the covert op that finally brought Eden home.

Ky pushed back his chair, hopeful, please God, that he'd find her this time. That this was the last wild goose chase. That he'd finally end Cameron Levine's treachery. But most of all, that Eden was still alive.

Forgive me. Eden stood at her open deck door facing west one last time, projecting her heart and soul across the gray Atlantic. To the land that she loved. To Ky. For what it was worth.

She hadn't had a vision since this ordeal began, and her second sight remained useless. Or dead. As quickly as she'd been kidnapped from Ky's home that terrifying morning, the end of her world had begun. She wasn't entirely sure he'd been left alive.

Cameron Levine boasted that he'd gotten past the FBI guards and killed Isaiah and his father, but he dwelled on how he'd killed Ky, or rather, how one of his mindless drones had killed him. Levine enjoyed sharing the minutest of gory details. That Ky had cried out for her when he'd died. That he'd begged for mercy. That he'd been left gutted in his bed, his belly split open and his blood and entrails poured out on the floor. Over the sheets. Dripping off his fingertips into the carpet below.

At first she'd been too traumatized to think clearly. She'd blamed herself, especially after Levine had punctuated his wicked control over her by shooting one of his poor drones at point-blank range. Right in front of her horrified eyes. She could still smell the poor man's blood in the air. The horror never faded.

But doubt persisted and logic had prevailed through her shock. She, after all, had been with Ky in his humble home. He didn't own a bed, so how could he have been murdered in one?

And yet, Levine had made it sound so real. Almost believable...

The liar.

A truly frightening man, he'd lost the human capacity for compassion somewhere during his miserable life, which was the reason for the upcoming visit to his diamond mine. He hadn't said specifically what he intended to do with her there, but she had every right to suspect that the foulest play in this horrific chess game she was caught up in was yet to come.

Eden meant nothing to him, was merely intended to be the queen who controlled the poor pawns—if, that was, she ever got her second sight back. He'd kept back at least two dozen of Zaroyin's drones instead of sending them north to be rehabilitated at the doctor's hidden medical facility in Canada. What were they good for? Assassinations. Abductions. You name it. They did whatever Levine programmed them to do, and none of it was good.

His greed responded to one thing only. More power. More wealth. Despoiling the already impoverished country of Sierra Leone. He wanted the titanium and bauxite. The gold. The rutile, the lovely red crystalline known for its refractive powers and technology's need for it. But especially the diamonds.

His insane plan hinged on spreading panic and chaos amongst the diamond-rich countries of Africa. He banked on it. Literally and figuratively. At that very moment, two drones were in transit to assassinate the president of Liberia, a neighboring diamond country where unrest and corruption had led to civil war in the past. Where it soon would again, only now the mayhem would enable Levine to step in and assume control of eighty percent of the world's diamond trade.

But she worried. Something in that foul-tasting shake Levine forced her to choke down every morning had compromised her second sight. That was the only thing that made sense. The drink gave her horrific night-sweats, bad dreams, and migraines similar to the ones she'd endured in Canada. It made her dizzy, weak, and nauseous all day long.

But Bick was dead, and his wife, Cassandra, was in jail. Or was she? And why was Levine so anxious to visit the diamond mines? A chill suffused Eden's trembling faith in herself. Under his thumb, she had no choice in what she ate, drank, or wore. He'd even forced her to cut and dye her hair, to paint her nails. Black. All black. The sad, dark color of her life.

Her poor heart fluttered like the wings of the gulls outside her deck at the thought of what very well might be the last day of her life. Eden was like that bird, only she was trapped in a cage too small to survive. And now, if her suspicions about the upcoming trip to the diamond mine were correct, she'd be left to die below ground. Without breath. Without light or air or space. Without Ky.

It didn't make sense, Levine's abducting her only to kill her, but the sense of dread remained. Wiping the sweat of the hot day off her brow, Eden inhaled deeply of the salty breeze from the ocean unfurled at her feet. Normally gray and dotted with whitecaps, today the Atlantic seemed calmer. Bluer. A ribbon of turquoise unraveled in the relentless breakers shattering on shore. Caught in early-morning sunlight, they offered a glimpse of beauty to a desperate soul in need of hope where there was none. In desperate need of rescue.

She glimpsed him then. A young man on a bicycle. With binoculars. She'd seen him on the dunes before, but this was the first time he'd seemed to be watching—*me?*

Eden held her right hand up, her palm forward, just in case. He waved. *Oh snap. He saw me.* Her foolish heart catapulted to life in her chest, thumping so hard she could feel it against her breastbone and ribs. She dipped her hand from side to side, and he waved again, just like a little kid wanting her attention. He really waved.

But just as quickly as she'd wanted to shout for joy, she froze. Whoever that brave soul was, he was no small target. He'd be killed if seen. She couldn't risk another's life so she stepped out of his view, but—he had waved. *At me!*

She combed her fingers over her head, daring to believe. These last three months had been utter hell. Tossing her short inky hair into spikes, an oddly sympathetic reflection of her poor, withering soul, she gulped her trepidation down to a manageable lump in her throat.

I can wait, she promised Ky, wherever he was, with all her heart. *I've done it before. I will do it again.*

Chapter Thirty-Five

People were so damned poor in Freetown, the capitol of Sierra Leone. Mostly Muslim. Mostly black. All scrounging for survival. And thin. Even the little ones, with their little extended bellies and wasted frames. It took a hard man to look away and not empty his pockets to the pitiful beggars at the roadside.

Since he'd touched down in Africa, Ky had rented a car and a dive hotel room on the poor side of Freetown to call home for the duration of his trip. He'd dropped his duffle bag in his room, lowered his Ray-Bans, and ventured back into the one-hundred-degree-plus day to find Tate, one of Alex Stewart's best.

There was a day when Ky had held that distinction. No more. Now he worked with the guy, not for him, and he was a far cry from being the best of anything. Truth be known, Ky relied a helluva lot on Alex's deep pockets. There'd be no Operation Find Eden without him, but Ky also knew nothing would stop him from searching for her. Deep pockets or not, FBI assistance or not, Ky was in this to the death.

The search had proved fruitless and demoralizing thus far. The first failed lead came from Cambodia through a trusted informant of Tucker's, some guy named Smoke. But it had proved dead, damned wrong. That Levine look-alike was an

American working with Doctors for Charity. He could've passed for a twin, but he wasn't Levine.

The second lead came from one of Alex's trusted agents in Peru. He'd spotted a man fitting Levine's description with a dazed version of a woman fitting Eden's. Ky had roared to her rescue, because along with that info came the ugly intel from Thailand that Levine had contacts inside the sex trade. Ky had saved the Eden look-alike, but that Levine was the wrong man, too. Yes, he was in the sex trade, and yes, Ky had disrupted the sale of more than a dozen poor girls and women in the bastard's possession. Just. Not. Eden.

Tate didn't wave, just stared him down from the open truck door where he stood with his arms crossed and his usual perpetual scowl.

"Hey, brother," Ky muttered, gripping his buddy's arm up to his elbow. A friend was a godsend when you were on the mission of your life, and Tate more so than others.

Tate returned the hold with a hearty backslap. "You've lost weight."

"Nah, I'm good." Ky rolled the tweak out of his neck. He hadn't slept in the past three months, and food was not high on his list of worries. He ran on caffeine, and when he needed to drop, a few shots of whatever was handy. Usually Jameson. Africa better have a decent substitute for Irish whiskey.

The only comfort he took came from the thin piece of fancy silk Eden had left behind. Her panties. Yes, he'd gotten freakishly obsessive and maybe he was going crazy, but he kept that intimate piece of apparel deep in his front pocket. Just. Damned. Because. He needed something of hers to hang onto, and her bra had straps. It would've been more noticeable.

Yes, he was mentally unbalanced. Losing his heart made a guy that way.

"Chappy is quite the informant," Tate offered as Ky climbed onboard. "You met him yet?"

"No. I thought we'd do that first. You?"

Tate nodded one short, quick nod. "Yeah. I've been staying at his place."

Ky glanced sideways at Tate. There was a different tone in his voice today. "No kidding? Alex didn't put you up in a hotel?"

"I don't like hotels." That was Tate for you, a minimalist through and through. "'Sides, I like Chappy's kids."

"How many's he got?" Ky's mind pinged over what he already knew instead of listening to the answer. Cameron Levine. Ex-FBI. Wanted man. He seemed to come and go abroad as he pleased. Alex still hadn't determined how Levine had gotten Eden out of the country.

"Hey. You listening?" Tate grumbled.

Ky shook himself out of his trance. "Sorry. What'd you say?"

"I said we're here." Tate climbed out of the truck, a battered excuse for a Chevy.

It would've been nice knowing where *here* was, but Ky hadn't listened. He lit up a Marlboro Red and joined his buddy.

Like every other building on the street, this one sported a flat roof with an industrial-sized air conditioner in one corner that must not work. All the windows in the joint were pushed open. No screens.

Inside wasn't much better. The blades of a large fan spun lazily overhead, barely moving the air in the empty room. Mud brick floor. Tables and chairs scattered in disarray. A piano in one corner and a grimy-looking bar along the far wall. A section of the floor masking-taped off for dancing. Suffocating heat. Meat sizzling on the grill behind the bar. Flies buzzing everywhere.

Ky joined Tate at the rickety table near the window, on the lookout for the man he only knew as Chappy. He dusted the ash off the tip of his cigarette as a slender black woman smiled from behind the bar. "I see you have brought a friend," she stated, every last pearly white on display in her dark, shiny face.

"Ky Winchester, ma'am," Tate answered respectfully. "He'll be here for a while."

"Does he need a room? I can put him up."

"No, thanks." Ky put an end to that. The only thing he needed was information, and *where the hell was Chappy?*

"Very good, Mr. Winchester. May I get you gentlemen something to eat?" she asked in perfect English.

"Beed," Tate replied as he held up two fingers, "and two glasses of Star, please." He'd certainly made himself comfortable in Freetown if he knew which foods were safe to eat and the local beer on tap.

"What's beed?" Ky asked as he puffed out of the corner of his mouth.

"Marinated meat. Don't worry. You'll like it." Tate's nose wrinkled at the cigarette smoke. "Thought you quit that shit?"

"Yeah, well..." Ky didn't make excuses. Cigarettes were the least of his problems. Meat on the menu was good, though it would've also been nice to know what kind. No mystery meat for him. The aromas wafting from the kitchen at the end of the bar stirred his appetite, but swallowing had become an effort, most likely because his body remembered what solid food felt like on the return trip up.

Without Eden in his life, he'd become similar to that heroin addict on lockdown, the one deprived of his fix and going out of his friggin' mind. The guy who no longer required sustenance because food didn't cut the high of one line of pure horse. The guy driven to one end and one end only.

Find her.

He drummed his fingertips on the table, lost in the world without Eden. There was no color to the sunset without her. No reason to breathe, and nothing to look forward to except the day he had her in his arms and on her back in that king-sized bed he'd bought out of sheer stupid optimism. But that was what he'd done. He'd planned in advance for the celebration that grew more distant with every failed intel. Every pointless search.

Ky ground out his smoke in the half-filled ashtray. It had been a helluva three months. Tate was right to be disgusted with him. He was not the guy he used to be. God, he just needed a solid clue. Just one.

The kindly barkeep shuffled over with a tray of food and drinks. Beed ended up being char-grilled meat on a skewer alongside three slices of dried, brown bread. The aroma drifting up from the sizzling platter watered his mouth, but his stomach grumbled and not from anticipation. Ky shoved the plate back and cast his eyes to the far corners of the joint, searching for the men's room. A guy with a bad stomach needed to be prepared.

"You are not well," the woman said, her dark brown eyes soft with concern. "You need soup."

"Nah, it's okay," he protested, a cold bottle already to his lips and on its way down. "I'm good."

She shot him a backward glance as she hustled away. "Of course you are good. Being sick does not make you bad. Soup it is."

"No, I meant... ah, forget it." She'd stopped listening, and he didn't need the aggravation of a nosy woman in his face. He had Tate.

Ky took a long swallow and wished for another cigarette. The woman was headed his way again, another tray in her hands. Why didn't people listen? He wasn't hungry for food, damn it.

He looked away. "Where the hell is this Chappy guy I'm supposed to meet? When'll he show?"

Tate tilted his cold one and smiled, but it was the woman who said, "I am right here."

Ky looked up into the beaming face of his benefactress, her forehead and cheeks shiny from the stifling heat. "Mama Chappelle," she said proudly, her chin-lift hard to miss. "But my friends call me Chappy. You may also."

"You're Sam Becker's friend?" Ky nearly choked on his beer. "I thought you said Chappy was a guy?"

Tate shrugged. "I may have said him instead of her. You wouldn't know. You weren't listening."

Chappy replaced Ky's plate with a bowl of creamy soup. "This is potato and leek—my own recipe. It will rest easier on your stomach than meat and bread. You have not eaten well lately, true?" she asked, her brow wrinkled.

"I'm good," he said, but Chappy wouldn't be dissuaded. She cupped his jaw, her thumb smoothing over his cheek. "You are a big man, Mr. Winchester. I think maybe you need more than soup."

Mama Chappy was one of those women who mothered everyone. Ky could read it in her eyes. A swath of red, yellow, and orange fabric clothed her slender frame from shoulders to sandaled feet, draping her arms up to her elbows. A scarf wrapped her head in pinks, greens, and blues, but her eyes were soft espresso with a splash of concern, not what Ky expected in a CI, a confidential informant. Perfect English rolled off her full lips in a smoky West African alto, deep with self-confidence and character.

He let her handle him. Some women were touchers, and it honestly didn't bother him since he'd been with Eden. His phobia had all but disappeared. If only the nightmares would. They'd come back with a vengeance.

Chappy ended the motherly moment. "Eat. Then we talk."

He ladled one spoonful to his lips, intending to pacify her. Then another, but just because she'd taken the chair across from him and rested her elbows on the table, watching. Every spoonful garnered a twinkle in her eyes. "How is it? Good or bad?"

He offered a quick, "Good," another mouthful on its way. Who would've thought potatoes and leek would go down so easily?

"My special recipe will make you better and stronger," she said with a nod of approval. "It is full of rich cream and my secret ingredient. A man cannot run on cigarette fumes and anger. You will come to Mama Chappy for breakfast and dinner every day you are in my country. While you eat, I will tell you what I have discovered, and we will become good friends."

Damned if that didn't sound like a good idea, but the soup was gone. While Mama Chappy returned to the kitchen at the end of the bar to remedy that, Ky leaned into Tate. "Why the hell didn't you tell me Chappy's a woman?"

Tate set his fork to his plate. "You'll see, brother. Just wait."

A group of five men and a young couple entered the bar. The men assembled at a table in the far corner while the couple settled at the bar, their heads together like lovers. Mama Chappy chattered at them, then took their orders, the five men, too, but Ky looked away. The sight of couples in love only reminded him of all he'd lost.

"Shit," Tate hissed.

Ky's sixth sense ramped up. He glanced over his shoulder at the men in the corner. "What's up?"

"Not them." Tate stuck his chin toward the entrance. *"Them."*

"Sam!" Mama Chappy called to the two shadows blocking the door—Sam Becker, and on his six, Tucker Chase.

Shit indeed.

"Morning, Chappy. Morning, boys," Sam said over a hearty handshake. "Good to see you again, Agent Higgins."

Tate reverted to a grunt, but returned the handshake.

"Why are you guys here?" Ky had to know.

"Because your boss has a business he can't seem to leave, and my boss is too smart to let the Bureau go to hell," Tucker responded with his usual snark.

"And mine's running the country. You know how it goes," Sam said with a wink. "Have you located Levine yet?"

Sam Becker. Ex-Navy SEAL. Ex-FBI sniper. Current Secret Service Agent assigned to the President of the United

States. Must've been on extended administrative leave. He stood a good six-feet-five, give or take. Broad shouldered. The man needed a decent haircut and a closer shave. Hell, his razor must've barely grazed the stubble on his ugly face.

Dressed in khaki pants and a flowered safari shirt with pockets, at the moment he looked the part of a guy on vacation instead of a covert operator with that five o'clock shadow scruffed over his cheeks and chin. Brown-eyed and grinning, he tended to assume you worked for him.

Tucker Chase, also ex-Navy SEAL. Current FBI special agent, and always—as in *always*—the biggest jerk in the room. Women, no doubt, might think he was a tall, dark, and handsome cliché of a guy, but he radiated nothing but ego and smirk behind that big, square chin of his. Jeans and a too-small black T-shirt. Black boots. The guy thought he was a rock star, that he knew it all. Like now. He slammed a meaty palm to Tate's back and leaned over his shoulder, getting square in his face. "You miss me?"

Ky blew out a snort through his nostrils. *Here we go again.*

"I don't miss shit," Tate growled, shrugging the unwelcome jerk away.

Tucker grinned. "Good one, Higgins. Can we get a beer over here?" he called to Mama Chappelle, then swung a chair backwards and straddled it. "Thought you boys would've done more by now."

Boys? Ky tamped his temper down. The way Tucker said it implied ridicule. Disgust.

It had taken Ky the last three months to understand this particular FBI agent. He didn't know what gnawed at the man, but in many ways, Tucker Chase was not so different from Ky—driven and filled with impatience when things went wrong. A hard charger who didn't know when to stop or back up—or shut up. Honestly, the guy cussed worse than Alex, and that was saying something. But Tucker cared for Eden, and he'd come to respect that she meant the world to Ky. There were rare moments when Ky thought Tucker's ears actually worked.

"Grab a chair, why don't you," Ky offered sarcastically. "I just got in a couple hours ago."

"How was the flight?" Sam considered himself the old man of the operation, that he needed to keep an eye on all operators, but in no way did Ky or Tate subscribe to that theory. One boss was plenty.

"Long," Ky offered as little personal information as possible. Sam didn't need to know how much difference that one bowl of soup had made, or how depleted his emotional reserves were. The only cure for what ailed him lay in the emerald glow of a certain lady's eyes.

"My friend," Mama Chappy purred at Sam, her tray filled with steaming plates and opened long-necked bottles. "You did not call. I would've made my special dessert for you."

Sam winked at her, the flirt. "You know why we're here, Chappy, so take a load off. Join us. Let Serena run the place for a minute or two."

"Ah, Serena," Mama Chappy huffed. "That girl is giving me the grandbaby I always wanted. She cannot stand the smell of the wonderful food I cook, so..." She turned toward the kitchen and yelled, "Bobby!"

A slender girl in an apron and a shift of all the colors of the world peered around the door. "Yes, Mama?"

"I'm taking a break. Keep my customers fed and happy," Chappy ordered with a wave of her hand.

"Yes, Mama."

Mama Chappy doled out two more full plates and bottles to Sam and Tucker as well as the bowl of soup for Ky. Of course, Tucker noticed. "You on a diet, Winchester?" he mocked as he sliced the sizzling mystery meat off his skewer and stuck one entire piece into his big mouth.

"Ah, no, no, no," Mama Chappy scolded before Ky could reply. "This is not soup for losing weight. Only for strong men. Not you." That almost helped until she finished with, "And soon Mr. Winchester will be strong again."

Ky rolled his eyes. *Well, shit. It sucks to be me.*

Tucker grunted, but Sam ignored the whole song and dance, just sopped up some of that dry bread in the juice brimming his plate. "So spill, Chappy," he said with his mouth full, and his smiling eyes on Mama Chappelle. "Where is he? Who's watching him and how long before we can make contact?"

Finally! Intel.

"When Little Sammy comes home for breakfast, he will tell me if your friend is coming into town today." She peered out the open door as if divining Little Sammy's approach. "He has kept a close eye on him. Do not worry."

"*Little* Sammy?" Tucker asked, one brow peaked at Sam. "There something you want to share, buddy?"

Sam didn't bat an eye, just kept on eating. "Chappy and I have been working together for years," was all he offered.

Interesting, but Ky cared less who Sam spent his time with. "Does he have her with him?" was all he wanted to know.

Chappy narrowed her eyes and whispered, "I have seen Mr. Levine twice with a young woman at his side. I believe she is the one you seek. She is a white Christian woman, as skinny as the branches of the red mangrove in the swamp with hair as black as the char in my stove. I tried to make talk with her, but she only met me in the eye one time. The second time I saw her she wore dark glasses."

"Only looked you in the eye," Tucker corrected.

Whatever. Ky leaned in to avoid being overheard by the other customers. "Where's he live?"

"Between Sussex and York."

Ky shot Sam a questioning glance at those very proper British cities in western Africa.

"On the beach?" Sam asked Chappy, still chewing and slugging down his beer.

She nodded wisely. "Levine owns much land. Many ears and eyes in town, too. You are safe to speak here because I know my customers, but be careful what you say and who you say it to on the streets."

Sam translated. "Sounds like Levine's got Eden stashed on the Atlantic side of the peninsula. There are a few mansions of the rich and famous along that shore. The Peninsular Highway will get us there, but it might be better to go in by sea. What kind of security does he have, Chappy? How many men?"

She frowned. "Maybe twenty, but these men are... different. They do not make nice with the young girls in town, and they do not drink or eat. Always serious. Never smiles. Not friendly. They wear dark glasses, and they look like—"

"Drones," Ky hissed.

"Yes," Chappy's head bobbed, "if drones are machines that can walk and breathe and not just fly, then yes. These men are drones."

Aw shit. His eyes locked with Tate's. That changed the game, but Ky caught the glint of one-upmanship in his buddy's dark eyes. "We can still take 'em, right?"

Tate nodded once. No doubt.

"Are you sure that young woman is the one we're looking for?" Sam asked Chappy, his plate cleaned and dabbing a napkin to his moustache. "The woman we're after has long blonde hair. Green eyes. She's about the same age as your Bobby."

"Ah yes." Chappy nodded. "The proof is not in the hair, it is in the eyes. The dark-haired little girl who looks like death and walks like a ghost has eyes like sad emeralds. No fire. No life. And another thing. There is a different scent in the wind around her. A scent of—"

"Menthol." Ky grabbed at that definite proof that this woman was Eden. His slim hold on control slipped. What the hell had Levine done to her? Bought her a fresh jar of Vicks? Why the hell? Was he kind to her? Bribing her with a few niceties? Charming her? The thought riled his gut. "Was she well?" he asked. "Is she hurt? Did she look healthy?"

"Eucalyptus and menthol," Chappy corrected, nodding at Ky. She reached for his hand. "My dear man, I see now why you are unwell. You are lovesick."

Ky could've bawled. He wasn't sick. He was dying without Eden.

"Where the hell's your boy?" Tucker muttered, his neck stretched so he could peer around the place. "When's Little Sammy getting here?"

Mama Chappy released Ky. She leaned back into her chair, her gaze narrowed on Agent Chase. "You have met my son?" she asked, and Ky sensed a heap of trouble headed Tucker's way in that quiet, imperious tone she used. A woman could pack a load of humility in one word if a man wasn't careful.

Tucker never saw it coming. "No, ma'am," he replied, wiping his mouth with the back of his clenched fist and still gawking toward the door, "but we've been on this asshole's trail for months and have yet to receive good intel, so your kid better be right."

Aw shit. If calling Chappy's son *boy* wasn't bad enough, now Tucker questioned her integrity, and he'd used crude language in the presence of a lady. The dumb jock stared her down, totally not getting it, and she stared right back.

"My son is twice the man you are, Agent Chase," she declared civilly, her chin lifted in pride. "I think you will eat your tongue before the day is over."

"You mean eat my words," he corrected her yet again, the know-it-all.

Her eyelids reduced to mere slits, like a lioness before she went in for the kill. "No. I meant what I said, and I said what I meant. You will eat that smart tongue of yours because I will grill it on a stick and feed it to you."

Ky scrubbed a hand over his chin and mouth to keep from laughing out loud. *You go, Mama Chappy.*

Tucker took the hit like a man. He coughed. He sputtered, but then he ducked his head and offered a sincere apology. "You're absolutely right, ma'am. I tend to forget where I am sometimes, and whom I'm with. I spoke out of turn. I'm sorry, and I apologize if I've offended you. I'm particularly anxious to meet your son. He sounds like quite a guy."

Appeased, a gentle sigh eased from her flared nostrils. "I do not have a telephone to call him, but he will be here. He is a big boy and he needs his breakfast. You will wait."

Ky settled. Mama Chappy had just gone up a hundred notches in his estimation.

Shortly, little Sammy arrived. Little nothing. The man dwarfed his mama. Tucker, too. A toothy grin cracked his mocha-colored face when he spied Sam. "You came!"

Sam introduced everyone and ended with, "You're looking good, LS."

LS looked straight at Ky. "You are her man?" he asked simply.

Ky nodded, his heart on his sleeve.

"Then we must leave now or you will not see her again."

"How do you know that?" doubting Tucker asked.

LS met him head-on. "Because it is my job to know. Mr. Levine drives a car when he comes to town, but today his helicopter is being prepared for travel. He plans to fly."

"Where?" Ky asked, that heart on his sleeve now stuck in his throat.

LS never flinched. "He is going to the mines."

Chapter Thirty-Six

"Faster," Ky growled.

With Tucker driving like a madman and kicking up dust, Tate had a hard time keeping pace despite the light traffic. Right-hand driving was the rule of the road, a pleasant change for a country that had once been a United Kingdom Protectorate. He and Tate were fast on Sam and Tucker's tracks, eating dust as they flew south from Freetown along the Peninsula Highway to a place Sam called the old garrison. When they reached the curve in the road at Sussex Beach, the Atlantic loomed to the west.

But why take a woman as dainty and delicate as Eden Stark into a man's world as inhospitable as a diamond mine? To bury her? Imprison her? Kill her and hide her body so no one would find her? Was this about concealing the evidence of her murder or did it have something to do with more drones? After what Ky and Tate had stumbled onto in remote Canada, anything seemed possible, and none of it was good.

Faster," Ky urged, his need for speed choking him with regret for letting Eden get taken in the first place. This was all his fault, and he accepted full responsibility. If anything happened to her, it was all on him. If he hadn't been so tired after they'd made love... If he hadn't kept her awake all night. If he'd been a smarter, better, more thoughtful man... God. He could've made so many wiser decisions in his life.

At last, the highway veered to the east. "There," Ky ordered, pointing at Tucker's taillight off the highway and barely visible through the billowing dust. Tate hit the dirt road that branched to the right and kept going.

Sam's calm voice came over the earpiece tucked deep in Ky's ear. At the moment, he ran the show. He knew the lay of the land. "We're going to park in the grove of cotton trees up ahead. From there, we go in on foot."

"Copy that," Ky answered, his throat so dry he could barely speak.

"Take it easy, son," Sam cautioned. "We'll still have a couple miles to go, but this is the only way we'll get inside without being seen."

"Yeah. Understood," Ky spoke up, his palms sweating and his heart about ready to climb up his throat. Little Sammy had sounded so sure he'd seen Eden, but Ky'd been sure before.

Tate pulled in behind Tucker, the dense cotton trees providing cover from Levine's place. Ky hit the ground before their truck rolled to a stop. Sam and Tucker were on their feet by then, and LS, too. Tucker had the tailgate of his SUV opened and all men were strapping on tactical gear. Camouflaged body-armor vests. Ammo belts. Plain, gray ball caps. Multiple pistols and... *I'll be damned.* Omni 9000s. Too bad Alex hadn't been convinced to absorb the high cost of the rifles yet.

Tucker noticed Ky drooling. "You want one?" he asked while he strapped a holster to his thigh.

"You got extras?"

"You didn't think I'd go into hell without the best sharpshooters at my back, did you?"

Damn. Just when Ky thought he had Tucker figured out— he didn't. The son-of-a-bitch handed one Omni 9000 to Tate another to Ky. Of course, then he spoiled it. "You sure you can handle 'em, boys?"

Again with the boys...

Tate had already balanced the butt stock into his shoulder. "Where's the helmet and heads-up display to this system?"

"No helmet," Tucker explained, two gray ball caps at the end of his fingers. "Flip the visor on these bad boys down. Trip the built-in heads-up display to line up your shot. It syncs instantly with your weapon. There's a pressure pad where you'd normally activate your laser. Tap it once to paint your tango. Twice to delete the setting if you change targets. Once you're lined up, all you've got to do is pull the trigger and watch the asshole you're aiming at fade to dust."

"Do you have one for me?" LS asked excitedly.

Ah, the innocence of one who'd never killed shone bright on this young man's face. If he only knew the soul-sucking responsibility he'd just asked for.

Tucker shot Sam a spiked brow instead of answering.

"You ever shot a high-powered rifle, son?" Sam asked.

"No, but I am always willing to try." The kid just wanted to please.

Sam unholstered his pistol and checked the safety on it. "What say we start with something a little smaller, but just as powerful?" he asked as he handed the pistol over, grip-first to Mama Chappy's son. "Grab that black nylon holster next to the ammo box. Strap it on. Gear up."

Ky lost track of the momentous first for Little Sammy. He was too busy familiarizing himself with the new technology at his own greedy fingertips. He slapped a ball cap over his head and flipped down the visor, sighting in what appeared to be a large seagull sitting out on the water. Ended up being a yacht.

Holy shit. He double-checked his scope. A Rapid Fire Blacknight Z-18, 5-25x50. Friggin' amazing. That was a fifty-millimeter diameter lens that offered a twenty-five times magnification ability for those of you without a clue. It meant your target appeared twenty-five times closer through that fancy scope than by the naked eyeball.

Ky had no more than targeted the yacht again when windage and elevation flashed in a muted green digital readout on his HUD. The rifle system automatically self-corrected, advised how many microseconds to make the shot, and he was sold. There was no reticle, just a red laser dot in his sights where the round would ultimately go. Ky lowered the weapon. Alex *had* to invest in these bad boys.

"Which way?" he asked, ready to rock and roll.

Sam nodded straight ahead. "LS will lead until we're at the wall. Then he'll hold position for retreat."

"But I will go inside with you, will I not?" LS did not understand the concept of hold the position. It meant he got to carry a gun, but most likely he wouldn't get the chance to kill anyone. He'd stay at the rear. Outside the frag zone. Safe.

Ky rolled the cramp out of his neck. This was not the time to train an FNG, as in friggin' new guy. Still, it wasn't his call. He kept his mouth shut.

"You'll hold where I tell you, son," Sam replied firmly, sounding exactly like the dad he hadn't admitted he was, "or you won't go in at all. Understood?"

LS got it. He nodded, his lips clenched thin, but obedient. "Copy that," he offered, saving face with the operator lingo he'd heard.

"Tucker, bring up the rear," Sam ordered. "You guys ready?"

Grunts and affirmatives responded, and the infiltration was a go with a possible extraction within the hour. LS led with Sam following. Ky and Tate branched to the left and right. Tucker brought up the rear. Crouched low in the tall grass, they were camouflaged ghosts on the breeze, moving like snakes toward their target. No one spoke, not even the new guy.

Ky studied the pristine white concrete wall ahead. At five feet high, it ran east to west, ending at the gray-blue Atlantic. Rhythmic breakers crashed against the sandy shore. Gulls and other seabirds floated overhead. Some kind of a hawk hovered over the wall, its wings outstretched and its beak downward, no doubt stalking some unwitting prey. The predator matched the hope of Ky's soul. LS had better be right about his recon. Ky needed Levine to be inside this estate and unwitting.

They traversed an open stretch of the tall grass and sand before they hit the wall. By then they'd rotated positions. Ky was out in front, Tucker and Tate at his rear with Sam and LS bringing up the tail. All appeared calm.

Sam nodded for Ky to proceed. Ky produced a small plastic case from one of his pants pockets. With a flick of his wrist, the cap snapped open to reveal a tiny pen-shaped device. TEAMdragon, a drone so tiny it resembled a dragonfly in flight.

Most folks wouldn't have given the insect a second look when it spread its gossamer wings, imbued with a forty-one-thousand-tensile strength, the same as ultra-pure fiber optic strands. They wouldn't think twice if it zipped over their perfect white wall and into their fortress.

Ky lifted it out of its case and activated the tiny spy from an app on his cell phone. It took less than a second to orient the device, and bingo. They had eyes inside Levine's encampment.

"What the shit's that?" Tucker muttered, now intently peering over Ky's shoulder.

"TEAMdragon," Tate replied. "Quiet. It's got ears. We may be able to pick up chatter."

"No shit?" Tucker whispered, sounding like Ky had earlier. "You got extras?"

Ky stopped listening, his whole being now over the wall with that tiny watcher. For as small a camera as it had, it provided a crystal clear picture. Two guards stood at attention at the patio glass doors on the south, facing Ky and his team's position over the wall. By the time the tiny dragonfly had circled the lavish estate, Ky knew the position of twelve more guards, three gardeners, and the pool guy. The double door to a garden shed in the back was open, a riding mower parked inside. The upper level deck revealed an open patio door.

TEAMdragon hovered at the deck rail. *Do I dare?*

Hell yes, he dared, and inside Levine's secure home drifted the baby spy by a foot. Then two. It hovered while Ky maintained perfect pitch and yaw, not willing to risk losing contact with the drone or to endanger Eden.

The drone entered a lavishly decorated bedroom. Gold brocade curtains. Billowing white sheers that he had to be careful not to ensnare his pet in. Black painted dressers and a matching trunk at the foot of the queen-sized bed. A sea-foam green comforter with too many pillows. The door to an en suite bathroom stood open to the right. The closed bedroom door to the left. No sound invited him in, and he had no way to tell if anyone slept there. It looked too clean to be anything but a guest room. His hopes at catching a glimpse of Eden faded.

"Well?" Tate asked, genuine hope in his voice.

Ky rested his baby drone on the deck railing. He shook his head. "No sign of Eden yet. You guys are welcome to watch the display. Mama Chappy said there were maybe twenty guards. I can see twelve at various stations around the yard. All armed. Helmets. Omni 9000s. There's no way we're getting inside. We're outmanned. Four to one if Chappy's guess is right. Maybe more."

"So?" Tate took a step forward, the eternal optimist. "I'm not going in to ask 'em to dance. They'll never see us. Come on, Ky. We've had worse chances than this."

Tate was right. They'd infiltrated sight unseen quite a few times over their joint TEAM careers, but this time felt different. It was Eden's life on the line.

Ky cast his heart to the surf where seagulls played catch with the wind. She'd love it there. She deserved the luxury this edge of the ocean hideaway evoked. Just not with Levine.

"Ky? Is that you?" a timid voice asked.

Holy hell. Eden? Ky pressed one finger in his ear to shut out the sounds of sea and surf that TEAMdragon also transmitted. There was no way to reply if that voice belonged to Eden. The drone didn't come with a mouth, just radar ears.

Ky took the chance. He maneuvered his pet back through the open deck door, his heart in his throat, praying to God he'd find her this time. And there she was. Pale as a ghost. Made paler by that cream-colored safari get-up she wore and her short black hair. She was so damned thin. It broke his heart to see the dark smudges under her eyes.

"Ky?" she asked again, her voice too small, more breath than substance. She reached for the drone, and Ky let it happen. He hovered that baby dragon until it rested on her trembling outstretched index finger. Shit. Her nails were long and painted as black as her hair. What the hell was going on in that house?

"You're here?" she begged to know, her bottom lip bitten and her green eyes glistening. "Ky? Are you really here? Is this you?"

And God, he wished he were close enough to grab her in his arms and steal her away from Levine. "Yes," he whispered as if she could hear. "Are you okay, baby?"

The air stilled. Eden didn't answer. Instead, she dropped her hand and spun toward the door behind her, unsettling the drone. "Yes?" she called out, her hand behind her back and waving as if brushing the dragonfly away.

He retreated his wobbly pet at the open window beyond the edge of the sheers.

"I'm here," she called again. "I'm—"

"Why aren't you packed and ready by now?" The asshole himself slapped the door open and stalked in to where he had no damned business being. Cameron Levine in the flesh. Around one hundred and seventy pounds. Six-foot-nothing. Dark, trimmed hair. Clean-shaven. Pressed white shirt open at the neck, the cuffs rolled to his elbows. Tan slacks. Dress shoes. Smug smirk on his lying lips as he scanned the open deck door behind Eden. "I asked you a question. You know we have to leave. What have you been doing up here? Wasting my time?"

"N-n-no. I wanted to take one last look at the ocean," she answered quietly. "It's my last chance, and I... may never see it again."

"You might. It could happen." He tossed the wide-brimmed hat he'd brought with him to the bed and stepped too far into her personal space, crowding her.

Eden held her ground, and Ky held his breath. *You lay one finger on her, and so help me, you'll die.*

But lay a finger on her Levine did. He grabbed her roughly by her jaw and peered down into her face, his lips twisted as if he might—kiss her. And Ky wished TEAMdragon was the kind of insect that breathed hellfire and almighty brimstone.

Eden's spine stiffened. She lifted her chin, but not in flirtation—more like she meant to bite him if he drew any closer. "But it won't happen, will it?" she asked, an edge to her voice. "You'll never let me leave alive, will you?"

"Don't toy with me, Stark," Levine cajoled, his tone surprisingly tender given his hold on her. He ran the backs of his fingers down one side of her face. "How many times do we have to go over the rules? They're straightforward to me. You comply? No one dies. You strike out on your own? You pitch a fit like that last one? You even think of running out on me, and I'll make sure they all die."

Ky stopped breathing as his team stilled around him and waited. *You make sure* who *dies? Me? Director Strong? Exactly who?*

She took a step back from Levine, leaving his hand suspended. "At least don't make me drink that energy shake every morning. It makes me dizzy."

She whined! His brave little Eden whined! Ky couldn't believe the temerity in her sweet voice, the one that reminded him of the deep throaty notes from his mother's wind chimes. The one who'd trekked through frozen friggin' Canada to escape the monster she had every right to believe meant to murder her. The sweet woman who didn't want to kill the mindless male drones who would've killed her. That Eden.

Levine scrubbed his hand over his head, his eyes shut as if it took willpower to endure Eden.

"You could've let Dr. Zaroyin and his son live," she declared, and Ky could almost detect her defiance. "You didn't have to kill those drones, either. And why murder the president of Liberia? Do you have to kill everyone?"

Oh shit. Ky stilled. Eden was passing some heavy intel on Levine's plans right under his nose.

"Eden, Eden, Eden," the deviant coaxed, his voice reaching beyond the open deck door like the first chill of a bitter winter wind. "Let me make this perfectly clear. I don't have to kill everyone, but I *will* kill Drake Franklin if you don't do what you're told. Isn't modern technology wonderful? All I have to do is make one call, and my faithful servant in Virginia puts a bullet in your father's head. Two bullets, if I ask nicely, and three just because you piss me off by continually defying me!" His voice ramped up with every word. "Remember, my guy has no fear of repercussion or death, so think before you open that pretty little mouth of yours again. He'll do it in broad daylight and video the gore for you to watch if you're not careful."

"You didn't have to kill Isaiah," she declared bravely.

"Then why'd you make me? Why can't you do what I ask without everything resulting in a power struggle? Why do you test me every goddamned day?" His tone tightened until...

SMACK! He backhanded Eden. She fell onto the trunk at the footboard, her hand to her mouth, her knees on the floor.

Ky's hackles lifted off his spine. His nostrils flared wide. Cameron Levine was a dead man, he just didn't know it yet.

"I'll kill that son-of-a-bitch," Tucker snarled, and honestly, Ky had forgotten he still watched over his shoulder.

"No, Chase. I will," Tate growled, the quiet man finally heard from.

Sam racked his pistol, the barrel already skyward and his voice pure acid. "Not if I get to him first."

"No," Ky ground out, needing to do the killing, but to do it once and do it right. Eden couldn't defend herself against this monster. Ky watched her throw one arm across the fancy trunk and use it to pull herself upright until she stood, swaying, but on her feet. As carefully as possible, he withdrew TEAMdragon from the deck and brought it back over the wall to rest at his feet. Ky didn't need to see any more. He knew exactly what had to happen next.

"The bastard's lying to her," Ky growled as he secured the drone. "He's threatening to kill her father. That's how he's getting her to do what he wants. She thinks Zaroyin and his kid are dead, too. Tate, call Alex. I need Eden's father in protective custody. The Zaroyins, too."

"If Zaroyin's dead, that's news to me," Sam grumbled.

"Me, too," Tucker piped up. "I've got an FBI app for news like that."

Ky kept going. "Tucker, get Strong on the line. Tell him to contact the Liberian government. Their president's in danger. Now!"

For once, Tucker had no snippy comeback. He simply nodded compliance and obeyed.

"And me, sir?" LS spoke up like the willing FNG he was. "How may I help your pretty lady?"

Oh, God, where to begin? "I think you've done enough," Ky murmured. "You brought me to her. If not for you—"

"Bullshit. You're going in with me, son," Sam growled. He doffed his gear, including that pistol he'd just armed. "For now, we are just two lost tourists, understand? We're a father and son out to see the sights, but our vehicle broke down a couple miles back. We need a drink of water and to use a phone. Maybe a bathroom. Nothing more, nothing less. We go in and we stall Levine to keep him from leaving while everyone else gets Stark out of there."

LS handed his weapon to Tucker, his eyes wide and his heart in the right place, but damn. This could go wrong in so many ways.

"Are you certain of this?" Ky asked. "I mean, your son..."

"Yes. He's my son," Sam declared gruffly, a bite of pride in his tone, "and I've never felt better about a decision in my life. Once Sammy and I get inside, get Eden out of there. Don't take no for an answer. Tucker, you stay behind. You're comm support. Now go. Let's get this bastard."

Chapter Thirty-Seven

With her chest heaving, Eden wiped the blood off her lower lip and swallowed her rebuttal. There was no sense in it. This wasn't the first time Levine had hit her. And if help was just a wish and a dream, if that dragonfly drone was just another of Levine's sick jokes to torment her, that slap wouldn't be the last.

"You're right," she pacified meekly. "I'll be good from now on. I'll pack."

"Excellent," he purred, that hard fist of his now lifted to the corner of his mouth as if he'd slapped himself. "It hurts me when I have to discipline you, Agent Stark. It's not how I see our relationship developing. I hope you know that."

She nodded quickly, needing him to stay focused on her in case... in case Ky really was out there. It seemed the wildest notion, but when a person was drowning, they'd grab anything to stay afloat, even something as small as a dragonfly. And she'd been drowning for weeks. She'd become—*Black Eyes.*

"Put the hat on before you come down and keep it on from now on. I hate freckles." He turned to the door, his back to her.

But you don't mind bruises and handprints. "Yes, sir." She added quickly to make sure he knew she meant to obey.

"I want you looking your best today. You'll be meeting someone important. I hope you'll behave yourself."

Her stomach pitched. "Aren't you going to tell me who?" she asked timidly.

He paused at the door, but didn't offer anything but a twisted smile and a kiss blown from his fingertips before he shut her in. Ah! She jerked in revulsion at the hint of anything from his lips touching her, even an imaginary kiss.

"Ky," she murmured, needing one more glimpse of that mechanical bug. It had to be from him. Tossing the billowing sheers aside, she ran out onto the deck, desperately searching. Peering over the railing, nothing but the wide concrete patio and shimmering blue swimming pool below glared back at her. The shy pool guy offered a friendly wave. A seagull squawked from the shore. It might as well have been Edgar Allen Poe's raven.

All she saw was—nothing more.

Wordlessly, Ky signaled for Tate to head out with him. The thick row of flowering shrubs that TEAMdragon identified during its flight shielded their quick entry over the wall and down the other side. Once inside Levine's manicured yard, Ky dropped to his belly behind the shrubs and sighted the guard to the right of the side door in his Omni 9000 scope, if one could call the lavishly carved wooden masterpiece a side-anything. The door dominated this aspect of the mansion, but Ky had already seen the magnificent spectacle that faced the ocean and its opposing twin to the east. Levine must have a thing for grand entries.

"I don't want to kill these guys," he murmured at the last second.

Tate's head jerked to Ky. "Not that crap again. Goddamnit, why not?"

"Because Eden wouldn't want me to. She's right," Ky replied, his throat as dry as the sand on the beach. "These are not the bad guys here. Only Levine. We need to put the drones out of their misery, but not by killing them. They might thank us for it later."

"And just how do you expect to do that?" Tate hissed, his stoicism in shreds.

"Remember that wolf in Canada? We had bear spray, but we also had a couple dozen Diazepam-filled darts. You wouldn't still have them with you, would you? How about we give these guys a dose of peace and quiet instead of the crap they've got in their heads?"

"Shit," he growled, fumbling in the leather gear bag at his hip. "Now that you put it that way..."

"Serious?" Ky dared to hope. "You've brought those tranqs with you? Here? Now?"

Of course Tate had them with him. He was a Boy Scout to his bones. Always prepared. "A bullet would be faster," he grumbled.

Ky didn't argue. He'd learned long ago not to push Tate once he'd been convinced to do something he didn't want to do. This definitely qualified as one of those times.

"Here, damn it." Tate handed a box of darts over. "This better work."

"It will," Ky murmured as he swapped his fantastic Omni 9000 for the only thing in his gear bag that could handle a tranq dart—his specially modified pistol. He knew a little about being prepared, too. "You ready?" he asked his surly brother-at-arms as he loaded it up.

"I am now," Tate grumbled, but reloaded a single Diazepam dart into his modified pistol. That was the only drawback. There was no magazine designed to preload tranq darts. Each had to be chambered by hand, one at a time. Once they started shooting, reloading would require speed and luck.

"What if the dose is wrong?" Tate asked. "You might kill 'em just the same."

"I'm more worried if it's not enough. Either way, it gives them a chance. On my count," Ky whispered. "One. Two. Three."

Z-z-z-zip! The first two drones never saw what hit them. They folded to the ground and let loose of their smart guns. Ky scrambled to his feet and crept toward the side door, his rifle up and ready for close-quarters warfare. Tranqing an unsuspecting target might work under perfect conditions, but he couldn't take the chance if he was the one surprised.

He crouched to make sure both guards were alive. Their pulses were slow and steady. Good enough. He shouldered his rifle, then he and Tate positioned the drones against the home to make it look as if they'd simply fallen asleep. It might buy a few extra seconds.

For a split second, Ky deliberated over taking out the rest of the drones the same way. It would slow Levine's security response time down to nil. It would also cause confusion, and might direct some of the danger from Sam and his son. But it could also create suspicion, maybe chaos or a total lockdown. Where would that leave Eden?

A loud pop sounded from the east. Ky reached out to Tucker. "What was that?"

"Not sure. I'm on it."

Ky tried the side door, anxious with that one unidentified variable now thrown into the mix of what had always been a suicide op.

Of course, the door opened with ease. Why lock any doors when killer drones were on patrol? Ky angled inside. Tate followed and silently shut them in.

The open staircase to the second level lay beyond. Ky led the way. The place shouted wealth. Mother-of-pearl insets decorated the beige-tiled floor, if that was what you wanted to call the tiny pieces of individually cut tiles that comprised an elegant version of Poseidon, or some other Greek water god, amidst a flurry of turquoise and gold waves. Hell, it could be a Roman god for all Ky knew, but holy shit. Who paid for this kind of stuff just to walk on it?

Once he reached the open entryway, itself as big as the entire ground floor of Ky's home in Silver Spring, the rules changed. They were exposed, out in the open. Ky didn't have time for second-guessing or those tranqs. He wasn't God, and he wouldn't sacrifice Eden's life to save another. Any staff that intercepted him, if armed, would go down hard. Cold-hearted rules to live by, but he was one of those hard men.

Satisfied no hostiles were in the immediate area, he took the steps two at a time. At the second level, Levine could be heard from the open door at his left. "You heard what I said. We're leaving now!"

Eden's room. Now or never. Ky pressed his rifle to his shoulder and palmed the door wider.

God, no.

She stood there with Levine's arm around her neck, her face blanched white and his cheek next to hers. The gun barrel Levine pressed under her chin stopped Ky's heart, but Tucker's panicked voice in his ear shot all plans to hell. "Man down!"

Chapter Thirty-Eight

"Winchester. Higgins." Levine's sarcastic greeting curled Eden's blood. "I should've known you two would show up. Where's Stewart? The rest of his TEAM? Or did he just send you?"

Eden followed while Levine dragged her past Ky to the staircase Tate grunted ominously, and Eden was never so happy to hear his disgust, but Ky? Amber death radiated from him to Levine. If looks could kill...

"Let her go," he ground out, his short-stock rifle poised on target.

The entry below filled with drones. Laser dots danced over Ky's chest.

"Please don't Ky," she warned. "He will kill you. I know he will."

"Listen to your girlfriend, Marine," Levine ordered as he pushed her down, step by step, "or she dies first."

Sideways, she descended, her gaze transfixed on Ky's angry, rugged face as her only hope transformed to despair. His chest heaved. His Adam's apple gulped with their awful predicament, but there was nothing to be done. Levine held all the power.

"Why the mines?" Ky demanded, following closely, his weapon tucked in tight.

"Just be thankful I let her live," Levine purred. "Keep moving, Stark, or I'll change my mind, and your boyfriend ends up in Arlington."

The FBI drones shifted at that implication, and Eden was scared. Someone had turned off the air-conditioning, and in the brutal African heat, the lavish home was instantly stifled. Every breath suffocated.

Ky stood less than five steps up from Levine, his weapon still on target and her life pitted against his. His eyes gleamed with his rage. Beads of sweat trickled down his temple and brow. The drones would kill him, but she knew he would die before he let Levine hurt her.

There was no other way.

He meant to save her.

She meant to save him.

It had to end. She did what she'd seen Ky do all those months ago in the frigid north. She summoned the sweet moment she'd spent with him. She rolled her shoulders, she closed her eyes and...

She let go.

The east door burst open in a hail of gunfire and one angry son-of-a-bitch. Thank God for Tucker. But his bullets sprayed wide. The first to die slipped out of Levine's grasp and tumbled down the staircase. Eden!

"No!" With a panicked "Get the hell out of my way!" Ky shot the stunned kidnapper. Levine dropped dead down the steps, landing between Ky and Eden's body. The ensuing gunfight reverberated in that enclosed space, but goddamnit! Ky had never been more shocked. Tucker had just shot Eden!

Ky stumbled over Levine's body on his way down the steps. He couldn't get to his woman fast enough. Skidding on his knees at ground level, he choked when he gathered her blood-spattered body into his arms and cradled her ashen face. "Baby. God, no."

"Ky. I'm okay," she murmured, opening her scared green eyes. "You're alive."

I'm alive? She had it backwards. Hunching over her, he sheltered her, willing to take whatever bullets came her way, ready to protect her to the death. "I love you," he ground out, his voice harsh and ragged, wrecked beyond belief. So damned found. So damned saved. But in so much danger.

She clung to him, sobbing, and he could've held her forever if not for the war zone they were caught in. When the racket finally eased off, Ky peered sideways to survey the carnage, shielding her from the gruesome scene. She didn't need to see it.

The Omni 9000s had done their job, but surprisingly, Tucker and Sam were still on their feet, their faces grim. Many of the black-garbed security guards lay dead or mortally-wounded on that pristinely tiled floor, although several sported darts in their chest or arms. Ky shot a grateful glance up to Tate, still positioned topside. The damned guy shrugged like those darts were no big deal, but they were. Eden would be proud of him.

Ky smuggled her out the patio door and away from Levine's version of the future. She sobbed into his chest, and she was plenty scared, but not broken. He knew better. This was her first firefight, but Eden was strong, maybe stronger than him. He let her cry until she squeaked out a muffled, "I love you so much."

He sank to the far side of the crystal blue pool. The poor pool guy and gardeners stood there with their hands raised, but Ky waved them off. They beat feet out of there like he knew they would.

It was odd the difference one woman could make in a guy's life—how now that Eden was safe, Ky felt like a man again. Like he could take on the friggin' world and win. Content for the first time in months, he took a deep breath to steady himself. He pressed a fervent kiss to the top of her sweaty head and just held her tight. A whisper of the breeze off the ocean cooled his brow. It brought the wild, fresh air into his lungs, a nice change from the rank odors that now filled Levine's mansion.

"He... he..." Eden couldn't seem to get the words out.

"He what, baby?" Ky soothed her shattered nerves as much as he could. Tipping her chin up with his index finger, he blessed her with a hello kiss that quickly morphed into a God-I-can't-live-without-you branding. Breathless and so damned grateful that Tucker hadn't shot her like he'd first thought, Ky pressed her under his chin. "Breathe, baby. Slow and easy. I've got you."

Eden nodded against him, her voice stronger. "I think I'm full of those hormones again, and I'm positive she's at the mine."

"She who?"

"Cassandra Bick."

"Her again?" Ky chuckled drily. "She's supposed to be in jail, but I'll contact Alex to see what he knows. You'll be proud of Tate. He didn't kill anyone. He used tranquilizer darts instead of bullets."

"He what?"

Ky peered over her sweaty head at the mansion. He would've laughed at her surprise, but Tate and Tucker were still securing the bloody battle scene. Not Sam, though, and Ky had yet to spy LS since Tucker's 'man down' alarm. A double-shot of acid dumped into his gut. *Not Sammy,* he prayed to the Lord above. *Please, not Sam's boy.*

"Hey, I need to go back inside for a couple minutes," Ky murmured. He wrapped Eden's fingers around his still warm pistol. "Keep this and use it if you need to. I'll be right back."

"Oh no, you don't," she muttered, sounding more like herself. "You're not leaving me."

"It's Sam," Ky admitted so she'd know what to expect. "Levine might've hurt his son."

"Sam has a son?"

"You'll see." He tugged her to her feet, and together they circled the home, now deserted of guards. "Sam?" Ky called out as they approached the east entry. "Everything okay, man?"

"Here," came the gruff reply. There knelt Sam on the front steps of the building alongside a bloodied LS, who looked a little gray. "The bastard shot my boy."

Surprisingly, Eden dropped to her knees alongside LS. "It's you. What are you doing here? You're Sam's son?"

"Hello, pretty lady. It is nice to see you again." LS grinned. "He is my daddy."

"Yeah, well, your mama's going to feed me to the lions for letting this happen," Sam grumbled as he tied the makeshift sling around his son's neck. "I'll never hear the end of this."

"What happened?" Ky asked.

"I really didn't think Levine would recognize me," Sam admitted. "I'd left the Bureau before he came aboard. We never worked together, but shit. He took one look at me and fired on Sammy."

A weary Tucker and a grim Tate exited the estate of one despicable and very dead Cameron Levine.

"We're not finished yet. Someone's waiting for us at the mine," Ky told them in no uncertain terms.

Eden had a full head of steam by the time the chopper with Sam and LS flew to Freetown to face the wrath of Mama Chappy. Worse, she'd channeled Tucker again.

The local authorities had been notified. An army of ambulances had already arrived at Levine's estate. The medical examiner, too. Director Strong and Alex Stewart were on what had to be an uncomfortable conference call with the President of the United States and the President of Sierra Leone, but hey. That was what they made the big bucks for.

Eden was headed east in a second chopper with Ky and Tate. Tucker piloted the craft while Ky sat with her on the bench. By then, Tate had gotten word from the Alexandria office that both Zaroyins were alive. Isaiah, still recovering from torture at the Bicks' hands, rested comfortably at a well-guarded military hospital in Maryland, while his father awaited due process while under FBI custody. The President of Liberia had been warned about the assassination attempt and was secured inside his palace. Alex had Drake Franklin stashed at one of The TEAM's safe houses, and finally, all known drones were neutralized and accounted for.

Honorably, Ky had assured Alex he'd bring Senator Bick's wife in alive. Too bad Eden had made no such promise. Today was no day for honor or mercy. Only comeuppance. Only one hundred percent surety that no future child would suffer one second of Cassandra Bick's evil parentage.

Mrs. Bick should have been in jail, not let loose on her own recognizance to flee the country at the first chance she got. It had taken her two months to connive her way into that plea bargain, but once she did, she'd come straight to her buddy, Agent Levine.

Ky's wide palm resting intimately on Eden's thigh should've soothed her after the hellish day she'd just lived through, but her heart was on all those unborn children the Bicks had been so eager to exploit. The ones she had no doubt *Cassie* still planned on stealing. Every last one of those innocent babies conceived through in-vitro fertilization would've been her sons and daughters. An uncommon warmth flooded her heart at the emotional predicament she found herself in, caring for children she hadn't yet given birth to.

She rubbed her abdomen, thinking of all those tiny fingers and toes. Giggles. Boo boos. Pinks. Blues. Bedtime stories. First words and first steps. That first tooth. Baby powder. Diapers. All of those wonderfully delicious baby things.

Why she'd become so emotional over children that weren't alive yet was a phenomenon she couldn't explain, but she was. Her heart had become increasingly tender these last three months. She could cry at the drop of a pin. What was that all about?

Isaiah might have been a level-ten psychic, but there was no way she loved him. Yes, he was kind and handsome enough. He just wasn't the man she wanted to have those future babies with. She glanced sideways at Ky. Until then, motherhood hadn't been a blip on her radar, but now...

There sat the man who would father her children. He looked fierce, his spine ramrod stiff, his jaw jutted forward, tense with the upcoming confrontation, and so darned handsome she wanted to climb onto his lap and eat him up. This man who'd come to her damaged, who'd once hated human contact, now radiated authority and a powerful energy. His passive aura flared with bright red amidst the crystal blue. Ky Winchester was not only back in the game, but he was in it to win it.

She shivered, astonished at her body's reaction to his. Every aching part of her salivated at the sight of him. Her thighs clenched in feral anticipation of getting him alone and ripping his clothes off. Yeah. There she was, tenderhearted and hormonally charged to the hilt. Horny as heck and needing her man to take care of her needs. All of them.

Darned if he didn't respond as if he'd just read her mind. Very deliberately, he turned to her and lifted his dark glasses. He winked. That devilish, lazy smile flickered across his lips. And she was his. Heart. Mind. Body and soul.

Eden took a deep breath of her brand new extended warranty on life and faced forward toward Kenema. She could hardly wait. Ky was so getting his when she got him all to herself.

Before long, the chopper's skids bumped down to the dusty landing pad at Levine's diamond mine, and there *she* was. The depraved rich bitch. Stealer of other women's unborn babies. The blackest heart of all. Cassandra friggin' Bick.

Dressed to the nines in a lovely cream-colored safari get-up. Long black hair. Comfortable boots. Her hands on her hips. A wide-brimmed hat on her head, no doubt sheltering her painted-on brows behind those dark sunglasses and...

Oh snap, kill me now. I look just like her. He tried to make me—her. Cassandra and Cameron had planned for this meeting. Worse. They'd planned to replace Eden with—*her.*

Eden cast her gaze past the maniac on the landing pad to the clean white building behind her. The one beside the industrial-sized generators. The one with the tanker labeled 'Danger—Nitrogen' parked alongside. The dastardly game that Senator Bick and his wife had started was still in play, only the characters had changed. Levine and Cassandra had teamed up, and Eden had no doubt that there was another level-ten psychic in restraints in that building. A male. They still meant to kill Eden and steal every last one of her future babies.

Tate dropped out of the chopper first, his weapon tight to his chest. Tucker did the same. Both were on guard, and both waiting on Eden and Ky. But Mrs. Bick must not have gotten word Levine was on his way to the morgue. She'd met the chopper without so much as a chauffeur to back her up. Her proud chin tilted in greeting. She waved and smiled those perfect red lips, offering a regal queen-of-the-parade wave.

A funny red blur tinged Eden's vision. All of her five senses honed in on the maniac dressed for a safari.

Call it rage. Call it insanity. The FBI's secret weapon came unglued. Eden pushed out of the chopper and hit the ground running. Ky had thoughtfully supplied her with a holster and pistol before lift-off. Eden nailed that prissy hat with her first shot.

Darned if Mrs. Bick didn't look surprised to see her. She went down on her knees in shock, but not enough awe, shrieking, "Kill them!"

Guess again. Tucker and Tate weren't Levine's drones, and they sure as heck weren't implanted with any mind-control shit.

Eden fired again. A lovely red blossom sprouted out of the evil queen's left shoulder. Then her right, and Eden was more than a little surprised she'd actually hit her target all three times, but still, the woman—Would. Not. Die.

"I should've killed you in Boston," the missus had the nerve to hiss even as she tilted to the left, one hand to her shoulder.

Eden walked straight up to her, the business end of her pistol now dead center between those haughty, painted-on brows.

But by then, Ky had come up quietly on her right, the perfect position for an avenging angel. Eden gloried in his calm presence. "It's not self-defense, Eden," he declared without a hint of self-righteousness in his tone. "She's not armed, and she's got no back-up to save her scrawny ass. Look around. This mine's deserted."

Eden grunted. "You look around, Ky. See the nitro? Why don't you ask Tate to go check inside that medical facility? Ten-to-one she's got another poor level-ten strapped to an autopsy table in there. Ten to one she's got a cryo-lab set up and waiting on my death." *Ten to one she's not going to live the day.*

Tate ran to the building and kicked the door in, but he didn't have to verbally confirm what Eden already knew. Apparently, Ky knew it, too. "This is nothing but a revenge killing, baby. I'll back you whichever way you decide to take this, but you need to think about what you're doing before you pull that trigger. Think about what this says about you." He kept appealing to her higher reasoning. Her compassion. It just wasn't getting past that red haze in her mind.

"But a head shot would be merciful," big mouth Tucker offered from Eden's left. "Maybe a double tap. Just to be sure. That's how us SEALs do it."

"Or a tranq. Maybe two," Tate offered just as unemotionally, back from the portable medical building. "She's right. There's a guy in there. He's in rough shape. Someone's been cutting on him. Has to be her."

Eden snorted. "Couldn't you make him mind meld with me, Cassie?" she bit out. "What? Isn't he a strong enough level-ten for you?"

The witch on her knees had the gall to sneer.

"This is not about Cassandra Bick, guys. It's about Eden," Ky breathed.

Darn. Until that point in time, Eden hadn't truly understood how deep Ky's ingrained sense of honor went. He was making this snap decision harder than it had to be. Worse, he'd given her time for that red haze to fade. He'd made her think, and Eden didn't want to think. She drew in a deep breath of *what the fuck should I do?* (Tucker's words. Not hers.) But they certainly fit the quandary in her head. The scale of justice tipped in Cassandra's favor, until...

"Look at you, Stark. You're still a weak little girl. A nobody." The woman didn't know when to quit. "You won't kill me. You don't have what it takes to do something right for a change. You're just like your father."

Eden calmed. "You know, you're right. I am like my dad, and I'm like my mom, too. They were both good people who did the best they could with what life threw at them." Eden licked her dry lips and swallowed hard. "Did you hear what I said, Mrs. Almighty Bick? They were a couple of nobodies, but they chose to do good in the world. Tucker and Tate are right. You deserve to die for all the men you've put in harm's way without a second thought. You deserve to be dead for the people you got killed, and for all the children you meant to use to your evil end. But Ky's right, too. I don't deserve a stain like you on my conscience, so guess what? You win. You get to live."

Cassandra growled. Even if by some miracle she got life-flighted to the nearest medical facility, her chance of survival was slim. Eden lowered her pistol into her holster, her work done. She might have to come to grips with her conscience, but for now, she turned her back on the evil queen. Surrounded by wealth and the best life had to offer, Cassandra Bick was still the poorest woman on earth.

Ky's arm snaked around Eden's waist, and that should've been the end of it. But it wasn't.

Eden's second sight kicked up a red flag. She twisted just in time to catch the glint of sunlight off the tiny silver gun in Cassandra's shaky hand. She'd raised it to the back of Ky's head and—

BLAM! Eden whirled and fired. One shot and one shot only. Ky grabbed her against his rock-solid body in a reflexive protective hold.

Tucker jumped, his rifle on target and a gruff, "Holy shit!"

Tate just grunted, but Mrs. Bick? Her scrawny ass folded backward onto her cream-colored safari get-up with a hole between those pointy brows, her two merciless, unseeing eyes staring at the hot African sun.

The chess game was finally over.

Eden offered one last puff of false bravado. FBI training, you understand. Lifting her weapon to her lips, she blew across the blistering-hot barrel and grunted. Tate would've been proud. "Ain't nothing holy about it, Tuck. Shit's just shit."

Epilogue

Nine months to the day

"Faster," Ky urged Tate.

The TEAM vehicle flew through D.C. traffic. Tate banked a hard right at Constitution then headed northwest on Pennsylvania to Georgetown University Hospital on Twenty-Third.

"I knew I shouldn't have taken that escort assignment," Ky grumbled. "Not this close to Eden's due date."

"You'll get there in time," Tate replied stoically, still maneuvering the SUV like a professional racer through the crowded traffic.

"Did you see her? That obnoxious brat had her hands all over me."

"Hollywood's children tend to think they always get what they want," Tate offered.

He'd been on as many escort assignments as Ky. Most of the time they were an easy day's work, but this wannabe starlet had had definite nympho tendencies. No fifteen-year-old should dress so provocatively—or be that horny. Miss Glam—not her real name—had earned a meeting with the President, but when she'd shown up at the hotel lobby in skintight spandex, most of which did not cover what had to be silicone knockers, Ky was embarrassed for her—at first. Then he was worried for the President. The girl was fast. She had more moves than a pickpocket at the Saint Patrick's Day parade.

"She probably gets off on guys in black suits and dark glasses. You know, the whole bodyguard thing."

"I'm not so sure. She was in D.C. all by herself. Her parents were too busy filming their latest and greatest to accompany her. I think she's starved for attention."

Tate grunted. "Must be why she kept calling you Daddy."

Ky shot a sideways glance at Tate. The truth was a little scarier. Ky wasn't exactly cured of that sneaky haphephobia, his aversion to human touch, but the weirdest thing had happened since he and Eden married the day after they'd come home from Sierra Leone. Somehow, he'd gotten more... sensitive. Yeah, that was the word for it. He could shake most people's hands and nothing would happen, but every once in a while—he'd see things.

Like the frantic loneliness in Little Miss Hollywood's purple-tinted eyes. That young lady was headed for trouble, but the people she needed most in her life seemed oblivious. Not good.

Or the desperation in Javier's eyes, Ky's waiter-buddy down at the best Mexican Cantina in Crystal City. That one was easy to fix. Ky had a guy-to-guy chat with Javier, confronted him about the bank robbery he'd been planning, then hooked him up with an interview for a better-paying job, and Javier stopped worrying about his wife's medical bills that, until then, were eating him alive.

Yeah. This gift of seeing through people, if that was what it was, was damned scary. Eden had beamed when he'd discussed it with her. That was the first time she'd blurted out, "I told you so." Not the last. She thought he had psychic talent with animals, too. She wanted him to take some psychological achievement test. He'd laughed it off, but damn. She might have been right about that other thing, too. Maybe he had been the one who'd reached around the world from Kabul for her that fateful day. Maybe he was—psychic.

Okay. No. No, as in *no way in hell.* He wasn't a mind reader, but he was going to be late if Tate didn't step on the gas. "Can't this bucket go faster?"

Tate made that SUV fly, and he knew where to park at GW, too. Ky led the way in, all but running up to labor and delivery where the Bureau's one and only psychic had better still be waiting for him. He lost track of Tate, his heart pumping at this—the second greatest moment in his life. The one night of unprotected sex with Eden in his sleeping bag would always stand as the first. It had led him to this day.

Ky couldn't hurry fast enough. Time meant everything to a covert operator. *Everything!* What was it that Alex preached? Never late? Never wrong? Never miss? Well, today was that day, and Ky would *not* miss it.

"My wife," he barked at the first nurse in the hall. "Where is she?"

"And that would be...?" the nurse prompted.

"Sorry. Eden Winchester." He stifled the need to run and look room-by-room for her himself.

"Ah, so you're Ky?" She nodded to the door at her right. "It's nice to meet you, Mr. Winchester. She's been asking for you. Are you ready?"

If that meant that a guy's heart was climbing out of his throat, then yes, Ky was friggin' ready already. He followed the nurse into the pleasantly lighted birthing room where Libby

Houston, Kelsey Stewart, Judy Mortimer, and Shelby Cartwright attended Eden.

"You made it," Eden exclaimed, her poor face flushed and her brow sweaty. "Did you see my dad?"

"She's dilated to an eight," Judy advised. "You timed that close."

"Your dad? No. Is he here? An eight? Is that good or..." Ky's head was spinning, but he took his place at Eden's side and planted a kiss on her cheek.

"An eight means you won't have long to wait. She's been bearing down. You know what that means."

I do?

"Oh God, God... God, Ky!" Eden told him between gritted teeth as another contraction tightened her poor belly.

"I'm here," he said helplessly while the woman he lived for clutched his fingers like a friggin' vice. Libby shoved a chair behind him and whispered, "sit," but Ky could no more sit than tap dance with his fingers being dismantled like they were.

"It's coming," Eden's obstetrician declared calmly, and honestly, Ky hadn't seen Dr. Logan at the end of the bed until then. Guess he couldn't see through the tears in his eyes.

Dr. Logan peered over horn-rimmed glasses. "Today's the day, huh? Here we go. Push down, Eden. Ky, help her. You two know what to do."

Ky tugged his fingers away from his murderous wife and cradled her while she grabbed the side rails. They tilted forward together and—

"Bah!" the tiniest little brown-haired baby bellowed.

Dr. Logan beamed as he lifted the little guy up for Eden to see. "That was easy. Congratulations. It's a boy."

"It's a boy," Ky repeated in awe, and his world, his life, every good and bad thing he'd ever lived through, imploded into—Eden. He cupped her face between his palms, hardly able to see through the tears he let fall all over her. "You're a mother," he whispered, as if she hadn't known all along what that baby bump meant.

She smiled through her own tears, her chin tilted up. Ky closed the distance, craving the taste of eternity on her lips. A man didn't get any luckier.

"Is he healthy? Ten fingers? Ten toes? All the right equipment?"

Ky shot a questioning look at Dr. Logan for the answer to Eden's question. "He's perfect." The doctor laid the newest member of The TEAM on Eden's flatter belly. "Time to cut the umbilical, Dad. Are you ready?"

Dad. Wow, that's me. Hell yeah. Ky did the honors, so damned proud of his beautiful wife and his newborn son. The ladies oooh'd and ahhh'd before they stepped out of the room. Dr. Logan wrapped things up and left, and once the little guy was documented and wiped clean, Ky got to hold his pride and joy. He held his son, too.

There were no words for the tender storm swelling up in his heart. Sitting beside Eden, he pressed what would be the first of many kisses to the top of that tired little guy's head. When his newborn son opened his eyes and looked into his father's face, the vision came to Ky slowly. Like starlight. Like grace. The most pure outpouring of love. Ky choked on the tender connection between father and son. This was no ordinary little boy. This baby was—perfect.

"Have you decided on your son's name?" He had to ask his wife before he bawled his eyes out.

"I like Kyler Lee after you and Lee Hart," Eden said quietly, her hand tucked inside of his, "but I'm open to suggestions."

Ky breathed in the heavenly scent of his firstborn, touched beyond words at Eden's choice. She'd done it again. She'd read his mind. "Hmmm. I like that, too. We'll talk more after you get some sleep. Can I get you anything? A juice? Some water?"

Eden shook her head, her eyes drowsy. "I already have everything. I have you."

Somehow it felt more like the other way around.

Ky Winchester had come full circle. His once austere little starter home now sheltered a comfy king-sized bed and other furniture he and Eden had selected. She tended to lean toward buying family-friendly, but his purchases were made purely from a full-blooded male's perspective. His tastes were simple and direct. Whatever he could picture her sexy naked body draped over, bent over, or lying on top of, he'd bought. She'd insisted on a china hutch to go with that solid oak dining table, but honestly? He'd just wanted the table. Clothes on the floor. Eden on her back on top of it.

He now knew why she'd been pushed from the East Coast and ultimately, to Alaska. It was Matt Hartigen's idea to use her as the runner, and Isaiah as the tracker. Matt and Cassie said it was to beta test their control over a level ten psychic, but Isaiah knew different. Matt and Cassie were just mean.

Mother and Ember had untangled why Cassandra Bick hated Eden, why she wanted Eden's unborn children for herself. Why no other level ten would do. Cassie didn't just want a baby, she wanted revenge for a wrong done to her that Eden had no way of knowing she'd committed. Of all Eden's

FBI rescue operations, the only hostage she'd ever lost was an elderly drunk named Churchill.

It was nobody's fault. The steel locking carabiners on the rescue chopper's ladder broke while he and his rescuer, a twenty-four-year old Navy SEAL with a wife and two children, dangled over the Everglades after escaping the burning barn where Churchill had been kept for days. They both plummeted to their deaths. Hollywood never knew that hostage was Cassie's father because she'd never told them the truth, that she'd disowned him on her climb to the top, that he made her look bad with his foppish, alcoholic ways. In a bizarre twist to the story, Cassandra Bick suffered a miscarriage within days of her father's death. According to the gossip rags, the poor thing never tried to get pregnant again. Life was just so, so hard. It was no wonder she was crazy.

When Find Eden ended, the creepy hold of Ky's other nightmares ended, too. Nizari's death grip. The Bicks' narcissistic concept of world domination. And smoking. Ky still missed the nicotine rush on occasion, but Eden convinced him that life with her was enough of a stimulant. He didn't keep that pair of panties in his pocket any more. Didn't need to, not when he could strip a new pair off of her delicious derriere anytime he wanted, and come up smiling.

He'd repainted the baby's room, then the utility room for her three-legged poodle, a cuddly bundle of apricot energy called, of all things, Spike. The poor thing came from one of those pet adopt-a-thons. Spike looked like he could've and should've won an Ugliest Dog contest, he was that kind of strange. He'd been born with a deformed jaw that resembled a bulldog's, and a canine tooth that hung over his bottom lip like a vampire. His fur came in patches, leaving him bald in places.

He was blind in one eye, and he drooled, but Eden loved him, so Ky did, too.

Spike guy tended to ping when he'd sat too long in his kennel on long workdays. Ky knew how he felt. He hated small spaces, too, so the cute little ugly guy now accompanied Ky on his nightly jog. It hadn't changed Spike's looks any, but spending time with the poodle's big heart smoothed the wrinkles out of more than a few bad days for Ky. The furry friend was inclined to snuggle with him more than it did Eden, and you know what? Ky didn't mind.

"I'm touching you," Eden whispered, fading fast, her eyes still closed.

Ky planted a lingering kiss on each of her knuckles, planning for the moment they could start making another baby. "Dr. Logan said I can do more than touch you in thirty days."

Eden sighed. "Plan on it."

He looked down at his wife's slender fingers now snug in his hand, his son's tiny fingers wrapped around his little finger. Ky's heart swelled. His eyes brimmed. His tenderized spirit quivered with revelation. He'd come so damned far from the wreck he once was, and all because an angel with green eyes had reached into the universe and had taken a chance to hold on and hang tight. To believe in him.

All Ky needed was Spike climbing onto his lap to sit with his newborn son, and he'd be holding his whole world. He didn't understand it and he'd never deserve it, but life couldn't get any better than it was right then.

Ky drew in a long, sweet pull of the best God had to offer, and he knew to the deepest depths of his being...

A man with hope could do—*anything.*

THE END

Sneak Preview of Hunter

Book 14

In the Company of Snipers

"Oh, man. I'm hit."

Junior Agent Ky Winchester fell to his knees with a pain-filled groan. Tilting forward with both hands clasped to his red-stained crotch, his weapon hit the dirt seconds before his face did. He was dead. Killed by an unseen and relentless team of assassins.

Revenge flamed to life in Hunter Christian's heart. Ky didn't deserve to die like that. Shooting a man's family jewels was just plain dirty. Could a female shooter be in the enemy's ranks? A sicko with a vendetta against men? Hunter faded into the mesh of jungle foliage behind him. Assuming firing position, one knee to the hard jungle soil, he meant to find the answers to those questions.

This ambush had quickly escalated into one helluva tough battle he hadn't expected and was barely prepared for. It was no wonder Ky had fallen so quickly. Barely geared up and boots to the ground after they'd fast-roped into the jungle, the four TEAM agents were immediately overwhelmed with a swarm of near misses. The enemy's steady onslaught continued. How could it not? The enemy was invisible, the four men from The TEAM weren't. Who the hell called this a fair fight?

Hunter bit his tongue instead of cursing out loud. Junior Agent Eric Reynolds didn't seem to follow that same line of combat reasoning. "Shit," he hissed not twenty feet away, right before he fell. Eric should've known better than to have opened his big mouth. He was agent in charge, for God's sake! He was leading this bungled op!

Damn it to hell. Two men down and within seconds of each other? The TEAM had been cut in half, Hunter and Seth. Shitty odds on a good day, but if that was the hand they were dealt, Hunter meant to play it to win.

Seth had gone silent, a good sign. Dread crept through the thick jungle's underbrush with Hunter, compelling his number one ROE, rule of engagement. *Stay angry. Let it simmer. Let it build. And just when all seems lost, let it out to obliterate anyone standing in your way.*

Someone on the opposing army was either one helluva sharpshooter or damned lucky. Hunter stifled another curse before it could fly, a burdensome feat for a wicked man with a prolific, combat-honed vocabulary at his disposal, crafted with explicit care and plenty of practice to artfully condemn a man to the lowest circle in Dante's hell.

Yes, he'd studied the epic poem a long, long time ago when he cared a fuck about English Lit. He'd even lived through a few of the tortures within the concentric levels of Hell himself, from Limbo to the most rancid, Treachery. He understood full well the Italian admonition at the gates where evil men like him were consigned for all eternity: "Lasciate ogne speranza, voi ch'intrate." That line was nothing more than the story of Hunter's life—"*Abandon all hope, ye who enter here.*"

A twig cracked portside, jolting him out of his foolish self-recrimination. Crap like that could get a man killed. Not him.

He took one quick step backward into the shadow of brush, a single tree at his back. Adrenaline spiked. Fight or flight. He chose fight. That'd be the day he ran from an enemy. Women maybe. Bastards never. Holding position, he stilled, hoping Seth kept his head and did the same. *Stop breathing, Hunt. Hunker down. Wait for opportunity to come calling. Then— smooth and easy. Slow and sure. Line 'em up and waste 'em.*

Another movement caught his peripheral, but he didn't turn to look directly at it. Male, female, or animal, it would have to come a lot closer before he'd risk firing the deadly short stock pressed tightly into his chest and under his chin. The custom made, bolt-action tactical rifle fit his steady grip perfectly. His intentions, too.

A barely discernable ripple fractured the scenery in front of him. Leaves, light, and shadows shimmered. Hunter allowed satisfaction to lift the corner of his right upper lip into a snarl. That blur in the all-green landscape of Venezuelan jungle was the tell of an enemy soldier. Donned in the latest ActiveCamouflage System out of McCormick Industries, the bastard had to be the one who'd taken Ky and Eric down.

Barely flexing his index finger, Hunter compressed the trigger. Once. Just once, and—

Blam! Finally. One enemy combatant down.

"Son of a bitch! I'm hit! One of them got me." It seemed the enemy didn't know when to shut up, either. The dead guy hit the dirt ahead and to the right of Hunter's hastily selected sniper hide. Satisfaction added to the ferocious sense of competition in warfare. *If I can kill one, I can kill two. Maybe more.*

He stilled again, fairly sure there were only three of the enemy left, certainly better odds, but the fact remained. *Fire your weapon; give your position away.* Hunter was now a target, but he chose not to move. Not yet.

He let the jungle do its thing. Close him in. Hide him. Camouflage the lines and angles of his six-foot-three build. He kept his head on a swivel and waited, let his heightened senses magnify the sights and sounds in the rainforest around him. He'd stand for a damned long time before he gave his position away, before he tired. His arm could atrophy and drop off before he'd squash the mosquito on his sweaty cheek. Or the three long-legged bugs on his hand. Or whatever crawled up the back of his bare neck.

This was what he did best. Hunter simply became one with the universe. He melted in and blended in to the lay of the land. He endured and he overcame. He was a USMC scout sniper, for God's sake, a living devil of a man trained to win, not to simply try, damn it. Trying was for kids and losers. Let the enemy walk into his LOF and never know who'd waited in the dark, much less who killed him.

The enemy would come looking for him if only because they'd made two kills and they were cocky. They thought they were winning. *Guess again.*

The silence in a jungle stretched, eerily quiet. Hunter's sniper sense tingled, alerting him to the quiet rub of clothing against a leaf at his six. It helped the leaf was a huge, rubbery banana leaf. Still—someone was coming up behind him, into his line of sight. Seth? Probably not. Seth knew better than to move.

The sound of a plastic zipper shattered the deadly calm, the trickling spatter of fluid spraying into shrubbery. *You've got to be kidding me. Some guy's taking a leak? Now?*

The smallest smirk tweaked Hunter's lips. His target had a nervous bladder and a bad sense of survival. Had to be a civilian, certainly not a spec ops guy. Did he think just because he was invisible, he couldn't be killed? The fool. His zipper went up with the quiet buzz of plastic against plastic, not the type of sound Mother Nature created. Not even close. The idiot moaned in typical guy relief of a job well done. Holy shit. Hunter nearly grunted. To make it worse, the enemy passed so close to Hunter's position, he pushed a branch out of his way, the tip of it making contact with Hunter's elbow.

This kill seemed too easy. Too cruel. Hunter had never shot a person in the back before, but fair play didn't apply in war. Squeezing off another single round, the second enemy combatant fell. At least, he didn't have to worry about wetting his pants any more.

Two down, two to go.

Fifty-fifty odds ratcheted up Hunter's confidence. Maybe he and Seth could win this no-win situation after all. He willed the thought away. Stupid thinking jinxed an operation. Thinking you were invincible or untouchable for even one split second, and that was the day a guy met his maker, call him God, Allah, or the Great White Spirit. It didn't matter. Over-confidence and stupidity brought the same kind of bad luck. *Bang. Bang. You lose. You're dead—and Aljazeera boasts how easily American soldiers die.*

A large part of being a good sniper depended on the covert operator's internal mind game. Is that idiot in the bright red and white striped shemagh going to bob his dumb head up one more time looking for you? Oh yes he is. Wait for it. Squeeze the trigger. Pink spray in the evening sun and another lying insurgent gone to claim his fifty virgins or whatever those guys told themselves they deserved for killing good American men and women.

Damn it. Eric shouldn't have died today. Ky neither. There was a time Ky was a mess, not any more. Alex Stewart, the owner of The TEAM, seemed to collect broken men and turn them around. Like Ky.

And me...

The telltale crush of a light footfall interrupted Hunter's melancholy repast. He eased his mind back to zero. *Concentrate. Focus. Only breathe if you have to. Only kill when you're ready. Don't waste a single round. Make 'em all count.*

It didn't take long. This soldier moved too quickly. Too confidently. When the blur of man-made camouflage halted several yards directly in front of Hunter, for one split second, he experienced a tremor. He panicked. Also included in the ActiveCamouflage System was one damned fine weapon. At that precise moment, its sights could be aimed directly at him, but he'd never know it until the round struck.

"Teague? Is that you?"

No idiot, it's not. Quickly and smoothly, Hunter squeezed off one round before the invisible soldier had the chance to fire. Bright red blossomed where he'd estimated the man's head was. The bloody red looked odd, the droplets suspended in the air like they were, the trace evidence a ghastly crime against God. The body fell without any verbal expression, most likely because Hunter had shot the man in the face.

He didn't waste time on compassion, not for an enemy intent on killing him, not now when the odds had just gotten better. But being good spelled trouble. He also now had three dead bodies in a tight circle around him. They gave him away. It was time to re-locate. On the double.

Where the hell is Seth?

Another shot rang out, definitely not one of theirs. Birds screeched. "Damnit, I'm dead," answered Hunter's unspoken question. *Great.* Only Seth would go down with a one last proclamation on his lips for all to hear. He was another one of Alex's rejects. *Weren't they all?*

Now the game changed. One-on-one made for an intense wait—or a heart-pumping hunt if the opposing team's last killer was anything like Hunter. Shit, this could take days. Hunter opted for vigilance and the patience of a saint. It was better to wait the guy out than hastily relocate. Force him to come courting. Let him double down, play his ace in the hole, and go for broke.

Or die trying....

Meredith Flynn crouched in the dense foliage, sure The TEAM's last-man-standing was right ahead of her and to her left. He'd been quiet taking that last shot, but bodies were stacking up in one specific quadrant of the playing field. Teague Horton, her lead engineer and favorite weekend warrior, had gone down without a sound only minutes earlier. Too bad he was the only one of her team who'd taken her up on a solemn oath of silence when, or if, they were shot. The others should've. Maybe they'd still be alive.

Her senses reached out through the jungle, feeling for any unnatural sound that didn't belong—the brush of khaki against khaki, the squeak of leather or the jingle of a belt, anything that would mark her target once and for all. Her ears became radar, listening for human noises made without thought. A burp. A sniff. A scratch. The slightest exhalation of breath.

Her eyes widened to detect horizontal lines where none should be, shadows that didn't blend, the shiny glisten of sweat on a hidden forehead. Her nose twitched to inhale shaving lotion or body wash, the signs of an arrogant guy who thought he was tough. But darn. Nothing but nature came back to her on the breeze. This last guy was good, but he needed to die before she did. She owed Teague that much.

Suddenly, the tiny hairs on the back of her neck lifted. Her gut clenched. Her inner alarm system roared. Meredith held her position despite the panic climbing up her spine like a little kid on a sugar high. The dastardly assassin had to be close enough to touch and watching, but he couldn't scare her. Meredith gritted her teeth, determined he would die. But where could he be? And who was he?

A brightly colored macaw screamed overhead, startling her, but not enough to make her jump. Meredith allowed her eyes to scroll upward without tilting her head. The cursed birds were pretty enough, but not the sweetest music makers in the jungle. They were big and boisterous, more like the rowdy boys from a Delta Phi frat house. The macaws roved the highest upper branches of the tallest trees in giant flocks, blessing everything below them with layers of slippery droppings and raucous racket. With another squawk, the scarlet gold flew off to torment some other creature. Thank heavens. One surprise was enough.

"Don't move," a deep voice rumbled from behind.

Darn! He's got me. She froze, the barrel of his gun jabbed sharply into her spine where his shot couldn't miss. How had he gotten so close? She'd been alert. She hadn't missed the signs, the crushed grass from heavy boots, the tiny bent tips at the ends of the branches, all proved he should have been ahead of her, not behind. How'd he get back there?

"Name, rank, and serial number," her soon-to-be murderer ordered.

Meredith swallowed hard, her throat day and her doom sealed, darn it. This guy had to be black ops as stealthy as he'd been. As good. She could feel his body heat, something else, too. It rolled off of him. Pure male power. Raw masculine strength. His heated breath on her collar. Even concealed beneath her camouflaged facemask, she could smell him. Clean sweat. Just a hint of deodorant. The tiniest whiff of cigarette smoke.

She stiffened as a large male hand reached around her without coming into contact with any part of her ACS suit. Adeptly, he lifted the invisible automatic rifle from her hands—like he knew precisely where it was and which way it pointed. A black tattoo extended from the sleeve of his OD T-shirt, a snake of amazing detail wrapped around his forearm, the wedge-shaped head flat on the back of his hand.

She nearly shrieked as an ungodly shiver arced up her spine. The tattoo looked alive, the scales of the reptile glistening as if the snake slithered along this guy's very tan rippling muscles. More ink stretched around his wrist and under the cuff of his black and green cammie long-sleeved shirt. Its red inky eyes stared unblinking at her from the back of his hand, its matching red forked-tongue stretched to the end of his middle finger in a continual obscene gesture. The blade of a knife pierced the serpent's head, the handle grip declaring USMC.

Ex-Marine, huh? Well, didn't that just figure? She'd been bested by one of America's best. The good guys.

Her heart set to pounding. Thinking she could delay her inevitable surrender, she whirled on him with her elbow cocked high and hard, intent on bringing him down, going for his Adam's apple. It could happen. She was agile and light-footed. Fast thinking. The rules of engagement clearly established death as the only end to the conflict. There was still the possibility she could wipe the smirk off his—

"Stop it," he hissed. That same heavy hand caught the back of her neck in a solid grip, his thumb just below her ear, his fingers turning her to his lips. He had her dead to rights. He was all man. Solid. Deadly.

Meredith melted, suddenly damp and hot for all the wrong reasons. She didn't even know this guy, yet her feminine side responded on an elemental, animalistic level. The urge to rub against him like a cat came out of nowhere. The minty scent of spearmint wafted out of his mouth. Spearmint and tobacco. Like an impala on the Serengeti, she inhaled deeply, committing that unexpected male odor to memory for the inevitable death match. It would come. Maybe not today, but soon.

"Go ahead. Make my day," he taunted, his voice hard, his nose nearly at the edge of her face shield. "Are you man enough? A shot this close will hurt like hell, but I'm game if you are. Where do you want it, head or crotch like you bagged my first guy?"

She bit her lip at the threat. A dare? A promise? Who did he think he was, Dirty Harry?

"Name or yield, either way works for me, Sally."

Sally? Was that how he belittled his adversaries? Huffing her disgust at his caveman tactics, Meredith pressed the pad in the middle of her gloved palm to shut down her ACS. This moron needed to know who he was dealing with, and it wasn't some idiot weekend gamer.

Section by section, the densely woven, metallic fabric of her all-in-one invisibility suit blinked into view. Each sensor-impregnated panel now reflected nothing more than the charcoal gray cloth of the uniform and the matching helmet. Still, there was a chance she could prove she was more than that ridiculous name he'd tossed at her. She wasn't anyone's Sally.

Slowly, Meredith lifted one booted foot sideways to give him something to think about, and—

His fingers clenched her neck, twisting her head to the side as if he meant to snap it to get compliance. "Say it or die," he demanded, the barrel of his rifle now stuck in her ribs, hard enough to really hurt. "I'm good either way."

She rolled her eyes beneath her visor, but belted out the requisite, "Yield!" for all still standing on the battlefield to hear. That would be just him, Mr. Tough Guy, the winner she hadn't yet seen.

Meredith meant to congratulate him for a job well done. Well, sort of. Half of her still wanted to shoot him between the eyes, the other half to kick his legs out from beneath him and knock him to his arrogant ass. Easing her visor up, she shrugged his grip off and turned to meet the only man who had bested her in a while.

Surprise sucker punched her hard. She leaned in to make sure her eyes weren't lying. What were the chances of running into an old friend in the middle of a South American rainforest?

"Hunter? What are you doing here?"

But it wasn't surprise glowering on Mr. Tough Guy's chiseled face. More like disgust. Hunter's top lip curled. He grunted, but offered no sign of recognition or welcome, just a quick nod and a polite, curt, "Ma'am," before he jerked away from her, performed an abrupt military-style about-face, and walked away.

"Wait," she called after the wide shoulders angling through the curtain of vines and away from her. "Don't you recognize me? It's me. Meredith Flynn."

But he'd literally vanished—just like last time.

Thank you for reading Ky!

Be sure to check out the rest of the guys and gals of Irish Winters' series: *In the Company of Snipers*

Other Irish Winters' books:

King of Hearts, Deuces Wild Series, *#1*
Joker Joker, Deuces Wild Series, *#2*
Smoke, Hearts and Ashes Series, *#1*
Ash, Hearts and Ashes Series, *#2*

Coming soon!

Seth, In the Company of Snipers, *#17*
One-Eyed Jack, Deuces Wild Series, *#3*

YOU are the key to this book's success!

Please tell other readers why you liked Ky and Eden's story by leaving an honest review at the retail site where you purchased it.
Recommend it to your friends. Lend it.
Most of all, enjoy it!

The best way to keep up with my new releases, giveaways, and actionable intel is to sign up for my spam-free newsletter at IrishWinters.com.

About the Author

Irish Winters is an award winning, Amazon best-selling author who, when she isn't writing, dabbles in poetry, grandchildren, and rarely (as in extremely rarely) the kitchen. More prone to be outdoors than in, she grew up the quintessential tomboy on a dairy farm in rural Wisconsin, spent her teenage years in the Pacific Northwest, but calls the Wasatch Mountains of Northern Utah home. For now.

She believes in making every day count for something, and follows the wise admonition of her mother to, "Look out the window and see something!"

Connect with Irish!
On Facebook: https://www.facebook.com/author.irishwinters
On Twitter: https://twitter.com/irishwinters1
Or at www. IrishWinters.com

www.ingramcontent.com/pod-product-compliance
Lightning Source LLC
Chambersburg PA
CBHW031049110726
47900CB00003B/862